Life's Only Promise

* * *

Sid Kara

* * *

Asad and Amanda —

Thank you so much for your interest in my book. I hope you enjoy it, and I wish you all the best.

— Sid Kara

AmErica House
Baltimore

Copyright 2000 by Sid Kara
Cover art by Lilian Crutchfield
Author photograph by Livia Corona

All rights reserved. No part of this book may be reproduced in any form without written permission from the publishers, except by a reviewer who may quote brief passages in a review to be printed in a newspaper or magazine.

First printing

ISBN: 1-893162-52-4
PUBLISHED BY AMERICA HOUSE BOOK PUBLISHERS
www.publishamerica.com
Baltimore

Printed in the United States of America

This text to Lilian,
Who taught me my heart;

These words to Laurie,
Who made me a prince;

This work to my parents,
To honor our blood.

Acknowledgments

I would like to thank the following people for their invaluable roles in this project.

Sean, for showing me Parchman.

Professors Shelton and Porter, for challenging my writing and awakening my literary mind.

Miles and Dawn, for helping me see when to remove my words from the stove.

Taffy, for mentoring me from thousands of miles away.

Charlie, for your generous and keen editing.

AmErica House, for taking a chance on me.

This book, for showing me parts of myself I had never seen.

Cornelia - - - for understanding what no one else could understand. For being there when the sky fell and fell again. Without you I would have failed. You are a gift.

And finally my ancestors, for these words in my heart and the freedom to write them.

Preface

This novel is based on history but is a work of fiction. Though some of the individuals and places in this story actually existed and have been realistically represented, the book is fictional and is not intended to represent the precise history of these characters and places.

One

LIFE'S ONLY PROMISE

The Lynching Tree

"With one voice which is wondrous
He giveth utterance to thoughts innumerable,
That are received by audiences of all sorts,
Each understanding them in his own way."

Sarvadharma - pravrtti - nirdesa Sutra

Long Chain Charlie had dragged them for miles through the sogged Yazoo Delta, and now, arriving at the front gate of his sentence, Fulton was neither thinking about his daughter nor that it was the rainy afternoon of his thirty-third birthday. Instead, he concentrated on silencing the cacophony of the rusted shackles and the stinging whips assailing his delirious mind. Later, as he waited in another line to be registered, Fulton thought about his friend Jay. Looking up, he saw Jay's dagger in the shapes of the clouds above him, and he wondered where he was. *Must be another one for white folk. Maybe somewhere else down fiftyfive, closer to Jackson.* Beneath his rattled consciousness Fulton clung to the hope that Jay would save him. Then in a whisper, he asked Moondog how far he thought they were from home, but before Moondog could respond a rifle struck Fulton's head, for trying to speak. He fell to his knees and watched his blood spill in sinuous drizzles to the ground, just like the tumbling rain. Each droplet was thick with the scent of dread.

***

It smelled like unfulfilled dreams, mournful with a tincture of serenity. Both sensations resided within the rhythms of its rolling and its sipping and its mystic permeation. Both sensations resided within its spice of somber memory, the recollection of loss. Sometimes Fulton wished he could drink it with his eyes. Extinguished, he rolled another. Unlike the cotton, the tobacco from his field was for him alone. It was only a few days to Settlement Day, October 1, when he would take all the cotton he had gathered since late August to Anderson. But now it was sweet tobacco time. He inhaled and watched the heavy smoke swim into the subtle but agitated presence of his ancestors, around and around themselves like chanted verse. Unrhymed. He saw her and smiled. With each sip he slipped deeper into their deliquescent consciousness and the soothing dance of the gypsy within him. But the ghosts remained discomposed, doleful, in search of serenity.

LIFE'S ONLY PROMISE

Through the smoke he watched the silhouette of his daughter skip up the dusty road towards him. The rusty sunset descended behind her into the color of unfulfilled dreams. He awaited her on his wooden rocking chair on the drooping porch of his dilapidated cabin. It creaked as he rocked back and forth. She arrived at its splintered steps, waiting for her father to return. In these entranced moments he seemed to simultaneously inhale and exhale his tobacco. In these moments he smelled like ash, sometimes like old books.

As she stood behind the mist of their ancestors, she seemed to melt into her mother's form.

"How's Orlando?" he asked.

"He's alright. We looked at his pitcher books en helped his mama tend they mules. He's startin' to smoke like you."

"Fifteen. That's the right age."

"I dunno 'bout that. Stinks to me. I don't see how people ever up en decided to start smokin' that stuff anyhow."

"Well it's the right age nevertheless. It's the age when a man starts to recognize his duty to his ancestors. But it wasn't always that men was smokin' tobacco. See, long time ago there wasn't no tobacco in this world. There was this man en his wife en his children, en they lived in a village with other families. One day this man's wife went to pick a chicken for supper, but she got a strange look in her eye en she started to eat all they chickens raw. The man told her to stop, but she kept on eatin'. She ate all they chickens en all they mules en all they dogs until there wasn't no animals left. Blood en bones was all drippin' out her mouth, en her tongue was just waggin' in the air for more food, but she promised her husband she wudn't gonna eat him or they children. Then that night when they was makin' love, the wife ate up her husband, meat, bones en all.

The next day her children threatened to run away, but she told them if they did she would chase them en eat them all up. So they prayed to the spirits en the spirits gave them a plan. That night the children dug a hole in the ground en covered it wit leaves en sticks. Then the next day when they tried to run away, they mama started to chase em, but she fell into the trap. She was rantin' en ravin' en threatenin' to eat them alive if they didn't help her out. But them kids turned they backs on her en started fillin' the hole wit dirt. They mama started eatin' the dirt they threw in the hole, but she couldn't eat fast enough. Soon she got too full en they was able to fill up the hole en bury her inside. Then the children returned to the village. Several weeks later a strange plant started to grow from the earth where they had buried they mama. No one had ever seen it before. The oldest child was a boy a fifteen. He took the plant en started to smoke it, en soon all the men in the village came en smoked wit em. That's where tobacco came from, en that's why men smoke it."

Simbi was silent after her father finished. Just like her mother after she and Fulton made love under the fig tree at the Banks Junction. Both seventeen. Both hypnotized by the other's rhythmic panting, each the whispy chorus to the other's desperate soliloquy. That night, under the swirling clouds, the lovers swam within each other until dawn. Then, when the sun rose they each ate some of the fig tree's bark before returning home. Uma got big and two-hundred-sixty-one days later Simbi was half-way born when her mother died. No one had ever seen such a thing. It meant that demons were in the family. Simbi had scars across her chest and head from her violent gestation and birth. Fulton buried Uma's ashes under the apple tree by the west side of his cabin to cleanse her demons, right next to her resplendent flower garden, which Simbi revived when she was old enough. Tulips and lubem lilies. Those were her favorite, with honeysuckle circling towards the sun. Simbi spent hours in silent rumination in the flower garden, staring into the thirsty blossoms as she traced bereft circles around her belly button. She was growing more and more like her mother, uncompromising and fierce. And she dreamed big dreams too, because Fulton told her that dreams were the difference between the living and the dead.

"Go on inside en light the stove for supper," Fulton said as he exhaled.

Simbi bounced up the steps to the porch, kissed her father's forehead, and pulled open the rusty screen door which whacked shut behind her. It was the end of September, so she knew Fulton was exhausted. These were the days when he returned from the fields laying flat on his mule without the strength sit up.

Fulton watched Simbi's feet as she moved inside. He watched her shoes from behind the smoke, the same as his -- torn, worn, and crumbling, like their house. They were the only shoes for sale at Anderson's store. But he wanted her to glide over the earth in golden slippers. Such a failure. As he brooded, he removed his own shoes to rub his swollen feet. Their skin was chapped and thick like leather. Croppers joked that they were not afraid of fire because they could stamp it out with their thick feet. Maybe that is why some of them were burned to death from time to time. Fire reminding them to fear. As Fulton rubbed his toes and heels, he wondered how his feet could still ache him everyday, as armored as they were against his journeys over the earth.

Simbi poked her pigtails through the screen door and dropped a dented saucepan on the porch, "Daddy, ken you go to the well en fill the pot?" Fulton raised himself with a groan and walked down the porch to the well behind the apple tree. He walked gingerly, with his back bent. He liked to imagine that the well was older than Mississippi and that it came from some distant place many years ago, maybe from some time when the earth was only populated by wells that roamed the land looking for a bubbling spring in which they could rest forever. But then one day they were cursed never to move again. So since then they fill each day with the fresh tears of their sorrow. Weeping Wells. Perhaps since Fulton drank their tears, he would never be cursed to spend his life yoked to the same earth without a place to rest.

As he raised the earthy tears from the Weeping Well, Fulton gazed down the dusty road at a shadow in the sunset so large that it could only be Moondog and his moonshine. Even though Fulton was just over six feet tall, Moondog was half a head taller, and even though Fulton was stronger than any man his size, Moondog was half a man stronger. They were each as fit as any man around, sculpted with robust and jagged features, ready for war. Fulton waited at the well, and when Moondog arrived they both walked in silence to the porch. Fulton sat on his rocking chair, informed Simbi that the saucepan of water was waiting, and relit his tobacco as Moondog took a seat on the second step of the porch and sipped from his jug. Moondog had a still at his cabin, and he sold pints and jugs to the other croppers across Anderson's land. He was the only one Anderson would allow to keep a still since he and Anderson shared the same father. "What ya'll cookin' tonight?" Moondog asked.

"Same collards en sweet taters we been cookin' all summer. Ain't your wife cookin'?"

"Yeah, she cookin' some special meal for some special gatherin' up at Andesons. Wit them countants, ya know, jes before Settlment Day." Moondog paused to sip his jug and look into the placid twilight sky, "I feel good en snakebit tonight."

"I never liked the sound a that word," Fulton scowled.

Fulton and Moondog had been friends since before either of them could remember. They had both spent their lives on Anderson's Land, just west of Hernando, sowing and reaping the earth since they were boys. Moondog had been called Moondog since his father found him in his pantry when he was four, lying upside down off a chair after sampling some of the shine. Twenty-seven years later Moondog still had moonshine in his hand. Not that he was a drunk. He could drink all day and still outlast the strongest man in the fields. He was a mammoth presence of nature -- full and thick, with deep, white eyes that could crumble a man with their stare. And he was covered with scars, which he said came from wrestling with gators and wolves. Fulton knew that Moondog had to drink because otherwise he would burst from his body. No veil of skin could contain his fury if he were ever sober long enough to remember his childhood sorrow. A sober Moondog would end up getting himself lynched, so Fulton did not mind his drinking at all.

They sat and watched the last rays of crimson sunlight slip beneath the horizon. Each sipping his respective gypsy. There weren't as many mosquitoes now that October was near, so they could enjoy a longer evening on the porch before retreating inside. Fulton inhaled his tobacco to summon the warm memory of lost love. Moondog drank his shine to cool the inner burning of his memory of loss.

Inside, Simbi tended to the dinner while pondering how hot water makes sweet potatoes soft. The cabin itself had three rooms. One big room, with a stove, a couch, and a small round table with four wooden chairs, and two bedrooms. The sheet metal ceiling drooped just above Fulton's head, and nothing decorated the walls. The cabin was always dark inside because its windows had no screens, so Fulton had to shroud them with covers to keep the insects, dust, and cold from entering. Each night before he slept, Fulton thanked his cabin for standing another day to shelter his family from the world.

Behind the cabin lay the sixty acres of cotton fields that Fulton and Simbi cultivated for Mister Anderson, the owner of the land. Stories among the croppers have it that Anderson's great-grandfather came from Virginia and built the mansion still standing atop the hill at the west end of the land. Grandfather Anderson courted a belle from Memphis, used the rest of his money to buy twenty slaves, and fornicated with the six that were female. He conceived one child with his wife and thirty-six with his slaves, but within two generations, thirty-five of them had died from everything from pellagra to malaria to a mule kick in the face. The one who survived fathered Mister Anderson, Moondog, and Neshoba. Moondog was the oldest and Neshoba the youngest. But only Mister Anderson was white. Moondog's, Neshoba's, (and Fulton's) colors of black were somewhere in between.

As he sat, calmed by the chorus of the Mississippi night -- bullfrogs, owls, crickets, and the hollow breeze -- Fulton yelled for Simbi to check the collards and the sweet potatoes. She always burned them otherwise. As soon as the food was on the stove, her thoughts began to wander. Fulton blamed himself for her wandering inattention because he almost suffocated her when she was seven months old. He could wield a scythe and wheelbarrow as well as any man in Mississippi, but he never developed the supple hands required to hold a baby, especially since he had to work his field and carry her at the same time.

For a time, he solved the problem by transporting Simbi in his wheelbarrow. He would place her in it and wheel her into the shade behind his cabin while he worked the field. But one day he forgot she was in it, and he buried her alive in some buckshot that he was carrying from the field to his tobacco garden. She would have suffocated if a hawk had not shat on his shoulder causing him to spin in disgust and spill over the wheelbarrow, revealing his daughter silent beneath the dirt. (Years later, Fulton would realize the hawk saved his daughter because, like her mother, it was not her destiny to be buried as flesh.) From that day forward he carried her in a sack strapped to his back no matter where he went. He promised himself he would never remove his eyes from her again.

Simbi called Fulton and Moondog when the food was soft, and the three of them sat down at the table to eat. They ate slowly, with honor and gratitude. The food was like an army banishing their hunger. Later, Simbi broke the silence, "Daddy, it's a clear night. Ken you play your harp?"

"I think so. I was thinkin' bout it earlier when I saw the clouds clear."

Fulton played his mouth harp only on clear nights because on cloudy nights the music could attract the mischief of evil spirits. They returned to the porch where the night air was moist. Moondog lit a small fire and placed damp leaves over it to repel the few remaining mosquitoes. Even in September, some were still as big as hummingbirds. The moon's milky glow awakened the teeming chorus of the night's hidden life. Night spoke to them in sonorous movements; night said everything they wanted to say. Fulton thought to himself that life abounds with unwanted noise, but night is music.

Fulton took his mouth harp from his pocket and began to accompany the night's song. His harp breathed with slow, fistulous moans. Moondog and Simbi felt Fulton's song dance through their spines like the fire's flickering shadows danced across their faces. They melted into the melody because it was the sound of their ancestors.

Years ago, Fulton and Moondog had learned to play the mouth harp from Old Willie. Old Willie was an ancient, gray man who spent his life sitting under the tree from which his father was lynched when Old Willie was seven years old. His father was lynched for looking at Grandfather Anderson's daughter with lascivious coon eyes. Decades later, Moondog's (and Anderson's) brother Neshoba was lynched from the same branch of the same tree with Old Willie still sitting beneath it. Neshoba was lynched by some of Anderson's men for claiming (while snakebit) that he was Anderson's brother. Anderson knew the truth of the bloodline, and when he learned of Neshoba's murder he was saddened, but he tried to tell himself that Neshoba died because he was a stupid nigger. Nevertheless, he could not forget the games they played together as children. Nor could he forget that Neshoba had actually saved him from drowning off the pier of the Mansion's Lake. But none of this saved Neshoba from dying for what he said, and from that day forward, Anderson could proceed in life only by reducing niggers to being nothing more than niggers. Except for Moondog. Though they never spoke again after that day, Anderson protected Moondog from Mississippi and allowed him to have a still and miss a cropping season without evicting him.

Fulton stood with Moondog the night Neshoba was lynched, both of them staring at the dangling body as it swayed in the autumn breeze. Old Willie saw himself reborn in their tormented eyes. Moondog had cried to the mob that Neshoba was not lying and that all they had to do was ask Anderson. But no one ever asked Anderson anything, so Neshoba was lifted from the earth. As he kicked and jerked, the tree's autumn leaves tumbled like afternoon rain. Then, just before the moment of his suffocation, Neshoba coughed Moondog's name, extended his right hand forward, and closed it in a tight fist that remained aloft and strong even after the final breath of life was squeezed from his lungs.

That night, Moondog and Fulton sat with Old Willie under the Lynching Tree, and Old Willie spoke words for the first time since he was seven, "there ain't nothin' I ken tell you gonna make the pain go away. There ain't nothin' nobody could tell me when I was a boy like you. So I decided back then that I was gonna sit under this tree 'til it told me why my daddy was lynched from its branches. And this here mouth harp's the only way I know how to speak to a tree." So that night, Fulton and Moondog sat until dawn as Old Willie sang a plangent melody to the silent Lynching Tree. After a few days, Fulton and Moondog returned to Old Willie with mouth harps of their own, and they mimicked their voices to his as Neshoba still swayed above them. They wanted to learn to play the moutharp because they were afraid their sorrow would otherwise expire unanswered. They listened and sang and learned to ask the questions words could not ask and men could not answer. Crowds occasionally gathered, drawn by the haunting meter of their sonant discontent, but Fulton, Moondog, and Old Willie never noticed them.

Then a few months later, Moondog returned to the Lynching Tree, gazed at the branch scarred by his brother's final struggles, put one hand against its trunk, and stopped asking. He buried his mouth harp next to Old Willie, and Old Willie frowned as he foresaw the suffocating heartache that would descend on a colored without a song. But Moondog had decided that no answers resided in a tree, and that is when he started to drink everyday, to keep himself narcotized to all the pain and loss of his past, to keep him from erupting into the world. Fulton, though, kept his mouth harp and played it from time to time, because he knew that one day Old Willie would die, and someone would need to continue breathing their song to the silent Lynching Tree.

LIFE'S ONLY PROMISE

Settlement Day

Settlement Day arrived. "It's like judgment day," Fulton's father Bukka used to say, "cept down here in Mississippi ain't nobody fit to judge." All forty cabins lined their mule carts and cotton around Anderson's mansion and down the dusty road along the southern perimeter of the land. The mansion itself was a sprawling Victorian structure, prefaced by forty foot ionic columns and containing over thirty rooms. The accountants' annex where the Settlement Day transactions occurred was about a hundred feet beyond the mansion. As they waited in line, the croppers all hoped that the accountants' arithmetic would leave them enough profit to retain their cabins another year. Success meant living on the land from one Settlement Day to the next.

For his part, Anderson paid his illiterate croppers whatever he wanted, and he primarily paid them in coupons worthless outside of the general store he stocked and operated on the east side of his land, in which everything cost four times what it should. So after all the rigorous months spent tilling, planting, thinning, clearing, and picking, Anderson's croppers had nothing to show for their labor except a few coupons worth just enough to feed and clothe them until Limit Day the following March when Anderson gave them a $40 coupon advance against the arriving season's cotton crop to keep them clothed and fed until Settlement Day. Fulton despised always being in debt, a condition that precluded him from realizing his dream of liberating his family to a better life. The debt at Limit Day was the residue that kept Fulton entrenched in the sharecropper's cycle of poverty. He felt incarcerated in a prison that stretched to the end of his cotton field. But such was the system of things, the order of his place and time, and he had to accept it because life in Mississippi in 1903 outside his sharecropping prison was an even more brutish sentence.

Two accountants sat behind a glass window in the annex awaiting the croppers and their cotton in order to tabulate their respective coupon and cash payments. Anderson's men inspected and weighed the contents of each barrel of loose cotton and then the accountants calculated the payment to each cropper, deducting the Limit Day advance and expenses for other supplies or livestock provided throughout the year. The croppers never saw the books; they accepted their always-disappointing remuneration as better than what they would otherwise receive outside the cropper's cycle. Sometimes arguments arose, mostly from new croppers, but the presence of Anderson's dozen or so riflemen generally dissuaded any problems. Anderson then took the cotton, bailed it, and sold it to distributors and manufacturers at ten times the value he paid his croppers for it. Thus, while cotton was nothing more than the currency of a sharecropper's subsistence, that same cotton was also the currency of Anderson's swelling wealth.

Fulton and Moondog sat next to each other in the line with their barrels behind them in their mule carts. As usual, both had gathered somewhere near five tons of cotton, as much as the families with several sons. This year a new cropper was in the line, two carts in front of them. His name was Stoka Lee. He was as tall as Fulton, but thinner, with sharp cheekbones and a contagious smile. He and his family had moved into Terrell Jamison's plot after Jamison's entire family died of pellagra. Terrell's family sat in its cabin and festered from the inside out. When the other croppers could smell that the family was dead, they burned the cabin with the corpses inside, and much to Anderson's displeasure, they burned both the mules as well. Stoka arrived from Tennessee the next day and erected a new cabin with scrap logs and sheet metal. But because Stoka arrived so soon after the Jamisons' death, some croppers feared that Stoka had cursed Terrell and his family with voodoo. Why else would he smile so much?

Nevertheless, Stoka worked tirelessly the next season. He played the guitar and invited the other croppers to his cabin on Saturday nights to share his music. Fulton would occasionally join them on clear nights and accompany Stoka with his mouth harp. Stoka's presence vivified the land and seemed to charm the cotton into more robust growth. It was not quite hope, but in a year Stoka brought a new energy and camaraderie to Anderson's croppers, even if they did fear his voodoo. And then one day Stoka became a true hero after he saved Tommy Dean's life when no one else would.

Tommy Dean was the unsuspecting clown of Anderson's land. Everyone liked him because he was less intelligent than they were. He worked diligently and sincerely, but he could not even keep track of how old he was. Every day seemed like the first day of Tommy's life, and therein the daily and seasonal cycles of sharecropping never became burdensome and monotonous to him. Moondog often wished he could be more like Tommy because then he would no longer be haunted by the memory of Neshoba's death. Fulton often wished he could be more like Tommy too, but he didn't really know why. Perhaps it was because Tommy had found the secret fountain of immortality -- the dismissal of his inimical self-consciousness.

Several months earlier, Tommy was in his fields late one night when he heard an ominous howling just beyond his vision. He had fallen asleep in the fields, and he knew enough about the howling to awaken and hurry home. Whenever the wolves descended from the higher plains, it meant they had exhausted their food and would not leave until they had gorged their hunger. Many mules had been stolen in the night by the plateau wolves, and anyone standing between the wolves and their dinner was asking for trouble.

As Tommy tried to hurry home that night, his mules were too terrified to flee in any direction at all. He did not want to abandon his mules and then be responsible to Anderson for their inflated value, so he did the only thing he could figure to do, he screamed for help. The agitated mules began to neigh and kick, and in an effort to calm them he caught one of their hooves square in his head and fell unconscious to the ground. Several neighbors, hundreds of yards away, heard his screams, but they also heard the howling, so no one dared attempt a rescue. Tommy's wife heard his screams, so she locked her terrified children in their cabin and ran up and down the dusty road in front of the neighboring croppers shrieking for help. But no one would volunteer for the doomed mission, no one except Stoka.

When Stoka heard the screams, he grabbed his scythe and oil lamp, burst from his cabin, and ran to Tommy Dean's wife, "You go on inside to your children. I'll bring your husband en his mules back." Tommy Dean's wife retreated to her cabin in hysterical tears. Stoka turned and bolted like a wildcat into the dark fields.

As he raced under the broken moonlight across the fields, growls and snarls began to fill the darkness. Stoka realized that he was upwind from the wolves, so they would smell him. Maybe that would distract them and buy Tommy more time. Then suddenly there was silence, and he stopped to listen. Nothing. He gazed in every direction, but he saw only darkness. He ran in one direction, then another, and then another. Still silent. And then he was lost.

Suddenly, the rabid growls and snarls returned, directly behind him. Stoka spun around, and just beyond the dark horizon of his vision he saw a mass of wolves with crimson faces jeering at him from behind the remains of a shredded carcass. The wolves growled their displeasure with Stoka's interruption, and with flesh dripping from their jaws, they inched beyond the carcass towards him. Stoka raised his lamp to better illuminate their slow, deliberate movements as they circled him. He tried to count them, four, five, six, but they moved in and out of the light, eluding his faculties. Stoka began to flail his lamp in an effort to keep the wolves at bay, but just as one retreated, two others advanced, snarling as if warning him to back away. Understanding his predicament, Stoka tore off his clothes, lit them on fire in front of him, dropped his lamp, and wrapped his long fingers around his scythe with taut precision. The light blazing from his makeshift pyre revealed the location of all the wolves, and Stoka announced to them, "I ain't leavin' without Tommy en his mules!"

So before his courage flagged, Stoka charged at the wolf in front of him. The wolf backed away, but from the side another hurled itself forward and lunged its fangs at Stoka's throat. With a reflex, Stoka slashed his blade at the wolf and opened its neck to the spine. The wolf collapsed straight to the ground and twitched as its blood steamed onto the earth. Without a moment to calm his heaving lungs, Stoka watched as the remaining five wolves slowly enclosed him and his receding fire. Sensing they intended to lunge at him in unison, Stoka slowly knelt to the ground and waited as the gnarling wolves inched towards him with their heads held low. Waiting, waiting, and when they were breathing over him, Stoka threw his lamp at the wolves to his left and jumped with his blade at the wolves to his right. He slashed at both of them, but they jumped back to avoid him.

At that instant, as he rebalanced himself from his empty slash, Stoka sensed the other wolves behind him rearing to pounce. He spun his blade just in time to catch one of the wolves falling upon him. The force of its attack pressed the wolf into Stoka's blade as it fell atop him. The wolf raked Stoka's neck with its left claw and yelped as its innards spilled onto Stoka, who was pressing his blade upward to rid himself from its dying weight. The confusion stalled the other wolves long enough for Stoka to free himself and jump to his feet, covered in the blood of his second victim.

Stoka was panting for life, and his neck was bleeding profusely. He felt surrender creeping into him and weakening his arms. Bent double and wheezing, Stoka watched the remaining three wolves surround him again. Along with his will to live, his fire was rapidly dimming. He passed a moment regretting his decision and worrying for the future of his family. He was not the hero he thought he was. But in the peak of his distress, an ally arrived from the shadowy perimeter of the scene with a furious blow to the head of one of the wolves sending it sprawling into a companion and falling still to the earth. Re-energized, Stoka conjured one remaining burst of energy and slashed his blade at the wolves. Stoka and his ally flailed with the fury of their unfinished lives, and the wolves, realizing that their numbers were no longer as favorable, retreated into the darkness back to the higher plains, living to descend for fresh flesh another day.

Stoka dropped his scythe and fell to his knees in exhaustion. The other stood behind him panting. Stoka was oblivious to him, hypnotized by the lingering fear of the previous minutes.

"Thankya Stoka."

Torn from his hypnosis, Stoka replied, "Yeah Tommy."

Tommy placed his hand on Stoka's trembling shoulder. Stoka rose and turned towards him, shocked by what he saw. Tommy was barely standing; most of his right thigh was missing. His milky femur glowed like the moon, and blood steamed down his leg in torrents.

"What happened?" Stoka asked.

"I was stuck under my mule. They was mostly eatin' him, but they got my leg too." Raising his hand, Tommy continued, "I took apart my cart axle to help you." And as suddenly as he had arrived, Tommy collapsed to the ground. He remained conscious, but too weak to stand from the loss of blood. Stoka tore off Tommy's shirt and wrapped his leg. The midnight winds had finally overwhelmed his fire, and surveying the darkness, Stoka prayed for the energy to carry his friend home. After Stoka lifted him over his shoulder, Tommy's eyes rolled into his head and his next memory was waking to his wife's face and the fiery stinging of Moondog's moonshine being doused on his leg. Stoka sat on his porch until sunrise, covered in the wolves' blood.

The story of Stoka's heroism spread quickly through the fields. Stoka had embraced his impoverished life and risked it for another man whom he had known only a few months, and who could not even pick fifty pounds of cotton in a day. The story even reached Anderson's ears, who was angry that he had lost a mule and almost two croppers, but mildly impressed with Stoka's courage, "Sometimes those coons show themselves to be worth more than the cotton they pick."

***

As they waited in the Settlement Day line behind Stoka, Fulton and Moondog tried to gauge the volume of his barrels to determine whether his superhuman valor manifested itself in fieldwork as well. He did not seem to have gathered any more than either of them, but of course he had only one mule. As they waited, each successive cropper wheeled himself to Anderson's accountants with hope shining in his eyes, and then each turned from the window with disappointment weighing against his face. But the disappointment was not embittered, for each cropper understood it was the nature of his role in Mississippi on Settlement Day. Each except Stoka.

Stoka had worked tirelessly for the entire season, even singing to his stalks in May to strengthen their skyward reach. Now, as he muttered and fidgeted in the slow line, Stoka watched the melancholy faces ride away from the accountants, and he refused to be cast a similar fate. He had plans for his money. He was going to trade in his coupons for another mule so he could harvest even more the next year and take a few of his extra barrels to Memphis for cash; after a few years he would take his money and move to Kansas City and work in the city for real money. Thus, this first Settlement Day represented the first step in Stoka's plan of liberation. If only the years could condense into days.

Fulton and Moondog noticed Stoka's impatience and told him to relax, "Your time wit the countants will come en go sooner than you think."

Stoka scowled, but soon enough he arrived at the accountants' annex, and he helped Anderson's men remove the barrels from his cart and place them in front of the scale. Stoka watched as they inspected each barrel to ensure they were not stuffed with rocks or otherwise defective. Then they weighed each one and recorded the weights on a pad which they shared with the accountants when they were finished. Stoka nervously attempted to discern what they were writing and how they were calculating his remuneration, "How much is that one? ... I know ain't one of em under a hundred twenty pounds ... They gotta be six ton here ... Ya'll figurin' it like Anderson said, right ... three dollar a barrel right ..." But Anderson's men and his accountants remained silent during Stoka's interrogations. When the captain had finally heard enough, he knocked Stoka in the chest with his rifle butt, and Stoka fell to the ground with a scowl. He watched the accountants scribble and calculate in their books, and after an unbearable length of time, they finally called him to the window, "Stoka Lee."

"Yessuh."

"Your payment consists of sixty dollars in coupons and twenty dollars in cash. You may begin to redeem this year's coupons in the General Store beginning next Monday."

Stoka closed his eyes and envisioned his wife and children. Calmed, he told himself that the accountants had miscalculated and that their error could be easily rectified. He tried not to think about the number of years their erroneous arithmetic would add to his plans.

"You musta made a mistake," Stoka said in calm words.
One of the accountants looked up at him from behind his wire glasses, "What do you mean, boy?"

"I calculated myself I should get more than double what ya'll sayin'."

"Then you calculated incorrectly, now take your payment and go."

"Lemme see your books," Stoka demanded.

"No," the accountant with the wire glasses shouted. They were displeased with the audacity of his challenge. No one ever asked to see the books.

Stoka's body began to tighten. Agitation pulsed over his brow, and his voice began to crescendo, "How do I know you ain't cheatin' me?"

"No one sees the books."

The accountant without wire glasses pushed the coupons and cash through the opening at the base of his window. Stoka looked at the payment and gnashed his teeth. It was unacceptable. Stoka could not control the anger of the sense of injustice boiling within him, so he crashed his fist into the window. The window shattered into shimmering shards spraying over the accountants' books and across their faces. Anderson's men pounced on Stoka with their rifles. The other croppers jumped down from their carts and hurried forward. Fulton and Moondog were the first to arrive, but they did not know how to help Stoka, who was buried under a mass of flailing rifles and fists. As the others crowded around, Moondog yelled at Anderson's men to release Stoka, which they did after they had beaten the resistance out of him. The guards removed themselves from the mass of bodies to reveal Stoka's broken and bleeding remains contorted on the ground. Everyone watched in silence as Stoka lifted himself to his wobbling feet, coughed blood onto himself, and then asked again, "I wanna know why my payment's so small."

"It ain't your place to ask questions," the captain responded.

From a distance, Fulton and Moondog tried to encourage Stoka to yield and accept his payment. This was the way things were. This was not a fight worth picking. But Stoka could not yield. It was not his nature to submit, not like the others. He tried to concentrate on the faces of his wife and children to cool his embers of rage, but the stakes were too precious. As he struggled to stand, he demanded again, "I wanna know why my payment's so small!" The croppers' anxiety increased along with the guards' ire. Then the accountant with the wire glasses, wiping the cuts on his face and arms, submitted to the tension of the moment and stepped forward to explain to Stoka that, among other things, his payment was adjusted for a new $40 new-resident tax, "These are new regulations that all new croppers must submit to. Now please, take your payment before this gets worse."

But Stoka was furious, "no one told me 'bout that tax when I came here."

"No one needed to," one of the guards barked in response.

Stoka felt helpless. He despised that feeling.

As his anger fumed within him, Stoka realized that he had already crossed all the lines that caged him and would probably be lynched before he could be evicted, and with that realization the foundation of his dreams crumbled beneath him. He had chosen not to submit, and now he had to follow that decision to its conclusion. His head began to swirl. The croppers were buzzing on one side, the guards were clenched on another, and the thieving accountants presuming to rob his dreams sat at the center of it all. The world felt heavy, threatening to crush him. What was the purpose of breathing, if he could not breathe life into his own dreams? And if there was no purpose in breathing, then it was no longer of consequence if they lynched him. And if they were going to lynch him, then he would not greet death without a fight.

So Stoka pounced on the nearest guard before the latter could raise a hand, snatched his pistol, and placed a knife at his neck. He shot at everything white in sight as he shielded himself with the guard's body. The croppers fled to their wagons, and Stoka injured two guards before he turned his fire to the accountant's annex, demanding to be paid. At that moment, Anderson and twenty of his men galloped up to the annex, surrounded Stoka, and pointed all of their rifles at his face. Anderson yelled at him, "Drop it Stoka!" Stoka whirled around with the guard still shielding him, "You didn't tell me 'bout no tax."

"You work for me, boy, you live on my land, and on my land the only man who has the right to ask any questions is me."

"That ain't right! I ain't no slave!"

"You'll wish you had been, because then I'd probably just whip you and forget this."

Anderson nodded his head, and in an instant a thick rope swung over the branch of a tree and two shotguns blasted into Stoka's legs from behind, collapsing him to the ground and allowing his hostage to escape. Stoka writhed in the dirt as he looked down at the shards of bone and flesh that remained of his legs. Moondog attempted to lead a riotous response to the violence, but he was driven back by shotgun blasts into the sky and by Anderson's stern eyes.

As Anderson's men dragged and beat Stoka towards the noose, Stoka's only thoughts were of gratitude that his wife and children were not present to witness his death. Hopefully, after he was lynched, the other croppers would ensure that they never saw his body. One of his eyes hung down from its socket, a few shattered bones poked out of his thighs from where his legs used to be, and blood saturated the earth beneath him. Anderson's men threw his neck into the noose and raised him from the earth. His lungs burned, but he could not open his mouth to refill them, so he jerked and heaved and clenched for life. As they watched, the other croppers felt Stoka's dying within them. As he watched, Anderson promised himself never to accept another cropper from Tennessee. Stoka's last thoughts were filled with images of his stoic wife, his bereft children, and his unfulfilled dreams for them. And with that final thought his head fell forward, lifeless. Blood flowed like ribbons from Stoka's body long after his consciousness had faded from the earth.

That night Fulton sat on his rocking chair and sang into his mouth harp while Moondog sipped his shine in silence. Simbi curled in her bed and cried until she fell asleep.

Later, Anderson's men removed the body and burned it. Anderson informed Stoka's wife she had two weeks to vacate her cabin. Most of the croppers visited her but had nothing to say. Silence substituted for that which could not be said.

The Crossroads

The autumn leaves colored themselves the various shades of sunset and fell to the earth. Time trudged forward in weary senescence. Fulton and Simbi passed the autumn days watching the seasonal metamorphosis from their porch. Rocking and napping and smoking the passage of time. The air grew cooler, and the symmetric fields yawned in beige somnolescence towards their spring rebirth.

And though winter's sleep was descending around them, Simbi's heart blossomed with love for Orlando. Fulton wanted to see her married, and Orlando was a strong man, so when he asked for Fulton's blessing he gladly offered it (even though, like Fulton, he had a widow's peak). They were married in early November. The croppers' preacher officiated their marriage ritual with the sun and moon together in the sky, and then the judge in Hernando notarized the marriage certificate and mailed it to them a week later. After the wedding, Simbi and Orlando each recited a prayer to the earth which Fulton's grandmother had taught him when he started working in the fields.

Liloba, she called it. *Liloba* was heavy with many things. *Liloba* was heavy with the purpose of their lives. *Liloba* was heavy with the journeys of their ancesotrs, and *liloba* was heavy with the force of their love. All of history resides in one pinch of her surface, and that was why on cloudy nights Fulton could see his grandmother still wandering for a place to rest, her diaphanous ankle still bleeding from the moccasin bite that killed her. When Orlando moved into Fulton's cabin, he and Simbi spent the first three nights of their marriage in silence, out of respect for their great-grandmother's search.

Though he was happy to see his daughter married, Fulton wrestled with a brooding agitation throughout the winter hibernation. Of all the lynchings he had witnessed in his life, he could not release Stoka's from his mind. He still saw the dangling eye staring at him when he reclined to sleep. Would that be his eye one day? Would this image haunt him forever? Too much time to think. Then in January a blizzard blanketed the land with a wintry sleep more white than when the fields were awake with cotton.

Simbi loved the snow, especially early in the morning, before any creature had tread across it. The snow made her feel she had gone somewhere far away because it hid the old earth, the furrows and scars reminding her of the past. For these same reasons, all the croppers needed the snow. It was an endless white that did not represent backbreaking toil, and therein it cleansed the emotive anguish of white's other associations. Snow opened the possibility of the future by veiling the past. But during this snowfall Fulton did not feel cleansed. No depth of pristine, white frost could bury his unhappiness. All he could see was himself in Stoka's fate.

And as duty to his daughter and ancestors, he could not allow his life to end so distant from its dreams.

So when the Gulf and Ship Island Railroad fliers began appearing on trees and posts throughout the land, Fulton foresaw the means of fulfilling his dreams for a better life. He decided he would seize this opportunity to make enough money to move his family to a place where they were paid for their work and could own their own lives. He travelled to Eudora where he listened to solicitors explain that the Gulf and Ship Island Railroad construction had begun in 1876 to open Mississippi's pine forests for export, but then stalled without funding during Reconstruction. Now, in 1904, the project was being completed, catalyzed by the proliferation of steam engine locomotives. Workers would learn on the job and be paid $3 a day plus food and tents to finish the Hernando to New Orleans leg.

But almost everyone who read the fliers and listened to the solicitors scoffed, "You gotta be a fool to think you ken work all day all winter long sleepin' in a tent for six months... all the former workers is probably dead, and that's why they here lookin' for more fools." The plan seemed obvious. Work the men to death so you don't have to pay them, then hire more again and again until you get to New Orleans for free. Nevertheless, some like Fulton recognized that $3 a day for six months was a lot of money. It meant the beginning of a new life. But the security of cropping was a lot to abandon for the perils of an unknown world and six months on a railroad. Nevertheless, each night that he slept in his cold, leaky cabin, Fulton began to discern the logic of the journey more and more clearly. It seemed to be whispering in his ear, compelling him -- *free yourself. free your family. Start again in a new place with a new life.* It was Stoka's ghost whispering, with hosts of ancestors by his side. They appeared as body parts -- a leg, an ear, an eye, a pointing finger -- and they charged him to take this journey to a new place where history had not already inscribed his fate upon the color of his skin. Maybe this was the answer to his mouth harp songs.

Fulton was afraid to make the railroad journey alone, so he told Moondog his plan. He needed Moondog's eyes behind him and his strength by his side, but he knew it would not be easy to unfasten Moondog's inertia.

"This is a chance for us to be free a this," Fulton pleaded.

"This is all the freedom I need," Moondog replied, "sides, wherever you think you gonna find more freedom you jes gonna find more troubles anyway."

Fulton tried to feed Moondog a dream, painted with the liberating colors of a new day. He told Moondog about all the people he heard who were moving to St. Louis and Chicago for opportunity and freedom. He told Moondog about the meat packing and steel industries up North where a colored can work and keep and honest day's pay. And he told Moondog that tickets on the Illinois Central Railroad from Memphis to Chicago were only $15. But Moondog resisted, "I kent jes up en leave my family . . . what 'bout the next season?"

"They ken start the tillin' witout us, en they can sow, en when we return in June we ken jes leave. 'Sides, what if the boll weevil come again like two year ago? There won't even be no harvest then anyway, en we jes be in more debt like last time."

Moondog remained silent as Fulton continued to plead, "Listen, you kent tell me you don't still see Stoka or your brother in your dreams every night. You wanna be next? You ain't no more safe than Stoka, even if you en Andeson is bruthers. What 'bout your children en they children after that? Bad things happen when you standin' in the wrong place wearin' the wrong skin."

Moondog did not want to be born again, but beneath his trained inertia he understood Fulton and had always placed his faith in his wisdom, "I do think 'bout Stoka. He didn't deserve that noose."

"No he didn't, en it's our duty to make sho he didn't die like that for nuthin'."

"And after a few months, if things ain't workin' out on the railroad, we ken always come back, right?"

"Yeah. En we will return, one way or another, either wit a new life for our families, or knowin' we tried."

Moondog realized what Fulton was telling him -- that Stoka was no different from Neshoba and that neither of them was different from him. They were all colored. Nothing more. And if he did not want himself or one of his sons to be next, then he needed to find a place where he could be more than a colored. He wasn't sure if that place existed, and he wasn't sure whether the railroad was the way to get there, but he had always trusted Fulton like a father, so on Fulton's word he decided to try.

"What you gonna tell Simbi?" Moondog asked.

Fulton sighed and responded, "I'm gonna hafta tell her our plan, en she en Orlando gonna hafta survive wit it 'til we return." Moondog scowled at Fulton with doubtful eyes.

Fulton turned his glance to the sky and inhaled deeply. He saw blood in the sunset; the same blood from his grandmother's ankle and from Stoka's dying body. Fulton felt bathed in that blood. He could smell it, and it smelled like failure. He despised its unforgiving color and its mocking scent, and he wanted to wake up one day cleansed of its torment. Using the railroad to find a life of freedom was the only way he knew how, and he foresaw that day when he returned and everyone before and after him would finally be cleansed of the blood spilled fighting for freedom. That would be the day they all could rest.

That night Fulton, Simbi, and Orlando sat together for dinner. Silence thickened the air in the cabin. Eating was never more than a routine, a flexing and grinding of certain muscles until the food was finished. Simbi and Orlando looked at each other as they watched Fulton eat his food like bitter medicine. As he stared into his plate, Fulton watched blood drip onto his food. He was too hungry to push the contaminated morsels aside, and he despised having to eat them. As self-loathing burned through his veins, Fulton found the courage to announce his journey to the world. To Simbi. He raised his eyes from his plate and broke the promise he had made years before when he almost buried her alive, "Simbi, I hafta leave for six months."

Her face unfolded in shock, "What you mean you gotta leave for six months?"

"I'm gonna work the railroad from Hernando to New Awlens. I'll be gone six months. When I return I'll have money to take us up North to a better life."

Simbi heard his words, but she did not understand. She trembled at the thought of such a separation. She did not know how to respond to his announcement, so she tried desperately to expose the flawed logic of his plan, "But six months! How we gonna start the crop? The winter'll kill you in a month if some crazy white foman don't first! 'Sides, we ain't railroad people, we cotton people." She stopped and began to cry. Orlando put his arm around her shoulder and asked Fulton, "How much they payin'?"

"Three dollar a day. After six months I'll have enough for us to move to Chicago en live a better life, a free life." Tears fell into Simbi's food. Her bond with her father was thick. He had been both her mother and her father, and she could not abide the rupture he was proposing. She already wore the scars of her mother's death, and she did not want to awaken one day to find her father's seared atop those. Fulton understood her fears; they were his own, so he tried to reassure her, "I ain't goin' alone. Moondog's comin' wit me."

Simbi was startled, "Moondog?! He'll get you kilt in a week!"

"That ain't true Simbi. Moondog's strong en smart. He'll keep me alive."

Fulton paused for a moment as Simbi cleared her eyes. He wanted her to understand his feelings before she suffered any more pain. He wanted her to understand that he was leaving her because he did not want her to live a life like his, one in which pain was the only origin of memory. And most of all, he did not want her to feel he was abandoning her. Fulton extended his hand across the table, beckoning her to take hold, and he continued in a soft voice, "Simbi, you kent take any a this too seriously. That's how all the problems in this world git started."

"But daddy . . . " she quivered.

"I know baby, I know... But you gotta see that I want you to have more than this, en that's the only reason I'm goin'."

They sat in silence and shifted their senses to the sounds of the Mississippi night. Hollow and brittle. Fulton immersed himself in the loathing within him. He had always felt it, but he told himself that colored folks could not remedy such things. Now, for the first time in his life he understood that he must. For the first time in his life he cast his imagination beyond his field's horizon. He held his daughter's hand and prepared to saturate himself with the labor pains of their unborn destinies.

Fulton and Moondog spent the next few days ensuring that their families had enough firewood and food for the remainder of the winter. Moondog's family was as uncomfortable with his decision as Fulton's, but Moondog's two sons were old enough to care for their mother and prepare the fields for the next harvest. Moondog also instructed his family to watch over Simbi and Orlando.

Fulton remained serene and detached from the anticipation that should have been preoccupying him. Simbi moved about the cabin like a cub lost from her den.

The evening before their departure, Fulton and Moondog sat alone on Fulton's porch. The sky was clear and cold. A single crow sat perched atop the drooping apple tree next to Fulton's cabin, watching. Watching with black eyes.

The two friends inhaled the history of their kinship and invited it to subdue the anxiety pressing against their chests. At length, Fulton retrieved his mouth harp from his pocket and began to play. Recumbent notes, more serene than nervous. After the song, Moondog arose to return to his cabin to spend the remaining hours of the night with his family. "Meet you at the crossroads tomorrow," Moondog said as he departed into the darkness with his oil lamp, his fist held aloft at his side. Fulton watched him drift into a haunting bounce of light fading into the night.

Fulton returned inside his cabin to discover Simbi seated on their couch in the cold darkness of the room. He placed his lamp on the table and sat next to her. She wore a stolid face.

"Where's Orlando?" he asked.

"He's inside layin' down." Simbi responded as if speaking to a ghost.

Fulton took her hand in his, and for the first time in his life he was overwhelmed by his daughter's presence. He was amazed by her. She was a miraculous creature -- living, breathing, and beautiful. The life that burned within her was perfect.

At the same time, Simbi looked into her father's shadoweyes and saw the spark of his love twinkle in the lamplight. And within that twinkle she understood why he was leaving with the sunrise. Her throat constricted as she laid her overwhelmed heart into his lap. Fulton caressed her hair and tucked it behind her ear so that it was not in her face. The gesture reminded Simbi of her childhood, when her father would return exhausted from the fields but still find the strength to sing her to sleep. Bereft of mother and wife, they were always each other's other selves, and now the purposes of this new journey in life.

That night before falling asleep, Fulton searched his memories and wondered how they would be changed in the coming year. What new memories awaited him?

Thirty years from now he wanted a war chest of nostalgia with which he could strike back against his dying days. But thirty years seemed too distant, so he chose instead to concentrate on the warmth of his bed, beneath his tattered covers, and the heat filling his cabin from the glowing stove. This would be the last bed in which he would sleep for months, and the last sleep whose dreams could reach across to the other room and kiss his daughter to sleep. He thanked his ancestors for bringing Orlando to his home in time for his journey.

When Fulton awoke, Simbi and Orlando were replenishing the stove and warming some grits. Fulton wore his brown work clothes and gray jacket. He ate his breakfast while packing his rucksack with some canned sausage and vegetables, a canteen, tobacco, a washcloth, and a knife. A mile away, Moondog packed a similar sack with a pint of shine as well. They would meet at the crossroads and walk a day-and-a-half to the Hernando Railroad Station from where they would begin to lay track to New Orleans. Six months later they would return with freedom in their pockets. Fulton took leave of his family with long hugs and reassuring glances. He told Simbi never to doubt that he would return, and then he threw his rucksack on his back, stepped down from his porch, and walked towards the crossroads.

As he left, Fulton refrained from taking a last look at his house and family, for such a glance would surely signify to the world that he did not expect to return. As Simbi watched her father depart she felt a constriction squeeze her heart, and she grew dizzy with the feeling that she had lost her reference in the world. As Fulton walked to the crossroads, he was invigorated by the new search for his.

The Poetry of Rain

They met at the crossroads and walked aside each other towards Hernando. It was cold but sunny. They walked in silence, each taking some time to digest this journey to a new life that every new footstep promised. They wanted to reach Banks by sundown so that they would have only a half-day to walk to Hernando the next morning.

Fulton walked with his hands in his pockets, observing the world around him. It smelled like after rain. That was his favorite smell, other than the smell of Uma's neck.

After they had traveled a sufficient distance beyond the perimeter of their former lives, Moondog finally broke the silence, "What's the name a that foreman we supposed to find in Hernando?"

"Simmons somethin' . . . I think it's Simmons Hill."

"That sounds right."

They continued towards Banks, and their thoughts began to fill and shape the space around them. Fulton saw the sinuous skeletons of kudzu suffocating a defenseless tree. Even in winter. The kudzu was spreading north like a rainstorm, and had just begun to arrive in this area. In a few seasons it would overwhelm Anderson's land. Fulton had heard that farther south during the spring the kudzu devoured the horizon, leaving all the trees and plants groping for scraps of sustenance. Soon enough, he would be farther south and would see the fabled kudzu horizon for himself.

As for Moondog, he began to see all the things he had not seen in years, since the day after his brother died and he decided to stop looking at the world. The earthy color of trees, the clouds that swim beneath the morning sun... he saw all these things again with a sensation of novelty. He walked down Highway 304 like a child at a circus, trying to drink in all the wondrous sights through his wide eyes.

After a few hours they sat by the roadside to eat their sausage. Fulton enjoyed its salty, spicy taste, while Moondog pondered a gathering of ladybugs on a rock, stretching their polka-dot wings under the sun. The pair ate quickly as the wind was beginning to chill them through their tattered clothing. In the distance Fulton spied a wagon approaching perpendicular to them. Then as the wagon turned onto 304, they saw two horses leading a colored man who sat on the cart behind. They waited for the cart to arrive near them.

"Where you headed?" Fulton asked.

"Few miles yonder, to Banks to leave my tobacco at the station."

"You mind if we ride wit you?" Fulton asked.

"Sho ya'll ken ride. I ain't goin much faster than walkin', but you welcome to take your weight off your feet en set on the cart wit the tobacco."

"We much obliged for your kindness," Moondog replied as he and Fulton climbed into the cart. The other smiled and led his horses forward towards Banks, Mississippi.

His name was Coltrane, and he seemed like the kind of man who could sit on his porch, chew tobacco, and ponder a day away. As they rode, they talked about the land and whether things had changed at all since the War. Coltrane was older and gray, and had fought in the War, "Not on account a my wantin' to get my head blowed off, but on account a not wantin' to get twenty lashes a day from my master." Fulton was fascinated by Coltrane, by his earthy voice and by the humble manner with which his face greeted the world. Like his father. Coltrane's furrowed skin mapped the tribulations of his life, and he spoke as if he had been alive for hundreds of years, "things is as they is, 'cause it's only History, not the Nowth, that ken emancipate us, en History kent emancipate us 'cause we live in a time without poets."

They continued in silence for a time, and Fulton and Moondog ruminated on the meaning of Coltrane's words. What is a poet and what does he have to do with freedom? How could history make them free? Wasn't it history that imprisoned them? When they arrived in Banks they helped their new friend unload his tobacco at the rail junction and then saw him off on his return home. They could not help feeling that Coltrane was some spirit from their past who had arrived to guide them on their journey.

Banks was a town that stretched about ten minutes on foot, but not many of its thirty or so permanent residents had ever stepped foot beyond it. It was a town of a few cabins and a Juke Joint surrounding a junction of the aging railroad that The Gulf and Ship Island railroad would replace. Other than the locals who operated the junction, Banks was home to several nomadic exiles who found a temporary home at the Juke Joint run by Naga Reed. Naga's tenants were the displaced and transient refugees of the South, who like Banks, awoke each morning to the same life from the previous day. It was a place and a town frozen from time, even more so than the remainder of the South, and that is why Fulton wanted to conceive his child in Banks, so his love for his family would be frozen forever (though on this return to Banks he looked away from that sacred fig tree). You would never find a white man in Banks, but Banks existed because whites lived everywhere else.

Fulton and Moondog walked straight to Naga's Juke Joint; they knew they could sleep in the stables for the night and then continue to Hernando the next morning. As they walked through the center of the town, several people were outside with drinks and smokes despite the cold. Others, like zombies, sat motionless as they stared into the sunset, waiting. Moondog sipped his shine as they neared the Juke Joint, which was surrounded by a mass of emptyeyed coloreds.

An arid listlessness enclosed the place so that it seemed deserted, and yet the sounds of Mississippi life pulsed from within. Moondog turned to Fulton with a smile, "maybe I ken open a place like this up Nowth wit my money when we get back." As they entered Naga's, only a few of the three dozen eyes present lifted to notice them. Those that did, nodded and returned to themselves. Fulton and Moondog stood for a moment at the front door and inhaled the scene. A long bar lined the back of the Joint with a giant colored behind it laughing from his belly as he served drinks. Most of the other people were gathered around another colored in a black suit and top hat, sitting on a stool in the corner strumming his guitar as if its strings were dogwood petals. The haunting rhythms seemed to commiserate with the morose wanderings of those present. The man in the black suit tapped his foot as he played and was as hypnotized as those who listened. Fulton and Moondog melted into the music as well, unaware of all the somnambulant people gathered around the tables playing dice and cards. Soon, they were no longer aware of themselves, simply adrift.

They walked to the bar, slowly, and sat at two oak stools to await the giant bartender. Once he noticed the two new faces he carried himself to Fulton and Moondog to serve them, "What you boys need today?"

"We lookin' for Naga," Fulton responded.

"That's me."

Fulton smiled and explained where he and Moondog were headed and asked if they could sleep in the stable for the night. Naga rubbed his belly as he poured them each a gill of whiskey and told them there was no need to ask to sleep in the stable; anyone and anything was welcome to whatever piece of ground they could find. After their drink, Moondog asked Naga about the guitar man. "I don't know his name," Naga replied, "but he been here a few days, come from the south lookin' for some woman who left him wit some other man . . . you know the story."

"He should be in some club in Memphis," Fulton said.

"Should ain't a word we use 'round here," Naga rejoined with a smile.

Fulton offered an apologetic face as Naga continued along the bar serving drinks. Moondog looked around and tried to absorb the distance from his world he had traveled in just one day, "world's a mighty big en strange place, ain't it?"

"Sho is," Fulton responded, "it sho is big en strange, en I don't know where we supposed to fit in it."

Night arrived quickly in Banks, and Fulton and Moondog found a place in the stable to sleep, but their sleep was not restful. Drinks, singing and other noises filled the night until the first peeks of morning. The stable was completely dark, so the night's sounds assumed frightful forms that swam through the darkness. Couplings to the rhythm of the Guitar Man's chanting. Couplings with the sounds of every combination, indiscriminate, and the scent of burning flesh. They peered into the inky darkness, but could never see.

In the morning Fulton and Moondog saw the night's remnants and could not imagine what had transformed the stable into what was before them. Bodies lay strewn across the stable, half naked and covered in blood and whatever other fluids living creatures could expel. And it seemed that some of the occupants of the stable had half-transformed into cottonmouths and were all inter-coiled, either eating each other or eating dirt. A smell of fresh blood saturated the stable and choked their lungs. When they left, Naga Reed was still standing behind the bar and offered a wave goodbye. Outside, four falcons were resting in the trees above the Juke Joint, perched in wait, as if they knew that Banks was the place which introduced snakes into the world.

They hurried away from Naga's and out of Banks, Mississippi. Zombies and cottonmouths littered the road, and various birds of prey began to descend on them. Fulton and Moondog were certain that some manner of hellfire and voodoo had overwhelmed the town, and they agreed to walk around it on their way back.

Once out of town, Fulton took a moment to think of Simbi, awakening a few miles away for the first time in a house in which they were not both present. The emptiness of those few miles ached his chest and constricted his breathing. He imagined that she would turn to her childhood history picture books for comfort. Neither of them could read, but from an early age Simbi had been fascinated with cars and trains and boats, so Fulton used their precious savings to buy picture books for her of the cars and trains of the world. From the *Parnhard Larvessor* to the *Ford 'Lectric Car* to the *Steam Loco* to a *Pirate Sailboat*, as a child Simbi imagined herself captain of her own train steaming across the unknown frontier, or driving a car to Washington to become President and make a law for everyone to have a house and a job and a school, or sailing to an island with no name where she could be queen and rule her happy people.

Fulton bought her an atlas for her tenth birthday so she could see America and where they were and all the other countries and seas across the world. Simbi would pick a country and transform Fulton into the car or train or sailboat that would take her there (travelling from the front room couch called Mississippi to Fulton's bed called Brazil). They would meet the kings and queens of distant lands and take sweet potatoes as gifts. After a regal dinner it was off in the train to another unknown land, "Oh what strange habits these villagers have, they eat they food wit they noses . . . have you heard that the prince a The West Sea has one hundred children who ken swim all across the ocean? My oh my, ...A farmer in Mountain Land told me his people live four hundred years... Oh what wonders the world ken share." Fulton smiled and imagined sharing those wonders with his grandchildren.

As the hours passed they realized they were reaching their destination; the first step. Several grain silos lined the last few miles of highway 304 into Hernando. Some of the silos were sixty feet high, and all of them were filled with grain. The bounty amazed Fulton and Moondog. Just one of these, and most croppers would never have to work again. The silos towered over either side of them like storage vessels from a land of giants. But not even the silos of the giants were immune to the kudzu, whose skeletons coiled up their ladders and blanketed their silver dome roofs, waiting to be reborn in the spring.

Then they crossed the Hernando city limits. Hernando was a small plantation town, but it was the biggest town either of them had ever seen. Hernando's proximity to Memphis was largely responsible for its size and the traffic north and south which passed through it. Twenty-five miles due north would find you on the Memphis bluffs of the Mississippi River and all the steamboats docked for a day or two during their journey to New Orleans. In New Orleans, they transferred their cargo to international trading ships which crossed the open ocean to South America. The Gulf and Ship Island Railroad was intended to alleviate the river traffic, speed shipments, as well as open Mississippi's pine forests to the profits a few men foresaw within them.

Fulton and Moondog knew that despite the dangers, there would probably be more volunteers than needed, especially poor whites. They were confident that they would be selected, but they feared being part of a colored minority in the workforce. That possibility presented a danger that could undo their plans.

As they searched for the rail station, Fulton and Moondog walked by a library, a courthouse, a steakhouse, and a pack of slim-eyed deputies on horseback. Almost every building was shrouded with posters of a man's face, under which were written words which Fulton and Moondog could not read. In due time, Fulton spotted a sign with the picture of a train on it. They followed similar signs to the railroad station and arrived a few hours before the scheduled 3 o'clock meeting with Simmons Hill.

There were not more than twenty people scattered about the platform, so Fulton and Moondog walked to the front and sat on two adjacent benches. Fulton removed his shoes and rubbed his feet while Moondog laid back to rest his head on his rucksack. They shivered in the cold even though they were sitting in the sun. One lone cloud floated across the sky like the tail of a sleeping dragon, like the silver suspiration streaming from their lungs.

A half-dozen men were sleeping nearby, five coloreds and one white. The white man slept apart from the others. He wore a light brown shirt, dark brown pants, torn brown shoes, and he had long brown hair. A peculiar smell weighed in the platform air, like mud. Fulton and Moondog decided to join the others in a nap (Fulton with his eyes half-open), and twenty minutes later a train from the north pulled into the far track along the other platform, awakening Fulton. A mass of coloreds unloaded beef and chicken from the train and loaded cotton back into it. But the beef and chicken were frozen. Fulton thought to himself that the meat must be frozen because of a refrigerated car. He didn't believe it when he had heard about it a year ago, but now he was seeing it. It must have come all the way from the slaughterhouses in Chicago. *You could take Cue a thousen miles to the Prince a the West Sea en it'd stay fresh.* The thought sent a refrigerated chill through Fulton's spine. Fulton slapped Moondog awake to show him the car, but Moondog told him to get back to sleep so they would be fresh and strong for the selection of the workforce. So Fulton drifted back to sleep with the sensation that the world ahead of him held a thousand opportunities to liberate him.

Fulton woke with anticipation a few hours later. He rubbed his eyes, picking the sleep crust away from their corners, then awoke Moondog, who sipped his shine to wash down the sleepy taste in his mouth. Moondog counted thirteen whites. That left at least seven spots for the others. No one who looked like he would be Simmons Hill was present, so they decided to meet some of the other men. It was never too soon to make allies. But Fulton's attention remained on the white man with all the brown clothes who was now sitting alone a few benches away writing in a small pad. Fulton had seen people writing only a few times in his life (mostly Anderson's accountants), and something in the look of that white man made him want to ask him what he was writing. But Moondog took Fulton by the arm and led him to a group of coloreds.

The coloreds gathered around and shared their histories. Some were croppers, others were nomads, but one man endeared himself to Moondog more than the others. His name was Corliss Tindel, and he was a cook in his plantation owner's house in Corinth.

Corliss arrived at the railroad because he was fleeing his plantation owner, Waynes Wallace. Waynes, had been sleeping with Corliss' daughter for months, but Corliss did not know because Waynes had threatened his life should his daughter say anything. Corliss finally discovered the abuse when late one night another servant saw Waynes mounted behind Corliss' daughter in the kitchen. When the servant told him, Corliss was furious. The next night he burned Waynes' house to the ground and fled with his daughter to his brother's house in Ripley. A few days later he heard about the railroad and marched to Hernando. He knew that a posse was hunting him, but they were also hunting the dozen other suspected servants who fled that same night. Corliss came to the railroad to make the money that would take him to Mexico, where he could sleep through the night without jumping awake in a sweat from fear that the posse had found him and was about to unleash vengeance on him and his daughter. Fulton and Moondog saw shades of

Stoka in Corliss, so they felt an immediate kinship to him. He was about the same size as Stoka, but his smile was not as strong.

All the while Fulton kept one eye on the solitary white man, scribbling secret words in his pad. He watched him from the corner of his eye, wondering why this white man was the first one who had ever intrigued him. Maybe it was the forlorn air that surrounded him, as if he were ancestorless. Maybe it was the secrets he could share from his pad; or maybe it was that sitting alone in the shadows he appeared a shade too dark to be white.

Simmons Hill arrived on a brown horse followed by eight other men on horseback. He ordered silence and attention with a trained, resounding voice. He was an even six feet tall, fat, and a knife scar spoiled several inches of his left cheek. He wore a gray, three-pointed hat, and a bullwhip hung by his side. He presented the task at hand in terse, punctuated words. There would be hardship and hard labor, and always strict discipline. Disputes among the workers would be settled in hand-to-hand combat, and disputes between the workers and his men would be settled however he deemed fit. Two-dozen of them would be selected, and they needed to be in New Orleans by the end of June.

Simmons ordered the men to remove their jackets and shirts and line up. The men shivered in the cold as Simmons' men rode down the line inspecting each of them. Fulton caught a glance of the solitary white man and was surprised at how much bigger he was than he had seemed. He possessed the defined, muscular contours of most coloreds, but he was still not as big as either he or Moondog. Relentless labor with the earth had sculpted them into manifestations of her most formidable contours - mountains resided within them.

After a few minutes, Simmons' men gathered around him. Simmons explained that he would point to the selected men and the remainder should return to wherever they came from. Fulton's heart began to race; in an instant his entire vision could be aborted. He wanted to, but he could not close his eyes. Simmons rode down the line, selecting each white man and an occasional colored. Sweat began to bead across Fulton's and Moondog's brows as Simmons neared them. They should have stood apart, or at the beginning of the line before the spaces for selection were exhausted. *What if I'm selected en he ain't? How ken I go without him? How ken we return so quickly wit failure?* Fulton felt his heart beating like a drum, thumping the air from his lungs. And then he was not breathing at all... arriving at him, Simmons offered Fulton a look of curious familiarity which tormented him in its infinite duration. And then in an instant he could breathe again as Simmons pointed to him, Moondog, and Corliss in succession. Fulton was dizzy, and Moondog needed a drink.

Later, as the selected workers gathered just beyond the station among the rail tracks, Fulton remembered the not-so-white white man and searched for him. He had been selected. And he was standing alone again, at the edge of the group, and Fulton laughed. He and Moondog were surprised, for it was the first time either of them had heard him laugh in sixteen years, four months and eleven days -- the day before his daughter was born.

The men slept on benches in the station waiting room that night. Three trains eased into the station and continued on, carrying goods and profits into the Southern night. Fulton and Moondog huddled with Corliss and continued to share their stories. Simmons and his men returned early the next morning and divided the men into six groups to share supplies and a tent, which would all be stored in one of the supply and material cars which followed them to New Orleans. Laying the railroad required six tasks, which each of their six groups would rotate performing: one to unload the materials car, two to pass and place the rails and crossties, two to hammer the rails and crossties into place, and one to follow behind with hammers to ensure the security of the construction. One day for each task, then rotate. As for pay, they would receive a certain percent of their salary whenever they passed through a city and then would receive the difference whenever they arrived in New Orleans, or whenever they quit. Stealing would be punished with dismissal and a forfeiture of wages. They would spend one day in Hernando learning each station of the railroad operation, and then they would build alongside the current railroad until it veered off to Baton Rouge.

It had not occurred to Simmons Hill at the time, but by selecting all thirteen whites for the workforce, he had condemned one of them to working and sharing a tent with three coloreds. The moment Fulton heard they were to be divided into groups of four he offered to include the solitary white man in his group. And so it was that with a reassuring eye and a bold request that Fulton, Moondog, Corliss, and the lonely white man were grouped together. "This must be the first mixed group to ever build a railroad in Mississippi," Fulton said.

That night, after a long day of training and sweating under the winter sky, the men slept in their tents, and Moondog shared sips from his unending flask of shine. The tent was just big enough for four men to sleep side by side. Shortly before midnight, the sky filled with gray clouds and a windy rain began to fall. Fulton knew it was going to rain because he could always smell the swelling of clouds before they released themselves to the earth. He loved that smell because it smelled like love. The hypnotic patter of the droplets on the tent melted Fulton into a state of contentment. As he relaxed, Fulton watched the white man write in his small pad by lamplight, and after Corliss fell asleep and Moondog began to snore he found the courage to finally speak to him, "What's your name?"

"Jay Collins," the other answered.

"What you writin'?"

"Words. About my life. About where I've been and where I might go. And some stories that happen to me along the way." Fulton nodded, and then Jay continued, "Truth is, I don't know why I'm writing this journal. I'm mostly content to stay in the same place and wait for necessity to move me. I suppose I'm writing this journal for whatever reason it ultimately manifests."

"Mani-fests?"

"Yeah. Whatever reason happens to it. I'm not really in control."

Fulton could see that Jay felt helpless in life, so he tried to offer some encouraging words, "When my daughter feels that way she pretends to become the president, so she ken change all the things that make her unhappy... me, all I want is to be the president a my own life, wit a piece a land I ken pass on to my children. That's what I hope this railroad does for me."

"I hope you get what you want. As for me, this railroad isn't much more than a new set of pens for me to write with for a while. I dont know what else to ask for from life."

Fulton did not understand how Jay could be completely unobsessed with the direction and progress of his life. He could never be a colored, even if in the shade he did not appear altogether white.

Then Fulton noticed a long dagger inside Jay's rucksack and asked if he could see it. Jay offered it to him as a secret. It was a clean silver blade with an onyx hilt from which two dragons curled into the blade. It was longer than a dagger but much shorter than a sword. As Fulton traced the elegant contours of the dragons along the hilt into the blade, Jay explained, "That dagger descended to me from my Irish ancestors. I keep it near me as a charm against evil and bad luck."

"I wish I had a blade that could fight evil and bad luck," Fulton responded, "maybe so many things in my life would be different." With that thought, Fulton went to sleep.

The first few days on the railroad passed without incident. The workers quickly learned that Hammer Duty was the station of preference. Just swing, bang, and move on. The twelve foot rails weighed three-hundred eighty pounds each and were sharp like knives at the edges. More than once a worker gashed his finger or belly against the sharp edges. When a worker became too injured or ill to continue Simmons recruited new workers from the nearest town.

The geography of the journey was uneventful to Fulton. Everything looked exactly like where he had spent his entire life, except that the land was not divided into neat rows of cotton, and there was more and more kudzu the farther south they traveled. Also unlike his fields, there was an emptiness that spread across the horizon that Fulton had never felt before. The land on which he had lived always seemed filled with the lives and spirits of this world. This other Mississippi seemed absent of any life at all -- no plants, no animals, no people, and no spirits. Just

LIFE'S ONLY PROMISE

brown. This world felt frighteningly empty. The ominous malevolence of the ever-cloudy sky was the only other presence Fulton felt.

As the days passed, Fulton and Jay spoke more. Jay continued to claim to have no dreams, but Fulton did not believe him. He could not believe that a man could be white and not embrace the fortune of wearing the skin that allowed him to realize his dreams, "Dreams are the only possessions a the living," he would say, "and in Mississippi white is the only color a life." Nevertheless, Fulton was surprised that he and Jay had become friends, and he wondered how many friendships had eluded him because he had spent his entire life rarely wandering more than a mile from his cabin.

Jay understood Fulton's self-consternation, for he himself was the son of sharecroppers. Jay's parents despised their lives and wanted to provide their son with the academic opportunities that would facilitate a life in the pursuit of knowledge instead of grain and cotton. Jay's parents saw their son teaching literature or law or medicine at Oxford and sowing knowledge into the fields of his life. But Jay's father died of malaria when he was twelve, and he and his mother were forced from their field. They moved to Jackson where they found work at a corner grocery.

Jay's mother fought valiantly to fulfill their dreams for him, but three years later she was stabbed and killed by a colored man she caught attempting to steal from the store. The colored claimed only to be stealing bread for his starving children, but because he killed a white woman a mob lynched him within twenty minutes. The public empathized with Jay and paid for his mother's funeral and helped him with work and housing for a few years. But in time, as other white women were offended and new coloreds were lynched, people forgot about Jay. At seventeen he began wandering and writing. By the end of the next eleven years he had walked the South from Georgia to Louisiana, always returning to Jackson on the anniversary of his mother's death to rest his feet near her tombstone. "I may not be a professor," he would say to her grave, "but I lead a good life and I'm blessed you gave it to me." Fulton told Jay that his life sounded like a colored's, but Jay responded that not all white people lived white lives. Jay maintained that tragedy was colorblind, but Fulton did not agree. Maybe it just looked for a little variety from time to time.

Corliss and Moondog were the rail gang's best workers. Especially on Hammer Duty. Their tree-trunk arms hammered the rail stakes into place in half as many blows as anyone else. Even Simmons was surprised by their strength, so their group received preferential treatment, especially during mealtime. The best workers needed to remain strong and well fed. Some of the white workers were envious, but Simmons knew that the presence of his men was sufficient deterrent from violence against his favored workers. As far as Simmons was concerned, he was simply protecting his profit, which was directly linked to the speed with which they arrived in New Orleans with a finished railroad behind them. Profit motivated his brazen disregard for racial hierarchy.

After two weeks, heavy rain stalled work for three days. Violent winds ripped the rain into the earth. Huddled in their tents hour after hour, the workers grew restless and irascible. Their tents leaked and the rain sopped the muddy earth inside. They were wet and cold; the rain was unrelenting. Fulton began to worry that the earth might melt into a soup with horses and people and cows and buildings floating across the soupscape for miles and miles. Then when the rain stopped and the earth hardened, all the peoples and things of the world would be lodged upside down and in all the wrong places. The Queen of China might end up next to his house. That would make Simbi happy. Or maybe while the earth was a soup, the weight of their evil would sink the wicked to the bottom so that when it hardened they would be buried forever, and only good people would walk the surface of the world. Fulton liked the idea of this new world. New mountains and trees and oceans would grow and people would have a second chance to live with justice. And there would be no history that some could use to justify the persecution of others. In this world men could live and prosper on the merits of their efforts and up to the limits of their dreams.

So while the other men grumbled at the deluge and its unending thud against their tents, Fulton secretly wanted the storm to continue. If the earth did begin to melt, he could use the crossties for flotation. The rain fell day after day and then droned them sleep.

"Fulton."

"Here I am." *He turned as he spoke and saw it. Swimming through the soupy earth beneath the endless rain, was a dragon (a snake with wings) with eyes more brilliant than the brightest star. It swam through the lengths of planets with a single undulation, and within seconds it reared its majestic face like a galaxy above Fulton's unblinking eyes.*

"I have come to devour your world."

"What is your name?"

"You cannot name me. But you may take this." *An eyelash fell from the dragon into a necklace around Fulton's neck. It contained a circular pendant with a lotus in it, endlessly unfolding upon itself.*

"Thank you. But why have you come to devour my world?"

"The losing throw was cast thousands of years ago, announcing the final age of strife in which sacrifice and sound are no longer purposeful. Life trudges forward until the weight of its emptiness collapses it. I have come for that moment."

"I don't understand. I'm not ready to be devoured."

"Mountains rise and fall like ocean waves and take no note of your readiness in between." And with his final, thundering words, the dragon dove into the plumbless soup and swam beyond the world's horizon. Fulton stood, suspended above the cosmos like a lost sound, looking deep into the indistinguishable expanse with the lotus in his hand, awaiting its assassination.

Love in the Time of Uncolored Gods

"Lawd have mercy!" Corliss bellowed the next day, "this rain done finally cleared away." The men burst from their tents like butterflies from cocoons. The sun blazed from behind the parting clouds, and the earth wore a pristine scent of rebirth. Birds splashed in the puddles and feasted on the bounty of worms exposed by the rains. Meanwhile, the men spent the day cleaning their supplies and drying their spirits under the golden sun.

They passed through Grenada a few days later. Simmons offered his workers the weekend to enjoy the town, provided they returned to camp by midnight, and he ordered his foremen to patrol the city to ensure good behavior. Some of the workers had fallen ill during the rain, so Simmons took them to a doctor. Others were invigorated by the sounds of human life and followed them in pursuit of the nearest Juke Joint. Fulton's group and another group searched the town together, thrilled by their presence in a new place with new people and things all moving about the earth.

They found a colored Juke Joint named Mojo's. Seven coloreds and Jay arrived with ivory smiles across their faces. Mojo's facade was covered with the same posters from Hernando. The posters were on all the buildings. They featured the stately print of a man's bust; his broad shoulders were thrown back and his focused eyes glared angry messages from beneath his heavy brow. He commanded attention and deference. Jay read the posters to himself. The name *J.K. Vardaman* was written in bold, capital letters beneath the bust, followed by smaller letters, *Vote Vardaman for Governor on March 1 and reclaim your South.*

When Fulton asked Jay what the posters said, Jay pondered his answer. He knew Vardaman's story and the depth of his colored hatred. During his campaign, Vardaman had injected himself into unsure times as a promise to recapture the South's glorious past. Jay saw him speak in Vicksburg, and his rhetoric was powerful and persuasive. So Jay decided to tell Fulton that the posters were for a man named Vardaman who had recently been elected governor and would begin serving his term very soon, but that Vardaman was the last man in Mississippi he wanted in the Governor's Mansion in Jackson. Fulton told Jay that he was the only white man he had ever met that he would want living in the Governor's Mansion. Jay turned a wry smile, and they entered Mojo's.

Jay's entrance turned several angry eyes, but he was adept at hiding unseen in shadows, so as the night wore on Mojo's ignored him. The air was filled with hanging smoke and the scents of sweat, shine, and sugarcubes, which Mojo's passed out free to all its customers to keep them sweet instead of sour. The rail workers spent the raucous night drinking and hunting for women, but Fulton and Jay sat together with a few drinks and talked. Fulton rolled some tobacco and the two shared its serenity. After a while, Fulton asked Jay about voting - "Ya know, I've heard that coloreds ken vote, but our landowner told us that we couldn't, en if we tried to he'd evict us."

"That's not right," Jay responded, "the Law says that coloreds can vote." But Jay went on to explain that Vardaman and his cohorts intended to pass legislation that placed literacy and land-ownership restrictions on voter registration, "and if they do that, then many poor whites such as myself would no longer qualify to vote. Meanwhile, Vardaman and his Whitecaps have been travelling the South for years frightening coloreds from even thinking of voting by burning their houses and fields and even lynching some of them."

"I heard a them Whitecaps," Fulton interjected, "I heard a them 'cause some a my landowners men is part a them. I remember jes last year a cropper named Sanford tried to vote, but a gang a Andersons men beat him before he even entered the voter booth. Sanford lost both his legs en Andeson evicted him sayin', 'serves that nigger right for tryin' not to be a nigger.'"

At that moment both Fulton and Jay jumped from their chairs to the sound of shattering glass. They spun around and saw Corliss standing over a gashed face with half a whiskey bottle in his hand and shards of brown glass across the floor. He hadn't eaten enough sugar. The scene was frozen like an angry painting, but only for the brief, kinetic moment before a storm erupted. Two men jumped on Corliss, who immediately threw one to the ground and fell atop the other. Moondog and the other rail workers pounced on the other brawlers, and before it was too late Fulton pulled Jay out of the bar and ordered him to stay outside until he returned. Jay waited in the shadows and listened to the tables and chairs and bottles crashing across the Joint. Jay knew that the police would only arrive if the brawl made its way outside, which it never did, because even in the fury of battle, all the coloreds understood that to lead their disagreements outside Mojo's would result in incarceration for them all.

Twenty minutes later the brawl had spent itself and Jay returned inside. Bodies were strewn across the floor, mingling spilled blood with spilled spirits in meandering streams. Three of the motionless bodies belonged to rail workers. Fortunately, Fulton, Moondog, and Corliss had suffered only a few cuts and bruises. But before they could compose themselves and flee the scene, Simmons arrived at the Juke Joint with his foremen. He was furious. He fired the three workers on the floor, but spared Corliss, Moondog, Fulton, and Jay only because they were the best workers, the friend of the best workers, and white, respectively. Simmons hired three more coloreds to the workforce and everyone was ordered back to work again the next day.

Simmons shouted for an hour that any similar performance would be met with dismissal into the barren Mississippi plains without food, water, or fire. Simmons worked the men around the clock the next week; supplies followed behind them on the rail and were exhausted as quickly as they arrived. Corliss and Moondog had both suffered knife slashes across their chests which burned them throughout the workday, and a chair had broken across Fulton's head which left him with an acorn knot and severe headaches which the banging hammers only aggravated. After ten days Simmons slowed the pace of labor and the exhausted workers barely had the energy to sleep at night.

The third week of February arrived, and Fulton wondered about Simbi. He told himself that he could not get involved in any other fights because he needed to survive to return to his family. He could not lose sight of his plan in the flashes of whirlwind moments. And though he yearned to be home, he told himself that each day was another three dollars. Three dollars closer to freedom. As the days passed, Fulton began to talk to Jay about his daughter. He told Jay about the Train Car Boat Game and how Simbi climbed on his back as he sailed or railed across the earth, "When she pulls my ear I toot like a horn, en when the train needs more steam she puts a cracker in my mouth."

After a brief respite, Simmons returned to a more rigorous schedule. He yelled and kicked the workers who displeased him, white or colored. At night the workers were not allowed to socialize around the campfires; Simmons ordered them into their tents, and whoever broke the night silence would not eat the next day. Fortunately for Fulton's group, Corliss understood his precarious position since the fight in Mojo's, so he focused on not drawing any attention to himself, suppressing his need to be the center of the universe.

Instead, Corliss began to share more about his previous life with his tent mates. He whispered a new story each night before falling asleep. Stories were like water to him, nourishing and necessary. Corliss' need to tell stories reminded Fulton of his own passion for storytelling, and he wondered where all his stories had gone. In the meantime, Fulton listened to Corliss' stories, and the story he most remembered was the one with the white girl named Mary.

Seventeen years earlier, before Corliss became the cook of Waynes Wallace's kitchen, he cooked for another landowner outside Biloxi. And there, he and a young white woman who was the step-daughter of the landowner had an affair. Her father was a priest for some white folks in Biloxi, and he preached to his congregation that the New Union was an abomination, that the Bible demonstrated that the negros should be slaves because they were the cursed descendents of Noah's evil son who knew him when he was drunk. Like their first forefather, the negro was a lascivious creature whom God punished for his disregard of the Word and the Law. No matter what Northern Law said, the negro was the negro, and in time the Lord would descend to re-order the world and return each to its kind.

LIFE'S ONLY PROMISE

But her father's words kindled the passions of forbidden fruit in Mary's heart. She lay in her bed at night swooning for the touch of this charcoal beast. She imagined him, black as night, floating through the window and descending on her. Then one day she met Corliss on a visit to her step-father's mansion. Their eyes met in the kitchen amid the swirling of chili and coriander spices in the wild sea air. In that instant they both undressed their illicit passions to each other, but Mary stole away her eyes in shame. Nevertheless, the spicy scent of the Negro in the ktichen had been implanted, and for the next several days it dizzied Mary's mind and fevered her blood. So Corliss was not surprised when, a few days later, Mary slipped into the servants' quarters at her step-father's mansion and found him. He silently led her to a brook behind the stables where he laid on the wet spring grass and let her devour him. They shuddered, both entranced by the rhythms of their chiariscuric union.

They shared their passions by the midnight brook for weeks. Mary begged Corliss to come to her house, to her bed, but he feared moving their lust beyond the familiar shadows of her step-father's land. Corliss knew where and when they could embrace without fear, and for him to venture into Biloxi, into her father's house, would certainly tempt disaster. But she wanted him in her bed, so that every night she could shroud herself in the scents of their passion.

Compelled by his affection for her, Corliss finally acquiesced and arrived by her window on a stormy spring night. And there, in her bed awaiting him, she was like a dove, opalesque and panting beneath the crest of her luminescent plume. The cool rain had washed his body taut, and she swam into the curves of his muscles as he descended upon her. Tepid water dripped from his brow into her parched throat, easing its impassioned constriction. They felt loose upon the world, but in the peak of their anarchy, the bed beneath them crashed into splinters onto the floor.

They were frozen, like the moment they met, and then they heard movement below. Corliss jumped to his feet to dress. Mary was on the floor, panting and dizzy, and just as Corliss kissed her on the brow and was climbing out the window, her father burst through the door and choked at what he saw. He screamed bloody rape and murder as Corliss fled for his life. Within minutes neighbors gathered with lamps and shotguns and bloodhounds and nooses. The bloodhounds inhaled Corliss' scent in the stormy sheets and raced into the night with the town behind them. The hunt had begun.

Corliss ran east all night, through the storm towards Alabama. The wind howled like the hounds behind him. By sunrise the storm had abated and Corliss was exhausted. Fear had carried him through the night, but the mob's anger was more powerful, and they inched closer and closer to him hour after hour until he felt them at his heels. At sunrise he arrived at the Wolf River where he collapsed and awaited the mob. Within minutes they were upon him, kicking him and throwing stones as they dragged him back to the city. They did not allow the hounds to devour him, for they had decided to lynch him in the presence of The Father and his daughter.

Once they returned to Biloxi, the mob dragged Corliss to the square where the gallows stood. The sheriff and his deputies arrived at the gallows with The Father and his daughter. Mary's awareness had long since abandoned her and the mob understood her blank face as the consequence of her shocking rape. The Father looked at Corliss, beaten, bloody, and collapsing on himself, and repeated his charge, "This nigger has raped and attempted to murder my daughter, and I demand justice for his crimes!" The sheriff looked at Corliss, looked at The Father, and then gazed across the wide-eyed crowd, gleaming with anticipation. He turned to his deputies and said, "String em up." The cry for Justice had been answered.

The mob roared with delight and yelled "Hang the nigger," and "Make him suffer for his crimes." Corliss gathered his energy and attempted to explain his innocence, but he was too weak to speak over the mob and spat out blood instead of words. The deputies dragged Corliss up the gallows, from where the orange sunrise cast long shadows across the crowd. The sheriff climbed the gallows and held Corliss' head in a commanding pose just in front of the noose while the deputies tied his hands behind his back. The mob silenced and the sheriff spoke, "This boy has been charged with the rape of The Father's daughter." The crowd spewed its agreemnt, and the sheriff looked at Corliss and continued, "Your crime is punishable by hanging. Do you have any last words to redeem yourself before God?" Corliss stared at the bloodhungry mob below him. He could not focus his eyes; all he saw was a blur of anger. He tried to find Mary, but he could not discern her. The world around him was a vortex of hatred, so all he could think to say was, "I didn't rape her . . . I loved her." The crowd snarled, and rocks flew at Corliss. One of them hit the sheriff in the knee, who responded with skyward gunfire to settle the mob.

The sheriff placed Corliss on a stool and noosed his neck within the frayed rope. Suddenly his world went silent and clear. He looked again at the crowd beneath him and realized that the entire town had gathered to watch him die; his death was the singular focus of their morning, like breakfast. As the sheriff reached around Corliss' face to tie the black blindfold over his eyes, Corliss refused it, shaking his head, because he wanted to see everyone staring at him as he died.

So he watched as the mob snarled and howled for justice. Suddenly, the world grew silent, and Corliss saw the mob's anger swirling around him. Then, in the chaos of that moment the Sheriff kicked the stool from beneath Corliss and he plunged for miles through the center of space, until the frayed chord snapped his voyage . . . but not his neck. He hung, kicking and suffocating, but able to suck tiny jerks of air into his burning lungs. The crowd stared in disbelief and swelling discomfort as the minutes passed. Mary cried tortured tears which burned inside her eyes. Corliss kicked and gasped in utter confusion . . . was he dead? Was he dying? How long would this last? Some in the mob eventually turned their eyes away. And at that moment of frenetic disbelief, a raucous commotion diverted the crowd's attention to another mob directly behind them. A second mob was dragging another negro and claimed he had burned down the church in which The Father preached. The Father ran from the gallows and headed for the alleged arsonist with the sheriff, deputies, and mob following behind. The accused was tied to a pole and dirt stuffed in his nose and mouth so that he did not die from asphyxiation while they doused him with gasoline. Corliss was stunned. If he was going to die then everyone had better witness it, and if not, then he was not going to die. So he twisted and kicked and hurled his body trying to crumble the gallows to the ground. Meanwhile, the other mob began to ignite the other negro, one limb at a time, slowly, so that he could watch himself turn to ash. Not fifty feet behind them, Corliss struggled so violently that the frayed rope began to untether to its last threads. The analogous kicks and struggles of generations of lynched forefathers had worn away the rope's knot, such that with his final kick before suffocating, Corliss managed to rip the rope and fall to the ground. No one saw or heard him fall. They were obsessed with the irony of an arsonist's screams to God for mercy from being burned alive. So Corliss filled his lungs with air, and fled to the ends of Mississippi with his hands still tied and the noose dragging from his neck like a tail. Two years later he was a cook for Waynes Wallace and the father of a beautiful daughter named after the woman of his morose and unfinished love.

The Dying Womb

Cold Canadian air blew far south into Mississippi and brittled the bones of the railroad workers. Several workers fell ill, slowing progress to New Orleans. Then, when they were four days from Jackson, Simmons Hill awoke in the middle of the night with pneumonia. He was bright red and feverish. He coughed green and yellow phlegm and his lungs gurgled as he breathed. Jay had read several medical books, so he offered his help. He boiled mint leaves which he ordered Simmons to inhale while he spread various vulnerary herbal pastes across his chest. On the second night of Jay's medications, Fulton and Moondog wrapped themselves in jackets and slipped away for a walk.

Fulton asked Moondog whether they would be paid in Jackson if Simmons died. "Of course we gonna be paid," Moondog responded, "this a govment job." Fulton was not as confident as Moondog, so he found himself praying for Simmons' survival. They walked along a little farther in silence, each listening to the recumbent sound of the wind swaying through the naked trees. The sound made Fulton think of his family, and he wondered whether Moondog was thinking of his, "You worryin' at all 'bout your wife en boys?"

"No, I'm sho they ok," Moondog responded, almost coldly.

"'Cause I been worryin' 'bout Simbi en Orlando. I been worryin' everyday. I feel like I abandoned her en like somethin' bad gonna happen while we gone."

"Thinkin' like that ain't gonna help you or her."

"That's the only way I know how to think."

"Then you better get used to feelin' bad up 'til the day we get back."

Fulton was not satisfied with Moondog's advice, but he knew Moondog could not really understand the pain of his separation from Simbi. Fulton knew that Moondog loved his family, but he chose not to suffer from that love, as he had with his brother. On the other hand, Simbi's smile defined Fulton's purpose in life, so if she was not smiling, his purpose was empty.

The next morning when Jay entered Simmons' tent, Simmons was dead. His eyes were wide and his mouth was open, as if in the middle of a word. The workers struggled to dig a grave in the frozen earth and buried him. The first foreman, Benbow Brence, assumed control of the workforce, and the team continued to Jackson.

Benbow assured the workers that they would receive the next portion of their payment once they arrived in Jackson, so the workers toiled diligently despite the frosty days, until they arrived in the Capital three days later. Jackson was the first milestone of their journey, half way to New Orleans. Benbow calculated that despite the weather and sickness, they were still on schedule. Three of the workers, all white, told Benbow that they wanted to quit the journey, so Benbow paid them for their work to Jackson and recruited three more coloreds to continue to New Orleans.

Fulton and Moondog had been anticipating Jackson since they left Hernando. Neither had ever been this far from home and neither had ever been to a city this large (even though Memphis was only a day away and was much larger than Jackson). All along the route Moondog dreamt about the first-class Juke Joints Jackson must possess, but now that they had arrived, he was not interested in sampling pints of local shine since he had been dry for the last two weeks.

After the incident in Mojo's, Simmons banned all alcohol from his men. Moondog was furious and was ready to start walking home until Fulton pleaded with him to remain. So Moondog stayed and stopped drinking. He poured his shine onto the frosty dirt like it was blood draining from his body. For the first week he shivered all night and hallucinated all day. One day he thought all the rail bars were demon-faced cottonmouths like in Naga's stable, and he fled screaming into the forest. It took Simmons and two other men an hour to catch him and convince him to climb down from a tree. Then, slowly, Moondog returned to himself, though he remained irritable and suffered from acute, needling headaches. Fulton knew Simmons was planning to fire Moondog in Jackson, so he secretly believed that Corliss had cursed Simmons with voodoo and caused him to die. But now that they were in Jackson and they were paid and allowed three days to relax in the city, everyone was happy and forgot any previous grudges. Even Moondog was calm, because the work kept him sufficiently exhausted to suffer from his childhood memories.

Even though it was late by the time the workers pitched their tents, several of them ventured into downtown Jackson to enjoy the nightlife. But Fulton and Jay were among those who remained near their campfires to relax and keep warm for the night. That was the night Fulton's understanding of the universe changed forever, the night he felt less significant than he had ever felt before.

Even though the night was clouding, enough of the sky remained for Jay to explain to Fulton that the stars they saw were countless other planets orbiting countless other suns like theirs. And not only was the sky filled with millions of planets and suns like theirs, but all of them were millions and millions and millions of miles away, "Think of them just like the moon except infinitely farther away. From what I've read, you could walk around the earth a thousand times and you wouldn't even have walked half way to the nearest star. And it's entirely possible that on one of those planets a thousand walks away, there's some manner of life standing there gazing back at us and seeing nothing but the glimmer of a distant star, a thousand walks away." Then Fulton asked Jay about the sun's black light and about the moon's milky light, and Jay told Fulton that the sun's black light was called an eclipse, and eclipses occurred when the moon crossed directly between the sun and the earth. He told Fulton that the moon was not full of milky light, but that it only reflected the sun's incandescence into the night, like a shiny stone.

Suddenly, the sky Fulton had seen a thousand times appeared menacing and alien. It was deep. Fulton had always believed that the stars were the remains of the first man whose sparkling ashes God had spread across the sky after he died. And he had always thought that an eclipse was dead spirits trying to devour the sun which made it shine black light (so his family used to bang pots and shriek and eat rotten wood and throw out their water to frighten the spirits and save themselves from deadly contamination). And he had always thought that the moon was full of light like the sun and that the woodpecker passed the fire back and forth between them, and that was why he wore a fiery headdress. But all of this was wrong.

"So that other creature on that other planet lookin' at me like I'm just a star -- do you think his life is like ours? Do you think he struggles like me 'cause his color is darker than some a the other creatures he lives with? Or maybe on his planet they don't got no colors at all."

"We may never know the answers to your questions Fulton, but one thing's for sure, if they ever come visit us, then they'll probably be smart enough to have learned not to waste any time getting angry about whether somebody is one color or another."

As he listened, Fulton's mind was reeling at the dizzying possibilities unfolding from Jay's universe. He had come a long way from seeing his first refrigerated car. He felt like an ant in a world of men, so unaware of the complexity around him, so focused on narrow tasks. Fulton shuddered with fright, and a cool breeze passed through him, carrying with it the scent of wintry memories.

***

"It's chilly tonight."

"I'll keep you warm."

Fulton wrapped himself around Uma to shelter her from the chill of February winds. They sat together on the near side of Anderson's hill surveying the symmetry of the world below them. The sky was a speckled sheet of black, cut cleanly at the horizon by the flat, Mississippi plains. She was his Sweetest Queen, but a discomfort sat between them that night, a sense of unfamiliarity. Uma breathed with the fear of assassinated love. Her family had arrived in Anderson's fields three years ago, and she had been friends and then lovers with Fulton ever since. He remembered first seeing her during that transitional time between the first buds of puberty and the opulent wardrobe of womanhood. She was on her porch swing in the sunlight, with her nimble femininity peeking through her childhood dress. The moment Fulton saw her, she burned an imprint of desperation in his heart, and he wanted to save her from the world. He introduced himself as the only child of the Chapman family that lived four cabins east. He began walking to her cabin everyday, sitting with her on her swing and talking about dreams and better places. Everyday she was more beautiful than the previous, and everyday Fulton found it harder to breathe. They passed the time sipping tea in the sunlight and laying under trees picking grass and stealing kisses.

Meanwhile, as time passed, Uma taught Fulton how to love a woman. She taught him that she didn't want protection; she wanted the thoughtful things - the little things she never expected. That's what makes love strong. And she told him that "the memory of love is life's best gift, so each moment we share is the best moment people have." When they were together she would rest her head against his breathing chest, and he would pass hours caressing her hair, tucking it behind her ear to keep it out of her face.

But Uma's father, Lee, was not interested in Fulton's passion for his daughter, and as soon as he detected the first scents of love, he forbade Fulton from seeing Uma. Lee had been born a slave, and though he thanked his ancestors that his daughter was born free, he intended for her to marry above the sharecropper's lot and thereby liberate herself from it. As far as Lee was concerned, it was not enough to be content to slave in the fields and not be lynched. Though Lee did agree to meet with Fulton's father and though he was impressed by the similarity of Bukka's ambitions, he would not allow his daughter to enjoy anything more than friendship with Fulton. Nevertheless, their emotions and the craft with which they found opportunity to express them would not be denied, even if it meant hitchhiking to Banks and back.

But that night on the wintry hill, a discomfort sat between them for the first time since they met. Uma brought Fulton to the hill with something to say, and Fulton feared the demons her words might unleash on his heart. The night was eerie, with clouds swimming across the celestial waters, glaring. So foul and fair a night. To calm her, Fulton began to sing. His voice tingled as it passed through her, and tears began to fill her eyes. Both their lives had been losing battles against loss, and she shuddered at the thought of losing him. "Dry your tears," he said as he took her hand in his, "put my love on the ground in front a you en speak to it whatever you need to say." She turned to him and opened her worries, "It must be that night in Banks under the fig tree. I'm almost three months big. My daddy found out. He says I kent never see you again en at the end a the winter we gonna move far away."

Fulton choked. He placed his hand on her womb and said, "There's a little life inside, a life made a you en me." He left his hand on her womb for another moment, feeling the whispers of life. But the complications of their circumstance left him without an understanding of how to save their future. He felt powerless, like trying to capture mist in his hand.

Fulton turned to his father for help, and the families clashed, each protecting its perceived rights against the trespasses of the other. For Lee, Fulton did not even approximate his expectations of a son-in-law. For Bukka, Lee had no right to sever their relationship and cause the child to enter the world a bastard (he knew, of course, that Lee would probably destroy the child at birth in order to preserve Uma's value). They were separated from each other for weeks, and from his window, Fulton could hear Uma's forlorn cries from her cabin, locked and bolted in her room all night. As the weeks passed, Bukka encouraged Fulton to forget Uma, "After your heart bleeds you'll find a new love."

But Fulton could not abide the thought, "my heart ain't gonna stop bleedin' 'til there's no blood left to bleed," and the weight of his misery pressed against him until he fell ill and laid in bed for twenty days, thinking only of his beloved, so near yet so far.

Then there was silence the last month of winter. The parents presumed their children had accepted their fates. Time always wins. Both Bukka and Lee were tormented by their children's pains, but also pleased that they were capable of such sadness, for as slaves, the opportunity for such freedoms of love and loss had never existed. Fulton and Uma both grew thin during the winter, especially Uma, who was so thin that the outline of the child pressed against her skin. Lee eyed the lines with contempt.

Once spring awakened, Uma redoubled her efforts to free herself from her father's plans. But Lee would not be convinced, "What is this freedom for then, if you gonna imprison yourself in this life like slavery?" Uma did not understand. She felt no enslavement in Fulton's arms; she felt the freedom of pure love. Uma grew desperate, and Fulton could smell her desperation from his room. And even though Moondog visited him and tried to distract him with laughter, Fulton boiled and brooded each impotent night he slept apart from his Uma and his child.

And then the child awakened. Tossed in between the desperation of its mother and the torment of its father, as if they had climbed into its heart through its chord, the child began to scratch and claw against its womb. Uma was terrified. All day and night the child tore and clawed and gurgled inside her. She feared it was shredding itself apart, until no conflict remained. Her suicidal fetus. It was floating in an amnion of anguish, boiling within her until the heat rose into her throat to choke her. March remained cool, so she spent hours on her porch, exposing her womb to the breeze, but April brought a warm spell and the verge of self-combustion. Lee consulted the croppers' Spirit Guide who told him that Uma's sadness had transformed the child into a demon that would devour her.

Then one afternoon as Uma sat rocking on her porch eight months big, she placed her hand against her womb and felt a witch's hand press back against hers. Startled, she withdrew, but the wind swirled curses all around her. She saw the bony fingers poking, beckoning, and she returned her hand to it, screaming at its touch. It was horrible, her child, horrible, as if from the morose realm of demons. The hand pressed against hers and announced its intentions, *the time has arrived. I will enter your world soon.* Uma wept.

At the same time, Fulton was struggling with the fading vigor of his memories of Uma. He was frightened by the waning immanence of his memories of her. Her face in his mind, once brighter than the summer sun, now paled and could no longer ignite even the pulse of his heart. He knew that he loved and missed her as dearly as ever, but his emotions were no longer desperate. Fulton denounced this discrepancy and tried to force the quality of his memories, but he could not dictate the terms of their persistence. They were aging like bones, sloughing away until they broke and life was no longer whole. Time was stealing his love; his most precious gift was a fading ghost.

That night, from the depths of these struggles, Fulton awoke with the suffocating sensation that he was entirely alone in the universe. He could no longer abide the separation, so he jumped to his feet and ran to Uma's cabin. As he neared he heard screams of torture. Uma's screams. He raced faster and faster to her cabin, the screams growing more and more shrill. He cried her name into the night so that she would know he was racing to save her. Neighbors emerged from their slumber as Fulton raced by; some followed, others rubbed their eyes as if dreaming.

Fulton arrived at Uma's cabin and banged on the locked door, screaming her name. She heard him and cried for him. Moments later Lee opened the door with terror frozen in his eyes. Fulton threw him aside and ran to Uma to hold her hand. Blood was drowning the cabin, and her eyes were rolling into her head, "I don't know what's wrong . . . it's too soon . . . it's killin' me." Fulton tried to calm her as he removed his shirt to wipe the steaming sweat from her face. He kissed her and reassured her and held her hand, but her agony had transported her to a world of swirling colors, distant sounds, and a macabre hissing that filled the air.

She was breathing rapidly and struggled to speak in between her breaths, "You - gotta - help - me - wit - this - baby... you - gotta - pull - it - out." Fulton felt the world crumble upon him; he wanted to save her, but he did not know how. He looked into her mournful eyes and at the bed weeping below, and he felt powerless. Then as they breathed and pushed and prayed together a form emerged from Uma's grieving womb. Fulton reached inward to retrieve it. Uma shrieked and cried as she pushed; she felt a needle pierce her heart.

A crying head and torso emerged, with fresh scars atop old ones. A palimpsest of anguish. Fulton tried to guide it into the world. At that moment, several women arrived, and witnessing the scene, they rushed to bring warm water and cloths to Uma. Fulton moved aside as the women converged. They held Uma steady, instructing her to push and breathe in rhythm. Fulton held her hand and tried to explain to the women what was wrong, "That child's fightin' her and tearin' her up from the inside." Then he turned to Uma and promised never to abandon her again.

The child emerged to its chest, and its crying deepened into a dolorous moaning. Scars covered its head and torso, but it was more beautiful than any child anyone had ever seen. Fulton felt more comfortable as the women delivered the child, but Uma remained preoccupied with her increasing pain. She squeezed his hand more tightly and began to pant irregularly. Fulton caressed her soaking forehead, but her heaving reached a fevered pace. The other women did not understand her suffering and grew concerned, "What's wrong child? You gotta tell us what's wrong." But Uma could no longer speak, so the women told her to, "push en breathe. Push en breath." The child moaned like a prisoner and felt like a ravenous blade inside Uma, and she cried to the world, "Oh God!"

Though her hand remained within his, Fulton felt that Uma could no longer see or hear him and that she was slipping from this world. The child howled and began to toss itself wildly and knot itself in its cord, which in turn slithered around its neck. But before Fulton could move to help the child, Uma began to crush his hand. Her body tightened and her head fell back. She looked at Fulton with a mournful glance, and Fulton screamed, "Uma!" as if to reclaim her. He cried and tried to shake the life back into her, but Uma's face was empty and her breathing began to choke. Through her tears she stuttered and shook and tried to speak, but said nothing before her eyes rolled back into her head and she fell to the bed, gawking and lifeless. The room was heavy with silence, except for the hissing sound of the infant's suffocating.

Before anyone could apprehend Uma's death, they all turned to the choking child. While they watched and wondered, no one moved. Then in a fury the women went to Uma's hips to try to free the infant, but they could not loosen it without the assistance of its mother's push. The child was wide-eyed and its arms went limp as it turned from blooded black to crimson blue. Fulton stared as if trapped in someone else's nightmare. As he watched the women desperately struggling to release the suffocating child, the moment when he first placed his hand atop the womb of new life on Anderson's hill flooded his mind. The little life was in jeopardy. Realizing this, Fulton pried his hand from Uma's and charged to the stove in the other room. He returned with a slicing knife and severed the cord from the infant's neck. The cord shuddered as it fell.

LIFE'S ONLY PROMISE

The hissing sound stopped, but the child was still choking. The weight of its mother's hips continued to crush it, and everyone understood what had to be done, but only Fulton had the knife, and he froze again. The women cried to him, "Open her up boy! You gotta free that child! She already dead, en that child gonna join her if you don't free it!" The blade was steaming red in his hand, and he could not bear to violate the body of his cherished with such violence. She was beautiful, like jewels in the night sky, but the world left him no choice. He turned his mind from the task and focused on the act itself, the opening of Uma's moribund womb.

He plunged and it was done. When the child began to cough and cry, Fulton dropped the knife and ran outside. He could not bear to look upon his violence nor the cabin drowning in Uma's blood. The women gathered the scarred, mournful infant and washed it clean with warm water. Lee remained frozen in the corner and blind to the world around him. One of the women carried the child outside to Fulton, and he held her in his arms. Her little heart was beating for precious life. She was no longer crying, and her lids were closed, but when she opened them he saw the profound and black depth of the universe in her eyes. Fulton kissed her eyes and caressed the delicacy of her scarred fontanelle, "Your name is Simbi, en you are my new purpose in life." Then he turned to Uma's house and announced to her still-frozen father, "I'm takin' my daughter home to raise her. I'll be back to bury Uma."

When he returned, the women told Fulton he would have to burn Uma and bury her ashes to cleanse the demons, so he carried her body to his home and dug and dug for hours under the apple tree next to his cabin, aided by his angry tears which singed the earth. Simbi was wrapped in a bundle of cloth and slept by his side. Memories of Uma flooded his heart, and he struggled to abide the expanse of their pain. His life another loss. Together they were an immortal couplet, but now he was cursed to live and die incomplete, forever unrhymed.

By the next morning Fulton had dug the deepest grave anyone had ever seen in Mississippi, and he carried Uma's wrapped body to the edge of her tomb, next to her daughter, and sat with them to speak. He could see the peace behind Uma's closed eyes when he spoke to her, "My Sweetest Queen. I promise you our daughter's gonna have more from this world. I promise you I'll never forget your place in my life. En I promise to meet you before God en ask him why his plans are more importent than ours." Then Fulton lit her, beneath the drooping apple tree. That was the day all its fruit became sour and that was the day that Fulton began to smell like ash, or sometimes like old books. He held his daughter to his heart as they watched, his love to ashes and the loss of all their unborn smiles. The loss of precious love. The loss of memory. Fulton promised Uma her image would forever reside on a throne in his heart.

As he watched her burn, Fulton retrieved his mouth harp and sang a song to the mournful fire, asking the world why it had assassinated his love. The flames danced violently, glowing in his embereyes, and a turbulent smoke unfolded from the pyre into the coiling sorrow of unfulfilled dreams. Later, Fulton deposited Uma's ashes in the tomb, but he knew that her interloping demons could never be cleansed.

LIFE'S ONLY PROMISE

The Shackles of Circumstance

"Today's your lucky day," Benbow announced the next day, "'cause it seems the State Transportation Agency had reserved rooms in a half-way house for us 'til Tuesday, so we're gonna extend our stay here in Jackson two more days." The men were jubilant; they would enjoy beds for the first time in over two months.

The next day the city erupted in celebration with banners and flags for the beginning of J.K. Vardaman's term as governor. Thousands of people cheered in the streets, and Corliss, for one, was entirely spooked by such a jubilant gathering of white people. He feared that, along with whatever other evil they had gathered to celebrate, someone would recognize him and have him lynched, or tortured and then lynched. Fulton, Moondog, Corliss, and Jay chose a spot at the far end of the town square to observe the celebration until they were ready to return to their beds. As the evening progressed, a mass of people gathered at the east side of the town square, many of them staring with vexed expressions at Fulton and the other coloreds speckled throughout the crowd. Jay agreed to investigate the gathering while the others remained on the sidelines.

The night smelled at once joyous and embittered, and Fulton was always wary of nights with conflicting smells. A few minutes later, Jay returned with a concerned expression on his face. He told the others it would be best for them to return to the half-way house. As they walked, Jay explained that Vardaman would be beginning his term as governor tomorrow and that all his supporters had gathered in the town square to celebrate. Vardaman was actually in Biloxi at the present and would be arriving by train tomorrow to deliver his commencement speech.

"That's the colored-hater you told us 'bout, right?" Corliss asked.

"Yes," Jay replied, "and I don't think we should be anywhere near his speech tomorrow."

"Yeah, well I think I want to be right near his speech tomorrow . . . jes to see why you think I shouldn't," Corliss replied.

"Look Corliss," Jay pleaded, "I don't think that's a good idea. The reason you should stay away from the town square tomorrow is not just because Vardaman hates coloreds, but more importantly because he won the election based on that hatred."

"I don't know what you're talkin' about Jay, all I know is the South lost the War, so this Vardaman fella kent go en make us slaves again, en I'm gonna show my face at his speech tomorrow jes to remind him a that fact."

As they walked west the city lights grew dimmer and the street lamps less frequent. Their half-way house was halfway between where the whites and the coloreds lived. It was an old brick building full of shadows that seemed to shift and slither under the moonlight. And that night even though Fulton was lying in a real bed for the first time in over two months, he could not sleep. He was not troubled by the other drunk railworkers and half-way residents stumbling in and out throughout the night, or by the alarming clunks and clanks of the house as it struggled to remain standing under the weight of its age. Instead, he trembled under the glowing moonlit sky and its amorphous gray clouds, clouds like the night on Anderson's hill. They grew misty and circled down as if to garland his neck before swimming back up to the moon.

The next day, Jay convinced Fulton, Moondog, and Corliss to remain outside the half-way house and learn to play fantan instead of going to Vardaman's speech, though Corliss demanded several gills of shine for his compliance (Benbow agreed to let them drink during their stay in Jackson, but only at the half-way house). They gathered around a tree stump and Moondog imagined he was the bartender in his first Juke Joint, serving his friends their shine, though no one drank as much as Corliss. The half-way house served eggs and grits for breakfast reminding Fulton how it was like at home eating breakfast with Simbi. She loved her eggs with ketchup, and she always saved her sunny-side-up yolks for last, like a golden treat.

Later, when the other workers ventured into the city to witness the celebration and Vardaman's speech, Fulton and his friends remained behind to chew licorice and play cards. Their game was an exercise in fate, with each card thrown a new turn was taken, possibilities were excluded, and destiny was narrowed. After several hours they tallied the scores; Corliss won and Fulton finished last.

The afternoon darkened into evening, and Fulton and the others grew restless. Jay continued to warn them to keep their distance from Vardaman's speech, but Corliss, saturated with shine, no longer appreciated the logic of Jay's advice. He saw no danger in words, and he wanted to hear the historic speech.

"What ken he say," Corliss asked, "that he gonna lash us en make us pick cotton again? Les jes go see what he gonna say. He's our govner too, maybe it ain't as bad as you think."

The others remained inclined to heed Jay's warning, but as the time for Vardaman's speech drew near, Corliss announced that he was going to walk to the town square and witness the speech, with or without them. And as he marched off, the others bit their lips knowing that they could not allow him to venture into the square alone, and snakebit. This was the trap Jay feared. As the others walked ahead, Jay felt inside his jacket for his dragon dagger, and then he followed his friends to the town square. Corliss sipped his shine as they walked.

Thousands had gathered, and only a handful, standing in the shadows of the perimeter, were colored. The air was raucous with victory. The crowd stood before a huge stage rounded by unbloomed azaleas and centered by a large podium. A large banner hung from two trees behind the stage reading *Welcome Governor Vardaman*. Pamphlets entitled *Free the South* were circulating. Jay opened one and read a vitriolic discourse on the black plague crippling Mississippi and Vardaman's promise to resurrect its glorious past. Jay was glad his friends could not read.

Fulton, Jay and the others stood under a tree at the far end of the town square. Against their protests, Corliss climbed up the tree and sat on the first branch above them in order to see the stage better. As Fulton looked up at Corliss, he noticed that the sky was clear. The moon was full, but he could not see any stars from all the lights below. Fulton was glad the haunting clouds had passed on to other skies.

Beneath the clear sky, the crowd churned with anticipation. Victory whipped through the air. As a fever swelled in the crowd, Jay began to regret their decision to accompany Corliss to the speech. Then a horse-drawn carriage arrived from behind them, splitting the cheering crowd as it trotted to the podium. Fulton looked up and saw Corliss cheering with the crowd, lost in his intoxication. The crowd filled in behind the carriage as it passed through, and when the immense brown horses arrived at the stage, the savior's hand drew back the carriage's red curtain and the intense face of J.K. Vardaman mounted the stage. The crowd erupted with chants of "White Chief," and Vardaman drank their oration as a toast to his victory. He stood behind the podium for several minutes as the unflagging cheering blared into the night.

He was a titanic man, outfitted in his traditional white linen suit and black broad-brimmed hat. His thin brown hair rested on his shoulders, and his right arm lay limp by his side. He raised his other arm in totalitarian supremacy. The crowd quieted under the weight of his gesture, a silence that tingled its spines in anticipation of Vardaman's words. Vardaman lowered his hand and spoke with a bellow that resonated into the psychology of everyone present, "My fellow citizens of this fair state, today we have won a victory for the safety of the home, the security of our women and children, and the inherent supremacy of the white race."

The crowd erupted in cheers and then quieted for the next sentence, "My fellow working men, you no longer need fear losing what little you have. Your land will be safe from misguided negroes demanding social equality; your women will be safe from the black fiend's compulsions to rape; and you will be safe from our growing coon problem as I promise to abolish negro education and repeal all frivolous safeguards relating to race, such as the fifteenth amendment, which in my view does not apply to wild animals and niggers. I aim to manicure our society like a garden, and I will not have nigger weeds running wild like kudzu." The crowd exploded with approval, and fearful anger began to swell in Fulton, Moondog, and Corliss. Jay sensed their discomfort and urged them to return to the half-way house, but their flaring anger froze them. Corliss yelled down at Moondog and Fulton, "He kent say that shit! He gonna eat my fist before he say another word like that!"

"Shut your mouth before you get us killed!" Jay yelled, "and get down from that tree!"

But Corliss ignored him and elevated the volume of his displeasure. Fulton and the others began to suspect the mistake they had made as Vardaman continued, "Our victory is a slap in the face of Roosevelt's criminal policy of social and political equality. All our problems arise from the Yankee conspiracy of nigger-loving politicians in Washington. But you need not fear the negro any longer. As Governor, I promise to send Militia and Minutemen to protect you from the negro whenever you may need them . . . but, if I were a private citizen today, I would head up a mob and string up any brute who looked like trouble, and I don't have much respect for a white man who wouldn't!"

The crowd roared again as Vardaman's animated words boomed like cannon fire at them. The presence behind each word weighed in the air like a lion upon its prey. Fulton and the others felt that presence gnawing at their innards. Anger burned within them, and Jay's anxiety escalated as Corliss continued to mumble and curse. Jay tried again to pull them away from the speech, but to no avail. A collective resentment had swelled amongst the handful of coloreds standing at the margins of the town square, and Jay foresaw its eruption as Vardaman filled his lungs for one final strike, "My loyal citizens, celebrate this day, for it is the last day the negro will bring fear into the Southern home. I have a new plan with what to do with any negro who dares to trespass our laws... a plan which will replenish the wealth of our state while reminding those negroes born after The War what the sting of twenty lashes feels like against their bare, black skin. The simple fact is this, the negro is a lazy, lying, lustful animal whose behavior resembles the hogs . . . "

"You resemble a fuckin' hog!"

Silence like death swallowed the crowd as it turned in disbelief and saw Corliss, sitting in his tree, with a triumphant smile on his face, sipping his shine. Fulton, Moondog, and Jay were frozen with terror. Vardaman gazed at Corliss with a hungry smile and asked, "What's that you say... nigger?" Fulton prayed for Corliss to silence himself, to recoil his neck from the executioner's block, but his prayers went unanswered, "I said, you resemble a hog, en you ken eat my proud nigger shit if you think you ken enslave me!"

Vardaman smiled and remained composed as flanks of armed men swooped towards Corliss. Fulton urged Corliss to get out of the tree, but he was too snakebit to coordinate his movements and remained coiled around the branch. A helpless image of Simbi appeared in Fulton's mind as the mob and the Militia Men moved towards them. Fulton did not understand why he was not fleeing. He foresaw the avalanche triggered by Corliss' outburst unfolding into a sequence of events ending in their suspension a few feet above the earth. But he was not fleeing.

He had a moment. A critical moment that held the difference between one life and another, if he would only run. Run to his daughter. But Corliss cancelled that whirling moment and eliminated any other possible outcomes by pulling an ink black revolver from his jacket, pointing the smiling end at the swarming mob, and firing vengeance into the crowd's ravenous belly. Two women, a man, and a child received the death sentence of Corliss' judgment. Fulton lowered his face from Simbi's image, and a lucent fog swam into the square. A bullet entered Corliss' arm, dropping him from the branch onto Moondog and Jay. Fulton found himself standing before his fallen companions as the enraged mob arrived to tear their flesh and bones. Just then, Vardaman's voice calmly bellowed through the fog, "Please stand aside and allow my Milita Men to bring those negroes to me." The mob obeyed, but they rained sticks and stones on Fulton, Moondog, and Corliss, along with whatever other coloreds who happened to be standing in the way as the Militia Men dragged them to the platform. Corliss did not feel the bullet in his arm, but he was shocked by the sight of his rich, redspilling blood behind him. Meanwhile, the mob was too obsessed with the spectacle at hand to attend to the fallen who pleaded for medical attention.

When the coloreds had been dragged onto the stage and thrown at Vardaman's feet, Vardaman walked to Corliss and stood before him, (white) face to (darker) face, and spat in his eyes. The crowd cheered. The captors were smothered in bruises and bumps and cuts and blood, and the crowd cheered. Vardaman began to pace back and forth across the line of almost a dozen coloreds, who were all trying to mask their terror with faces of strength. When his thoughts satisfied him, Vardaman stepped back from the line and spoke in a curt, calm voice, "So you niggers think you can show your nigger faces at my speech and kill innocent women and children." Vardaman slapped one of the coloreds in the face and then erupted, "Well you're wrong, you hogs!" The crowd howled with approval of Vardaman's display. "You are going to be my first examples. You are going to show all the other dumb niggers in my state that we will not tolerate your animal behavior any more!"

Vardaman turned to the crowd and continued, "This is the New Mississippi. One where we rule and the nigger obeys!" The mob cheered again and began a chanting chorus of "White Chief! White Chief!" to hail their savior. Then they began to cheer for a lynching, and in fact, a rope had already been draped over the nearest branch.

Vardaman returned his focus to Corliss, who was now standing in a scarlet pool of his own blood and staring at the reflection in it of the full moon above. As he felt Vardaman approaching, Corliss turned his face forward just in time to greet the pistol Vardaman pointed square against his forehead. He did not close his eyes, and the crowd chanted for blood. "If I wasn't Governor," Vardaman groaned, "I'd kill you where you stand by my own hand. But since I am, I have to let Justice decide your fate." So Vardaman turned to the crowd and asked, "What punishment will satify your cry for Justice?"

"Lynch him! Hang him!" the mob roared.

So Vardaman released Corliss to his Militia Men and informed the other coloreds that they would receive a trial tomorrow for their roles in the murders. Fulton and Moondog stood in shocked silence at how far they were from only a few months ago.

The Militia Men dragged Corliss to the tree at the far side of the stage where the rope had already been draped. Onlookers kicked him and spat at him as he was dragged by. Fulton and Moondog could not believe what was happening, so quickly and so irreversibly. Meanwhile, Jay had separated himself from the crowd and was trembling atop the small perimeter wall around the town square. Tension squeezed his eyes while Fulton and Moondog felt their hearts choke through their spines. Once they arrived at the tree, the Militia Men stripped Corliss naked. From the stage, Vardaman looked across the spectacle like a sculptor at a finished work. Fulton could not bear what he was going to see, so he turned to Vardaman and begged him for mercy, "Please Mr. Govner suh, please have mercy..."

Vardaman turned with a grave face and interrupted Fulton with a grave tone, "Mercy abandoned that nigger the moment he crossed me." Moondog pulled Fulton's arm and squeezed him into silence. Vardaman returned his attention to the display.

Within moments, Corliss was in the noose and pulled to his toes. The inch before suffocation. Vardaman waited; anticipation dripped from the onlookers' mouths. They wanted to taste the fire in his emptied lungs. They wanted to see Justice dispatch of their devil. Meanwhile, those on the stage saw the devil dispatching the image of themselves.

When Vardaman sensed the moment, he raised his hand for quiet so everyone could hear the final rasps of his negro enemy. The crowd silenced and the coloreds on stage held their breath. Before giving the signal, Vardaman looked at Corliss and asked, "Do you have any final words or pleas for your soul's mercy?"

Corliss raised his wobbling head and saw the culmination of a terminal course of events initiated before he yelled at Vardaman, before he first met eyes with Mary, and before he was born. He coughed blood onto himself and wondered why he had done what he did. He looked away from the faces gnashing at him, "Lawd, oh Lawd - guess I done alotta things wrong, en the last one was stayin' in Mississippi jes a day too long." Disapproval spewed from the crowd, and Vardaman's ire lowered his hand with a violence which signaled that Corliss should be raised.

Corliss was dangling, clenching his neck against the constricting noose but able to suck in quick tufts of air so that after several minutes he was still alive. The crowd grew apprehensive, but Vardaman enjoyed watching him suffer. And he was suffering, and burning, and wondering what cruelty had consigned him to this curse. Maybe they didn't tie the rope right. Or could it be that he could not die from lynching? Fulton and Moondog watched, and for the first time they believed the story he had told them. After several minutes, Corliss gathered enough air in his lungs to scream, "For God's sake, cut me down en hang me from a gallows!" The crowd and the Militia Man who was suspending Corliss turned to Vardaman with dumbfounded faces. Vardaman laughed. But before Corliss could suffer any longer, three gunshots pierced the confusion and killed Corliss where he hung. Everyone turned, some with anger, some with misunderstood relief, to see Jay Collins standing atop the perimeter wall with a smoking pistol pointed at Corliss' slumped body.

That night all the coloreds on stage and Jay Collins found themselves in Jackson's prison holding cell. Fulton, Moondog, and Jay huddled in a corner with their eyes fixed on the floor. Not looking at each other helped them disassociate themselves from the present state of their lives. Later, Fulton told Jay that sometimes he wished he could do what Jay had done. Meanwhile, one of the other coloreds in the cell was squatting in the corner, relieving himself with steaming pungence.

The next morning, Vardaman ordered the men brought to him in his statehouse chambers at the center of the town square. They were chained and led through the quiet morning, twelve coloreds with a white man in the middle. When they arrived Corliss was still dangling from the tree with hawks pecking at his flesh and eyes. The guards led them to the third floor of the statehouse where they waited outside Vardaman's chambers. The rosewood doors to his chambers were almost twelve feet tall, and after they had waited an hour in anxious silence, the door opened and the guards led them to Vardaman's desk.

He sat with his back to them in a chair larger than he was. Thick cigar smoke drifted above him. Two large statues stood in the back corners of the office, one of Robert E. Lee and the other of himself. Seven paintings and hundreds of books filled the walls, including a ferrotype of Vardaman on the wall opposite his desk, and a large cabinet full of gleaming black and brown shotguns stood against the wall behind them. Vardaman was looking outside through the four large windows behind his desk. They stretched from the floor to the ceiling, and he was thinking to himself that the world could fit in them.

Without turning, Vardaman addressed the men, "Boys, I'm very upset with you. You killed some of my citizens, and then you disrupted my execution." He paused to puff his cigar. Fulton thought about his tobacco. "Those citizens you killed are the citizens who elected me Governor. They are very angry because they need Justice for their loved ones." Vardaman turned his chair to face his captives and rose to his feet, "So you see, I have to try again to deliver Justice to them. I have to respond to the *vox populi*. That's what I promised I'd do when they elected me." Vardaman walked to Jay and stood above him with a quizzical look on his face. Jay looked back at him with untrembling eyes. "As for you. Because you killed a nigger who should have been killed, I applaud you. But because you killed the nigger I wanted to kill, I denounce you. You stole him from me, so now you owe me a debt, which you will repay."

Vardaman returned to his desk and stood behind his chair. "For the rest of you niggers, I have a very special place I'm going to send you. I'm not going to kill you or lynch you or burn you alive. You owe a debt to the state of Mississippi, and you will settle your accounts. I am sentencing you to fifteen years for abetting that negro murderer." Vardaman returned to his chair and puffed his cigar in satisfaction, "That's it. Take them away." The guards led the men from the office, each resigned to whatever fate awaited him. Except for one. The youngest. He refused to accept the maleficent progression of events around him, "Wait! Wait! Wait!" He turned and yelled, "don't we get some judge or some trial? I didn't have nuthin' to do wit that man killin' them folks. I was just in the crowd en got..."

"Shut up nigger! Shut up!" Vardaman slammed his fist as he screamed. "Don't you understand who I am and who you are?" Vardaman stormed at the insolent negro and slapped his thick hands around his throat, crushing his neck against the wall. He spoke as if gnawing his words, "I just spared your life and you dare to question me? Don't you ever forget that your life is mine, and I can snuff it out in an instant." Vardaman released him and composed himself while the other coughed for air. "The place you're going, you'll wish I had killed you. Now all of you, get out of my office and pray you never cross me again." The guards pulled them out of the office and closed the door behind them. Vardaman returned to his seat and looked beyond the town square thinking of his unwritten legacy germinating in the fertile furrows beyond.

That night they were in another cell, more cold and cramped. They whispered to each other about where they thought Vardaman was sending them, and after a few days they began to wonder when they would be taken there. Jay was not with them. Fulton did not know where he was, and he wondered how Vardaman would punish him. The young colored who had burst in anger at Vardaman sat near Fulton and Moondog, but they did not exchange any words. In fact, Fulton said nothing until a few days later when one of the others raised his voice at him, "You. I saw you near em. When he shot them people. I saw you talkin' to em before that." The accusing colored and a few others grew indignant and rose to their feet, "You're his friend. It's your fault we here!"

"I didn't know em," Fulton responded in a stoic voice.

"Yes you did," their voices escalated, "I saw you wit em. You supposed to mind your friends when they snakebit. It's your fault we here."

Fulton responded again, "I didn't know em."

But they were not satisfied, and the leader erupted, "I gotta family en children en that drunk nigger friend of yours ruined my life!"

Fulton exploded with an ancient, guttural anger, "I gotta family too! I'm in this jail too!" Moondog jumped to his feet with Fulton, and they both stood face to face with the half dozen other convicts breathing anger on them. Their lungs heaved and their eyes seethed at each other, and they would have erupted had the guards not circled around telling them to sit and be silent or be whipped. As they sat, anger smoldered in Fulton's chest, and with loathing resignation he whispered one last time, "I didn't know em."

After a week of sitting in their cell, of eating bread and water, and of relieving themselves in the same, unemptied bucket, a bond began to develop between the cellmates. The man who had questioned Fulton's relationship with Corliss was named Bedford Lewis, and he had heard stories about Vardaman and the New South his allies envisaged. He heard about Vardaman's Whitecaps who terrorized dissidents and coloreds, and he heard about all the new laws Vardaman intended to pass which would put coloreds in jail for looking at a white lady funny, or ten years for stealing a candy bar. "Or fifteen for standin' near a colored who shoots some white folks," Moondog said with a wry voice.

Along with Bedford, Kenge Lang and Bream "Mongoose" Blackman (the one Vardaman had throttled) emerged as the most prominent personalities of the cell. Their stories helped turn everyone's attention away from their hunger, their tormenting uncertainty, the roaches and rats that scurried across the cell, and their waste that had long ago begun to seep across the bottom of the cell.

As they gnawed on their bread, Mongoose shared stories of the fish he and his older brother used to catch in Willow Lake outside of Jackson. They lived alone on the lake and spent the day loading timber for the Morgan Lumber Company, and at night they caught big, fat catfish and roasted them. The night air would drip with their scent. He caught other fish too, but never the blossom carps, because he loved watching them wait beneath the trees for their blossoms to fall so they could gulp them from the surface like a candy treat. Mongoose liked to catch moccasins as well. His parents were half Issaquena, so they taught him, as their parents had taught them, how to catch snakes by moving across the earth and over water just like they do, like a river or a cloud. Mongoose figured he had caught hundreds of moccasins. He used their skin for boots and their fangs for necklaces. He made his favorite pair of boots and favorite fang necklace from one moccasin he caught just a few weeks ago that was over sixteen feet long.

Mongoose was sure that it was the biggest snake in Mississippi, maybe the mother of them all. He remembered catching her by accident when she bit onto his shiner. He and his brother had to use all their strength to get her back to their cabin, and she flailed her body for a whole minute after they chopped off her head. And of course, they burned her head right away, as they always did ever since their parents died, "The day after we moved to the lake as young boys my daddy caught en kilt a snake en prepared a feast praisin' the bounty of the land. A few days later a moccasin slithered into our cabin en kilt both my parents, en ever since then me en my brother believed that when you kill a snake, it keeps your image in its eyes so its lover ken avenge its death. So we started burnin' all the heads of the snakes we kilt from then on, en ain't no snakes done slithered into my cabin for revenge ever since." Those new boots and fang necklace were at home with his brother. Mongoose had planned to wear them next week for his birthday. Turning twenty-two.

Kenge and Bedford were croppers like Fulton and Moondog. Fathers of the furrowed earth. They were older though, in their sixties with children and grandchildren. They had cropped near Corinth since they could walk, born into slavery and awakened one day to their liberation from servitude. They looked much older than Fulton imagined he would look thirty years later. But a year like these last few months could steal three or four years from his life; maybe that was the true cruelty of Vardaman's punishment.

Meanwhile, as he awaited his future with escalating uncertainty, Fulton could no longer abide his own filth-coated presence, let alone the other eleven shit-steaming coloreds so close upon him. He was dying for some warm water so he could just wash himself clean. He felt himself going mad and feared he might soon explode from not knowing what the future held for him. Then finally, a few days later, the future arrived and stood outside their cell in the ghoulish guise of Long Chain Charlie.

They were asleep when he arrived. He announced himself from a hundred feet away with heavy shackles and chains clanking behind him as he bellowed his arrival, "Rise up negroes! Long Chain Charlie's here!" Fulton and the others shook off their sleep and rose to see a filthy, churlish, scarred white man towering above them with a malicious smile. "You niggers who hear your name, you're comin' with me -- Bream Blackman! Fulton Chapman! Rex Deakins! . . ." The oration continued until everyone in the holding cell heard his name.

The sheriff opened the cell and Long Chain's oily men arrived and shackled all twelve coloreds into a single chain and pushed them out into the cold morning. Wearing the same filth-coated clothes they had been wearing for weeks, Fulton and the others were herded with cattle prods into a wagon which took them to the train station where they were thrown into a dark, cold train car with a few dozen other chained coloreds. They were all filthy, exhausted, and frightened, and they kept their faces to the ground. There were four cars in all. Once the train jerked into motion, the convicts huddled near each other to keep warm. The cool mist of the morning settled into a heavy fog in each car, and Fulton could feel its thickness in his lungs.

As the morning hours advanced, light crept into the car and dispelled some of the mist. The chained men looked around to see who was in their car with them. Everyone looked similar, weak with sleepy eyes. Some of them knew who their captor was, but not much about where he was taking them. Some of them had heard about Long Chain Charlie, an infamous legend born with Vardaman's New Mississippi. For six months he had been rounding up arrested coloreds across Mississippi and shipping them to Parchman Farm. A scuffle with a colored two years ago left Long Chain with a deep gash on his face and vengeance in his veins. As far as he was concerned, the negro had no right to freedom and equality, so he was more than happy to take them to Parchman.

As for Parchman, the stories were numerous but uncertain. No one was sure where it was (other than somewhere in the basin of the Yazoo Delta), and no one was sure what it was (other than some big swamp land which was supposed to become a plantation). As the train rumbled along, Mongoose whispered to Fulton, "I'm scared, en I don't like not knowin' where they takin' us."

"I'm scared too," Fulton responded, "jes try to think of good things." So Mongoose thought about the mist in the train car which reminded him of his home at Willow Lake. But, now it was fading with the sunlight into iridescent spears piercing the darkness of the car. Contrary to Mongoose, Fulton was relieved to see the mist dispelled.

After two hours the train stopped. The guards opened the cars and ordered the convicts to the ground. Long Chain stood atop the train with a long cane in his hand. The negroes looked like moles to him, black moles who belonged in the dirt. He wore an angry face as he addressed them, "The tracks ahead are flooded. We can't take this train into Gordon Junction, so I'm gonna have to walk you niggers from here to there. Don't fall behind or I'll just have my men shoot you." Long Chain climbed down from the train and led the chained men along the tracks to Parchman - miles away. Fulton was exhausted and thirsty, and he began to pity himself, until he looked ahead and saw a child in the line, no older than twelve. How could he be here? What could he have done? Somewhere, his mother was sitting up all night wondering where her boy was and why he missed supper.

Fulton wanted to walk up to the child and talk to him, but he could not move beyond his fixed place in the line. So he showed the child to Moondog who curled his face in disbelief. They walked for hours, Long Chain at the front of the caravan with his dozen guards walking alongside the shackled convicts with their shotguns, almost hoping for temptation.

Fulton figured they were about ninety miles north of Jackson, headed north. If they walked all day to Parchman, that would make it ninety or so miles south of Memphis, maybe seventy miles south-east of his home. So he was walking straight back the way he came, shackled and without one Confederate penny for his work on the railroad. Empty hands and shackled feet. Mississippi had unraveled his plans and stripped him of what life and freedom he once had. And who knows what had happened to his family in all this time.

High above, an eagle soared like an emissary. It was as big as a man, crested and majestic. Its golden eyes saw into infinity and glanced below with curiosity at the long, winding creature slowly slogging across the patchwork earth.

After two hours the men arrived at a creek. Long Chain allowed the convicts to sip some water and rest their feet. This load would swell Parchman's population to just over seven hundred, enough to drain the marsh quickly so the land could be tilled for planting. Superintendent Flood wanted Parchman to be shipping cotton in two years and thereby resurrect Mississippi's cotton industry. As they rested, several convicts groaned and bled with the pain of the cold, rusted shackles which cut into their flesh with every step. Fulton was not bleeding, but his skin was raw and he knew he would have blisters in the morning. If only the skin on his ankles were as thick as the skin on his feet.

As he sat by the creek rubbing his feet, Fulton looked around at the other faces. He could see them hiding their thoughts. He saw two more boys, maybe fourteen, who had not been alive long enough to learn how to hide their thoughts from the world. They were frightened and shivering. Then he looked at Long Chain Charlie. He wore his thoughts on his face, because he could. Fulton could see Long Chain loved watching the convicts' blank faces struggling to suppress their fright. He imagined himself a tornado, ripping them from their lives, tossing them through space, and dropping them at the gates of Parchman Farm. The Long Chain Twister. *A dollar a nigger. Then I can retire to the coast. New Orleans maybe. Open a bar with gumbo and beer. Beer-battered gumbo. Call it Long Chain's Cantina. Vardaman can visit and remember the old times. Bet I could buy a boat too. Sail to Mexico and open another Cantina. Serve fajitas and tequila in the Mexico bar. And sail back and forth from one to the other. Damn tracks better be clear next time. A dollar a nigger ain't worth hiking a hundred miles with all these niggers. Smell like rotten shit.*

The pilgrimage to prison continued, and rain began to fall. The rhythmic clings and clangs of the shackles hypnotized the convicts, redirecting their minds from the chafing and slicing pain of every step. The shallow marsh turned to swamp and their progress slowed. The convicts trudged through the swamp with heavy, laborious steps, and the muddy waters rose to their knees. Kudzu swam all around them, more than Fulton had ever seen. Long Chain was cursing the swamp and almost shot a few negroes in anger. Fulton could not believe that Long Chain was cursing *liloba*.

Unlike the others, the clanging shackles did not mesmerize Fulton. Instead, their cacophony needled his mind, so he concentrated instead on the sounds of the swamp in order to endure the journey. Unlike the fields, the swamp was alive with a chorus of sounds and a banquet of smells. The earth smelled ancient in a swamp, unfurrowed and teeming with richness. It was unborn buckshot. A chaotic soup. Fulton now understood why Mongoose lived in a swamp. It was *Liloba* before men. But just like Anderson's grandfather, these white men intended to descend on this swamp and force the coloreds to drain the soup from the land and rape its riches for the swelling of their pockets. To them, the swamp was not untouched life, it was unborn profit. They would vampire the earth until only a desiccated, barren orb remained. They were like kudzu. Fulton realized that Parchman would be no different from the life he left three months ago, except that now he was no longer free. In three months he had managed only to move from the furrows to the bowels of Mississippi, the swamps of Parchman Farm.

Then it finally appeared before them, against the pinkish sky of the setting sun. They had passed Gordon Junction a half-mile earlier and now, after the trees cleared, they could see a few short buildings in the distance. As they neared the front gate, the land sloped upward out of the swamp. A mumbling passed through the convicts. This is Parchman? This is a prison? This is Vardaman's resurrection of the former South? No more than a half-dozen buildings stood behind the black iron front gate, with a colossal Victorian mansion standing at the east side of the installations. As they climbed the slope they could see flanks of barracks spreading out for miles to the east and west from the central, fenced compound. The sunset cast long shadows across the land, and the swamp's chorus was replaced by the delicate suspiration of the winds across the plains. The drenched and muddied convicts shivered in the breeze. When they arrived at the front gate Long Chain fired his shotgun into the sky and yelled, "Flood! I got your niggers, now bring me my money and something dry to wear!"

Several men emerged like cave dwellers from the buildings. They wore gray uniforms with rifles over their shoulders and were led by a bloated man with long, brown sideburns who responded to Long Chain, "you're nine hours late!"

Long Chain waited for the bloated man to arrive next to him and then responded, "Seems the land has inherited your name, so we had to walk the last twenty miles here."

"Very funny. Truth is, the levee at Mounds Landing collapsed. Half of Sunflower County is flooded. Some of the gunmen are rebuilding it right now."

"Well, here's your shipment. Now you can drain the ocean." Long Chain and Superintendent Flood continued to chatter as the others in the gray uniforms led the Long Chain of Negroes through the front gate into Parchman Farm. That's when Fulton finally silenced the shackles from his mind, and that's when he was not thinking about his thirty-third birthday, or about Simbi. But as he waited in the Administration Building line, he was wondering what had happened to Jay. Jay had been in and out of his life in fewer than three months, but his presence weighed on Fulton like an ancestor's. Fulton missed speaking to him and hearing all the things he knew about the world and the stars; he missed watching his hand move across his journal as he inscribed his thoughts.

How much did he write 'bout me? What's he gonna think in thirty years when he looks back on them ole pages? Maybe he's gonna save us. Or maybe me en Moondog ken get outta here, en we ken find him one day, sittin' under a tree wit his papers, en we ken all go somewhere where these things don't happen to honest men. Where a colored man don't get sent to prison for fifteen years just for standin' near trouble. Fulton asked Moondog how far he figured they were from home, and a rifle butt struck his head in response. He fell and caught the streaming blood in his hands. Delerious, Fulton did not feel the other convicts gazing at him as he watched his hands fill with blood and rain... until the offering spilled over and fell, like dread, into the thirsty pores of the earth.

Two

LIFE'S ONLY PROMISE

The Amnion Soup

" . . . what is the use of action, if the thought guiding it leads to the discovery of the absence of meaning?"

Tristes Tropiques

He was always too tired to sleep, but on this night he was also haunted. The mournful howling of the wolves streamed like ice water over his bones. As if with sardonic intent, Stoka and his eye had been resurrected in that moment. This uninspired repetition of miseries haunted him like the doleful repetition of the wolves' wails. Once again, the fury for liberation had ended with vengeance coiled around their necks and cleaved into their backs, like the furrowed earth that enslaved them. Had they come to accuse, or did the scent of blood arouse them? They were the rimy resonance of unfulfilled dreams, and they proclaimed the presence of sleepless ghosts who plague the purpose of living.

***

The guards ordered them to strip naked and then hosed them with wintry water to wash away the mud and blood. Fulton felt his bones chillsplit inside him. As the convicts shivered, Flood's guards unshackled them and corralled them in groups of four into the Administration Building for registration. The Administration Building was one of three buildings across a courtyard from the immense Victorian Mansion prefaced by the sign (not that Fulton could read it) *Superintendent William J. Flood, Parchman Farm*. It was almost larger than Anderson's Mansion. The entire area was called Front Camp and was rounded by a twelve-foot barbed wire fence.

When they emerged from the Administration Building they each possessed an identification number, a uniform with horizontal black and white stripes (which they later learned were called ring-arounds), a gray full-brim hat, and new shackles around their ankles. The identification number consisted of the cage number and bunk number assigned to each convict. Fulton's number was seven-thirty-two. Cage seven, bunk thirty-two -- his new home. Mongoose was in the same cage (number seven-forty-seven) while Moondog and Kenge were in cage eleven and Bedford was in cage four. Fulton felt afraid, but he did not have time to dwell on his fear, for as soon as they were registered and clothed, the convicts were prodded to their cages, "Get on to sleep boys," the guards yelled, " 'cause tomorrow you're gonna be workin'!" Seven-thirty-two. The number chimed in Fulton's mind like a death toll.

Thirty-two was a top bunk. The bunk beneath was covered in mud and filth. The cage was a long concrete space with a hundred bunks and a tin roof. Two small windows with thick metal bars peeked to the outside from the longer walls. The moment they entered, a thick, putrid stench convulsed their lungs. Its source seemed to be several buckets in the far corner of the cage overflowing with human waste. Fulton held his arm to his face, but he still choked. Mongoose, who was two bunks over from Fulton, puked on himself. The new convicts moaned nauseated vowels the moment the guards locked them inside. Atop his bunk, with his face tucked beneath his arm, Mongoose erupted, "I'm fuckin' sick in here."

Fulton tried to calm him, "Don't think 'bout it. It's killin' me too."

Mongoose wretched on himself again, "Are you crazy?! Don't think 'bout it? I'm gonna die in here!" Mongoose jumped from his bunk and charged at the metal door. He banged and clamored for air, and other convicts gathered behind him, equally unable to abide their noisome cage. Moments later they heard rifle fire behind the door, and a guard opened the peep hole and placed his rifle through it into Mongoose's face. Mongoose yelled, "We kent breathe in here. You gotta clean it or let us out for air!" The others shouted in agreement.

The guard calmly responded, "Ok. I'll give you a choice. You can go back to your bunk until you're ordered out for work tomorrow, or you can come out here and get shot." Mongoose and the others were silent. Tears of frustration burned in their eyes, and they slowly turned away from the door and returned to their bunks with their heads held low. Mongoose and several other convicts then mimicked Fulton, who tore two small pieces of his ring-arounds and stuffed them in each nostril. They breathed just enough to keep breathing.

As they awaited the arrival of their cage mates, hopelessness overwhelmed the new convicts. They all wondered how it was they had arrived in this place. Then, long after the sun had set, the other residents of cage seven returned from the marsh and climbed into their cold beds. They walked as if they had no bones inside them. Fulton later overheard one of the arriving residents explain that they were called gunmen, because they have guns pointed at their heads all day.

Long before sunrise, the guards arrived and yelled awake the gunmen. As Fulton lowered himself from his bunk, the gunman below him offered his hand and introduced himself, "Name's Cuttino Calhoun ... follow me." Cuttino was thin and dark with feline eyes, and he led Fulton and Mongoose outside into the cold. Most of the other gunmen walked to the far corner of the cage and relieved themselves before filing out.

"You boys look tired," Cuttino said as they exited the cage.

"It's that damn stink. Kept me up all night," Mongoose responded.

"Yeah, well you'll learn to stop smellin' anything soon enough, but you won't never sleep 'til you learn to stop dreamin' too."

Fulton and Mongoose sat on either side of Cuttino at a long wooden table next to their cage which Fulton did not remember seeing the previous night. They ate syrup, biscuits, and tea while three guards sat on horseback around them, one at the head of the table with a bullwhip coiled at his side. They all had .30-.30 Wincesters in their hands; Fulton recognized the rifles because Anderson's men had the same ones. Fulton counted around fifty gunmen at the table. At length, the guard at the head of the table with the bullwhip addressed them, "Since we have some new gunmen with us, I'm going to go over the rules again like last month. My name is Duke Judson the Second. I am your Morning Sergeant and these are your Morning Drivers, Stock Craven and Jimmy Thornton. Your Night Sergeant is Able Brace and your Night Drivers are Holman Jenkins and Fefa Blue. These are the rules. You work from four-thirty to ten Monday through Saturday. You have Sunday to yourselves. You'll get breakfast in the morning here at your cage and lunch and dinner while you work. You will be chained in groups of ten at all times. If you need to piss, you yell 'gettin' out' and wait for approval before you step forward to piss, or you will be shot. If you do not work or you disobey or you try to escape, you will be shot. Right now we are draining this marsh so you can start planting cotton on the land." With his speech completed, Duke Judson, II instructed his drivers to chain the gunmen and educate the new ones on how to drain a marsh as they were led out into it. The gunmen gulped their last bites of breakfast and washed them down with the tea, which was already cold.

Before they had begun to grasp what Stock and Jimmy were explaining to them, the new gunmen found themselves knee deep in bone-chilling water which spread for miles. It was an endless, watery chaos that reminded Fulton of the indistinguishable expanse from his dream. Stock and Jimmy explained that the previous six months had been spent extending the Mound's Landing Levee all the way west by south-west around Pinnekoke Lake to the far east border of Parchman's 20,000 acres. The extended levee from Mound's was called Pinnekoke Levee. They started draining the marsh about two weeks ago, but had been awaiting Long Chain's next shipment for enough gunmen to line the marsh to pass bucket after bucket of water across the marsh, up the slope of the extended levee and into Pinnekoke Lake on the other side.

On Fulton's first full day in Parchman Farm, around seven hundred gunmen stretched almost a mile through the marsh straight up through the barrow pits to the dump of Pinnekoke Levee. Hundreds of buckets were already bobbing in the marsh like eager children awaiting their arrival. "Bend down, fill up a bucket, pass it down," Cuttino instructed, "and step your feet up en down or they'll freeze right off." He pointed out several gunmen who had already lost toes and feet to frostbite from standing in the icy marsh all day, though he warned there was nothing they could do about having to sleep in wet frozen pants all night.

"How long you been here?" Fulton asked.

"Long Chain brought me here in the first shipment two months ago. I was friends wit the gunman who slept in your bunk before you, but he died a the flu three weeks after we got here."

Meanwhile, the Sergeants and Drivers sat on their horses, riding back and forth across the line, barking instructions. One guard could oversee forty or more gunmen at a time since they could not flee very far in the marsh before he could shoot most of them down. When they could, the gunmen relieved themselves in the marsh (after asking for permission) so that they would not have to squat over the buckets in their cages.

Fulton looked down the line trying to spot Moondog. But the day was too gray and too misty, and his eyes were too tired to see more than a hundred feet in either direction. However, he did discover the boy he had noticed during their march from the train. He was in the group of ten to Fulton's left. He must be in the same cage, Fulton reasoned, so he decided to stand next to the boy tomorrow. The child was struggling with the weight of the buckets and fell into the water more than once. Anger burned inside Fulton (but did not keep him warm), and he turned his face in shame from the sight of the child's frightened struggles. What if he were his own?

After a few hours, the sun helped to warm the gunmen. Still, along with their feet, their arms were numb from the incessant repetition of filling and passing and filling the buckets. "I'm hungry," Mongoose complained, "when do we get lunch?"

Cuttino responded with a scowl, "We get lunch an hour or two after midday, but you ain't gonna like what we get or how we get it."

Many of the other new gunmen were also growing hungry and tired, so they began to complain, "How much longer we gotta be out here... when we gonna eat lunch... my arms is tired suh... kent we get some rest..." so Duke Judson and his Drivers disciplined them with kicks to the head or cracks from a bullwhip. After Duke Judson whipped a gunman in Fulton's group for refusing to work, Cuttino whispered to Fulton, "That's Black Annie, every Sergeant's got one, en you don't never want to make her 'quaintance." The whip's hissing sound was still curling through Fulton's skin.

After another hour the guards finally ordered the gunmen to huddle for lunch. Fulton was exhausted and could not feel his legs or arms. He touched his face and felt nothing. He felt like a lump of senseless flesh and bones. He saw two horse drawn carts in the distance moving from the gunmen of cage six towards them. Mongoose looked at Cuttino, and Cuttino smiled, "Here comes your lunch... so get ready!" Cuttino and the other gunmen flexed themselves as if preparing for battle. As the cart neared, the gunmen pushed and huddled towards it but did not step too close. They had made that mistake before. The new gunmen mimicked their behavior, but they did not share the same urgency and soon found themselves tangled in their chains at the backs of their groups. The drivers of the wagons uncovered their carts to reveal a few dozen pots of steamed sweet potatoes and greens. The gunmen were wide-eyed and slack-jawed like dogs waiting for a bone from their master.

Then, in an instant that froze the new gunmen in disbelief, the wagon drivers flailed the steaming sweet potatoes and greens into the open mouths of the huddled gunmen. The gunmen jumped and grasped and fought like wolves for every scrap they could recover from the marsh before they sank under foot. And then it was over. Fulton and the others were paralyzed as they watched the food cart roll on to the next cage's gunmen. The new gunmen tried to jump into the icy water to recover some food, but they found themselves only with empty, groaning stomachs, and drenched with bone-shivering water. Fulton coughed and choked since he had swallowed more water than sweet potatoes, but before he could pity himself he saw the boy on his knees, crying at the edge of his group with a deep gash in his head. The Drivers ordered the gunmen back to work.

"Goddamnit!" Mongoose cursed at Cuttino, "why didn't you warn us?"

But Cuttino looked at him with hardened eyes and responded, "You need that anger to fight for your food everyday. You kent be told to have it. You gotta feel it burn to survive." They returned to the marsh, moving it from one side of the Pinnekoke Levee to the other. Fulton promised himself that he and the boy would enjoy as many sweet potatoes as they wanted the next day.

They worked well past sunset into the cold night. Fulton watched the sun descend into the horizon's lap and then watched the moon rise in the heavens. The moonlight danced across the restless marsh right up to his numb feet. Meanwhile, the night guards kept the buckets moving with roars and whipcracks, but they mostly kept themselves warm by sipping whiskey under the stars. Dinner was served just like lunch, just before sunset, and in the spreading darkness, all the gunmen struggled to find and consume the jejune food. Finally, several hours after he felt he had already fallen asleep, dreaming the motions of his continuing labor, Fulton heard Sergeant Brace announce the end of the workday. The night guards led the gunmen back to their cage, where they were unshackled and released to the two shackshooters of cage seven.

The shackshooters were both large, irascible white men with two rifles each. Cuttino said that no one knew their names. They inspected the gunmen on their way in their cage, checking their mouths, ring-arounds, and buttocks for anything that might facilitate their escape. As he laid down in his bunk, Fulton realized that the cage did not smell as putrid as the previous night, because his entire body was numb. From the cold he could not feel his legs, from the buckets he could not feel his arms and back, and from his fatigue he could not feel the world around him. He felt empty and unconnected to the world. Before falling asleep, his tired thoughts turned to Moondog. He wondered how he and Kenge had fared in cage eleven. If he could find him, and if they could talk, then maybe they could devise a plan of escape. *Them hounds from Front Camp, sittin' with them guards en gnarlin' growlin' at us, they kent track me en Moondog through that marsh or that forest on the other side. No way they ken track us . . .*

The next morning during the line-up after breakfast, Fulton and Mongoose stood on either side of the boy while Stock and Jimmy shackled the groups of ten together. The marsh did not seem any shallower than yesterday, and Fulton wondered how they could ever drain it. Soon enough, the rhythm of their labor consumed them. Full bucket to the right, empty bucket to the left, full bucket to the right, empty bucket to the left. Fulton and Mongoose joined to help the boy, and after an hour, Fulton tried to begin a conversation with him, but he was reluctant to speak, or even make a sound. He already had furrows of skin across his forehead like an old man, and his eyes watched the world like a nightmare. Fulton was sad to see a child who had already learned to mistrust the world, but after he helped the boy get food at lunch, the child began to look at Fulton as if searching for the courage to speak. And when he did, he told Fulton with a timid voice, "My name's James Harrington en I turned thirteen years old last week."

"Happy birthday, James. So tell me why a good boy like you is in a bad place like this." Fulton asked.

"I got a ten year sentence two months ago for burglary wit intent to rape . . . I did steal that lady's purse, but I wudn't gonna hurt her. I just grabbed it en ran. I still don't know what rape means."

"Where were your parents?"

"Far as I remember, I ain't got any. I lived in the streets a Gastonia wit a group a other kids, stealin' food en clothes to stay alive."

"Long Chain Charlie bring you here?"

"Yeah. I was in jail for two weeks in Gastonia when Long Chain came for me en the others," James' face tightened as he continued, "while I was in that cell, them older ones made me drop my pants."

Fulton wanted to place his hand on the child's shoulder to reassure him, but he could see that James was terrified of being touched.

"You don't have to worry 'bout any a that happenin' here 'cause I'm gonna make sure that both of us get outta here alive, en then you ken come home wit me en meet my family en stay wit me if you like."

James did not smile, but he nodded his gratitude. Fulton could see that the world was a nightmare to James, full of monsters instead of dreams, and that made him no different from the dead. *Ten years for stealin' a purse,* Fulton thought, *wit intent to rape? Difference 'tween that ana spankin' is the darker color a that boy's skin.*

The next day Parchman's sky filled with menacing swirls of clouds. They made Fulton nervous all day, and when night arrived, Fulton wanted to return quickly to his cage, but he could not move any faster than the slowest member of his group. Mongoose noticed the clouds as well and said, "These the kind a clouds that bring all the snakes from hidin' back at Willow Lake." Then Fulton heard his name whisper-yelled from the darkness to the east. He squinted and spotted Moondog trying to make his way to him, but he could not free himself from his position in his group. Fulton waved, and then their respective Drivers arrived and kicked them into silence. The gash on Fulton's head re-opened and bled again. Drip-drop into the marsh.

Cuttino could feel Fulton's gash in his own head, "Tomorrow's Sunday," he said, "en you ken try to find your friend then."

A bolt of lightning pierced the distance and the sky thundered in a foreboding rhythm. The gunmen quickened their pace back to their cages, and soon enough they were inspected and inside awaiting sleep to overwhelm them. All that night the sky opened and drenched the earth. Before falling asleep, Cuttino shook the cage with an outburst, "Fuckin' rain! It's fillin' up all the water I spent two months drainin'! Fuckin' rain!" Fulton's eyes widened as he understood all of his work and exhaustion and suffering was being washed back into the marsh. He cursed the rain as well, but then realizing what he had done, he cursed himself in shame, for he never thought the day would arrive that he would despise the waters of the sky. That was like cursing his own blood, or his mother's milk. Parchman had turned him against rain. All of a sudden, Fulton feared what he was becoming, after only two days. What then of fifteen years? If only they had remained in the half-way house that night. If only Jay were here to write him a letter to his daughter. If only...

Rain fell in merciless torrents the next day. The gunmen were locked in their cages since none of their Sergeants or Drivers wanted to sit in the rain all day supervising them. Lunch and dinner arrived through the front door in watery, rusty buckets of sweet potatoes and greens with some pork. And unfortunately for the gunmen, their cage offered them only marginal shelter. The ceiling was full of leaks that soaked them, their beds, and the floor. They had no sheets and no covers, so they had no choice but to lay in their beds with the rain dripping on them. And worse still was the rising lake of waste from the far corner of the cage as the water spread the miasmic swamp across the floor.

Cuttino told Fulton and Mongoose that the shit-and-piss swamp had swelled once before, and after it dried and crusted, the gunmen were allowed to shovel it into a hole outside the cage. Then the cage was less foul. But for now, they had to endure it. So Fulton stared into the ceiling; in its corrugated contours he saw images of his former life, his loved ones and former routines, but the images were fading, and he had to dive deeper and deeper to retrieve them. Fulton was losing another battle against loss. He wondered if one day he would reach for his former life and find nothing more than the ghosts of memories strewn across the arid battlefield of his empty life.

James and Cuttino both lost a tooth that night. They had been loosening and finally rotted out of their mouths. Cuttino threw his into the swamp rising below. James swallowed his. Some of the older children in Gastonia told him that if you throw your tooth to the ground it will make the trees sick where it falls, so he swallowed it. Meanwhile the cold, relentless rain fell for two more days. Fulton wanted to tear off his skin and scream. On the second day of the rain, no one brought them food, so tempers flared, fights erupted, and the walls bled. When the rain finally moved to the northeast, Fulton waited for the smell of the fresh earth to fill his lungs, but all he inhaled was the hanging stench of rotting negroes.

Sergeant Judson and his Drivers arrived late that morning with breakfast, and then lead the gunmen back into the marsh. Even though it looked the same, the gunmen knew that the marsh had swelled with the rains and all of their work was undone. Not that they were invested in the success of the venture, but the longer the water was on the wrong side of the Pinnekoke Levee, the longer they had to spend monotonous days passing and lifting buckets hour after hour after hour. A week later the gunmen were given shovels to clear the crusting sewage from their cages. The gunmen asked if they could bathe, but the guards said they would hose them and nothing more. Since it was too cold to be hosed, the gunmen decided to wait until the spring to be clean again. In the meantime, their filth and putrescence compounded the stench of their cages.

The next month Long Chain rolled into Gordon Junction and delivered another eighty negroes to Parchman. Most of them, like the ones before, had been arrested under the Pig Laws and then sentenced to Parchman. Fulton saw Vardaman's smile painted in the clouds that day. Six more gunmen, including another boy, joined his cage. The new boy slept four bunks down from Mongoose. His name was Will Evans, and he told Mongoose and Fulton that he was eight years old, and that he was sentenced to six months in Parchman for stealing change from the counter of the local dry goods store. Also among the new gunmen, sleeping just below Will, was the oldest gunman in Parchman, Sunday Slims, seventy-nine years old. The next day in the fields he told Fulton that he had been arrested for entering the room of a white woman with malicious intent. The judge ordered him to pay a fine, and of course, court fees. The fine was $50, plus a $6.90 Mayor's Fee, a $4.20 Officer Fee, a $2.80 Jail Fee, and $132 for court costs. But Sunday had only three dollars to his name, so he was sent to Parchman to work off his debt at two dollars a day, less a dollar and twenty cents per day for room and board.

The only new gunman Moondog noticed (everyone noticed him) in his cage was a giant colored, named Gerrit Faulk. His eyes did not look at the same thing at the same time, and he wore a gnashing scowl across his face. He mumbled and drooled and twitched his neck, and since he was almost twice as big as the average gunman (his ring-arounds barely reached past his knees and elbows), no one bothered to ask him what was wrong. Weeks later, Fulton and his friends speculated on what was troubling Gerrit, "Looks like he's sufferin' from snake poisonin," Mongoose said. "Naw," Fulton responded, "I bet he was dropped on his head as a baby." "Ya'll both wrong," Sunday chimed. "Problem wit that negro is that he's got the devil in him, plain en simple." Whatever his malady, everyone agreed he smelled dangerous, so everyone kept his distance.

Five Sundays after Fulton arrived he finally had the day off. No rainstorm or shit-swamp shoveling ruined his opportunity to relax. Fulton woke that day with Moondog in his mind, and he was ready to go find him, but first the Drivers led the gunmen after breakfast to attend Church services, officiated by the Reverend Gary Kibel. Kibel was a pious man from a long line of priests with mystical faiths. His world was defined by the history of spirits, and the Christian's duty was to merge himself into their movement toward perfection. Christ was God's gift to humanity as the archetype of that movement. Therein, Reverend Kibel came to Parchman each Sunday to officiate services for its guards as well as its gunmen. The guards received their service first, in the small chapel aside the Superintendent's Mansion. Then Reverend Kibel performed open-air services in the courtyard of Front Camp for the gunmen. The Drivers were perched on the buildings around the courtyard just in case one of the gunmen, who were not shackled on Sundays, decided to run for freedom.

Reverend Kibel opened each service pleading to God for the salvation of the wayward, "Lord, today we come to you asking that Parchman will serve as the first step towards the rehabilitation of these convicts and their desire to live better Christian Lives." Kibel also counseled any gunman who wished an audience, especially upon their arrival at Parchman. "What did you do? Do you repent your transgression? Do you open your soul to reform and salvation? Let me teach you how to conquer your feral nature and elevate your spirit towards God." But after a few services and consultations, most of the gunmen grew tired of Kibel's sermons. They initially hoped that he could be an ally, a source of leniency, but he never believed their stories -- that they had not committed the crimes of which they were accused, and of how brutally they were treated at Parchman.

Fulton initially found Reverend Kibel a decent and concerned man, except that he was not willing to help Fulton in any way other than his own way. He would not help Fulton write a letter to Simbi (Fulton was not ready to be received by her) and he would not help get the children released from Parchman (if you remove a serpent's fangs when it is young it cannot grow up to poison you). For his part, Mongoose despised the giant, golden crucifix Kibel wore around his neck, and he did not like his shiny black velvet robe either. Mongoose wanted to tell Kibel that a camel had a better chance of making it though the head of a needle. Cuttino did not trust Kibel because he felt like Kibel was always looking at him with more than two eyes, and he was always suspicious of the sanctimonious half-smile painted across his face.

So on the day of their first service the gunmen walked into the courtyard and knelt on their knees. Kibel blessed them and sermonized with his half-smile. Thirty minutes later the gunmen received the Lord's Blessing and rose, with the remainder of the day to themselves, but only in Front Camp under the watchful hawkeyes of the perched guards. Fulton found Moondog and they introduced their respective friends to each other. Moondog's friends, Stromyle Epps and Joe Graham, loved to play dice, so they all gathered at the steps of the chapel to play and talk about the place which had stolen them from their worlds almost six weeks before.

First, Moondog told Fulton about his friends Stromyle and Reverend Topeka, "cept Reverend Topeka's dead now. In the first week we was here, the guards started draggin' him from our cage each night, en then returned him bloody en beaten few hours later. Topeka told the guards that the Lord was gonna save him; but the guards took him anyway, night after night, 'til last Tuesday mornin' when somebody spotted Topeka's body floating face down naked in the marsh."

"Ain't nobody been treated like that in my cage," Fulton responded after the story, "but how'd a Reveren end up in this place anyhow?"

Stromyle told the story. Up until a few weeks ago he and Topeka lived in Tupelo where they tended the lawn of the Mayor's Mansion and lived with their families in a settlement for coloreds near the edge of town. Reverend Topeka Sanders was the Preacher of the settlement's congregation. Stromyle did not care much for God or Topeka's church, but they had been best friends since they were children. "Topeka liked jokin' wit me that I was only his friend just in case he was right about Jesus en Godly things." They each had a boy and a girl and a wife, and when one family struggled, the other was there to help. "That's what Topeka preached, and that's what he said would liberate us from our difficult lives. *Rise above*! he'd say, *The most beautiful flowers grow in swamps. And on your Judgment Day, let it not be said that you harbored anger gainst your lot in life en you held it gainst your brothers by not helpin' them in need. No matter what little you have, you always got somethin' for someone who got less than you.*"

But Topeka did not confine his preaching to the colored settlement. On the days when he and Stromyle were tending the mayor's lawn, or cleaning his house, or building his stables, the mayor would pass by them and Topeka would not miss the opportunity to harangue him. He would tell the mayor that "the kingdom a God is not open to those who idolize mansions on earth."

And the mayor would respond, "On the contrary, I think that God's mercy is with me and not with you since he made you the nigger and made me white. And what's more, my idolatry puts food on your plate."

"I warned him to keep his proselytizin' to himself," Stromlye somberly continued, "before we found ourselves witout work like the rest a the settlement. But he would jes say that you kent silence the Word en deep in his soul the mayor wanted us around en wanted to hear his sermons or he would have fired us both long ago."

But in the end the mayor became irritated with Topeka's sermons, and he had Topeka arrested for stealing silver from the kitchen. Two chambermaids testified in court that they witnessed Topeka abscond with the silver. But Stromyle knew that Topeka would not take even a penny from a dying man, so he protested during the trial and was consequently found guilty as an accomplice when the two chambermaids also remembered seeing him in the kitchen that night with Reverend Topeka. They were both tossed in jail, but not before Topeka forgave the chambermaids for bearing false witness against him. Once in jail, Topeka refused to face his family, even though they pleaded to see him. He was too ashamed to face his children, whom he had ruined by his own false ruination. Stromyle sent messages to both families that they were all right, but that he did not know how long they would be in their cell as they had been sentenced to time at Parchman Farm.

Meanwhile, the settlement rallied behind Topeka's innocence and cried for justice. They even paid for a letter to be written to W.E.B. Du Bois, who had just visited President Roosevelt in the White House, in the hopes that he would come to Tupelo and fight for Topeka's freedom. But Du Bois never arrived, and instead Whitecaps ravaged their settlement, burning down cabins and lynching eleven men, six women, and two children, one of whom was Stromyle's boy Willis. "That day, when my wife came to the jail tremblin' wit tears in her eyes en she hardly breathin', like the devil had his hand 'round her throat, en she told me my boy was lynched... I'll never forget that day. I wanted to tear this world apart. But I couldn't do nuthin'. I couldn't even reach out to hold my wife en wipe the tears from her eyes. Nuthin'. I just stood there en felt my chest turn to nuthin'. I was ashamed to be a man. So all I could do was curse Topeka en his God. I screamed for hours, 'til Long Chain arrived in Tupelo en brought us here. Later I apologized to Topeka for cursin' him en his God en blamin' them for the death a my son, but Topeka told me that he was not worthy a the apology en all he saw all around him was angels crashin' to the ground."

When he arrived in cage eleven, Moondog had gravitated to Stromyle and Topeka because he saw in them the kind of friendship he shared with Fulton. Proximity to Topeka entailed a serenity Moondog had missed since sitting on Fulton's porch watching the sunset. Like Fulton, Topeka spoke with an earthy voice and was never overwhelmed by his immediate circumstance. They both lived in a world that was soft and humble.

So when the guards began taking Topeka from his cage and returning him hours later beaten and tattered, Stromyle and Moondog wanted to help, but Topeka turned his head and looked into the ground. There was nothing they could do, and he did not want to entangle them in his suffering. He told himself that by receiving all the pain from the guards he was saving others from receiving it. So they watched him, dragged from the cage in the shadows of the night, and they boiled with rage in their bunks each night that they could not rescue their friend.

That Tuesday morning, when a gunman spotted Topeka, naked and bloated in the marsh, Stromyle and Moondog turned their eyes to the other end of the horizon so that no images of the cruelty could burn themselves into their minds. Maybe the mayor was right. Maybe God's mercy was not with them and that's why they were niggers. Or maybe there wasn't a God and being a nigger was just the consequence of the unfolding of human cruelty. Whatever the case, Topeka was found dead in a filthy Mississippi swamp. And with no discernable logic to explain why, they realized that any one of them could be next.

The Mask of Death

"What's it like bein' a sharecropper en a daddy," James asked Fulton the next day in the marsh.

"Well," Fulton responded, "sharecroppin' en bein' a father is quite similar. For both, you work from an obligation to a greater power, 'cept that in sharecroppin' that obligation is to your landowner en in fatherin' it's to your ancestors."

"Sometimes I think 'bout havin' my own children when I'm older," James responded, "boy ana girl. I would call the girl Shirley after my mama en the boy Fulton after you."

Fulton smiled but was afraid for James. As he was so many years before, so now was James a young colored with big plans.

Later that week, the inmates were awakened at four-thirty as usual, but instead of heading into the marsh after breakfast, they were led to Front Camp to the courtyard in front of Superintendent Flood's mansion. On the way over, Mongoose noticed that Sunday Slims' ankles were torn open and festering beneath their shackles. He walked with a labored, painful gait whose shadow even betrayed his affliction. "Shackle Poisonin'," Cuttino said, "happened to another a week before ya'll arrived. Shackles cut right through his skin en he got infected. Puss en blood gushin' outta it for days, all over his bed en clothes. He used to moan all night 'til them shackshooters stuffed dirt in his mouth to shut em up. Then he jes died one night. Looks like Sunday ain't got but 'til Friday or Saturday hisself." Fulton and Mongoose bereaved the fate of the old, old man.

The gunmen waited in the cold morning, watching the sun cast a yellow glaze across the flat horizon. Fulton fixed his eyes on a crested eagle soaring across the awakening sky; he felt its elegance swim through him in waves of supple wingstrokes. He wanted to fly into the sky and recline with the bird in the heavens, but before he could soar, gunfire ripped him from his vision and returned him to Parchman. The guards ordered the gunmen silent, and they all wondered what danger had arrived to disturb their routine. A few minutes later, Superintendent Flood appeared on his third-story balcony and surveyed his empire. The gunmen looked up at him, but they could see only his shadowy silhouette in the sun rising behind him. When he spoke, they could not see his mouth move or the look in his eyes.

"Some disturbing occurrences have come to my attention. I've ordered you here today to rectify these occurrences. Though I've not been the one to do these things, I do blame myself to a certain degree. This is, after all, a correctional facility in which you wayward negroes are supposed to learn how to be proper, hardworking, law-abiding negroes. Perhaps I've not remained diligent in my effort to rehabilitate you. Perhaps I've let myself assume that a strict, labor-intensive environment would be sufficient to discipline you. But then again, perhaps those of you responsible for my disappointment are only a few bad negroes ruining the image of the entire bunch. I don't know, but I see your guilty faces, and I know what each of you has done. I know everything you do."

The gunmen searched each other for the faces about which the shadowy voice spoke. Fulton wondered what they had done and what it meant would happen to them. He prayed Moondog was not involved. In the midst of their growing discomfort, the shadow escalated their fears, "So I have gathered all of you here today to eliminate the negative influences among you. As I see it, all of you should not lose the opportunity to become fine negro members of Mississippi society, and perhaps this display will deter you from following these negative examples."

Those who suspected that they were being spoken to began to fear for their lives, but they feared flight even more, which would mean certain death, for the perched guards could shoot them all in seconds. Then the shadowy voice continued, "Let it be said that your trespasses have been grave ones. Your homosexual and murdering activities have cost us several lives and sacrificed the quality of your rehabilitation. You have brought corruption to Parchman and insulted its mission."

Most of the inmates looked at each other in confusion; a few hung their faces below the eyes of the others. Fulton and Mongoose exchanged concerned expressions, and in an instant, Fulton smelled ash in the air just as the shadow spoke his last word, "One day you will remember Parchman and thank it for purging you." At that moment fire rained down on the gunmen. The guards shot simultaneously, and eighteen gunmen saw their brains fly in front of their eyes in the momentless moment before they fell to the earth. The other inmates piled over each other trying to protect themselves from additional fire, but no more bullets arrived.

Soon, their squirming and screaming subsided, and the gunmen untangled themselves from their shackled knots, wondering who had been shot. Unsure whether more fire would follow once they had calmed and ordered themselves, the gunmen remained apprehensive, with their hands over their heads, watching the guards above them to see where they might fire next. But the shadow ended their anticipation by ordering the gunmen back to their cages to prepare for work. The shadow also ordered some of the Drivers to dig a hole behind the chapel and deposit the bodies in it.

A crimson morning accompanied the solemn march into the marsh. The gunmen walked under the weary sensation of disassociation from themselves, as if they were the others, the dead and buried versions of themselves, squirming under the weight of the dirt above them. As the morning awakened, the marsh glistened. Other than the gunmen's watery movements, the world was silent; even the Drivers were subdued. Black Annie remained coiled by her Sergeant's side the entire day, sleeping. But there was no peace within the silence, and no energy to search for anything to say. Lunch arrived with little struggle. The gunmen were satisfied to receive whatever scraps of sweet potatoes and greens happened their way.

By afternoon the silence became heavy, pressing against their chests, as if they were standing at the bottom of a dark ocean. And then a voice resonated as if from a cavern, and it called the other thousand gunmen to its rhythm, "Lawd oh Lawd, they didn't mean no harm." Then silence, all heads turning to the call, reverberating through the marsh... silence awaiting their response in chorus, "But that don't matter to Parchman Farm." Another call and another chorus. The sound shook the horses and saturated the air and earth and water as its poetry unfolded in concurrence with its creation.

"I spent a thousand days wit a bucket in my hand,"
"Changin' ocean to land for the Cotton Man."

And with their call and chorus the gunmen elevated their minds beyond the marsh into the sonorous waves of their chants, singing as if watching themselves sing. Within that disjunction they located a space of peace in which they could momentarily abide the afflictions of their lives.

When the day ended and the gunmen returned to their cages, they awakened the night sky with the hummed rhythms of their songs. Each star was a different resonance. They hummed the songs of their deaths at Parchman Farm back to their cages and until they fell asleep. Then, as they rested, the families of roaches and vermin, swelling with the warming days, skittered back and forth across their bodies until morning.

The next day Sunday Slims died. He fell face first into the marsh. Sergeant Judson galloped to him and ordered him to rise. When Sunday remained motionless, Black Annie whizzed through the air and split open his back. Still nothing. So Sergeant Judson concluded that Sunday was dead. He ordered the Drivers to unshackle him so the gunmen in his group could bury him behind the Chapel. When they unshackled him, the Drivers uncovered his festering ankles, which had been reduced to putrid stumps of puss and blood with a mossy, green growth thriving across the exposed flesh.

It was probably better that Sunday died in spring, because by the time the summer arrived, he would have suffered an even worse fate. That summer, seven gunmen were half-eaten by alligators (and consequently discharged), three gunmen were killed by brown bears, nine caught fevers from cottonmouth bites, eighteen died from dysentery (from drinking the marsh water), and thirty-two gunmen and two Drivers died from malaria.

But the sun was the deadliest carnivore of them all. The heat scorched and baked the gunmen for months. By ten in the morning the marsh was a bubbling cauldron which boiled the gunmen alive, and by mid-afternoon the heat melted their bones and pounded through their minds. Not even the occasional bucket of water over their heads could cool them. As a consequence, heat stroke claimed forty-seven lives. Fulton and his friends all survived the summer, but the seething heat evaporated the air from Fulton's lungs, and for the first time in his life he began to have trouble breathing. He heaved and wheezed all day, struggling to inhale enough air to keep himself from collapsing. The air was like fire, and he felt like kudzu had taken root in his gut and was clamping around his lungs.

By August, Superintendent Flood wrote a letter to Governor Vardaman requesting an acceleration in (colored) arrests so that he could have enough hands to finish draining the marsh in time for next year's crop. Meanwhile, all the summer's victims were buried in the dirt behind the chapel. The next Sunday, Kibel expressed concern to Flood that so many gunmen were perishing without rehabilitation or repentance. Flood shrugged and told Kibel it was God's sun that made them sick.

The Sergeants and Drivers hated the summer months in the marsh as well. At least in the winter some whiskey and gloves could keep them warm, but nothing could cool them in the summer. So they often reduced their shifts, dividing their half-day shifts between the three of them so that no one had to be in the sun for more than two or three hours. The guards were initially worried that their reduced presence might tempt escape, but they soon learned the gunmen were far too weakened from the heat to even remain standing, let alone muster the strength to organize a flight through the marsh into the plains beyond.

Summer nights in the cages were no more pleasant. With only the two small, unscreened windows, the interior of the cages was more hot and humid than the exterior. The squalid air hung like steam inside, saturated with the noisome pungence of the bubbling shit swamps, which in turn encouraged every species of vermin and insect and fungus and parasite known to Mississippi to make a home in the cracks and mattresses and occupants of each cage. Centipedes, flying roaches, dung beetles, rats, mosquitoes, black widows, brown recluses, fire ants, ticks, chiggers, and horseflies buzzed and bit, bored into, and poisoned the sweating gunmen, night after night.

And on the worst of one of these morning, Fulton awoke to discover black widows crawling out of James' gaping mouth as if it were a gateway into their homeland. His face was swollen and red, and rats were gnawing his feet. Anger consumed Fulton. He screamed his anguish and threw the creatures from the corpse. They recoiled with patience, waiting. The remainder of the cage, initially alarmed by Fulton's cry, turned with indifference from what it had already seen too many times. Fulton held James to his chest. How could the world make him so vulgar? The world was the mother of this child, and yet it was also the rotting plague of his every attempt to do anything more than just survive.

That day, in the marsh, Fulton looked at the world with malevolent eyes, as if it were agent to the systematic disintegration of everything he valued -- family, freedom, friends, hope, and life. In the void of his hopelesness, Fulton saw himself as just a casing, dreamless, and no more purposeful than the water which he was moving from one side of the Pinnekoke Levee to the other. Death's face had masked itself over the boy's, swollen and infested, with eyes staring as if there were never anything behind them. The world was this mask of death. All around him, the clouds became the mounted heads of the lynched, the winds were infected with shackles and whips, and the helplessness of colored existence gurgled from beneath the marshy sea.

LIFE'S ONLY PROMISE

Freedom Offering

After malaria claimed Bedford and Kenge in July, Mongoose gathered Fulton, Moondog, Cuttino, Stromyle, and Joe one Sunday to the front of the cattle barn across from the chapel. He sat them in a circle and said "I'm gonna protect ya'll from malaria for the rest a your lives." They laughed, but Mongoose countered with confidence, "Laugh if you want, but me en my family been protectin' ourselves from malaria for years at Willow Lake with a simple ritual en concoction we learned from our Issaquena ancestors." The others moved from laughter to confusion. "All you gotta do is drink a potion I prepare, repeat the words I say, en you won't have to fear joinin' Bedford en Kenge, wit your whole body shakin' wit the chills en then the burns en you kent sleep en you kent see straight." Moved by the strength of his words, the others agreed to humor Mongoose.

Mongoose calmed his breathing and continued, "Now last night, durin' the inspection, I slipped through the shadows back to the marsh to gather the ingredients for my potion. The sky was cloudy, but I could find what I needed under the comin' en goin' moonlight..."

As he spoke, Moondog interrupted, "Wait a minute! You tellin' me that you was in the marsh, all alone, outta your cage, en you came back here?!"

"Yeah. I've been goin' an comin' from time to time for awhile. When the time's right, I'm gonna show you how. I'm gonna show you how my ancestors en me ken move like snakes through the shadows a the world so nobody ken see or hear you. For now, I figured I jes needed to protect us from malaria."

The others were stunned. They could not believe his words. With what voodoo had Mongoose managed to slip out of line, right past the guards and the shackshooters, past the hounds, past the prowling nightshooters and their floodlights and into the fields, without raising a peep or scent of attention? As if he were a ghost? "All creatures can do what I do 'cause there ain't no difference between the livin' en the dead. Animals ken do it by their instincts, but they ain't smart enough to master they potentials. Humans, on the other hand, is smart enough to master these movements, but theys born oblivious to em, so a special teacher gotta awaken the memory a this knowledge in em."

In due time, Mongoose promised to teach all of them how to disappear from the eyes and noses of the world and move without a scent or a sound or a trace, without weight or substance on the earth, like the dead. Mongoose had already escaped from the cage to determine the best route of their escape. "But first we need to be safe from malaria so we ken live to escape another day."

Mongoose had buried the ingredients of his potion in the ground outside the cattle barn the previous night. He circled the others around the spot and unearthed his treasure. Some of the Drivers watched with curiosity and approached them, but

Mongoose assured them, "Ain't nothin' here to be concerned 'bout. I ain't tryin' to dig a hole back home." The Drivers scoffed and returned to their Front Camp patrols.

Within a few minutes, Mongoose unearthed a seven foot moccasin, the soft, broad leaves of a swamp kudzu, half a handful of green moss, a few shoots of elephant ear root, and a glass jar. Fulton and the others stared at Mongoose as if he were a devil. Next, Mongoose chewed the swamp leaves, spat a green paste like cud into the jar, and began to mumble words from another tongue as he bobbed his head. Then he rubbed the green moss against the elephant ear root and placed it aside the jar. The others tried not to appear nervous, but with each movement Mongoose's ritual became more and more disturbing. He began to mumble more loudly, and his eyes rolled back into his head. Mongoose handled the snake with listless undulations, and it seemed to come alive. Its eyes glowed like night stars.

Fulton and the others were entranced by the rhythm of the snake's motions in Mongoose's arms; they could feel it slithering in their spines. In fact, the rhythm was so entrancing that they saw nothing when Mongoose lifted the snake to his face, bit off its head, and drained its scarlet blood into the jar. In one continuing motion, Mongoose then spat the snake head to the ground, took a bite of the elephant ear and sipped the potion, all the while mumbling words from another tongue. Fulton, Moondog, Cuttino, Stromyle, and Joe repeated the ritual, and when the jar returned to Mongoose, he buried the remainder of the root, the potion, and the snake back into the earth. Finished, they arose and walked to the steps of the chapel to play dice. In silence. None of them noticed the drops of blood trickling from their chins.

Unfortunately, though he was able to save his friends from malaria, Mongoose did not have a potion to protect them from the summer heat that desiccated all life. The gunmen joked that the Mississippi sun removed more from the marsh than they did, but their joking did not sustain their sanity through the brutal hours of unprotected labor under the summer's fire. They felt like they were being digested where they stood. Everything rotted under the sun, not only the gunmen, but also the food they received. The sweet potatoes were a putrefied mush swimming with vermin, and the greens were skeletal stalks infested by insects. But hunger forced every obtainable morsel down their throats. Food was nothing more than that which allowed them to continue working a few more hours. In the same way, life had become nothing more than that which allowed them not to be dead. So it should not have been a surprise to anyone when Joe came Knockin' later that summer.

Joe came Knockin' at the door of Joe Graham's sanity. He had been suffering all summer under the heat, the work, and the sleepless nights. With each day he became more and more anguished by all the hardships he endured, the stink of his cage, the heat of the sun, the weakness in his body, and the desperation in his mind. Moondog lent Joe his strength to support him through the months, but Joe's will to live was fading. It was only a matter of time.

And that time arrived in late August, when Joe collapsed in the marsh after puking his sweet potato and green bean lunch. Moondog went to pick him up, but he jumped back when his Sergeant arrived with Black Annie coiled to strike. He ordered Joe to rise from the marsh, but Joe did not move. He stung Joe in the neck with his whip, but Joe did not move. He was still alive, but he was not breathing and he would not move. So the Sergeant barked at Moondog and another gunman, "Carry him to the infirmary to be rehydrated. Once he wakes up, I expect to see him back in the marsh."

So Moondog and the other gunman carried Joe to the infirmary. There was no doctor in the infirmary; instead, the Drivers rotated duty during the day and tended to the light wounds and other maladies brought to them. For the most part, the infirmary handled heat stroke, nausea, and any light cuts or wounds that could be mended. If a gunman found himself with a more serious disease or injury (like an alligator attack), more often than not he was released from Parchman. Joe awoke from his unconsciousness after several hours and was allowed to return to his cage for the night. As he returned under escort, Joe wanted to die, but he feared taking his own life. Instead, he searched the distance between the infirmary and death, the space in which Parchman no longer wanted its gunmen, and that was the delirious realm into which Joe decided to thrust himself. He lay to sleep that night understanding what he had to do in order to return to his former life, even though he could barely remember what that was.

When Moondog and Stromyle returned to the cage later that night and asked Joe how he was feeling, Joe wore a calm smile as he answered, "Everythin's fine, and it's only gettin' better." He closed his eyes and lay in his bunk, calmed by a smile that was gently upturned, like a vessel fashioned to cradle an infant.

Several hours later Joe awoke. The cage was lit by a few moonbeams penetrating the thick air through the windows. Moths fluttered up and down the beams in ghostly procession. Joe looked at the other gunmen; they were all spread open on their bunks to try to cool their sweating sleep. With one gesture he could extricate himself from the torments of that sleepless sleep. One gesture to freedom. And he would rather have that than wholeness. After all, what would his gesture accomplish that Parchman wasn't already accomplishing with each passing day... cleaving his flesh and spirit until he walked the marsh like a patchwork of hopeless bones. What was he in Parchman other than the movement of buckets from the left to the right and back to the left, until he died? There was nothing to hold on to in this life. So logic and desperation dictated the ferocity of his gesture of liberation.

LIFE'S ONLY PROMISE

Joe turned in his bunk to face the moonlight and awaited the morning. Listening to his liberation knocking at the walls of his mind, he lifted his left leg towards his face and gazed at his foot, thick-skinned, black, cut open and raw. His eyes widened with the self-determining power of his impending action. He grew fangs and, like a snake, taut before the moment of strike, lunged at his heel and buried his jaws into his Achilles tendon. With blood and pain splashing across his face, Joe tore his fangs away in a guttural scream that sent his tendon flying across the cage to the bubbling floor.

His scream awakened everyone, and within moments the shackshooters burst inside and stuttered at what they saw. Joe was breathing with erotic heaves, inhaling his destiny through his wide, white eyes. He screamed, "I been attacked! I been attacked, en I'm bleedin' en dyin'!" The shackshooters searched for a culprit but found no one with fresh blood on his hands. So they ordered Joe carried to the infirmary where they could wrap his wound. Moondog and Stromyle (escorted by one of the shackshooters) carried Joe as he screamed to the sky, not in pain, but in delirious rapture, "It's done, it's done . . . I did it, en it's done." They gave him moonshine to ease his pain, and at length, his breathing slowed and he fell asleep. The shackshooters never found anyone who looked like he had attacked Joe, and no one thought to wonder why Joe's mouth was painted with blood.

The next day, Joe's Sergeant informed Flood that he could no longer walk. He would be useless in the marsh. So Flood ordered him released. Joe hobbled out of Parchman's gates towards the horizon of his reclaimed destiny. All the other gunmen were shocked, partially that he had been released, and also because he had succeeded in what they had all contemplated. Everyone knew that Joe had lamed himself, and now he hobbled free. With the precedent before them, "Knockin-a-Joe" inherited a nobility among the gunmen of Parchman Farm. It was a sacrifice for freedom and family and former lives. It turned a ghost back into a man. Later that summer, Natty Deeds chopped off his left hand with a hatchet and Otis Beeks broke his right knee. And even though Flood discovered the gunmen were mutilating themselves, he released both of them. By September, a few of the Sergeants began to express concern that if Knockin-a-Joe became too popular they would not have enough gunmen to drain the marsh and start tilling by the spring. But Flood responded, "Look, if those dumb niggers want to maim and disfigure themselves to get out of here, that's their business. I can get ten more for every idiot that pulls out his brains or chops off his legs. Besides, a lame nigger is no threat to Mississippi; he won't last a week out there, and I don't want his sinned blood dying in here on my hands anyway."

Reverend Kibel also voiced concern to Flood, "Something must be desperately wrong and potentially unChristian if all these coloreds are finding the courage to massacre themselves."

But Flood assured Kibel that Parchman was not driving its gunmen to desperate insanity and that the few coloreds destroying themselves were probably manifesting the same violent dementia that landed them in Parchaman in the first place, "Maybe it's God's way of keeping the rest of us safe from the most evil and dangerous of them."

Kibel wanted to see for himself how the gunmen were living and working, but Flood forbade him from ever leaving Front Camp, "for fear of his safety." And no gunmen were ever willing to tell Kibel what they were enduring for fear that their loose mouths would result in tight lashes. Kibel tried to convince the gunmen that harming themselves was a sin against God and his Creation (to which Stromyle mumbled that being a negro was a sin against Creation). Kibel tried, but he could not bring God into Parchman. So instead, the gunmen continued to invite the devil into their hearts, for just long enough to liberate themselves from their slow digestion in the bowels of Parchman Farm.

LIFE'S ONLY PROMISE

Mediterranean Blues

Despite all the disease, heat, and self-mutilation, by September there were only thirty empty beds in Fulton's cage. Mississippi's Pig Laws and Long Chain Charlie had outdone themselves. The gunman who had been sleeping below Fulton died of sunstroke, and an old colored named LaRue Bolivar arrived in his place in Long Chain's September shipment. LaRue reminded Fulton of his father, stone-faced and covered with the scent of autumn leaves. And he always walked as if he were wearing a robe. LaRue did not tell anyone how old he was, but Fulton and Mongoose figured that he was over sixty. He was silent most hours of the day (he did not even sing with the other gunmen in the marsh), but when he spoke he delivered his words like precious jewels, or like he was giving away a piece of himself. But what most surprised Fulton about LaRue was that from his first day he had been able to sleep in their cage without stuffing anything into his nose to palliate the stench.

LaRue slowly opened himself to Fulton and Mongoose, and he eventually agreed to play dice with them on Sundays, but he never spoke during their games. One day, searching for anything that would draw words from LaRue, Fulton asked him how he had always been able to sleep in their cage without stuffing anything in his nose. LaRue smiled and answered in an earthy voice, "When I was a young man, I made a trade with the devil. I exchanged my nose for the ability to read and write."

"You ken read en write?" Fulton asked in a shocked voice.

"Now don't go spreading that around," LaRue replied in a whisper, "or I won't get any peace. I'm trusting ya'll because you've been kind with me."

LaRue was the only gunman any of them knew who could read and write. The possibilities were spinning through Fulton's mind. He could write letters to Simbi, and she would know where he was and that he was alive. She could come to Parchman to see him and help him find a way home. Seven months had passed since he left her, and Fulton worried that she and Orlando would fail the crop and that Anderson would evict them.

As Fulton's mind was spinning with these possibilities, Mongoose looked at LaRue with a curious brow, "What do you mean you traded your nose to the devil so you could read en write?"

LaRue reclined and explained, "When I was seventeen I was cleaning fish in Biloxi for Jimmy and Sons Seafood. I hated the smell of the fish and the moldy docks, but I was afraid to leave my job because at fifty cents a day I wasn't going to make more money doing anything else."

So each night, after gutting and cleaning and gutting the fish, LaRue returned to his cot in the dock barracks feeling ill and trapped, like he could never escape the smell of fish. He felt their scales growing over his skin. But he told himself that he was doing as well as any illiterate colored in Biloxi. But literacy could change everything. The world would open its treasures if he could communicate with it, for the world did not progress through spoken words, but through words written on papers which passed from one mind to the next throughout History. LaRue decided he must find a way to enter the commerce of written words. "You never met a rich man who couldn't read," LaRue told himself in his youth, "and you never met a poor one who knew how."

So he fixed his mind on this goal, and the very next day, after fourteen hours of gutting fish, LaRue reached his limit, so he took his gutting knife to his chest, cut a bleeding cross into it, and announced to whatever spirits were listening, "I hereby exchange my nose for the knowledge of written words." He shuddered after his barter, but he told himself that smelling had taken him as far as it could in this world (and that there were no sweet scents awaiting his destiny), so in essence, he was exchanging nothing for the key to the world's treasures.

That same night a black elephant with six tusks appeared to LaRue in a dream, and without a word the elephant pressed its trunk against his nose and stole his air. LaRue awoke with a choking start just as men dressed in capes and swords and moustaches broke into the barracks and stole him and dozens of others onto a galley named the Santa Isabella (which LaRue still could not read). They were chained together and packed like rats in the ship's dark belly, forced at whiplash to row the ship to wherever they were being stolen. Their captors spoke a foreign tongue and tossed gruel at them twice a day, which most of them regurgitated with the queasy motions of the sea. After a violent, four-day tempest, LaRue fell ill with a boiling head and boiling joints; had he not been able to conceal the severity of his illness and continue rowing, he would have been thrown overboard. "I'll never forget those days. The wind was diseased with whips and screams and the crowing of men tossed into the belly of the sea." Then three days later, the pain of LaRue's aching head and joints disappeared, and with the pain so did his sense of smell. He had paid the price, and now he awaited his recompense. Until that day arrived, he was thankful to possess one fewer sense through which the misery of his life could assualt him.

Weeks passed at sea, until the Santa Isabella finally arrived at land. The coloreds remaining in the ship's belly (about half of the original number) were taken to Madrid and then led through the streets to the Queen's castle. LaRue could see that the streets offered a thousand smells -- breads and fruits and fish -- but he could not smell any of them. Instead, he thought of his family and the families of the others, worlds away still weeping and wondering how the world could so suddenly devour their children. "Next thing I knew I was in the castle of Queen Isabella II. She was covered in silk scarfs and golden jewels. The other coloreds and I were lined up before the Queen and assigned specific duties throughout the castle -- cooking, stables, gardening, and others. Soon I was the only one without a duty, and then the Queen told me I would serve her meals everyday and that I was more beautiful than the blackest, strongest horse in her land. She said I walked as if the night had grown legs and danced across the heavens. In time, the Queen taught me Spanish so I could speak with elegance, and she taught me all about the world so I could understand who I was."

As the months passed, the Queen taught LaRue that he was in Spain, which was the most powerful and enlightened country in Europe, and that she was the Lord of everything and everyone in it. She ordered her tutors to teach him to read so that he could educate himself and converse with her on matters of culture and intellect. LaRue enjoyed her company, but he reminded himself that she was responsible for the deaths and enslavement of countless coloreds, and that none of the other survivors was living the blessed life he was. Not only was he free from labor, but also he did not sleep in the cell with the other servants, chained to the wall; instead, the Queen allowed him to sleep in a small room of his own, adjacent to the kitchen, where he was glad he could not smell the Mediterranean fish cooking. And even though he missed his mother and sister, for LaRue, Spain was like a land from his dreams, where he could be more than a nigger.

Then one day LaRue summoned the courage to ask Queen Isabella why Europeans and Americans enslaved his people. The Queen said that he had been studying too much and it was time to take a ride through her city. The Queen and LaRue sat together in one of her golden carriages (though LaRue sat on his knees at her feet), and they rode through the streets of Madrid. He had not ventured one step outside of her palace since he arrived six years earlier, so he squinted and blinked like a child awakening from a sleep. The streets, the people, and the motions of their lives were alien to him. The Queen told LaRue that her favorite aspect of Madrid was its smell of sweet oils, and then she said, "Everything you see belongs to me. I have not made these people who they are, nor myself who I am, but it is the nature of things into which we are born. That is why I am their Lord, and that is why they are yours."

"But why is this the nature of things?"

"You shouldn't struggle with such questions. Since all of this is, it must be so."

LaRue frowned at the Queen's words, and sensing his displeasure, she placed her hand on his head and spoke again, "But that answer does not please you. Would you feel better to know that there was a time and a place where your people conquered mine."

LaRue's eyes furled in curiosity and his Queen continued, "The Almoradives, negroes just like you, but from another time and place. They conquered the

Europeans in Morocco and Spain, but they chose not to enslave or oppress us. In another world, perhaps their compassion would have been a virtue, but in this world it proved to be their weakness, for it allowed my ancestors to believe they could revolt. And when they did, the Almoradives joined you as our slaves. So you see, these are the natures History has precribed us."

The Queen and LaRue rode the streets of Madrid for hours, occasionally stopping for fruit, cheese, or bread. LaRue watched as her citizens bowed in obeisance and pleasure at the opportunity to serve her. Aside from that bowing, they could live their lives for themselves; that was the difference between the Spanish in Spain and the Negroes in Mississippi. But LaRue was not satisfied with Queen Isabella's dismissive explanations of his role in the world, so he pressed her again, "Why is it that in your church here and in mine back home we learn that the Lord and his Son love everyone and that we are all his children?"

"Yes. So he does. But remember LaRue, just as a mother loves her children equally, is it not still true that one child is born before the other, and that one child is smarter or stronger than the other, and that from those differences manifest the natural order of their destinies, one greater and the other lesser?"

"But why would God create some of his children lesser to others?"

"If we were all equal, the History of his Creation would be quite monotonous. Our lives would lose all meaning. We can't all be the Queen of Spain."

LaRue understood her words, but he refused to accept her logic, "Perhaps. Perhaps what you say is true. Perhaps it is my birthright to be slave to your people. But remember, given the opportunity, I have learned Spanish, history, geography, cooking, and the ability to debate with the glorious Queen of Spain."

The Queen smiled and placed her hand on LaRue's firm chest. She felt his breathing swim through her. He was alive like a mountain. Then she turned to watch the world slowly passing outside the window of her golden carriage.

They rode until the sun began to slip into Madrid's curved horizon, like the rounded arch of a lover's hip. As they ascended the incline to the palace, LaRue remained dizzy with conflicts of reason. "I remember how angry I was that day, listening to the Queen explain to me why I was a slave. I felt powerless. I wanted to know the truth, but the truth didn't seem to be anything more than the answer her History offered me."

"So I stayed with the Queen in Madrid for another four years, but the Queen was overthrown in a revolution led by Generals Serrano and Prim. She was exiled to a smaller palace on a hill in Barcelona overlooking the Mediterranean. I lived with her in that palace for another fourteen years. I remember waking each morning and melting into the blues and greens of the sea, losing myself in its waves and sounds, like the world would have sounded before human noise. That was the first time I regretted not having my nose, to smell the water and that feeling of solitude in the world. It's the opposite of love, but I like it the same. That's the feeling I want when I die. Finally, one day the Queen found it cruel to keep me with her and she offered to send me home to Biloxi. I decided it was my duty to return to serve my knowledge to the lives of those less fortunate. The night before I left, we made love on the beach of the misty sea."

When LaRue returned to Mississippi at the age of forty-four, Biloxi was exactly the same. The only work he could find was cleaning fish at the same docks as before, but at least now he did not have to smell them. He found no traces of his family, and he lived in the same barracks as thirty years before. His time in Spain seemed like the consciousness of another life inserted into his own, for back in Mississippi, its uniqueness sat in dormant slumber as he could find no way to improve anyone else's life. So LaRue spent the next twenty years cleaning the same fish at the same docks in the same city at the bottom of Mississippi. In his old age he wondered whether literacy revealed anything sacred in the world at all.

"Then one day they arrested me for back taxes. I didn't know what they were talking about, and it turned out that I didn't owe any back taxes, but I only had eighty dollars to my name, so I couldn't afford the two-hundred dollars in court fees and expenses, so they sent me here to work off the rest. And here's where I've been ever since."

Fulton and the others were entranced. Working on the railroad down to Jackson was as far away from home as Fulton and Moondog had ever been, and none of them had ever traveled beyond the borders of Mississippi. Fulton told LaRue, "You don't seem colored at all, especially from the way you talk."

"Maybe not, but I ended up right back in the same place as the rest. We all start and finish in the same place, without a trace. That's what being colored means. The middle is just passing time."

LaRue was happy to share his story. Fulton could sense that he hadn't told it often and that countless other tales from his life remained to be spoken. Fulton heard in his words that LaRue was beginning to feel that he would expire from the world without its ever having recognized the uniqueness of his life. He did not want to pass without a trace.

LaRue promised to write letters for his new friends, but not for anyone else, "Mississippi is no place for a negro to demonstrate dangerous talents." When they returned to their cage that night, Fulton, Mongoose, and Cuttino walked around LaRue like proud children.

But then, that night as he fell asleep, Fulton became agitated, for LaRue's life had become nothing more than his own. LaRue should be with DuBois, meeting the President and leading his people to equality with the power of his mind. But he was sleeping in a cage in Parchman, just like a thousand other coloreds, fed to the world and used for nothing more than the movements of his arms and legs for someone else's profit. A renewed displeasure festered in Fulton. He thought of Simbi and the Boat Car Train game. LaRue had actually traveled to the distant lands of Kings and Queens, only to be returned to the poverty of all colored lives. Even for LaRue, there was no escape. Then what of his family? This railroad, this jail . . . and now she probably thought he was dead. All this, when there never was any escape.

Before he fell asleep, LaRue told Fulton something he would never forget, "But I wouldn't want to be them, to trade humility for wealth and wake up everyday like I had something to teach the world."

***

My Dearest Simbi,   *September 24, 1905*

First, let this letter show you that I am well and that I love you. I should have already returned to you and taken you and Orlando to a better life. But I have not returned, and I cannot come home yet. I am in Parchman, about seventy miles south of you off highway 49. I am serving a fifteen year prison sentence. The details of all this are not important, but know that I committed no crime. Nevertheless, I am here and have been here since February. Life is not easy here, but I will survive. Moondog is with me. I have made some new friends, including a man named LaRue who is writing this letter for me.

You cannot visit me yet. Come in the winter with Orlando so Anderson won't notice. I pray every night that you are happy and well and that the crop has grown tall and full for you. I know that Moondog's sons have helped you, so thank them. Keep strong and know that I will return to you soon.

I am sorry now that I ever left you, but I needed to try to bring us better lives. I don't know anymore whether this is possible. For now anyway, Mississippi is not happy with my plans. I think Dean's wife who cooks in Anderson's house knows how to write, so go to her to write me a letter back. Then come in the winter so I can see your face and know that you are alive. You are my strength and my survival, and our ancestors will ensure that we are a family again. Until then, be strong and never doubt that I will return.

I love you,
Daddy.

"See Fulton, there's poetry in your heart too."

SID KARA

***

When LaRue finished writing the letter he placed his hand over his heart and then over the page. He looked at the words like they were his children, blessed and Godsent. They manifested his transcendence of skin and History; he felt most alive with the pen in his hand. With each word, each letter, he unfolded into the curves of the ink, swimming along their undulations with supple fingers. Lash and lynch him a thousand times and you could not suffocate them. Even after his hand no longer remained to repeat the ancient gestures of his lexicon, his words would still possess the winds that whisper meaning into the world. He only wished it were not necessary for so many mundane words to reside between the profound ones. The ones that steal your breath.

That Sunday, after Kibel's service, Fulton, LaRue, Cuttino, and Mongoose went to Parchman's Post Office to mail their letters. The Post Office was nothing more than a ten by ten shack next to the Administration Building, with a box for incoming mail. Fulton did not actually have his own address; all of the cropper mail was delivered to Anderson and then distributed, from time to time. None of them had ever tried to mail a letter before, so when they arrived at the front door of the Post Office and it was locked, they did not know what to do. The other gunmen watched from a distance, wondering how they had letters to mail at all. Fulton approached the nearest Driver and asked him how he was supposed to mail a letter. The Driver told Fulton that the Post Office was closed on Sundays.

Fulton protested, "But Sundays is the only day we got to come here en mail letters. How we gonna mail letters if the Post Office is closed on Sundays?"

"Well then. I guess you're gonna have a hard time mailing any letters then, aren't ya."

The Driver's nonchalance burned inside Fulton, "But Flood told us we could mail one letter a month en I ain't mailed a single letter in seven months, so there's gotta be some way for us gunmen to mail letters from here even if the Post Office is closed on Sundays."

From his outdoor pulpit, Reverend Kibel noticed the discussion and approached Fulton and the Driver. Sensing Fulton's desperation, Kibel interrupted him to ask the Driver what the problem was. The Driver explained that Fulton and some other gunmen were trying to mail letters but that the Post Office was closed on Sundays.

"But that's the only day we's allowed to come here to the Post Office!" Fulton protested.

"Give me the letters. I promise all of you I'll talk to Flood about mailing them, and in the future you can give me whatever letters you want and I'll be sure to include them in Flood's outgoing mail."

As Kibel extended his hand to receive the letters, Fulton looked at him with concern, "This letter's very important to me Revren. It's to my daughter, so she knows I'm ok."

"Don't worry Fulton," Kibel answered with sincere eyes, "I promise you I'll mail the letters."

Though Fulton remembered how Kibel had told him that he was not ready to be received by his daughter, he had no choice, so he handed the letters to Kibel.

"Don't worry," LaRue comforted, "Kibel's a man of God; he won't betray your trust."

Kibel mailed the letters the next day and then spoke to Flood the next week about mailing the gunmen's letters for them. Flood told Kibel that he had never received any letters from any gunmen, but that he would be more than happy to mail any forwarded to him. What he did not tell Kibel was that he would open and read and rewrite or even burn some of the letters, so that those who did receive them would not read anything about Parchman Farm -- where it was, who was in it, and how the receiver could help them get out.

As for Fulton's, Cuttino's, and Mongoose's letters -- Cuttino's wife never received his because she and the rest of his family had been terrorized from their cabin by Vardaman's Whitecaps; Mongoose's brother did not receive his because he was dead, and Simbi never received Fulton's letter because Anderson had forfeited all his Postal Service in a battle with the United States Postal Department over their decree that all his croppers should be supplied with individual mailboxes and addresses. The letters sat in a dead mail vault in Minneapolis for two years and were then burned. As the months passed without a reply, Fulton's imagination conjured nightmarish images of what foul fate had befallen his fair daughter and how she must have anguished over why her father had forsaken her.

Heroes and Monsters

Autumn arrived, and autumn was better for everyone at Parchman. As the nights cooled, the gunmen were able to sleep again. The Sergeants and Drivers enjoyed the autumn almost as much as their gunmen; the cool trans-terranean breezes eased the discomfort of their duties and they became more patient with their gunmen since they were not suffering from the summer's heat. The comfort of autumn also translated into more time for recreation on Sundays and occasionally on Saturday nights. Even Kibel's monologues seemed less punctuated with hellfire and burning, now that the scorching summer sun was cooling for winter.

But the leaves did not change color at Parchman. LaRue was the first to notice that none of the leaves in Front Camp, near the cages, or beyond the marsh were shedding their robust greens for the vibrant sunset oranges and crimson shades of autumn. When he asked Fulton whether it seemed strange to him that Parchman's leaves did not change color, Fulton answered, "I hadn't really noticed, guess I stopped lookin' around long time ago." In Spain, LaRue's eyes had been his passion, the textures of the day, the peculiar curves with which the Spanish filled space, and the colors of night above the verdant sea. But in Parchman the only colors to see were black and white.

When winter arrived again, the water reached only half as high as the previous winter. Nevertheless, by December, most gunmen were again losing toes to frostbite. Fulton had only six toes remaining, and he walked like someone was pressing against his back. When he slept, rats chewed on his dead toes, causing him to remember how his grandmother told him that the remains of the dying are always fated to nourish the rise of the living. Three of his teeth fell out, and his skin thickened and chapped until it resembled the bark of a tree. Many of the gunmen began sniffing lighter fluid in the mornings to narcotize themselves to the cold. Fulton and LaRue initially resisted, for fear they would lose their memories. LaRue feared that Spain would be erased from his mind and he would forget how to read, and Fulton feared that he would lose his most precious gift, the memory of love. But the incessant jittering and spineicy discomfort of the cold overwhelmed them, and they eventually succumbed to the narcotizing refuge of the lighter fluid's fumes.

The fluid reminded LaRue of the opium he used to smoke in Spain, and it reminded Fulton of his tobacco, which he had not enjoyed since his belongings were confiscated in Jackson. He could feel the gypsy suffocating inside him, suffocating from his inability to summon the ghost of his love. Without her, he wondered what of him would remain for his former life to recognize.

For every ten inmates who arrived that winter, six were buried in the pit behind the chapel. The winter of 1905-1906 was the harshest in memory. Snow blanketed the Yazoo Delta four times in January, completely freezing the surface of the marsh, so the gunmen were locked in their open-air cages for weeks. But the hiatus from the marsh was no relief. The gunmen were given only two small fire barrels in the center of their cages to keep them warm. They gathered their bunks around the barrels but still froze night after night. Dozens of gunmen, especially the old and the young, either froze to death or died of pneumonia. The incessant cold and their interminable isolation tested their composure, and fights erupted, painting the walls with blood. Fulton and his friends kept to themselves, huddled together across two bunks. They tried to think of summer nights at their homes, and the warm potion of nostalgia helped sustain them through the cold winter nights.

When they returned to the marsh in early February, the gunmen wished they were back in their cages. Not this, not that. A flu epidemic ravaged the cages in February killing one-hundred eighty-eight gunmen, and two Drivers. Superintendent Flood ordered a doctor to Parchman before anyone else died, and the doctor, named Kenneth Adelson (who became a doctor so that he could practice medicine in colored, rural communities), vaccinated the entire Farm in two days and ordered three days of rest. Upon his departure, Dr. Adelson requested an audience with Flood to voice his concerns over the health of the inmates in Parchman. On a Sunday afternoon after Kibel's services, Dr. Adelson walked into Flood's office and explained that the prison conditions in Parchman were brutal and unacceptable. Sitting in his large, leather chair and smoking his favorite Spanish pipe as he looked at his gun rack on the wall, Flood responded, "beautiful, aren't they?"

"Excuse me?"

"Winchester rifles. They're quite beautiful aren't they?"

"That's not my concern, Superintendent. My concern is with the inhuman treatment of these inmates." Though he was young, Dr. Adelson spoke in a forceful tone, and Flood appreciated the vigor in his voice, but he was in no mood to trifle with him, so he barked in response, "Look, I'm just following the regulations given to me by Governor Vardaman. If you have any suggestions on how to improve Parchman you should address them to him." Flood returned his attention to his rifles and waved for Dr. Adelson to dismiss himself.

Adelson left Parchman, but the sound of Vardaman's name awakened a forgotten anger in him, an anger that compelled him to fight. So he wrote an article in the *Greenville Gazette* describing Parchman's inconceivable conditions, but his attempt to curry empathy from his fellow citizens met with little response. No more than a handful of meek coloreds and liberal whites approached Dr. Adelson, and they soon realized that there was little they could do. Even Editor-in-Chief William Brewell of the *Greenville Gazette* refused to print any more letters from Adelson after he received several death threats for printing the doctor's first article.

So Dr. Adelson decided to follow Flood's advice and voice his concerns directly to Governor Vardaman, a man whom he had hated long before he saw

Parchman and long before Vardaman cut the public health budget to colored counties, making it impossible for Adelson and others to maintain their practices in rural, colored communities. Adelson had hated Vardaman for over four years, ever since his beguiling rhetoric hypnotized his blacksmith father into despising his poverty and blaming greedy-eyed niggers for its persistence. Adelson's father eventually joined Vardaman's Whitecaps at age sixty-six and spent his last year on earth terrorizing colored citizens, until one day a colored fought back and shot Adelson's father square in the left eye, dropping him dead on the spot. Adelson sought the colored who shot his father and discovered that he had been burned to death that same night. He was not sure what he would have said to him had he found him alive; he would not have cursed or damned him, for he had convinced himself that the man the colored shot was not his father, but a ghoul in Vardaman's army of demons. Thus, in order to continue with life, Adelson interred the ghost of his father deep beneath the layers of his memories. But when Flood spoke Vardaman's name he awakened the dormant residue of Adelson's father, so Adelson decided to wield his fury and confront its contemptible overlord.

When he arrived in Jackson, Dr. Adelson marched straight up to the front gates of the Governor's Mansion and asked to speak to the Governor about Mississippi's Penal System. To his surprise, he was led straight to the Governor's office and seated on a couch to await Vardaman's audience. Vardaman called Adelson, and the first thing that occurred to him upon entering his office was that it was exactly the same as Superintendent Flood's, except everything was bigger: the windows, the walls, the gun rack, the paintings, the desk, and the leather chair in which the Governor sat, smoking his pipe. Vardaman was studying the 1905 Cotton Crop Report, and without looking up he asked Adelson what he needed. Adelson explained that he had come to voice his concern over a place he recently visited, a place called Parchman Farm. The Governor's eyes lifted from his report and scrutinized Adelson. "What do you mean, Parchman Farm?" Adelson looked deep into Vardaman's eyes so that he would never forget them, and he explained that he had been called by the Superintendent to treat a flu epidemic, and during his visit he was shocked to discover the conditions in which the prisoners were forced to live. Vardaman stopped listening to Adelson after he heard that Flood had asked him to treat the gunmen, so when Adelson finished speaking, Vardaman told him he would look into the matter.

But Dr. Adelson would not be so casually dismissed by the arrogance of a man who terrorized coloreds and caused his father's misguided ruin. So Adelson banged his fist against Vardaman's desk and yelled, "No! That is not acceptable."

Vardaman was surprised, not even his nonchalant dismissal of the doctor merited such a violent response. He placed his Cotton Crop Report on his desk and looked into Adelson's turbulent eyes, "Have a seat doctor, and tell me what is acceptable."

Adelson remained on his toes, "The prison conditions at Parchman Farm are unconstitutionally and immorally cruel. Those men live in cramped barracks with walls bathed in blood and floors flooded in feces and urine. They are dying from malnutrition, disease, and cruel work conditions. The English language does not possess words sufficiently depraved to convey the condition in which they live."

"Maybe nigger language does . . ."

"I am not amused, Governor. Those people are people. They are entitled to a decent standard of habitation. This is the United States of America, and we do not treat our citizens like this, no matter what their crime is!"

Vardaman had heard enough. He was not interested in Adelson's prison philosophy or nigger ontology, "Citizens?! Those niggers have no rights. They're not martyrs! They are nigger criminals!"

Adelson stood in silence rubbing his head. He wanted to tear open Vardaman's throat and remove his words before they ever had the chance to be spoken. But with those very words he realized he had already failed. Vardaman's anger was incontrovertible and his philosophy irreducible; his fangs were always sharpened to tear colored flesh. Vardaman and Adelson were each the personification of everything the other hated, so neither could devour the other.

Silence stood between them until Vardaman, in a calm voice, spoke more of the words Dr. Adelson already knew he was going to hear (the words with which his father tormented him), "Doctor, you have to understand, the negroes will not work unless by hunger or force. Do you want thousands of negroes just loafing about staring at your wife and children? Parchman takes the worst of them and feeds them and clothes them and teaches them a skill so that they can return to society without their negro habits."

Adelson was fading away. He saw his father, sitting behind Vardaman's eyes, behind his words, and he no longer had an appetite to argue. Vardaman's logic was buried too deep within the very capillaries of his mind. So he turned to leave, "You and I both know that Parchman ensures those inmates are all dead before they ever have the chance to return to Mississippi society." Dr. Adelson left Vardaman and Jackson that day with the weight of his father's resurrected and wandering ghost in his heart. He pondered whether he or anyone else could ever win this battle. But he would not yield, not yet.

***

The spring brought warmth to Parchman, but no letter from Simbi to Fulton, even though he had sent her a new one every month. Fulton tried not to imagine the implications of the absence of any communication from his family, especially since he had not seen anyone receive any letter from anyone outside Parchman. Though the thought tormented him, he figured that none or only a few of the letters were ever mailed, and that meant that over a year had passed since Simbi had received any indication that he remained alive. The urgency to be home gnawed his insides, often pressing against his chest and scraping his already flagging lungs. Spring also realized the completion of the marsh's relocation. The gunmen had transported twenty-thousand acres of knee deep water to the other side of the Pinnekoke Levee. Superintendent Flood called his Sergeants to his Mansion to discuss the immanence of their first cotton harvest, "White gold my boys. White Gold. We will be the ones to make this state rich again." Flood imagined ambitious numbers, several thousand tons within a few years. But he would need many more gunmen. They had lost too many over the winter, so Long Chain and the Mississippi legal system would need to redouble their efforts.

But before he could till and plant the land, Flood had to address the first crisis to threaten Parchman's existence, not three years after it was conceived. Dr. Adelson. Adelson had continued his war against Parchman and managed to awaken a consciousness across Mississippi of ardent disdain for Parchman's alleged inhumanity. Stories raced through the countryside of torturous work conditions, inhuman living quarters, and an alarming death rate. Adelson galvanized an ideological and legal barrage against Parchman in an attempt to expose its brutality, free its prisoners, and destroy its physical and philosophical foundations. He gathered support from hundreds of educators, journalists, and lawyers and mounted an assault on Parchman's constitutionality. The war was his duty, to absolve his father's ghost. Fiery words describing his intentions arrived in Vardaman's ears, and Vardaman immediately journeyed to Parchman. He could not allow Adelson's crusade to be heard beyond Mississippi and awaken a national movement against Parchman (which would be a movement against his Mississippi and himself). He and Flood would have to crush Adelson before he could sting them. And as their luck would have it, they would have their chance within a few days.

Adelson learned of Vardaman's trip to Parchman, so he gathered his supporters, the *Colors of Liberation*, and took a train to Gordon Junction. Adelson planned to stage a tremendous demonstration right outside Parchman's front gate, including a gathering of the local and state presses to document the event and spread its word throughout Mississippi. Adelson also had a friend from college days who was an editor for the *Jackson Daily Chronicle* who promised to join them and print an article about their demonstration on the front page of the newspaper, bright and bold for Vardaman to read while eating his six-eggs and sausage breakfast. As soon as the government in Washington saw the headlines, Mississippi and Adelson's father would be purged, the coloreds would be free, and he would be at peace. These were his plans.

But from his sources, Vardaman discovered Adelson's plans, so he made some plans of his own. As far as Vardaman was concerned, plans were only as good as the power of the man who conceived them, so in Mississippi, anyone who planned anything against him may as well be planning failure. When Vardaman arrived at Parchman, he told Flood he had already decided how to destroy Adelson and his *Colors of Liberation*. But Flood was nervous, "Adelson has gathered dozens of citizens and they're ready for a revolution. How can we silence them all? We can't go killing our own citizens?"

Vardaman looked down at Flood with the eyes of the apocalypse and explained, "I don't think you comprehend the gravity of this situation or its potential to infect Mississippi, the South, and the Union. Our very mission and livelihood are at stake. The very platform upon which I stand as your Governor is in jeapordy. So we will do whatever we must, we will sacrifice whomever we must to retain the greater sanctity of our ideology and way of life." Flood's greatest fear was that Vardaman's words were not bound by consequences or cost, and those were the most deadly words of all.

Vardaman assured Flood that if his plan succeeded, the sacrifices would be minimal. Only if his plan failed would they resort to more bloody measures. Vardaman explained to Flood that Adelson and his misguided followers planned to protest with signs and slogans on Tuesday. He was to order every gunmen taken as far into the fields as possible that day, "I don't care if you just have them sit there for twelve hours, just keep them where they can't hear anything." They could not be allowed to learn that portions of the outside world (especially in Mississippi) possessed empathy for them. Finally, Flood would instruct his Sergeants to select twenty gunmen, the right twenty -- big, angry, stupid, and illiterate -- and he would leave the rest to Vardaman.

The day before the demonstration, those twenty selected gunmen were brought to Flood's office to meet with Governor Vardaman. Vardaman ordered the gunmen unshackled and seated on Flood's couches, and he told them, "Don't worry. I'm not going to harm you. Actually, I'm going to help you save your lives and the lives of everyone in Parchman Farm."

These were impossible words, but his face was sincere. He addressed them in a congenial but grave tone, "Boys, I'm going to offer you your freedom, and all I want in return is one small favor, one that you would probably do anyway." Vardaman allowed his words to seep through the ears and minds of his audience, and then he continued, "Tomorrow afternoon, a young doctor named Kenneth Adelson is going to bring a big crowd of maybe forty or fifty people to holler and carry signs that everyone of you should be executed instead of rehabilitated because you cost the taxpayers too much money - -"

"Hold on," one of then gunmen interrupted, still confused that Vardaman was offering to help them, "is you tellin' us that if we do one favor for you that you gonna let us free?"

Vardaman didn't appreciate being interrupted, but he nevertheless responded, "Yes."

"And this favor? It got somethin' to do wit dem people who want us dead?"

"Exactly," Varaman continued like a school teacher, "All you have to do is the following. First, you cannot breathe a word of this to any of the others. You cannot tell them that I am offering you freedom for this favor, or they will kill you to take your place. Second, tomorrow, in the middle of the demonstration, we are going to open the front gate and let you free. We will tell the protestors that you are being freed for good behavior, so they have no business crying for your execution. When you leave, put your hands over your ears and just keep walking. Don't say a word. Just keep walking to Scott and go to the Wilson Inn where we have arranged for you to spend the night, under the protection of your Drivers. You will remain there for the night until you have fulfilled your end of the bargain. Then, my friends, you are free."

Vardaman continued to explain his plan to the gunmen. He told them that Kenneth Adelson and his demonstrators would be sleeping that night across the street from the Wilson Inn at the Abbey Inn, and that with their Drivers' help, all they had to do was kill each and every member of the demonstration. "That's it. All these white folks want to see you hanged or burned or lashed or shot anyway, and if you saw them on the streets, as a free man, I wouldn't have any respect for you if you didn't throttle them dead. Once they're gone, you don't have to worry about them convincing the lawmakers that they're right and that each and every one of you behind these gates should be executed just to save the taxpayers some money. Do this deed, and you have your freedom, and you save a thousand lives. Your friends can then serve their sentences in peace and return to their families as free men. But your freedom comes tomorrow, not ten years from now. Take this opportunity, rid our society of these hate-loving men, and return to your wives and children for a better life. I'll even give you the blades with which you can do the deed." Vardaman paused from his vigorous oration to allow his audience to see the sincerity in his eyes, and then he finished with one, solemn sentence, "But if you try to escape, if you renege on your end of the bargain, you will be shot dead, or hunted by all the Sergeants in Mississippi and strung up wherever you are found."

The twenty big, stupid, irascible, and illiterate gunmen did not want to understand the implications of their bargain with Vardaman, a deal with the devil, because the taste of freedom in their Parchedmouths was too moist and too sweet not to swallow. And yet, they still did not understand how to trust Vardaman (why couldn't the Drivers just kill them?), "What if we say no?"

"Then you'll be returned to your cages and ordered to silence and twenty other inmates will be selected."

They knew what that meant, "ordered to silence," and Vardaman knew they knew what that meant.

"Let's be honest for a moment, shall we? You've all killed before, haven't you? That's why you're here, isn't it? You, how many men have you killed?"

"Well, uh . . . three."

"All at once, or at different times?"

"Different times."

"So why did you kill the last one?"

"He cheated me at cards."

"And what about you, how many have you killed?"

"One, for stealin' three a my chickens en a dog."

"Are we clear then? I'm not asking you to do anything you haven't already done. The only difference is that instead of cards and dogs, you are killing for justice and freedom. The difference is, instead of landing you in Parchman, this killing will land you free."

Vardaman felt them drifting towards him. He saw the transformation in their eyes, the subtle dilation of their acquiescent pupils. He could always sense that moment in an audience, when, as a group, they had allowed themselves to melt into his words and follow the consequences of their trajectory. That was how he became Governor. It was always only a matter of time before an audience began to devour his words, no matter how unpalatable they originally found them. And this audience, this selection from deep within Parchman's belly, was no different. They no longer wondered what motivations resided beneath his words; their passion for freedom compelled them towards the blade Vardaman held outstreched before them. The deed was of no consequence relative to the prize.

For the rest of that Monday, the twenty gunmen, Vardaman, and Flood all grinned secret smiles. The selected gunmen had only to remain silent as they impatiently counted each moment inbetween the present and their freedom. Meanwhile, Vardaman gave the Drivers who would be in the Wilson Inn their explicit instructions. He also contacted the reporters of the *Scott Daily Herald* and informed them that Parchman's officials were deeply concerned by Dr. Adelson's allegations, and in a gesture of goodwill, Superintendent Flood intended to release twenty gunmen, for good behavior and positive rehabilitation, at four in the afternoon during Adelson's demonstration. In respect of the inmates' wishes for an anonymous return to Mississippi society, they would be escorted by a handful of guards, without interview, to Scott, Mississippi, where they would board for the night and then return by train to their respective homes. But Vardaman did not tell the papers that another handful of guards would be waiting in the Wilson Inn to ensure that his plans were enacted, perfectly.

The stage was set, and History awaited Vardaman's order to raise the curtain so that each could enact his role -- some the role which had been enscripted to them, and some a role of which only the playwright was aware. This was Vardaman's world, a stage upon which he conducted the progress of his vision into History. Tomorrow's was a short act, but would nevertheless leave the stage littered with blood. Tragedy for some was victory for others, and the difference resided somewhere in the power of their willing.

Adelson's rally began the next morning. Over fifty lawyers, educators, journalists, and other activists gathered in front of Parchman's front gate with pickets and protests against the inhumanities perpetrated within. Vardaman and Flood surveyed the demonstration from Flood's third-story office. Vardaman respected Adelson's energy and sense of mission, but the philosophy beneath his mission was misguided, and more importantly, contradictory to his own. That is why Adelson and his protests had to be silenced.

For his part, Adelson wanted a revolution. His ideals painted the world around him with thick, heavy brushstrokes that compelled his action. Adelson had heard of Vardaman's intended show of goodwill and its obvious intent to diffuse the turbulence of his demonstration, but he was not concerned because he believed in the just nature of his cause and the redemption of his father's ghost, and when the curtain finally fell, his call for justice would be heard.

Later that afternoon, a dozen Drivers escorted the twenty selected gunmen from the marsh to Flood's Mansion. Of course, the marsh was not actually a marsh anymore, but an endless land of mud, dappled by spiked tree stumps which the gunmen had to clear away so that the land could be tilled and sown by spring. They were still chained in groups of ten, but instead of buckets they wielded shovels and sharp-shooters and axes to chop and uproot the stumps and drag them back to Front Camp from where the timber was shipped for profit. As miserable and tedious as the draining had been, the clearing was more exhausting and backbreaking. The weakest among the gunmen found themselves lashed daily by Black Annie for tiring too quickly, "Maybe that'll give you some energy to keep chopping!" And when Black Annie did not work, the Drivers used cattle prods. Fulton and his friends were strong enough to endure each day, though their muscles ached so miserably they could not sleep at night.

On the other hand, like the other older gunmen, LaRue was not faring well. By midday he could barely lift his axe, and he often collapsed into the mud, only to be writhing a few moments later under Black Annie's flesh-stinging fangs. Fulton watched LaRue's life slipping from his eyes, and LaRue began to mumble in Spanish from the depths of his fading consciousness. When Fulton tried to talk to him, LaRue would stare and respond with aposiopetic mumblings from other conversations, "I learned about some place called Metonymy... pero no se tomarlo fuera, I dont know how to make it stop burning... security is mortal's chiefest enemy, now I understand... donde las plumas pueden tajar separadas las espadas, maybe that's a place negroes are free... they can throw you in an oven and you won't burn... our lives are backwards... el sol no puede quemarnos si sacamos la flogisten... we enter this world crying, but we don't make a sound when dying..." Already, eight gunmen over age sixty had been worked to death, and Knockin-a-Joe re-emerged with alarming (to Fulton) frequency. With axes and sharp-shooters in their hands, gunmen recommenced removing hands and feet to receive a discharge.

The days were as long as ever, and unlike during winter, the amount of eating and sleeping became inadequate again. The lack of sleep was a seasonally repeated torment. For each gunman, the first few weeks of sleep deprivation left him exhausted, irascible, and buried beneath his zombified consciousness. The pattern was brutal. The morning Drivers awakened the gunmen after what seemed like only a few minutes of agitated rest. The syrup, biscuits, and tea helped freshen them, but within a few hours their exhaustion overwhelmed them, and that is when their morale drowned, their arms collapsed, and they were stung by Black Annie's whipping fangs. By nighttime, those still standing dragged the others back to their cages where they laid in agony, too tired to sleep. As they fought the advancing numbing of their minds, many gunmen succumbed to their misery and collapsed into the marsh, like a fallen sound, expiring on the spot. Those who survived the first few weeks emerged into a new state of disjointed consciousness, exactly how Vardaman wanted them. In this way the surviving gunmen were protected from the misery of each new day by the thick armature of their fragmented consciousnesses. That is why Vardaman knew the gunmen he released would walk through the front gate and fail even to notice the gathering of protestors, let alone apprehend the import of their slogans.

Inside Flood's office, Vardaman reviewed the plan with his gunmen and then released them to the Drivers who would escort them to Scott. When the front gate opened and the gunmen passed through it towards their first breaths of free air in years, the journalists swarmed them to try to record their thoughts. They rained questions at the gunmen, but their questions fell on finger-shut ears. Vardaman and Flood watched from the Mansion, only a hundred feet away, surveying the unfolding of their drama, and much to their surprise, Adelson apparently ordered his protestors to ignore the freed gunmen and to crescendo their voices with new chants decrying Vardaman's token display. They cried for Justice, not disingenuous gestures. So, just as scripted, the gunmen were disoriented by the chaos, and they ignored the histrionics around them as they marched to Scott, Mississippi, up one flight of stairs in the Wilson Inn, and directly to a furnitureless room 202, where twelve Drivers sat them on the floor and ordered them to silence.

The gunmen sat in a silent, circular huddle for the remainder of the day and into the night. They did not utter a word other than to say that they were thirsty. They were sweating with beads of nervousness, looking into their Drivers' eyes for answers, but they saw only scowls. Later, Adelson and his demonstrators arrived across the street at the Abbey Inn.

Waiting, still waiting. The bag of knives was sitting in the corner, and it floated into the gunmen's dreams as they drifted to sleep shortly after midnight. Three more hours to wait. Even the Drivers, not accustomed to the soporific monotony of such conditions, succumbed to the weight of their eyelids and slipped into a perilous sleep. Then the instincts of one of the gunmen awakened him to his opportunity. A bag of knives, six Drivers snoozing in the room, and six more smoking outside. He awoke the other gunmen and like cats moving through shadows, they each took a knife and raised them with hatred above the snoring Drivers, poised for the moment of their violent slash of liberation. Not even the heaving of their wild breathing awoke the slumbering Drivers. Hands firm, embracing their Freedom Blades, the irascible, stupid, and illiterate gunmen raised their arms in ritualistic simultaneity and entered their blades into the throats of their nightmarish Parchman lives.

The bloodied blades steamed with self-determination. The gunmen trembled, eyes beaming. If only the ground would shudder and the firmament tremble in recognition. But the gunmen realized that the thrones of their freedoms remained still a few moments away. Six Drivers were below. Not so many now that they had rifles and knives.

Without a word, the (almost no longer) gunmen slipped through the darkness down the staircase of the Wilson Inn and huddled in the shadows of the main lobby, just beneath the windows against which the six other Drivers were standing. They could hear them, talking just above a whisper about who would kill the most after they had slaughtered the demonstrators. The gunmens' lips curled in anger, which fed new courage into their remaining task. Their angerflexed muscles only required an instant, and in that instant they pounced through the door and sliced three of the guards before their eyes saw more than a shadow. The other guards lunged at their rifles, but the gunmen pounced again, like a pack, relishing the inversion of fates and aroused by the smell of white fear. But one of the guards managed to yell to the Abbey Inn, just before the flesh on his face was shredded to the underlying bone.

Then chaos intervened. Within seconds, a dozen Drivers burst through the front door of the Abbey Inn with rifles firing. In their attempt to flee for cover, the gunmen stumbled over each other and the ragged carcasses of their enemies. In less than a minute, the twenty gunmen were choking for their last breaths as they watched their once and fragile freedoms spill from them.

Lights and voices began to arouse, and the Drivers had only moments to drag the gunmens' bodies across the street into the entrance of the Abbey Inn while a few others ignited its foyer (Vardaman would later praise their nimble thinking). The inferno escalated, and the screaming and burning inhabitants of the Abbey Inn jumped and fled from every window or door they could find. A few minutes later the fire truck from Greenville arrived, but the building was little more than smoldering wood and bodies. Thirty-three of its sixty-four inhabitants were burned to death, and the headlines in the Scott newspaper read, "Freed Parchman Inmates Bring Fiery Hell to Scott's Abbey Inn."

The article continued to explain, as per the account of the surviving Drivers, that the freed gunmen slaughtered their Drivers with knives they had smuggled from Parchman, and then proceeded to burn the Abbey Inn and all the protestors in it. Fortunately for the town and for Dr. Kenneth Adelson (who survived with a few light burns), Vardaman had been astute enough to anticipate such a disaster and station a dozen Drivers with rifles in the foyer of the Abbey Inn that night. Adelson owed his life to Vardaman, and Vardaman was quoted as saying, "The negro is a reprehensible creature with a hog's sense of morality. If Parchman can't take the nigger out of the negro, then maybe we ought to take the negro out of Mississippi."

Whatever empathetic hearts had been residing and uniting in Mississippi were now either burned to ash or dismayed in confusion as to how they could have so misconstrued the nature of a negro. Across Mississippi, anti-colored movements embraced the incident as violent evidence of their philosophy and further justification for a return to the South of shackled negroes. And Vardaman emerged from the stage a hero, evidently possessing keener insights into human and negro natures than anyone else. Therein, Parchman was lauded as a proper laboratory of rehabilitation for wayward coloreds. Adelson's cry for justice died like a whisper on a solitary hilltop, unheard. Could it be that his father and Vardaman were correct? He clung to the belief that Parchman was an inhuman institution, but everything he had seen forced him to conclude that coloreds were less than human. He told himself that Vardaman had somehow duped them all (including History), but he was forced to leave Scott, Mississippi that day with his life in Vardaman's debt. He could point to nothing to demonstrate to everyone that the previous days had belied the (true) natures of Heroes and Monsters.

Cotton People

All the while, Fulton's attention was focused on LaRue, whose pejoration continued under the boiling summer sun. All life was wilting. The field was still too moist to sow, so Flood decided to let the summer dry the land and wait until next spring for Parchman's first harvest. Meanwhile, the gunmen spent hours each day clearing the kudzu and tilling the fields, until they formed the symmetric rows that were the birthmarks of Mississippi earth. Already suffering from his declining condition, LaRue was whipped more and more each day, and at night Fulton carried him back to their cage where he crawled into the corner and mumbled in tongues until sunrise, "Es muss sein, es konte auch anders sein." He spoke from his throat, harsh and hoarse.

After several days, the other members of the cage began to fear LaRue's incantations, afraid that he was summoning evil spirits or trying to curse them. The heat of the summer nights aggravated their fear, and Fulton sensed a violence swelling in the cage's thick, humid air. He tried to awaken LaRue from his trance, but LaRue was staring into an emptiness from which his battered consciousness refused to return. The last traces of who he was faded into these midnight mumblings until nothing remained except his absent eyes, which could no longer abide looking into the gaunt horizon of his destiny. LaRue mumbled and twitched and slapped his face, and his visage began to haunt the dreams of the other gunmen. He was a living ghost. And just before the cage could no longer support LaRue's haunts, he died, sitting in the corner with his mouth open, silent like the dusty ruins of a once proud and majestic kingdom. Fulton closed his eyes, and he felt the void in the world where LaRue once sat. Where was his Queen, to rescue him from this indignity? Fulton choked with the sadness that more than any man he had ever known, LaRue's particular time and place had robbed him of the destiny he deserved, and there was nothing Fulton could do to realign that tragedy.

That Sunday, while Fulton, Moondog, Mongoose, Cuttino, and Stromyle were playing dice, Reverend Kibel approached them and nervously asked about LaRue, "Hello boys . . . I was hoping to ask you about LaRue's last days and his fits." No one even looked up.

"The reason is, I just want to know whether the stories are true, because if they are, then only something horrible could have reduced such an impressive gunman to such a miserable state, and I intend to confront Flood to find out what that horrible thing might be."

Still silence, then Cuttino answered without looking up, "LaRue spent the last week a his life jes like any other man his age would if he had to till dirt all day under the hot sun."

"Do you think he was overworked or abused?" Kibel asked. The gunmen looked at each other unwilling to respond. The Drivers and Sergeants were spying them with suspicion.

"I need to know," Kibel entreated, "I want to keep this from happening again. LaRue was a learned and gentle man, and though he never told me why he was here, I am sure it was a minor offense."

But Kibel's empathy did not inspire the courage for a response. Gunmen who spoke too liberally with Kibel had already been painfully reminded that their place was to work, not to speak. Kibel saw that he was not gaining the trust of the gunmen, so he tried another approach, "I also need to be sure that none of the rest of you are in any danger." Fulton and the others looked up from their game of dice with quizzical faces. "I've heard that in his last days, LaRue was speaking in tongues, and perhaps, he may have been influenced by malignant forces which may have used him in this moment of weakness as a conduit to pass harm into this world, especially to his friends."

This sentence evoked emotion from Fulton, who rose to his feet and spoke with indignation, "Are you tryin' to say that the Devil took him?"

"I'm . . . I'm not sure."

"Now jes wait one cotton pickin' minute Revren, I don't know what LaRue was sayin' them last days, but I do know that whatever happened to him, this place here did it, en it didn't need no help from the Devil! If the Devil was in him, he woulda kept him livin'!" Fulton's emotions were ignited by Kibel's dishonoring of LaRue's memory (for that was all that remained), and Kibel realized that he had only succeeded in distancing himself further from the trust of the gunmen. The intentions of his God did not understand colored lives, so he dropped his head downwards and walked away, rubbing his golden crucifix for comfort. The Sergeants and Drivers eyed Fulton as Kibel returned to his horse and rode to his home in Greenville, far away from the devils and demons of Parchman Farm.

The next Sunday, Mongoose shared an idea with his friends. He had been contemplating it for a few days, so he decided to share it with Fulton and the others. "Softball," he said, "dice en cards en nappin' on Sundays is nice, but I want more, en I'm willin' to bet I ain't alone." The others were intrigued, so Mongoose continued, "see, dice en cards kent take us nowhere, but softball's another world, wit teams en leagues. We ken have one team a cage en have a regular season wit playoffs for the best teams. We ken start now en play 'til winter en then start again in the spring. En we ken tell the Sergeants en Flood that softball will help us be happier, better cotton pickers."

The idea caught on. Stromyle had coached softball to the children in his settlement, and Fulton and Moondog remembered playing stickball as boys. They encouraged Mongoose to approach Sergeant Judson, and for once things worked out. In a few weeks the gunmen were playing softball every Sunday.

The softball league was like a messiah. All week long the gunmen talked in the field about the impending matchups, boasting which cage had the best athletes, and wagering pints of shine or a mule (which they would repay after they had served their terms) on the outcome of each game. The response was so overwhelming that each cage had two teams of twenty gunmen each. The league was an even thirty teams, and they played a simple rotational format of two, five inning matches each Sunday after Kibel's service, which never ended soon enough. The other half of each cage, most of whom were too young or too old to play, cheered their cage mates under the summer sun. The gunmen's lives, and even their nightly dreams, now revolved around the Sunday softball games. For those few hours they were their own masters, they held the bats in their hands, and nothing except their natural talent to strike the incoming ball could determine the outcome of each swing. The softball universe was small and simple and not troubled by the complexities of skin and History. And to Flood's surprise, no violence ever erupted during any of the games. As a precaution, he had stationed several Drivers and Sergeants around the field (which stretched behind Flood's mansion past the front of cages eight and nine, in which there was room for eight simultaneous games), but within a few weeks he reduced the softball security forces to only a few Drivers on horses with the hounds. But the gunmen never noticed the Drivers or the hounds. They knew they would not get far before a bullet or a hound tore into them, so they ignored the open-field invitation to escape and instead lost themselves in the game. The games were not freedom, but they represented freedom enough to take the bat, hit the ball, and run around the bases like you were running for freedom.

Cages seven and eleven battled back and forth for the best record in the league, and Fulton and Moondog led their respective teams because they had spent countless hours playing stickball growing up on Anderson's land. When they were younger, Anderson played stickball with Moondog, Neshoba and the other coloreds, but as puberty arrived, the lighter brother was no longer allowed to play with his darker brothers. Even as youths, Fulton and Moondog demonstrated exceptional athletic talent. Moondog's father once told him that if they were not colored, both he and Fulton could probably play in the majors. Then Neshoba was lynched, and the demands of the cotton crop stole them from any recreation at all the day they were old enough to tote the nine-foot sacks behind them. So now, years later in the Parchman Softball League, Fulton and Moondog relived the careless days of their youth, playing stickball by moonlight until the mosquitoes finally drove them inside.

But reliving the careless days of his youth was also a dangerous experiment for Fulton, for the games resurrected the memories of his former self. And rather than comfort him, this momentary ghost haunted him whenever he had time on his hands. Time to brood.

By November it was too cold to play, and with the field tilled, and turned for the spring planting, the gunmen found themselves with significant amounts of empty time. These were the moments of self-reflection during which Fulton most anguished over the state of his life and its absent direction. These were the moments when his inertia suffocated him, and desperation overwhelmed his thoughts, especially since softball had reawakened the image of who he used to be. Lighter fluid helped him flee, but the residue of former selves always survived.

On one particular night, after Fulton inhaled the lighter fluid's rock-a-by fumes, he lay in his bunk watching the moonlight through the near window slowly slide towards him. He could not see the light's movement, but he could discern that after twenty minutes the light was closer than before. In the same way, he looked at the last twenty months in Parchman, and he could see that they had passed, but he could not follow their movement through time. The months were a blur, at certain moments seeming nothing more than a few days of his life, and in other moments (when his former life forced itself into his mind) seeming like decades. Fulton thought of the Dragon and his mountains that rise and fall like ocean waves. What was a moment to him? Were they sometimes centuries and at other times only a week? Maybe then, his time was just like the Dragon's, if these months can at once appear as days and years. In another life, such an elongation of time would be a blessing, but for him now, this slow, laborious passage of time was a cumbersome curse. *Walk a day in my skin. Ocean waves like mountains.*

As the moonlight neared him and rose up his body to his waist, Fulton reached out to take hold of the light, and for the first time in his life he saw the color of his skin. He had always seen the black, the (unexamined) color he resented, the color that devoured Moondog's brother and swallowed him into Parchman's belly. But in the soft moonlight of this night, Fulton saw the rich texture of his skin. It was deep like memory, and he did not resent it for the misfortunes with which it had cursed him. Instead, he saw a color born from the earth. Elegant.

When the moonlight passed over his head and Fulton was again lying in darkness, he found within himself a momentary neutrality towards the nature of things. He remained burdened with displeasures, but he carried his burden with serenity, *it is as it is*. Even his anguished thoughts of Simbi arrived with a gentle, sleeping smile, for at least he had those memories. He was, for a time, lost in a placid contentment, at least until the smoky scent in his mind died.

***

The gunmen enjoyed their special Christmas feast of pork and cranberry and cider and mash, but the remainder of the winter of 1906 was more deadly than the winter of 1905. One hundred and nineteen gunmen died of the flu and sixty-three died from various viral and bacterial infections. Since the land behind the Chapel was already filling quickly, each Sunday during this winter the gunmen gathered the corpses, which had been lying in their cages for however many days before Sunday they had died, took them behind the chapel, piled them one on top of the other, and burned them. Most of the gunmen tried to keep their distance from the fire, out of respect for the spirits of the dead, but its warmth was difficult to forego.

The weekly routine was grim. After Kibel offered his benediction and blessed the dead gunmens' souls, the Drivers saturated the pile of bodies with lighter fluid that they then trailed several yards away. As they fumbled for their matches in the cold, Fulton had just enough time to gaze into the gaping mouths and eyes of the contorted bodies. He saw release. Then, during those languid moments as the flame raced towards the pile, and before it burst into a skyward eruption, Fulton looked at the corpses and saw his own ancestors, charging him to endure his tribulations with courage. A moment later they turned to ashy red and said nothing more, erased from the world without a trace. The popping and crackling flames slowly descended into an even burn that summoned most of the gunmen to gather around for its heat. Their friends became dying embers that warmed them for a few minutes. Fulton remained transfixed, staring from the margins of the gathering, watching the hypnotic flames like a funeral dance. When the dance died to a slumber of cooling ash, everyone returned to their cages without a word.

When March arrived the gunmen were back in the fields weeding the kudzu and re-tilling the soil for Parchman's first cotton harvest. Once the rich buckshot was prepared, they carried their sixty-pound sacks of seed over their shoulders into the fields and sowed every inch of every row of Parchman's 20,000 acres. As the stalks reached out of the buckshot with the April rains, the gunmen spent the next two months tirelessly thinning the young stalks and clearing the rows of all the grass and vines and relentless kudzu that seemed to reappear each morning as if they had never been cleared at all. They also dug an elaborate system of furrows through which they passed water from the other side of the Pinnekoke Levee back into the fields to water the cotton. Since they used the same buckets as before, most of the gunmen felt that their lives were spinning in a meaningless circle, "Leave it to a white man to make a negro spend his life movin' water from one side of a levee to the other en then back again," Mongoose complained.

Throughout these months, the gunmen were still monitored by two shifts of one Sergeant and two drivers. However, it became increasingly difficult for three guards to supervise a cage of eighty or ninety gunmen. When Parchman was a marsh, the gunmen were too cold and too sogged to skirmish with each other, let alone consider an escape. But on the dry, warm earth, the gunmen had more mobility, and since they were shackled more closely together (only a row or two apart), they had to coordinate their movements and their chains over the stalks as they progressed across the rows. As a result, tempers flared, and there was not always a Driver or Sergeant nearby to arbitrate the dispute. More and more fights erupted, and more and more gunmen throttled each other to death. On one occasion, Zydeco Mills from cage six killed both gunmen on either side of him without ever being heard or seen by his guards. They only noticed a few minutes later when they saw eight gunmen sitting on the ground around two dead bodies. When their Sergeant demanded an explanation, none of the gunmen was willing to speak, so they all received lashes from Black Annie until Zydeco cried that he had killed both gunmen because they were unwilling to help him poison the bloodhounds who lived in Front Camp.

Unfortunately for Zydeco, his Sergeant was the bloodhounds' chief trainer, so he was quite irate when he heard Zydeco's confession. Those hounds were the only reason Parchman's fields were not fenced and the dozen or so attempts at escape had always resulted in a bloodhound blood feast. So the Sergeant ordered the dead gunmen buried behind the chapel, and he ordered Zydeco to stand in front of him. The Drivers unshackled him and the remaining seven gunmen in his line dashed out of harm's way. Zydeco stood trembling with half-closed eyes. If anyone had bothered to ask him why he killed the gunmen, he would have felt the question was being asked of someone else. But no one asked him anything. Instead, his Sergeant did not utter a word as he raised his .30 -.30 Winchester like a thunderbolt and shot off half of Zydeco Mill's face where he stood. He calmly ordered another Driver to bury the body, and he reshackled the remaining gunmen and led them back to work.

There were a dozen similar skirmishes during the next few weeks, and the Sergeants and Drivers were afraid the gunmen would sense the loosening noose of their control and organize a mass escape. Sometimes they would be distracted by gunmen at one end of their field while gunmen at the other end sniffed paint thinner from small bottles, or beat the life out of a disliked, weak gunman. The guards whipped and herded the gunmen like beasts to manifest their authority and control. But by June, as tight green bolls appeared throughout the fields and the winds were raucous with locusts, all the Sergeants and several Drivers approached Flood with their concerns.

But Flood already had the answer to their inability to monitor their growing prison population as well as a way for the most violent of the coloreds to unleash their anger in a manner productive to Parchman. "First, fights will be settled in a civilized manner. If an argument erupts into physical confrontation, you unlock the combatants and announce that they have ten minutes to resolve their differences.

Whether one of them dies or they just beat each other senseless, when the ten minutes is over they'll return to work, or you send them to the infirmary to recover until they can return to the field." As for the need for more eyes watching the gunmen, Flood was not willing to pay for more Sergeants or Drivers, so he announced a solution to create more Drivers for free, "I'm going to make some of the gunmen Drivers."

The Sergeants and Drivers were incredulous. Had Dr. Adelson's rhetoric somehow infiltrated Flood's mind? "The minute we put a rifle in a negro's hand there'll be mutiny, bloodshed, and mass escape!" Flood listened to the protests, and when they had begun to tire themselves, he calmly revealed his logic to them.

"Choose the biggest, meanest, dumbest gunmen, put rifles in their hands and horses under them, and tell them to guard the other gunmen with their own lives and they'll never have to pick an ounce of cotton again. Tell them, all they have to do is watch the gunmen like hawks and shoot anyone of them that causes trouble, and they'll never have to break their backs picking cotton under the boiling sun. In fact, tell them if they shoot a gunman trying to escape, they'll get six months off their sentence."

The implications of Flood's plan began to trickle through their minds. It's in the negro Driver's interests to maintain strict discipline and shoot a gunman who looks like he's trying to escape, and that would ensure enough fear in the other gunmen that they would think three or four times before attempting a dash for freedom. But the Drivers remained unwilling to admit any negro to equal footing with themselves, so Flood assured them that they could feel free to remind any negro Driver who forgot that there was a difference between white and black any way they saw fit.

"That's fine, but we can't call them Drivers though. We hafta have a different name for them. Just not Drivers."

"Fine," Flood assented, "call them whatever you want. But for now, your task is to find two gunmen from each cage and inform them of their new roles as . . . as whatever you decide to call them. Then you educate the remainder of each cage that they are to respect the two negroes the same way they respect you, and if they don't, the two negroes will have rifles to shoot them." Flood paused to scratch his chin, and then he assumed a more serious tone, "You have to be smart with your choices. You know those gunmen better than anyone, so you go find the type of negro who is selfish enough to care about nothing more than his own ass, and mean and unstable enough to intimidate the other gunmen. Otherwise none of this will work. We have to use the negro's nature against him, so you have to find the gunmen who most exemplify the unintelligent, selfish, and violent tendencies of negro nature. And you let them know that you will watch them and if they violate our trust they will be shot. Until then, they have our trust . . . so that's what we will call them. Trusties."

The Depth of Skin

With the cotton stalks strong and waiting to blossom, Flood allowed the softball league, which had been suspended since winter, to recommence until August. Mongoose walked through Front Camp, each Sunday reminding everyone that cage seven was the cage to beat and nobody could hit more home runs than Fulton, not even Moondog, who was third to Earl Jackson from cage three. In fact, everyone was amazed at how easily Fulton's bat crushed the ball week after week, and Fulton would just smirk, "it's 'cause I feel my arms in the bat, so hittin' is jes like catchin'." Even in the heat of July, when it was too hot to stand in the shade, the gunmen marched onto the softball field each Sunday. And the guards endured the heat as well just to watch them play. In fact, after the first few weeks of watching the gunmen play with dog-chewed balls and broomsticks, Duke Judson, II went into Greenville and returned with thirty Louisville Slugger regulation bats and sixty new balls. The kind they used in the real world. But when late August arrived and the gunmen's field work changed from weeding and watering to harvesting the endless eruption of cotton bolls they no longer had the energy to play softball each Sunday.

By September, Parchman's population swelled to near capacity, and its mission climaxed. Cotton picking, cotton picking. Six days a week, sixteen to eighteen hours a day. The nine-foot sacks, each man with a quota of 250 to 350 pounds. Miss your quota. Black Annie. Step across the line. Shot. As the sun blazed to its peak of broiling heat, the gunmen wobbled, went blurry eyed, and occasionally just dropped dead. Each day they returned to their cages in their ring-arounds, sticky with sweat and smelling like the insides of a rotten hog. Then the mosquitoes bled them all night until they were too fat to fly.

But before the harvest began, the Sergeants and Drivers decided to nominate their trusties. Two per cage. They already knew who their trusties would be, and the trusties already knew they were going to be selected, so on the first Monday of the harvest, late in the humid afternoon, the Sergeants all halted the picking and revolutionized Parchman Farm. Fulton would never forget that day, the day the white man gave a rifle to a colored and convinced him to relish the opportunity to shoot other coloreds, "If the end hadn't started yet, then this day is definitely the beginnin' a the end."

It happened just after Fulton asked to piss. The gunmen had just eaten lunch, and Fulton's group was unloading its sacks into the cotton cart (which followed the water cart and was led up and down the line of gunmen by the Cotton Boys so the gunmen could unload their sacks, which were weighed, and then they continue picking) when Fulton returned to his line and asked to urinate, "Steppin' Out!" He waited.

"O.K."

He stepped out, relieved himself, and quickly returned. Then it happened. Just as Cuttino had begun another chant, "Walk your proud row my friends"

"We walkin' walkin' proud."

"Pick your cotton proud my friends."

"We pickin' pickin' proud."

Duke Judson, II ordered his gunmen to drop their sacks and gather around him. The sun burned Fulton's forehead, and he smelled burning wood in the air.

"Quiet down, boys!" Sergeant Judson ordered so he could be heard. The morning Drivers, Jim Willard and James Seyd, sat on their horses on either side of Sergeant Judson with their rifles slung over their left shoulders. The night Sergeant and Drivers arrived from Front Camp and sat horseback around them. From the margins of his vision, Fulton could see the gunmen from cages six and eight gathering around their sergeants as well. All of a sudden, Fulton felt very thirsty and the kudzu constricted his lungs.

"Recently all the Sergeants and Drivers met with Superintendent Flood," Judson explained, "and we decided that we would reward the two hardest working gunmen from each cage with a promotion."

The gunmen furled their brows at each other as Sergeant Judson continued, "These gunmen will be promoted to a new position called trusties, and trusties will be given a horse and a rifle and entrusted with similar duties as a Driver, including the authority to shoot any gunman trying to escape, with time removed from his sentence as reward." Sergeant Judson paused to survey the fear his words were inspiring, and then he finished his speech by explaining that in order to discourage any personal jealousies or plots, the selected trusties would be exchanged into another cage. Silence shrouded the gunmen. Fulton could smell the words as they fell from Sergeant Judson's mouth. They smelled like the evil you never suspect, like your own brother slitting your throat when you sleep. Or like being lynched just because you're the brother of a white boy. Or like being jailed just for standing your skin too near to someone else's crime.

Fulton did not want to be selected, and his heart burned as Sergeant Judson lined up the gunmen and rode down the line making eye contact with each of them, but not yet selecting anyone. He approached Fulton and Cuttino. Fulton closed his eyes and prayed that he would be passed over. He did not want to become a demon to his own people. Only twenty men left in the cage, and he had not pointed to any of them. And then as Judson neared Fulton, he opened his eyes and watched him raise his hand. Fulton felt his heart arrest and his lungs constrict, just until the moment Sergeant Judson passed his finger over Fulton and over Cuttino and pointed to the gunman just beside them. Then he pointed to one more, and everyone watched the expressions across everyone else's faces shift from dumbfounded to liberated and back to dumbfounded.

"Them baboons?" Mongoose whispered at Fulton and Cuttino, "they's two of the dummest negroes I've ever seen. They likely to shoot each other just for lookin' stupid."

Cuttino agreed with Mongoose, but offered some relief, "At least they ain't the trusties for our cage."

But Fulton was not comforted, "Somethin' tells me the two trusties we get ain't gonna be much diffrent from these two they sendin' somewhere else. We gonna have coloreds shootin' other coloreds jes to be free, en that means trouble."

That night, Fulton had a dream. He was alone on the earth, and the earth was barren and arid. He was standing in the center of an endless plane of windy dirt, but he could see the rounded horizon of the world, as if it were only a few miles across. His shadow stretched for miles behind him, and he was calling for his daughter. But he could not yell loud enough because he could barely fill his constricted lungs with enough air to whimper. He felt suffocated by a heavy sensation of solitude, and his heart began to thump with urgency. The windy dirt whipped around him in a frenzy and soon he could not see his hand in front of his face. He was alone. In endless space without reference or boundaries.

Then the winds calmed and the dirt fell. Fulton cleared his eyes and gazed across the empty landscape. He saw nothing. He heard nothing. He tried to gaze beyond his solitude, but just as he did, the ground trembled, and four mammoth, monstrous, ivory fangs emerged from underneath the horizon and plunged into the four corners of the earth. The fangs plunged deeper and deeper, tearing to the core. The earth writhed, until its very seams released and it crumbled into a million fragments throughout space. Fulton was flung from the destroyed surface, and the fangs receded into the darkness. Silence devoured the universe and Fulton floated, unable to see anything except the thick color of absolute black. Like his daughter's eyes. He floated in the silence and the darkness and wished he had someone to whisper to.

The next morning Fulton awoke exhausted, as if he had been screaming. His ankles were sore, so he limped outside for biscuits and syrup. Then his heart limped into his chest when Sergeant Judson introduced two gunmen named Gerrit Faulk and Moondog as the trusties for cage seven. Fulton's gaping eyes met Moondog's shifting eyes. He tore his face from Moondog and refused to look at either Mongoose or Cuttino. He was drowning in the cruelty of his fate. How could it be, unless by malicious design, that his closest living friend had been handed a rifle and ordered to shoot him dead? This was the friend whose strength sustained him. And even though he had been in another cage for the past months, the knowledge of his presence bouyed his courage. Otherwise, one lash from Black Annie would have struck him into a pile of dust.

On that first day that trusties rode back and forth across their gunmen, the fields were silent. No chorus of chanting echoed across the furrows. There was only heat and cotton. The gunmen were unsure how to understand the trusties, and the trusties were unsure how to understand the gunmen. They tried to understand the gunmen like a Driver did; at least, they imagined looking at the gunmen through a Driver's eyes, *Pick that cotton or I'll kick your teeth in. Take one step outta line en I'll shoot your head off.* But each group waited for an incident, a precedent, which would verify the new order of the trusties and its superiority to the gunmen. Moondog and Gerrit Faulk rode back and forth across the line of their gunmen throughout the day and night shifts. They received their food in a box like the Drivers, and an acidic resentment festered in the gunmen's stomachs as they watched their trusties calmly dining atop their horses. They were coloreds just like them, until one day they were allowed to be white. Moondog chose to eat away from the gunmen; he could not bear to watch Fulton eating like an animal, nor could he bear to imagine Fulton's pain in observing the new difference between them. The gunmen scowled as they returned to work, picking pieces of Mississippi buckshot from their decaying teeth.

Though confused, by that afternoon, Moondog had already begun to feel his new power seducing him, but he refrained from barking at and kicking the gunmen as much as Gerrit did. Whenever he felt the urge to strike a gunman, he imagined the gunman was Fulton, and in that way he kept himself from forgetting he was colored.

When the first day was over, the gunmen dragged themselves and their cotton sacks back to their cages while the trusties rode to Front Camp with the Drivers where they would sleep in their new cabin (the third Driver cabin which was now for the trusties). But before the trusties turned to go to Front Camp, Moondog made his way to Fulton and rode alongside him in silence for a few yards. Moondog looked down at Fulton, but Fulton did not look up. Mongoose and Cuttino; however, did look at Moondog, and Cuttino finally broke the silence, "Your butt hurt from sittin' on that horse all day?"

Moondog smiled, "A little."

They continued in silence for a few more yards, and then Fulton looked up at Moondog and finally spoke, "So this mean you gonna be on our softball team in the fall?"

"No," Moondog responded as he lowered his head, "They ain't gonna let us play no more."

"That's too bad," Fulton responded, "I was hopin' that we could play together like when we was kids."

"Yeah, me too. But don't worry. We ken talk tomorrow at lunch, en then we ken talk more on Sunday, jes to figure things out." Moondog turned his horse towards Front Camp to meet the other trusties for their first night in their new cabin.

It did not take long for the otherwise uneasy and uncertain boundaries between the coloreds picking cotton and the coloreds guarding them to be more clearly defined. That is to say, it did not take long for the gunmen to discover that there was more to a trusty than the fact that he sat on a horse with a rifle and a scowl. A slow but steady escalation of disobedience finally culminated in a sudden and conspicuous moment, just as Flood had foreseen (Flood could not own their hearts as long as the gunmen clung to the notion that they were oppressed by another kind. But as soon as the oppressor wore the same skin, then whatever value they placed in that skin would unravel, and they would be left with no choice but to submit to their role in Parchman and in Mississippi. Those few coloreds he promoted in order to vanquish the will and pride of their masses were a small price to pay).

The center of the defiance in cage seven was Mongoose. From the first day, he openly ignored, disobeyed, and challenged Gerrit. Mongoose dared Gerrit to force him to obey, and with each instance of disobediance, Gerrit's anger swelled. Moondog warned Mongoose that Willard and Seyd were manipulating Gerrit and that something dangerous was going to happen. They had been saying things to him at night like, "You gonna let that lowly nigger disobey you? Kick him, put your rifle in his face, beat him down. Teach him who his master is. And if he still disobeys, then for God's sake shoot his face right off his neck!" Gerrit was confused enough that it took him time to understand that he could kick another colored and think that he was kicking him with a white foot.

Nevertheless, Moondog saw Gerrit arriving at a dangerous mental crossroads, and he warned Mongoose to back away, but Mongoose scowled, "I ain't submittin' to a system a coloreds as masters of coloreds, not without a fight." It was bad enough that he had been imprisoned for all this time without ever having committed a crime, but also to be forced to submit to the indignity of submission to a stupid colored was unacceptable. "If I don't take a stand now, I might as well be dead." Fulton was certain he had heard Stoka say something like that the day he died.

The next morning Mongoose did not pick half the bolls of cotton in his row. Gerrit barked, "Pick your cotton wit more care, or you ain't gonna get no water break."

"As long as you the one makin' me, I'm gonna pick it any way I choose."

Gerrit wrapped his hand around his rifle and raised his voice, "That ain't what I told you to do. I said pick your cotton en pick all your cotton or you ain't gonna get no water or nuthin' to eat 'til you do!"

The other gunmen in Mogoose's line backed away from him (as far as their shackles would allow), and the other lines of gunmen dropped their sacks to watch the scene unfold. Sergeant Judson and his Drivers did not mind the stoppage; in fact, they rode closer to watch it themselves.

"You better back away Faulk, en ease your hand off that rifle if you know what's good for you," Mongoose said as he fisted his hands.

Fulton and Moondog tried to catch Mongoose with their eyes to tell him to stand down (just like Stoka), that this was not a battle worth fighting, and it was not one he was going to win (just like Corliss). But Mongoose's eyes were locked in Gerrit's, and both men were looking into the other to see how far their words were buried within them. Unfortunately for Mongoose, it did not matter how deeply Gerrit's words were embedded within him because he had the rifle, so his words did not have to reside very deep at all. Just trigger deep.

Gerrit relocated his rifle from his shoulder to his lap and rested both hands on it. His right forefinger was coiled around the trigger. Meanwhile, everyone, the other gunmen, Sergeant Judson, Willard, Seyd, and Moondog had encircled Gerrit and Mongoose to witness the drama of their impasse. Mongoose was breathing heavily and flexed his muscles for action. Unlike every previous standoff with Mongoose, Gerrit's hands were no longer quivering. "I'm orderin' you one last time Mongoose, to pick up your sack en pick your cotton like the rest a the gunmen."

But Mongoose remained obstinate and unphased, "I hear you talkin', but I ain't listnin'."

"Then maybe you don't understand who I am." As he spoke, Gerrit led his horse until he was directly above Mongoose, "Maybe I need to make you understand."

Moondog watched with increasing concern, and he caught Fulton's beseeching eyes, but he could not undermine another trusty, for he would be beaten and lashed, just like they told him he would, and he did not want to be a gunmen again. Moondog felt trapped in a space smaller than himself, and he could not discern a course of action that would save his friend. But it did not matter, for with one more sentence Mongoose opened the floodgates of inevitability to come crashing upon him, "I ain't gonna do a thing, en you better back away before I throw you from your horse en remind you who you are."

The words inflamed Gerrit, and in a single, furious motion, he swung the butt of his rifle through the irrecoverable space between them and smashed Mongoose's head, knocking him to his stomach and opening his head so its scarlet blood could pour onto the cotton field. Fulton and Moondog both turned their faces away. Mongoose was twitching with his face in the ground, and a new creature was born on Parchman's fields. A trusty. Only time would unfold the gravity of the misfortunes that would befall the gunmen now that they could be beaten and shot by coloreds who were once just like them. And Flood was correct. Now that their own had embraced the capacity to brutalize them, the gunmen all felt the unity of their skin evaporate into a solitary helplessness. "Back to work!" Sergeant Judson ordered. Mongoose continued to spill blood, like milk, onto the earth.

Gerrit ordered Fulton and Cuttino, who were still chained to either side of Mongoose, to lift him from the ground and stand him back in his row. Fulton and Cuttino stepped forward and turned Mongoose onto his back, and they both skipped a breath when they saw that his left eye had been knocked from its socket and was hanging to the side of his face by a few tattered nerves. Fulton was not as stunned as Cuttino and the other gunmen. In that moment, he and Moondog shared the same lifeless reaction to the unimaginative repetition of negro miseries. It was, after all, the same sight that had spurred their journey from home so long ago. But having to see it again would cause Fulton's eyes to burn from this day forward as if relentless fires were raging behind them.

Mongoose opened his remaining eye and looked at the faces around him. He saw Gerrit watching him from atop his horse. He did not feel pain, but his head was spinning, and he was unable to orient himself in the world. Then he reached to his face and felt his eye dangling over his cheek. Anger scarred his face as he realized that for the remainder of his life he would see only half of the world. Fulton and Cuttino tried to calm him, but Mongoose was enraged, "My eye! My eye!" He felt the absence of his eye in its socket, and he watched the blood continue to pour in ribbons down his body. In his rage he screamed a deafening roar, ripped his eye from its nerves, and threw it at Gerrit. The eye sailed past Gerrit, who laughed as he ordered his gunmen back to work. Fulton tore the sleeve of his ring-around and wrapped a tourniquet around Mongoose's head. For the remainder of the day, Mongoose mumbled to himself, "I kent move no more. Not like the shadows. Now they ken get me. I kent teach you. Now we kent move in the shadows." The irony never occurred to him that the invisibility of his shadow walking represented precisely the kind of anonymity he needed to cultivate in life in order to remain alive in Mississippi. Like Fulton.

Fulton did not hear Mongoose's mumblings that day because he buried himself in his deepening sorrow. They would have to escape. Mongoose's eye made him promise. Already too much time had passed without the courage to flee. And every tomorrow awakened another demon to beckon at his mortality without warning or reason. So as the day turned to night, Fulton conceived a plan of escape. The next day he told Mongoose his plan and that he would talk to Moondog that Sunday, so Mongoose promised to teach them how to disappear into the shadows just like him, even though he had only one eye. Escape was the only hope that sustained them.

LIFE'S ONLY PROMISE

The Witness Tree

"They seem distracted," Moondog said to another trusty two days later while watching the Sunday softball games. He could feel that it was his presence that was distracting them. Before, there was only the game, its motions and sounds and smells and the trajectory of a ball through space. But now, the game was conscious of itself, exposed like the underside of a turtle. No one, not even Fulton, hit a homerun that day.

Before the games, the trusties joined the Drivers and Sergeants in the chapel for Kibel's first service. Then the gunmen gathered for their service, flanked by their recently blessed guards. Just before Kibel began, Cuttino spat in the dirt and scowled to Fulton, "You mean to tell me if you put a gun in a negro's hand that all of a sudden he is favored by the Lawd?"

Then Kibel issued an animated sermon against trespass and disrespect. He sermonized about Abraham's unconditional allegiance to God and how the weight of a man's sins carry him down to hell and not up into the kingdom of the Lord. Kibel denounced violence and lauded the other cheek. He decried the gunmen's recent behavior with words like arrows piercing their immoral thoughts and sinful actions. "There is no room in Christ's kingdom for your animalistic ways, and there is no room in human society for your disregard of civility and morals," Kibel harangued, "you are all in Parchman to find redemption from your wayward immorality. God has not forgotten you and wants to see you all redeemed, for it is not your nature that is sour, but it is your disregard for your natural morality that is abominable. The Law has exiled you here, and like Lucifer, you will remain exiled until you repent your evil ways and submit to God's Law."

With his final words still resonating through Front Camp, Kibel turned like a breeze and marched from Parchman until his sermon the next week. The gunmen watched him depart. They had heard every word he said, but like every other sermon, he seemed to be speaking to someone else.

After softball that Sunday, Fulton, Mongoose, Cuttino, and Stromyle played dice on the steps of the chapel. Fulton caught Moondog's eyes and invited him to sit with them. Moondog approached cautiously, as if to inspect their activities. He remained standing, next to Fulton with his rifle by his side, nervously watching about so that he was not seen speaking with his former friends for too long. "How's your eye," Moondog asked after a moment of silence. But just as the words left his mouth he realized their cruelty, for it was not Mongoose's eye that was the problem, but the absence of it that caused his suffering.

"Fine," Mongoose answered, "'cept from time to time I get these sharp pains in my head that won't go way 'til I sleep."

Moondog walked around the chapel and then towards the cattle barn, looking over the shoulders of other groups of gunmen, and then he returned to Fulton, "Don't mind what Kibel said to ya'll. He was startin' to ask about ya'lls well bein', but Flood en them Sergeants told him ya'll was hurtin' each other en tryin' to escape. Kibel means well, he jes don't know what's happenin' round here. Nobody does."

The others remained silent and continued their game. "Sevens!" Cuttino cheered after a roll. Though they did not want to, they felt uncomfortable with Moondog around them, and each day he was a trusty they trusted him less. Moondog sensed their discomfort, and he tried to maintain their trust, but on a deeper level that frightened him, he was beginning not to care, because after all, he was the one who was a trusty.

After a few more moments of silence, Fulton spoke to Moondog without looking up, "Let's walk yonder, to the cattle barn where we ken talk." When no one was looking Fulton and Moondog slipped into the cattle barn and hid behind a haystack. It smelled like Fulton's home.

"Flood had a talk wit us few days ago, the day after Gerrit hit Mongoose."

"What'd he say?"

"He told us that Gerrit was right en we shouldn't be fraid to use our rifles on any gunman that acts up, or tries to escape."

After a moment of silence, Fulton made an announcement, "I have a plan, Moondog."

"A plan to escape?"

"Yeah. After I saw what Gerrit did to Mongoose, en after I'm hearin' what they gonna let ya'll do to us . . . we gotta get outta here soon. But I need your help."

"You know you got it. You know you ken trust me. I ain't one a them gonna shoot ya'll like dogs. I don't even know why they made me no trusty anyhow."

"We gonna make that the first en last mistake they made," Fulton responded, "'cause you gonna be the one to make our escape possible."

Fulton and Moondog held their fists tight in the air, summoning the strength of their ancient friendship to carry them through the task at hand, and then they returned to their respective places in Front Camp.

But before they could escape, Mongoose had to teach his friends how to move without being heard or seen or smelled by living things. So each Sunday Fulton, Cuttino, and Stromyle learned the silent language of the swamp from Mongoose. They could never escape until they learned to communicate without words and eyes. Words can be heard by enemies, and eyes cannot be seen in the dark. But the language of the swamp was composed of clicks and the movement of shadows (so you needed a full moon to escape), and Mongoose had used it for seventeen years to evade snakes and white men before that night in Jackson. But without his left eye Mongoose felt uncertain as he taught them, and since he could see only half of the world, he was incessantly haunted by the sensation of something lurking for him just beyond the reaches of his sight. Mongoose also had grave concerns over Fulton's insistence of Moondog's inclusion in their escape even though he was not learning with them (and though he would not say it, because he was a trusty). But Fulton would not be dissuaded, "Moondog's the key to our escape, so for better or worse, he's goin' wit us when the time arrives."

But their darkest concern was that since the day they arrived, only one man had escaped past Parchman's implicit perimeter, and even he was caught two days later by the hounds. The gunmen all knew that he had been caught when they watched the hounds gnawing on human bones and tattered ring-arounds the next Sunday as Kibel preached the Sermon on the Mount.

Willis Covington was his name. He was a small, thin man from Oxford who was sentenced to Parchman for sleeping in a public place. He had arrived at the beginning of the year, and to his misfortune, he was placed in cage nine, the "Voodoo Cage." That's what the gunmen called it because of the cult that had grown around Tiberius Reed, a shaman from Haiti (but fabled to be a descendent of Naga Reed from Banks). Tiberius was a tall man with long muscles and mist for eyes. His face was covered with the sorrow of trapped spirits. He spoke in words that rhymed with frightful scents, and you could see the unseen sides of things in his ominous smile. Not even the Drivers and Sergeants were willing to cross him, so they left the Voodoo Cage and its dark rituals to itself.

Tiberius preached mostly against Kibel's white magic and the dangers of possession by the white demons who would open your soul and feed on it for eternity. "That's what the crucifixion is all 'bout," he preached. "They convincin' you to spread yourself open en helpless so they can tear out your soul en feed it to they fat god. Kibel wants to tear away your flesh from the power of the earth so you's powerless 'gainst his magic. That's why he calls you sheep. Drinkin' his blood makes you slaves forever."

Tiberius organized rituals in cage nine every week. Even though they were a half-mile away, the nearest cages could hear Tiberius and his followers, drinking each other's blood and eating small animals they caught with their hands. And unfortunately for Willis, Tiberius despised the weak as imperfect examples of his race and the reason his people had been enslaved for so long. So when Tiberius first saw Willis Covington walk into his Voodoo Cage with his slight frame and timid eyes, Willis became the next victim of the voodoo congregation. Tiberius' cult tormented Willis and those like him with haunting dances that ended in repeated beatings and rapings. Willis turned to Kibel for help, and Kibel tried to have him moved to another cage, but Flood was unwilling to move him. "And what happens when he gets beat in the next cage? And what happens when every gunman wants a new cage? No. Willis will remain where he is and he will learn to fend for himself. But to assuage your fears, I will talk to Tiberius and instruct him to leave Willis alone." Flood never spoke to Tiberius, and the torments continued. In his misery, Willis grew desperate and searched for the courage either to escape or Knock-a-Joe.

Willis chose escape. He possessed a nimble mind that he applied to the task. He had always wanted to be a civil engineer, building roads for people to drive on and buildings for them to work in, but the only job he could get was pressing pulp in a paper mill in Oxford, and when the mill went bankrupt he was left sleeping on the benches of the General Lee Park. So Willis devised a plan to escape one night during his return back from the dissipating marsh. After the gunmen had passed the marsh, and before their chains were unlocked at their cages, Willis would unlock himself and run for his life into the night. His plan presented him with two dilemmas. First, he would have to figure out how to unlock his shackles without the Sergeant's key, and second, he would have to be surrounded in the shackle line by enough allies who would not expose him as he fled for freedom. The latter problem was easily solved. At least a half-dozen other gunmen in the Voodoo Cage had been raped and beaten by Tiberius over the months (though none as severely and routinely as Willis) who would either try to escape with him or be willing to remain silent as he tried. As for the first problem, he was certain that with the proper tools he could open the shackles in seconds.

By early fall 1906, the marsh was cleared and Willis was ready to escape. He had found two, thin rusty nails near the cattle barn several weeks before and tested them on his shackles each night, jiggling and wiggling them until he heard the lock click open. He kept the nails in his mattress and practiced night after night until he could open the shackles in seconds. In the meantime, Willis had been whispering in the marsh to his allies of his plan and encouraging them to join him. But for whatever reason, despite their physical and psychological duress, no one was willing to join Willis and risk being shredded alive by the hellhounds and their dagger teeth. But they did agree to line around him and remain silent. In the end, Willis was happy to escape alone, for he was much faster than any of them.

Willis visualized his plan over and over in his mind, and when the day of his escape arrived, his heart pounded with the cusp of his destruction or freedom. He was exhausted from the weeks they had spent uprooting tree spikes and dragging the lumber back to Front Camp, but he had to escape in the fall, before it was too cold. His only fear was that after his escape, the friends who had been chained around him would be interrogated and tortured, but they instructed him not to worry, "Ain't no torture they ken devise that's worse than workin' this marsh eighteen hours a day en then bein' beaten en tonked by Tiberius all night. 'Sides, we ken tell them that if we was your 'complices weeda escaped to. We'll tell them you stole sum a Tiberius' magic en used it to escape." Willis promised his friends and their ancestors that he would repay their kindness.

On the day of his escape, Willis focused his thoughts on the details of his task, and when the day was done and the exhausted gunmen were returning to their cages, he summoned the strength of his ancestors to fill his legs with fire so he could run for days and days without stopping until he reached a land of freedom and rest. Willis and his allies walked slowly and remained near the back of the procession returning to the Voodoo Cage. Once the gunmen had cleared the marsh, the Drivers and Sergeants moved to the front of the procession to unshackle the gunmen so the shackshooters could inspect them as they filed in. This was Willis' moment. He looked to his friends and thanked them for hearing his cry for freedom. Then he dropped to his knees and within seconds he was fleeing back into the marsh.

Even though he was exhausted from the day's labor, the rush of unfettered motion swept Willis through the marsh and into the night. Within ten minutes, the shackshooters discovered his absence, and a dozen Drivers were gathered on horseback with Parchman's hounds ready for pursuit. The Drivers took the hounds to Willis' bunk where they saturated their senses with his scent, and then they charged into the field. Tiberius smiled as he watched them rush into the night. He whispered a small curse against them to help Willis' magic prevail.

Had he fled an hour later, or on a Sunday, Willis would have been caught within an hour. But the marsh was too fresh with the scent of a thousand gunmen for the hounds to locate and follow his singular scent. They sniffed and turned and sniffed again, waiting for the scent that would thump the tripwire of their senses, but they were overwhelmed by a chorus from which they could not extract Willis' singular voice. Without the precision of their hounds, the Drivers were left to deploy themselves in pairs into the endless landscape beyond, hoping one of their groups would discover him and signal the others.

Willis ran to the east, heaving his steamy breath into the cold, cloudy night like a silver train. He did not waste a moment to look back for fear that if he saw even a spark of light he would panic, and the hounds would smell his panic and close on him even faster. Instead, he watched the land passing beneath him, and he repeated with each step the thought that he was one step closer to freedom. He ran for two hours without stopping. He only stopped when he arrived at the banks of a raging river that spread over two hundred feet across. He knew it was the Big Black River, and it was freezing dark. But he had no choice, so without a thought he dove in, and the icy water immediately jolted the wind from his lungs. He surfaced and coughed for air as he felt his entire body turn to a senseless lump beneath his neck.

In desperation, Willis began to flail his arms and legs, but he could not feel them. Before he became a chunk of black ice sinking to the bottom of the river, Willis charged towards the other bank. He fought the rapid current with strength he had never before possessed, and when he reached the other side, he was panting for life and rubbing his body from the stinging of the brisk wind against his icy wet skin. He managed to run another thirty minutes before finally collapsing beneath a tree from dizziness and exhaustion. His entire body was numb, and just before he drifted from consciousness, he entertained the proposition of never awakening again.

When he did awake with the sunrise, Willis felt two stumps at the end of his legs. He had lost both feet to frostbite, and he was so dehydrated that he could not swallow his fear. When he tried to stand and run, the uncanny sensation of lumbering about on two, numb, stumps of feet left him collapsing every few steps. He clung to trees and branches and dragged himself as far as he could. Each step was one step closer to freedom. He dragged himself for one more day before he heard the distant howling of the hounds, haunting him with the warning that they were arriving to devour his freedom. Willis ran and stumbled and dragged himself with desperation, but the howls and barks seemed to close on him more furiously the more frantically he tried to escape. He knew that they smelled his panic and that his time was limited. He wanted to explode from his body and soar to freedom, but all he could manage was a crippled pace that his despairing heart could no longer abide. So in mournful resignation, Willis dragged himself up to the nearest tree, sat against it, and closed his eyes. He folded his legs underneath him and placed his hands on his knees, calling his ancestors to bear witness. No particular thoughts passed through his mind; rather, he experienced the gradual emptying of the panic and clutter of desperate thoughts. Perhaps this was what he had wished for. Perhaps his ancestors were granting his wish the only way they could.

Within minutes, Willis opened his eyes and saw four Drivers and their four hounds, growling and snarling in front of him. The Drivers restrained the hounds, which were jumping and gnarling to tear open his flesh. One of the Drivers fired a shot into the sky, scattering the morning's serenity, and then turned to Willis with a curious look, "You still alive, nigger?"

Willis watched one of them dismount and calm the hounds before he responded, "Nosuh. Not alive really, but still breathin'."

"Well, I don't think you're breathing's gonna last much longer 'cause these hounds are gonna tear you open and eat your guts for breakfast."

"That ain't particularly lawful, is it?"

"Lawful? Do you know how much trouble you've caused us? Look around you boy. . . you see where you are? Whose supposed to be your witness to what's lawful and what's not?"

Willis understood. He placed one hand on the damp, morning earth and rested the other hand open in his lap. The wind blowing amid the trees stopped, and Willis exhaled with a smile as he closed his eyes. In that moment the Driver released the hounds. They charged at Willis with hate-sharpened teeth and tore into his brittle flesh. Not a scrap of him remained where it had been before when the hounds began to fight each other for his bones. One of the Drivers placed Willis' ivory remains in his saddlesack, and they all returned to Parchman. Those bones with their tattered ring-arounds still clinging to them would be all that reminded the world of Willis' life, and watching the hounds gnaw on his residue during Kibel's Sermon on the Mount frightened every other gunman from ever trying to escape.

So a year later, when Fulton and his friends were planning their own escape, they were the only ones to have done so since Willis Covington's death. Legends arose around the ferocity of the hounds and their preternatural instincts, but Mongoose was certain that his instincts could evade theirs.

They decided to escape that autumn, after the harvest. With all the leaves scattering their scents, Fulton and the others hoped to make it far enough away that the Drivers and their hounds would resign themselves from the hunt. Meanwhile, Mongoose's lessons suffered for a few weeks during the harvest's peak in September. In retrospect, Mongoose wished he had managed to retrieve some of Willis Covington's bones from the hounds. He wanted the bones so he could grind them into a potion for everyone to drink. Like a vaccine. That was how you conquered History. But even without the potion, Mongoose was confident he and his pupils could remain in front of the hounds for at least a week, and that might be enough time for them to find their freedom and former lives.

LIFE'S ONLY PROMISE

The Field of Bones

By the time the harvest ended and autumn settled on Parchman, Mongoose, Fulton, Cuttino, and Stromyle were fluent in the nocturnal discourse of clicks and snaps and they could travel through shadows like a breeze. They moved like specters, like Mongoose's ancestors who mimicked the prey of the earth in order to evade those who slaughtered them. They practiced in their cages at night, moving back and forth from gunman to gunman without ever being seen, smelled, or heard. By mid October, their plan was ready, and despite continued protestations from the others, Fulton insisted that Moondog escape with them, for they were, after all, using him as the critical component to their escape.

The morning of their escape, the Mississippi horizon was painted in a bright sunrise that reminded Fulton of autumn mornings on his porch, after Settlement Day, with nothing to do. The crisp, light autumn air vivified Fulton and opened his lungs from the summer haze's constriction.

Autumn was the season of balance, unscorched and unfrozen, and the time of year when Fulton always thought of distant places. He thought about his home and his former life, more distant than any other place in his imagination. He had interred that life under unmarked tombstones in the cemetery of his past, unable to abide recollection of who he used to be. But as the time of their escape approached, Fulton discovered his former self insinuating its way into his mind, first through his dreams, and then in the middle of the fields in the middle of the day, triggered by a scent or a motion familiar to his past. He felt the schism between his selves begin to buckle under the force of his memories, and he felt that he was losing control over the architecture of his being. Though confused, Fulton understood the commingling of his past and present selves as a sign that perhpas forces beyond him were also ready for his return home. The only questions that he dared not ask were to what he was returning and whether he would be able to erase this Parchman life from his memories (or would Parchman's specter linger in him until he recoiled into a corner like LaRue).

By fleeing on a Saturday night, they could run for several hours before the Drivers arrived at eight the next morning to lead them to Front Camp for their services. That would give them three and a half hours to run and run until their legs collapsed. Mongoose instructed his pupils to spend the day concentrating on their cotton, "Don't you dare ruminate," he warned, "the world ken read your thoughts, so jes concentrate on them bolls. En make sure you meet your quota; the last thing you want before goin' to sleep is ten lashes."

Everyone heeded Mongoose's warnings, except Fulton. Fulton could not help worrying. First, he worried about Moondog's worries. He knew that Moondog was nervous because his role was the most critical and dangerous, and if they failed he would suffer the most. And second, before the day ended, Fulton also worried about the sky. Returning from the fields, he looked up and watched the day announce its death with a legion of thin, serpentine clouds swimming into the sunset above him. The clouds absorbed the sunset's rufescent color, painting a canvas of blood above the horizon, and in their ominous appearance Fulton realized it was precisely their powers he was appropriating in order to escape. The power from the stable at Naga's, the power from the town square in Jackson. Fulton did not know whether the clouds were painting his victory or his doom across the sky, but the sky was red with someone's blood, and that made him worry. However, since he could not abide twelve-and-a-half more years, fail or not, he had no choice but escape.

At that moment, Moondog rode up to Gerrit and Sergeant Judson and told them that he was feeling ill, so he asked to ride back to the trusty cabin and rest for the night. Sergeant Judson told him to call Dr. Powder (the doctor the Sergeants, Drivers, and trusties were allowed to call from Scott whenever they were ill) first thing in the morning. So Moondog galloped back to the trusty cabin, passing Fulton along the way and upholding a clenched fist to the night. Fulton felt the courage summoned within him, the purpose of Neshoba's and Stoka's deaths, and as he watched Moondog gallop away, he closed his fist as well, squeezing the history-heavy fibers of the cotton in his hand.

Moondog galloped with haste to his cabin. As always at this time of day, Front Camp was deserted and would remain so until the other guards arrived two hours later for their Saturday night festivities. Those from the morning shift were already in town enjoying a drink, and they would join the night shift in Front Camp with some women later. And Flood was either out drinking or in his Mansion entertaining a cotton distributor, so Moondog was alone with almost two hours to complete the most important steps of their plan.

As he arrived in Front Camp, Moondog realized that never before had his heart thumped so violently from fear. Because of his kinship to Anderson, he had never feared any violence against him. He had even taken Parchman's worst days in stride; a dozen open-skin lashes did little more than sour his mood for a few days. But now he felt fear flexing in his heart. It did not feel like he would have imagined. Fear felt peculiarly similar to making love.

Arriving at the trusty cabin, Moondog dismounted his horse and removed his clothes. He fumbled with the buttons and zippers of his gray shirt and trousers as he stripped himself. Then he placed his trusty uniform under his pillow, from where he concurrently removed a pair of ring-arounds that he had placed there the previous night.

Next, he dashed from his cabin and jogged to cage seven where the shackshooters had not yet arrived. He slipped into the cage, immediately gagging at the stench of feces and offal to which he had grown unaccustomed during his last few months as a trusty. He covered his nose, moved to Fulton's bunk and placed a copy of his keys to the front door of the cage as well as a six-inch gutting knife into the torn mattress. Before he suffocated, he exited the cage and relocked its door. With that step completed, Moondog jogged two miles to cage eleven and climbed into Stromyle's bunk. He pulled the tattered sheet over his head and placed his face into the stained, stinking mattress, which did not smell nearly as awful as the putrid air around it. Moondog breathed slowly to calm himself; as he lay, he realized that he was exhausted, but also in a few hours he would be required to run for miles, so he immersed himself in the steady rhythm of his beating heart and fell asleep.

Shortly thereafter, Fulton, Mongoose, and Cuttino were standing outside cage seven. The guards unshackled them and handed them over to the shackshooters for the night. Sergeant Judson, Willard, and Seyd then rode to Front Camp to join the others for drinks and women. The shackshooters called the names of each gunman, and each gunman sounded off and was inspected before entering. Once inside, Fulton felt the keys and the knife in his mattress while the shackshooters checked the cage to see that each bunk was filled. As soon as the shackshooters closed the door, Fulton reached into his mattress like the belly of a dragon and retrieved the treasures that would enable his liberation. Without saying a word, he told Cuttino and Mongoose that the keys and the gutting knife were under his pillow. Then he listened to the sounds around him; he heard the shackshooters laughing just beyond the thick metal door of the cage, and he realized that it had been over a year since he last laughed, the day Mongoose said he was going to protect them from malaria.

At the same moment, two miles north of cage seven, Stromyle followed the nightly ritual of the unshackling, the line-up, and the line-call. Because Moondog had shredded the socket wires, the floodlights at cage eleven did not burn, and the surrounding darkness with its flittering shadows from the shackshooters' lamps created the perfect environment for Stromyle's escape. At the precise moment after he answered the line-call, Stromyle disappeared into the spectral darkness around him like a shard of glass in a spring lake. Only a gunman or two who had been near him noticed his absence, but the intervening time before they were being inspected was so short, their day in the field so exhausting, and their inability to deduce what possibly could have happened to Stromyle so confusing, that they concluded their eyes had deceived them. Moments later, all the gunmen were asleep, and before locking the cage for the night, the shackshooters checked that every bunk was filled, but they did not think to wonder why Stromyle was snoring for the first time in his life.

Meanwhile, Stromyle was swimming through the night to Front Camp and the trusty cabin. He could hear the trusties, Drivers, and Sergeants beginning to gather as he slipped into the cabin, changed into Moondog's uniform, placed his ring-arounds under the pillow, and covered himself in Moondog's sheets. A few minutes later he heard the Drivers and Sergeants firing off their rifles, inhaling pint after pint of shine, and seducing their night-women with spirit-induced affection. The trusties gathered on the deck outside their cabin with a few jugs and some cards.

"Go on inside en see if Moondog wanna play."

One of the trusties entered the cabin and saw Moondog's body covered in his bed, "Moondog. You feelin' ok? You wanna come out for some shine en cards?"

Stromlye lay in the bed in sweating silence as the trusty walked next to him, breathing right over him. He shook the body in the bed, "Hey. Moondog. You asleep?" Stromlye grumbled.

"Well, never mind then."

Stromyle exhaled as he heard the trusty return outside, "He must be dead alseep 'cause he didn't say a word . . . now pass me some more shine." Two hours later the guards and their women were thoroughly soused and all collapsed into sleep.

Meanwhile, Fulton, Stromyle, Cuttino, and Mongoose had not been able to sleep at all from the furious traffic in their minds. They all calculated within a few minutes of each other (primarily from the location of the moonbeams through their respective windows) that they had an hour-and-a-half before they were to meet at Jefferson Hill at the outskirts of Parchman's fields. They listened for sounds or signs that something had gone wrong in someone else's part of the plan, but all they heard was an uproar of snores, frogs, owls, crickets, and the beating of their hearts inside their heads. And when the time for their escape arrived, they each summoned the goodwill of their ancestors and the potency of their magic to open a small rift in the world's order of things so they could slip inside it and escape unscathed to their families, their homes, and their former lives.

Four in the morning. Mongoose began to click at Fulton and Cuttino that it was time to head for Jefferson Hill. Morning mist filled the cage as Fulton lowered himself from his bunk, as if he were in a den of sleeping lions. He felt Mongoose and Cuttino just behind him, and the three of them glided to either side of the front door. They heard the shackshooters playing cards at the meal table. Fulton showed the others his silver blade, and he handed the keys to Mongoose while Cuttino watched behind to ensure that no one had awakened to notice them.

The lock to the front door was an old Whitman Lock which, though rusted and resistant, could be opened from the inside as well as the outside. Jennings Whitman designed the lock fifteen years ago after his wife burned to death in a basement fire from which she could not escape because the door locked behind her from the outside. Ordinarily, a prison would never use a lock such as the Whitman Lock, except that Jennings Whitman was the cousin of Vardaman's sister-in-law, so Vardaman was able to procure two-dozen Whitman Locks for pennies on the dollar to be used for the doors of the cages at Parchman.

Always looking for a bargain to swell his profit margins, Vardaman congratulated himself upon delivery of the locks, "Genius is manifest in success, success resides in the details, and the details will make us rich."

Mongoose was unaware of both Jennings Whitman's wife and Vardaman's frugality as he inserted the key into the lock and slowly turned it to the right with surgical precision so as to make the softest clicking sound possible when the bolt turned. But when the bolt clicked louder than any of them had anticipated and they caught a glimpse of the shackshooters snatching their rifles and turning for the front door, Fulton and Cuttino caught their breaths and felt their knees buckle, but Mongoose told them to be ready. So Fulton clenched his knife like the throat of his mortal enemy. They all hunched down beneath the grate of the door as the shackshooters arrived to search the darkness for trouble. Fulton and Cuttino prepared to pounce.

At that moment, Mongoose tossed the keys onto the floor so that they jingled, not loud enough to awaken the sleeping gunmen, but just loud enough to incite the forward shackshooter to insert his key into the door to investigate. And in that sliver of an instant, Cuttino erupted from his haunches and burst through the door knocking both shackshooters to the ground where he held them in disorientation for the additional second Fulton needed to lunge onto Cuttino's back and raise his bladed hand. The shackshooters caught their final glimpses of the world as Fulton slashed their necks. He relished each deadly slice left and right, left and right. Mongoose closed and locked the cage behind them with only a few snores and grunts from inside as response to their violent escape. They dragged the bodies into the shade behind the cage and kicked dirt over the trail of blood steaming into the sleepy sky. And then with a deep breath they charged past the floodlights and into the fields towards Jefferson Hill.

Thirty minutes later they arrived at Jefferson Hill where they found Stromyle sitting on the branch of a tree.

"Moondog here?" Fulton asked.

"No. Been up here ten minutes. Saw ya'll comin' through the flat, but I ain't seen him at all."

"Let's wait fifteen minutes," Fulton said, making the others uncomfortable.

Stromyle explained that Moondog had delivered his uniform just as they planned, and that once all the guards were dead snakebit, it was no task at all for him to slip through the floodlights and into the field straight to Jefferson Hill. "Your people musta sold they souls to the devil to get magic like this," Stromyle said to Mongoose.

"Ain't no devil involved, 'cept white folks. It's how my people learned to survive. Some say they still on mountaintops somewhere, others say they was finally caught between the ocean en the white man, en they all drowned themselves to the bottom a the sea. Not a day goes by I don't wish I could find them." Mongoose's slow, chilling tone silenced the night for a few minutes. The almost-free gunmen looked back at Parchman and its distant lights. They waited and paced anxiously, trembling under the sensations that they were standing at the cusp of freedom but remained waiting on the hill, until the fifteen minutes expired and they still saw no sign of Moondog.

"We gotta go, "Cuttino said, "the longer we wait here, the closer they'll be in the mornin' when they notice we gone . . . unless they already done captured Moondog en they comin' after us now."

The air thickened in Fulton's lungs, and he realized he could not detain his friends any longer, but neither could he abandon Moondog, even if it meant forfeiting his return home. He could never enjoy his liberation as long as he knew that Moondog continued to suffer. So even while standing at the doorstep of bliss, Fulton told his friends to continue to freedom without him. "Me en Moondog'll either meet ya'll at Holly Bluff by sunup, or wit our ancestors alongside God."

Stromyle descended from his branch and joined Cuttino and Mongoose in trying to convince Fulton to continue with them, "Come on Fulton, we're right here at our freedom. Moondog'd want you to take his freedom home wit you en tend his family en live your life."

But Fulton stepped away from them and explained that he had no choice but to remain, "I kent leave Moondog behind any more than I ken leave my arm or my leg behind." So Fulton turned his back as the others fled into the darkness beyond Jefferson Hill. Running to freedom. Leaving Fulton alone on the hill with only the chirps of crickets and the gurgles of bullfrogs. Alone, he sat down on the cool, dewy earth and dug his finger into the ground. He raised the moist, black buckshot to his face and inhaled its autumn scent. It smelled like the twilight of his life.

With the scent of *liloba* in his lungs, Fulton affirmed that he would wait on Jefferson Hill until either Moondog or the hounds arrived. He knew that in the case of the latter he would probably have to endure torture and finally death until he revealed the destination of the others. At least he would die on a Sunday. With any luck, they would take his body straight to Kibel's sermon for a blessing and burial.

An hour passed without Moondog, and Fulton began to convince himself that he never wanted to run away anyway. There was never any escape. LaRue had taught him that. Alone atop the hill, gazing across the endless fields of empty stalks, Fulton confronted his moment in History, and it did not provide space for the freedom he contemplated. He was, in fact, less significant than the cotton he picked. At least the cotton is noticed by the land on which it lives and dies, whereas he would live and die without a trace. So to where was he running? He would only find himself in another part of the world that would vampire his life for its comfort and profit. He should have never conceived the redirection of his fate twenty months ago, and he should never have cajoled Moondog to embrace his misconceived plan. Moondog told him trouble always finds a colored no matter where he thinks he's running to. In that way, it was an offense against his ancestors to jeopardize his life (their sacrifice) with actions pursued under the untenable assumption that their outcome resided within the force of his will. He had betrayed himself, his friends, and his family, and he would have returned to his cage were it not for the newborn velleity dragging through his veins.

So he sat. Listening to his own bereft suspiration and inhalation of the earthy air around him. Almost silent. Minutes and more minutes passed. Then he heard whispers of his name and saw, emerging from the far side of the hill, a form that was too large to be anyone but Moondog. He did not remove his open hands from his knees as he shifted his torso to face him. Moondog raced up the hill and arrived at Fulton, heaving for air so that his words were broken by his gulping lungs, "I-fell-asleep . . . where - the - others?"

"I sent em on 'bout an hour ago," Fulton softly responded.

Moondog reached down to lift Fulton so they could continue running, but Fulton would not be moved. He no longer understood the utility of motion.

"What's wrong? You hurt? We gotta get runnin' cause we ain't got but a few hours."

Fulton was silent for a moment and then responded, "I ain't runnin' nowhere."

Moondog went dizzy with Fulton's words, and his head was too befuddled to try to understand them. So he reached down and grasped Fulton's arm with the strength of twenty men, stared into Fulton's zombie-like eyes, and roared in stochaic words, "We ain't got no time for no second thoughts, en we ain't got no time for no fear. I promised you when we left I'd bring you home. So one way or thother you're comin' wit me. Now either gettup en start runnin' or you ken lay there while I drag you home. Either way, we done suffered too much for you to jes set there." Fulton was not moved by Moondog's words, but the fire in his eyes resonated with the pride of another life, and Fulton soon found himself on his feet, running, alongside his friend towards freedom.

They had run nineteen miles without stopping when James Willard and Jimmy Seyd arrived at cage seven to line-up the men for Kibel's sermon. When they did not find the shackshooters at their station they searched around the cage and found their mutilated bodies. It took seventeen minutes for eight Drivers, three Sergeants, and the hounds to charge into Parchman's fields through the endless rows of skeletal cotton stalks towards the forest of autumn-scattered leaves past Jefferson Hill.

The field songs that day sang the magic of four gunmen and a trusty and their brutal escape. The Drivers bet on the number of days before they were recaptured. Most everyone expected them to return to Parchman just like Willis Covington. As one gunman whispered to another, "Ain't no way them niggers ken outrun them hounds. I don't care how far ahead they started. Them hounds got the devil in em, en they'll run you down a hundred miles to a inch." Meanwhile, Flood threatened to replace every Sergeant in Parchman if the gunmen were not captured and returned to him, dead or alive. A successful escape was no way to finish Parchman's first harvest, for it would inspire additional attempts, and the growing pressure to repeal the Pig Laws was making it more and more difficult to round up and arrest the same multitude of coloreds as before.

So the hunt was on. Fortunately for Fulton, Moondog had the keys to their shackles, so they were able to run without the weight of their flesh-slicing edges against their ankles. On the other hand, Cuttino, Mongoose, and Stromyle went fleeing into the dusty morning with their shackles agonizing their every step. That is what every prison guard or slave owner counted on for catching any escaped negro -- sooner or later those rusty shackles will tear into his bones leaving him writhing in pain awaiting the posse's arrival.

Except for Mongoose, who lived south of Parchman on Willow Lake, the others all lived north and northeast of Parchman. Nevertheless, instead of running north or northeast through the forests and plains to their homes, they ran southwest through the Yazoo swampland in order to keep the hounds off their scent long enough to discourage the posse. They planned to run to Vicksburg, from where Mongoose would break from the group and head east to his home, while the others would circle through Louisiana and Arkansas before re-entering Mississippi somewhere south of Helena, whereabouts Fulton and Moondog would head northeast to their homes and Cuttino and Stromyle would continue east towards Oxford and Corinth. That was their plan. Stay in the swamp and then out of Mississippi as long as possible. Fulton and Moondog calculated five weeks for them to return home.

But Fulton saw their plan already crumbling as Cuttino, Mongoose, and Stromyle were miles ahead of them and there was no way to determine how they would ever meet. Moondog told Fulton that it didn't matter whether or not they ever saw each other again as long as they all made it home, except that they needed Moondog to unshackle them. They might not last long with those shackles gnawing at their ankles. Even if the posse did not catch them, all the bleeding might attract alligators. In either Parchman or in an alligator they were nothing more than a meal to this world. A pile of bones or a pile of shit, decomposing into the soil.

After running through the morning, Fulton and Moondog found a small hill with some trees, providing cover for them to take a short nap. The more Fulton thought about it, the more he doubted those hounds could ever find them, even if they had the devil's vengeance in their noses. They slept for an hour and then continued running. The autumn air kept them cool and helped them run. Fulton always wondered what it would be like to live in the North and not sweat eight months of every year. He figured that people in the North must be much happier since they only had to sweat four months of the year. Maybe that's why they didn't have slaves.

They ran another two hours without speaking, occasionally stopping to gulp some of the delta's swamp water to ease their parched throats. By early evening they were ready to collapse. As strong as Fulton was, his thirty-five year old body had begun to ache and fatigue more and more with each day he spent in Parchman. Even Moondog was doubled over in exhaustion. As evening approached, they still saw no trace of the others. They found another hill good for another hour nap, calculated they had three more days to Vicksburg, and then rose with legs heavy like logs and continued running away from those who devoured them towards those who fulfilled them.

They ran and napped and ran for another day, and when they were a day from Vicksburg, Fulton suddenly stopped with the expression of death on his face because he realized they had been running up and down the Delta still wearing their ring-arounds. Until that moment, it had not occurred to either of them that they had been fleeing in a uniform that you could only find in one place in Mississippi -- Parchman Farm. If anyone had seen them from even a mile away they would have gathered a posse on the spot and hunted them down. "How'd we overlook this?" Fulton asked in exasperation, "We shoulda been captured en strungup a long time ago."

"Maybe that's what happened to thothers."

"Maybe. But how'd we not plan for this?"

"Ya'll all been wearin' the same outfit for almost two years now. It's like your skin. En I didnt think of it neither when I changed from my trusty uniform."

"So what we gonna do?"

"Unless you wanna run naked, we gonna hafta keep goin' like we been goin' 'til we get to Vicksburg. Maybe we ken get somethin' less assumin' to wear there. 'Til then, let's rub mud on us to hide the white stripes."

So they wiped mud on themselves, caught their breaths, and continued to Vicksburg. Feet forward. Each step another step towards freedom. Each step realizing the success of their plan. And if nothing else, to be running at all, to command the movement of legs and arms for their own purpose, even that was a small piece of freedom. They were only ten miles from Vicksburg. But they had forgotten one detail, and that detail might ruin them.

They stopped for one last nap before continuing, and they were both asleep when they suddenly jumped from their skin at the distant but unmistakable rumbling of hounds barking for flesh. The growls sounded from ahead of them, closer to Vicksburg. Terror suffocated their hearts, and their mouths went dry with memories of Willis Covington. They balked in fear over what to do. Soon enough, their instincts to run overcame their indecision, and they jumped into the swamp and ran away from the hounds, back towards the general direction of Parchman Farm. Conflicting impulses to turn south then northwest then southwest zigged and zagged the pair through the swamp, and their desperation escalated as the growling of the hounds crescendoed. They arrived at a dense thicket of ancient trees shrouded in kudzu where the swamp became thick and muddy. Their pace slowed, but they felt less conspicuous. They tried climbing to the top of the thicket canopy, but as they strained to pull themselves upwards, neither possessed the strength to lift himself even a few branches into the trees. The growling and barking began to resonate through the thicket from every direction, as if the trees had joined the hunt, leaving them without a direction to flee -- the branches like hellhound fangs, the swamp's stench like the devil's belly, and the haunting growls like the rumbling of a hunger to devour them. Desperation decayed into disassociation from the overwhelming sensations of the moment, and Fulton and Moondog stumbled around in the mud with no idea how to save themselves. Fulton's mind returned to the truths awakened on Jefferson Hill. No matter the fire for freedom in his heart and no matter the fury against captivity in his soul, his moment in History would forever deny even his most humble wishes.

Stuttering and stumbling, the world before them began to twist and melt into a swampy torment. And it was into that swamp that they fell backwards, exhausted and unable to breathe, as they watched the impossible vision of eight Parchman guards, on horses but without hounds, riding as if to a funeral, almost as unaware and unprepared for what they saw as were Fulton and Moondog - two gunmen, stunned and breathless on their backs in the thick, muddy swamp.

The Drivers swarmed onto Fulton and Moondog like vultures onto carrion. Effortless conquest gleamed in their eyes. The guards clamped rusty shackles around their almost free ankles, and one of the Sergeants fired his rifle into the sky three times. They heard the hounds clearly now, arriving from behind them. So they sat in the mud with their faces down, wondering whether their tormented hearts would finally burst and spare them from the unfolding of whatever cruelty awaited them. The Sergeants and Drivers gloated, "Didn't think you could really get away did you? Haven't you niggers learned anything since you were born?"

Minutes later, six white men arrived on their horses; the only face Fulton recognized was Duke Judson, II's. They brought six brown hounds with them, which were not from Parchman, but sufficiently similar. One of the men tied the hounds to a tree and ordered them silent. The six white men also arrived with two extra horses, behind which Fulton and Moondog spotted Cuttino, Mongoose, and Stromyle, tied and dragged through the swamp with little more than an instinct to breathe supporting their gelatinous, naked, blood and mud smeared bodies. Duke Judson enjoyed the reunion. He led his horse towards his new captives, "You must be wondering how, outta all of this useless swamp we captured all of your friends and the both of you, all in the same day." There was a conceit in his eyes as he spoke. *If only the world would put you in my skin for a day.*

Duke Judson, II explained in victorious detail how the other three gunmen decided to stop in Redwood at a locksmith friend of Stromyle's to have their shackles removed. But what they did not plan for was that Redwood was Duke Judson, II's hometown and that the previous week he had returned there to retire from Parchman and bequeath his whip and rifle to his son, Duke Judson, III, who was present among the other white men and ceremoniously nodded at Fulton and Moondog. Duke Judson, II happened to see the three coloreds walking through Redwood barefoot, wearing gray trousers and uniforms, on his way from his house on Tate Street to the corner grocery on Chickasaw Street. "I couldn't see their faces from their brim hats turned down, but when they turned into the same grocery I was heading to and ran out a few seconds later with bread in their hands, I chased after them. I didn't have my revolver or my rifle with me, so I was yelling for my son while the shopkeep was yelling for help, and soon enough a whole mob of us fell on them, and wasn't I surprised when I lifted their hats and saw their faces so far away from home. I was mighty proud to accomplish one final good deed for Parchman and the state of Mississippi before passing the reins of my cage to my son."

Of course, after he had captured Cuttino, Mongoose, and Stromyle, Duke Judson, II assumed that there were others who had escaped with them. But when they would not confirm his suspicions, he dragged them to the town square, stripped them naked, and threatened to whip them until their confessions bled from them. Lashed, ripped, broken, and crumbling, they still refused to speak. But their sacrifice quickly became purposeless as Redwood's Sheriff discovered that Mongoose had a friend in Redwood, named Rusty Lamar, who had run the town's bait and tackle supply store for years. As fate would have it, Rusty Lamar raised Mongoose's father and then cared for Mongoose and his brother until Mongoose was twelve. Rusty left Willow Lake then because the land had gone bad, spoiled, evil, but Mongoose and his brother would not leave because the lake was the burial ground of their parents. Rusty sent word to his boys that he was in Redwood selling worms and crickets and fishing every weekend in a new lake, and he encouraged the boys to visit him, but Mongoose was never willing to leave Willow Lake, not until he had killed every snake that slithered across its surface. So it had been over eight years since Mongoose and Rusty Lamar had last seen each other when the Redwood Sheriff dragged Rusty into the town square, stripped his old body naked, and threatened to whip him silly if Mongoose did not speak. Two of the deputies held his emaciated frame steady as the whip hissed through the air and stung open his back. It only took one strike for Mongoose to speak, to keep his second father from suffering the same fate as his first, "Fulton en Moondog's escaped too."

"Where are they?"

"Don't know, maybe somewhere 'tween here en Vicksburg." Duke Judson, II immediately wired ahead to Vicksburg to send a posse heading northeast looking for two coloreds while he and his son led a posse circling back from Redwood towards Vicksburg.

"So you see, we had you sandwiched here in the swamp, all thanks to the betrayal of your friends. All I had to do was tell them I'd send them to Vicksburg's prison instead of back to Parchman and they sang like canaries. You negroes are so selfish you'll rat each other out just to save your own worthless skin." Duke Judson, II looked at Cuttino, Mongoose, and Stromyle as he continued, "instead, these three will get five more years for larceny and probably ten more for attempted escape. The two of you will just get ten." They tied Fulton and Moondog to the horses along with the others, and the posse without the hounds returned to Vicksburg while Duke Judson, II and his son turned for Parchman, dragging all five gunmen by their wrists through the mud. Fulton knew that Justice would not find them in the lost time of the Yazoo Swampland, so for the first time in his life, as he struggled to breathe from the burning in his wrists and the mud flowing over his face, Fulton wished that they would just kill him. However they chose to do it. He knew that at the end of their journey back to Parchman a full audience of trusties, Drivers, Sergeants, and Flood awaited, laughing and barking in chorus at the profound and indelible example they would make of each of them. They would become images burned into the wretched consciousnesses of the other gunmen, right next to Willis Covington's bones.

Though it took them two-and-a-half days to return to Parchman, the posse did not offer their captives any food or water. Meanwhile, back in Parchman another group of gunmen attempted to escape. A Sergeant from cage two named Minter Tipton, twin brother of Sergeant Terry Tipton from cage fifteen, uncovered another plan of escape involving twelve gunmen in his cage.

Several weeks before Fulton's escape, Minter had selected a young, nervous gunman named Jarvis Small, and told him that if he reported any suspicious doings, he would recommend him for a pardon. Minter ordered Small to strict silence about their relationship, or the deal was void and he would be lashed. Minter also hid his relationship with Small from all the other Sergeants and Drivers in Parchman. He knew that if every Sergeant tried to obtain a clandestine spy in every cage that the advantage of the system would crumble. Spies would be spying on spies and everyone would know not to trust anyone else, and the moment the other gunmen discovered the spies they would be dead.

So Sergeant Minter Tipton and gunman Jarvis Small kept their relationship silent. Things worked out as planned for Minter, but not quite so for Jarvis. One day, Jarvis overheard a group of a dozen gunmen mapping their escape like generals preparing for war. They were led by a thin, broad-faced colored named Winston Menard. Winston's plan was completely different from Fulton's in that it involved escape on a Sunday in broad daylight into a speeding truck driven by one of his four brothers, who would then drive them to freedom faster than the trusties and Drivers could follow. Those guards who did decide to pursue would be discouraged by the gunfire of Winston's other three brothers.

At forty-four, Winston was the oldest of his brothers, and he arrived at Parchman for stealing valuable parcels from the Post Office in Senatobia in which he worked for twenty-two years (ever since he taught himself to read and write). The fact was that Winston had been stealing a trinket here and a valuable there just like the rest of the office, but no one had ever cared until six months ago when Winston was charged, convicted and sentenced to eighteen years in Parchman on twelve counts of postal theft.

The one skill that Winston learned during his twenty-two years at the Post Office was the use of the carrier pigeon. He learned how to train and care for the pigeons, and he grew attached to his fleet of birds. He cheered with each successful mission and especially enjoyed watching the newborns learn and achieve their skills. He named them after the states in the North he wanted to visit, wishing he could fly there like them, Dakota, Montana, Vermont, New York.

So Winston was not surprised when his pigeons searched for him and found him at Parchman, perching themselves at his window and awaiting their missions. And their missions turned out to include several trips back to Senatobia as facilitators of his plan of escape. When everything was set, the day before his escape, Winston's brothers sent him a last message which read, "Maybe we eat some fish for dinner tomorrow night," with a Salem cigarette attached to the letter for Winston to enjoy.

In that way, no one was able to ascertain how Winston had organized his escape with his brothers. Trusties, Drivers, and Sergeants were later interrogated as co-conspirators, but no one, not even Jarvis, saw Winston composing his notes and releasing them to the night sky with Montana or Pennsylvania. But one night Jarvis overheard their plans, so he informed his Sergeant immediately. And when Minter revealed the plot to Flood, he was incredulous, "Another one? Damn brazen gunmen. I'm gonna have to teach them a lesson they'll never forget."

So it was a Sunday, after the morning service and during the afternoon softball. Winston and his eleven freedom-dreaming friends heard the old motor's congested rumbling approaching from the direction of Gordon Junction. And he saw his three pigeons, circling high above Parchman's front gate, as if to serve as celestial markings for the brothers to follow. Winston and his friends gathered around each other and moved from the fields to the front gate. Fulton was not there to see the fire in Winston's Stoka-like eyes the moment the truck emerged a hundred feet away, and he yelled "Charge!"

Every eye in Parchman whirled at Winston's roar. Winston and his eleven companions raced towards the front gate. Trusties and Drivers were perched atop the buildings, but in the few seconds it took them to weild their rifles, cock, aim, and fire, Winston's brothers were speeding past the front gate in a twister of dust, and three of his brothers rose from the truck's bed and fired at the trusties and Drivers exposed on their perches. The guards did manage to shoot three of the fleeing gunmen, but with their attention also focused on protecting themselves from the truck's counterfire, and with their vision obstructed by the truck's dust storm, Winston and his eight remaining friends hopped into the truck and sped off towards highway 49, leaving a trail of dust shrouding the onlookers in the obscurity of Winston's success.

But before Winston and his brothers were more than a hundred yards from the front gate, Flood, Minter, and every available Sergeant at Parchman sprang from the thicket along the clearing that Winston was following to highway 49. They fired from every direction at the truck. Winston's brothers fumbled to suppress their pursuers, but it only took a few minutes for Flood and his dead-eyed Sergeants to blow so many holes into the truck that the wounded vehicle nearly crumbled apart as it rolled to a submissive halt only a few hundred yards from Gordon Junction. Winston's brothers continued to fire, but they and their cargo were being picked off like limp ducks. Flood, Minter, and the other Sergeants encircled the truck like a treasure, continuing to fire even after the resistance expired. Only Winston and his oldest brother were left alive when Flood ordered the ceasefire and approached the remains of the escape. Winston did not look up to their triumphant faces, or below at the dead faces of his brothers and friends. He could feel that Flood and Minter were waiting for him to look into their eyes and acknowledge that they owned his destiny. So instead, Winston fixed his trembling vision on the gun in his hands, and he shot himself through the eyes, for there was no longer anything in the world he wished to see. Winston's remaining brother, the only survivor, was invited back to Parchman and given a ten year sentence.

Later, just as Winston's brother and the other gunmen were preparing to return to their cages, the former and future Sergeant Judsons emerged from the margins of highway 49 with their emaciated, bruised, and broken booty. Every gunman dropped his eyes to the ground, as if watching the dead crawl out of their graves, while the Drivers cheered the posse like mythical heroes. Their day could not have been more triumphant. The trusties cheered as well, though with less vengeance. Mostly, they cheered for their power to cheer.

The posse dragged their captors through Front Camp. They stopped in the center of the courtyard in front of Flood's mansion, and Fulton and the others finally had the opportunity to raise themselves to their feet. But they each collapsed in disorientation, weakness, and fatigue. Duke Judson, II dismounted and deflected the accolades from himself to his son, the inheritor of his empire. Cage Seven. Within moments, the commotion attracted Flood from his mansion, and he walked directly to the Judson lineage and embraced them as if they had recaptured Jerusalem from the infidels. Or in this case, returned the infidels to Jerusalem.

"This certainly is a special day. What do you say we should do with these troublesome gunmen and their treacherous trusty?" Flood asked.

Duke Judson, II responded as if he had rehearsed his lines for a performance, "Why, I don't know Superintendent. Seems it would be too easy to just let the hounds at them, or just hang them or burn them or shoot them. Seems more useful that we make a more lasting example of these gunmen so the others can learn their lesson without all the suffering and trouble. Ain't that the Christian way?"

Fulton and the others could not see or hear anything in particular from all the buzzing and whirling of glances and gasps and cheers. Fulton felt his skull swelling from confusion, as if it wanted to burst and leak onto the earth.

"I suppose you're right Judson. I suppose that is the Christian way. Why don't you throw them down and toss some sand on them. Looks to me like a healthy dose of lashes should teach them their lesson."

Several Drivers and trusties threw Fulton and the others to the ground and spread sand across their backs. Streams of sweat and mud and blood were already dripping from their bodies, like sobbing. With the full population of Parchman's gunmen held at gunpoint on their knees to witness the lesson, two trusties and three Drivers reached to their Sergeants for their Black Annies and lined up behind each prisoner. They felt her behind them, poised to strike with her fleshsplitting fangs. Like fire burning from the outside in and back out. Meanwhile, Duke Judson, II stood between Flood and his son. Flood instructed Duke Judson, III to lead the count. A silence strangled Front Camp as if to ensure that the lashes could be heard by every living creature present, so that months later the sound would haunt their dreams with painful clarity.

Duke Judson, III opened his wet lips to release the power of the word, "One!" Whirr-Crack. The gunmen clenched and swallowed the pain down their throats, and Fulton muttered into the ground, "If I knew this wasn't gonna happen again I'd forgive you this instance." "Two!" Whirr-Crack. "Three!" Whirr-Crack. Their breathing began to buckle. "Four!" Whirr-Crack. Their minds turned black. "Five!" Whirr-Crack. Blood flowed in streams. "Six!" Whirr-Crack.

"Wait!" Flood interrupted, "why don't we wait a moment. To ensure that everyone understands why this is happening." Flood turned to the examples and explained, "You see, it'd be too easy to kill you. No one would be any better for it. You have to be punished so you understand that you committed a crime." Flood turned to the audience of gunmen as he continued, "And all of you have to witness this punishment because Parchman is a correctional facility. Our purpose is to rehabilitate you so you can return to Mississippi society as civilized contributors to its enhancement."

None of the gunmen seemed to hear a word he was saying, but he went on anyway. "We are all suffering here," Flood pontificated, "from depreciated standards of living and quality of life, and we can only improve our condition if we work together by accepting our roles in our society. All of you are here because you have forgotten your part. Running away will not help you or Mississippi. You must learn along with these five convicts that all human beings organize themselves into societies, and each society is structured in its particular way. In our society, each of you has a specific place, and if you don't keep to your place, things will fall apart." Flood had riveted himself into a self-righteous frenzy infatuated with his own sound, as if the sound of his words was alone sufficient to validate them. Flood turned to his five examples and instructed Duke Judson, III to continue and then he returned to his mansion.

"Seven!" Whirr-Crack. "Eight!" Whirr-Crack. "Nine!" Whirr-Crack. Fulton's lungs constricted, and he could barely breathe. "Ten!" Whirr-Crack. "Eleven!" Whirr-Crack. Moondog was enduring better than the rest, though even his thick, equine muscles were shuddering. "Twelve!" Whirr-Crack. "Thirteen!" Whirr-Crack. "Fourteen!" Whirr-Crack. The bodies of the examples tightened from the acute pain and appeared like onyx statues in Medusa's promenade; they were petrified from the accursed moment they were born to inherit the misfortune of gazing into her Mississippi eyes. By the time the count reached nineteen, more lashes than anyone had endured at Parchman, Fulton and the others lost consciousness in an effort to escape the affliction they could no longer endure. Stromyle wretched his innards before his eyes closed. Even Duke Judson, II was surprised that his son had continued so far, and for that matter, so was his son. But he was mesmerized by his power. Like a lion toying with his prey before devouring it.

"Twenty!" Whirr-Crack. "Twenty-One!" Whirr-Crack. "Twenty-Two!" Whirr-Crack. "Twenty-Three!" Whirr-Crack. "Twenty-Four!" Whirr-Crack. "Twenty-Five!" Whirr-Crack. The count spilled from Duke Judson, III's mouth as if it could not stop. The examples had lost consciousness several lashes ago, and now their bodies simply flinched with each additional lash. Their cells and organelles oozed in amoebic disintegration from behind their crumbling walls.

No one, not even Duke Judson, III, knew it at the moment, but the examples only had one more lash to endure. The twenty-fifth lash had jarred Mongoose from his unconsciousness and awakened him. A falcon was soaring infinitely above, and it watched Mongoose's body slouch and his head turn just as the younger Judson trumpeted, "Twenty-Six!" and Black Annie ripped through the air for another bite. The thick, knotted tip of her fangs snapped just at the moment Mongoose turned his collapsing head around, and struck him in the uprolled white of his remaining eye, shooting it out of his face like a bullet straight into the palm of Duke Judson, III's reflexed hand. Splattered with blood and nerves, Mongoose's second, severed eye stared up from Duke Judson, III's palm. Gasps awakened the other examples, and the gunmen, Drivers, Sergeants, birds, lizards, and winds stared in uncanny witness to one man's hypnotized observation of a naked eyeball contemplating him from the perch of his own outstreched hand.

No one, not even Fulton, bothered to take notice of Mongoose's tormented writhing as his blood gushed between his fingers from his newly vacated orbital slot. No one even knelt to offer Mongoose a reassuring touch or a bind for his wound, for everyone was fixated on the dramatic spectacle of a man's hand staring back at him.

Duke Judson, III dropped the eye to the ground, and its gaze returned everyone to Mongoose. He was standing with his hands at his side, blind but content like a suckling babe against its mother's breast. Breathing little fairy breaths. Though he had no eyes, he turned his head back and forth as if to see himself in the faces of those watching. The world was dark and dense with seclusion. The sensations were so overwhelming that Mongoose no longer noticed his pain. In an irony that he did not choose to locate, Mongoose was seeing the world in a way he had never imagined, as if at peace for the first time. He understood his placement within it and where it was compelled to take him, and at length, he spoke, "Never thought I'd see a place like this. Like a dream. Somehow all the faces I kent recognize seem familiar. Issaquena. They're wearin' feathers en flyin' on top a mountain, past some field a bones where you kent see the difference tween people. En I ken fly too. Yes, I ken fly. I ken fly wit them, to the top a the mountain, jes past that field a bones." Then he collapsed to the ground. That night a few trusties interred Mongoose's body in the swollen tomb behind the chapel.

But Flood's Christian lesson was not yet finished. There was still purgatory. Every gunman was locked in his cage that Sunday evening, after they were fed their supper, just like every other Sunday. Everyone was surprised they were allowed to eat, but no one noticed the secret smiles of their servers, "Eat up!" the guards ordered with the same, clumsy monophonic voice of any white man telling you what to do. When they were locked inside their cages with a rusty cla-thunk, Fulton noted with fear the giggling guffaws from outside, laughs that would later signify the end of a period which Fulton would always remember like a profound scar slicing across the gyric history of a tree.

It started about half an hour later. That is when Moondog was no longer surprised he had been simply returned to cage seven, as a gunman. The Sergeants, Drivers, and even the trusties crowded around the tiny windows (cursing their small dimensions). The gunmen did not know what they had eaten, nor what it was going to do to them, but they knew they would be terribly ill when, like clockwork or curse, each gunman in each cage felt his innards knot and press against the base of his spine. Some wretched, others spewed their shit like upside down geysers, and within an hour, every floor of every cage was completely sunken beneath the gurgling, swelling, shin-deep swerswamp of every possible putrid substance that a human body could expel. They spent the next twelve hours wretching and shitting from their bunks, into the swamp or onto each other.

By the next afternoon the gunmen collapsed from dehydration and exhaustion, sucking air like fish out of water. Though the frequency slowed, they continued wretching and shitting through the next night, submerging those who already lay below, dead in the swamp.

They prayed they would be liberated the next day. They were certain they had suffered their sins and the sins of others several times over, and all they asked for was air, water, and some bread to calm their turbulent stomachs. But they did not receive anything the next day. No one was even nearby to hear them beg. They were locked in their cages, isolated from the world. And though their illness abated, three days later their skin was split and bleeding from dehydration, and no one could even produce enough moisture to swallow and cool his burning throat. Those who were alive watched with glazed eyes as the gunmen around them slipped into a silent, oblivious world.

Fulton, Moondog, and Cuttino conserved their energy by remaining still, as if hibernating. They kept their eyes closed and wished they could banish their sight all together. Or have it banished, like Mongoose. Like the others who remained alive, they survived by eating their hair and nails, but nothing could quench the inner desiccation that choked them. They began to believe that Flood was going to leave them locked in their cages until they were all washed away and dead. Then he would repopulate Parchman with another thousand negroes. Start again. They were furious and desperate, but none possessed the strength to lift a finger against his fate.

Four days later the cages were opened, and the remaining gunmen were instructed to clear the bodies to Front Camp for cremation. The guards threw bread into the cages for the gunmen to eat and sprayed them with water to drink, while also hosing the cages. But their ring-arounds could never be cleaned. Not even after they were scrubbed for hours. They remained stained with the death and filth that had saturated the last week of their lives, and the gunmen would live with that death until they shed their ring-arounds for new ones, like skin, with the new year.

It was a Sunday when they carted the bodies to Front Camp, and Kibel had prepared a sermon on the merits of purgatory. But as he watched the seemingly limitless bodies pile towards the sky, the fervor of his words turned cold and empty in his throat. Four-hundred-twenty-eight. They erupted into apocalyptic flames, and the living gunmen knelt to their knees to receive the words of a loving but vengeful god. Kibel looked across them, a field of black skeletons with sunken souls. None of the words of his God seemed worthy of utterance, so he descended from his podium and wandered to his home.

That night, the silent fields were awakened by the Gregorian howling of a pack of wolves. The sonorous, doleful wails traveled the night like a breeze blowing across damp hills. Whispy and resonant. No one could sleep, not Duke Judson, III, not the Drivers, the Sergeants, the trusties, or Flood. No one could sleep that night except the dead.

And far above, the falcon still circled. It surveyed the charred bones in Front Camp and the endless Parchman fields beyond, and in front of the fields the narrow forest of Oak that separated Parchman from the remainder of Mississippi. The autumn forest was jagged and spiked sharp, and it opened in the middle to the hilled clearing of Front Camp, across which was strewn an arid field of endless bones.

Three

LIFE'S ONLY PROMISE

The Sound of Furrowed Earth

"That for which we find words is something
already dead in our hearts. There is always
a kind of contempt in the act of speaking."

The Twilight of the Idols

" - the rest is silence."

Hamlet

The funeral flames fluttered like the sleep of unfulfilled dreams. After they raged into the sky in a tower of melancholy, they returned to the earth and glowed with the emptied serenity of life's final breath. The sound of forgiveness. Fulton shrouded himself in that sound, like meter from the poetry which unfolds and dissolves the world and then recoils into silence for the duration of the time in between. And though he could no longer hear it, he knew the cacophony of the fire's sorrow could be heard by the thousand other ears of the living and the dead. He understood that within that sound the earth remained unforgiven, and the dolorous poetry of wandering ghosts would forever resonate within the watery bellies of reclining dragons.

***

He had forgotten how loudly Moondog snored, almost like raging fire. But he was glad Moondog was with him again. A sloppy colored named Shaky Roach was appointed to take his place as trusty. He was not as large as Moondog, but much more likely to tear open a man for shaky reasons. Shaky was always looking at the world from over his shoulder, never turning to look forward, so at times he appeared to be riding or walking backwards. His cheeks twitched like horse skin flicking away flies.

Though he was happy Moondog was with him in his cage, the agony of the previous week would never fade from Fulton's mind. It would be weeks before he and the other escapees could sleep on their backs again, and even then their backs wore permanent welts, like rivers or snakes, from the lashes they had endured. And then there was the purgatory. Fulton feared that on some future night he would awaken from a nightmare of that week so vivid that he would wretch his intestines into the world again. Perhaps that was why they were returned to their cages. Living was their punishment.

Fulton was also surprised that Flood did not order any new procedures or precautions to circumvent future escapes. Things were just about the same as they were before, except of course for the additional ten years added to his and Moondog's sentences (fifteen for Cuttino and Stromyle, though Stromyle did not have to serve his since he died in Flood's purgatory). Three years for the escape and seven years for the shackshooters. Fulton contemplated the numbers, "Seven years for outright murder, en ten years for standing next to a colored who committed murder."

Moondog could not swallow the disparity, "I still wudn't used to my first sentence. Now ten more years atop that? Goddamn! Ten more years atop that!"

As for the murdered shackshooters, no one other than the gunmen who killed them and the Drivers who found them ever saw their bodies. They just disappeared. And no one ever spoke of them either. This erasure offered Fulton a kind of pleasure, for coloreds were not the only ones who could disappear from the earth without a trace.

The winter of 1907 passed and the spring of 1908 arrived without consequence or grumbling from the pen of Parchman's history. The ground was tilled, the seeds were planted, and the stalks opened to the world. Soon again, the gunmen stood at the footsteps of fields of cotton. Fulton often wondered whether cotton would be cotton if it were black. Would a negro then be white? They would have the white negro picking their midnight gold to support their black economy. Fulton could run a garment store. *Buy your own home grown American black cotton trousers. Best in the world. Hand-picked by the great American negro, born to harvest black cotton for a thousand years.*

Though the winter had been uneventful, beginning that spring and for the next few years, several more events occurred which the gunmen would never forget. These events blew the first winds of change through Parchman, bringing a sense of movement to its otherwise, thick, hanging air. The winds unfolded Parchman into its complex and diverse potential. Some of these events did not hurt the gunmen, while others sent them tumbling deeper into the dank dungeons of their virtual enslavement.

The next week, as if by special order and arrangement, Long Chain Charlie arrived with an extra-large shipment for Parchman. Flood had threatened Parchman's profit power by administering such a deadly punishment the previous year, but the logic of his decision seemed appropriate for the long run. So a mass of new coloreds rolled in, just in time for the next cotton season.

Long Chain Charlie's massive delivery became the next event after Flood's purgatory that would imprint itself in Fulton's memory, for of the three-hundred and two negroes unloaded from Long Chain's caravan that Sunday, Fulton recognized one of them as the blues man from Naga's Juke Joint. Fulton pointed him out to Moondog, and Moondog smiled, "That sho is the guitar man from Banks. Kent keep the negroes away. Wonder what he did to end up here?"

"Probably jes set in the same place for too long," Fulton responded.

Cuttino asked a question with his face, and Fulton and Moondog explained to him where and when they had seen the Guitar Man and what kind of guitar he played, "It aint like nuthin' you ever heard. The way he play, it'll take hold you en won't let go."

"What's his name?"

"Don't know."

Fulton and Moondog kept their eyes on the Guitar Man as he and the others were lined up in front of the Administration Building to become gunmen. Many of the current gunmen gathered around the new convicts and jeered and cheered their arrival, shouting "Welcome to hell," or "Today's the first day a the resta your afterlife." The soon-to-be-gunmen looked like frightened children staring into a dark room. *You, Willy the Negro. You get the pussbloody shitcrusty mattress a one Timmy the BeatenDead who formerly slept there. Number two-eighteen. Next. Walk in a negro, walk out a gunman, en let's see how long you ken last.*

When the Guitar Man received his ring-arounds, he turned to face Fulton and Moondog, who were standing in front of him like boys awaiting their father at the train station. He was their first and only link to the past to arrive in Parchman. He was a man with whom they had shared an evening before they stepped foot on Long Chain's caravan to hell. As much as Mongoose and Stromyle and Cuttino had helped them to survive the past few years, Fulton and Moondog shared no prior history with any of them. They could not talk of a place or a time, a sound, or a smell, which they had shared before Parchman.

They shared no anterior relationship that rooted at least some portion of their selves, no matter how distant or small, to some other place other than Parchman. And Fulton and Moondog could not gesture to their common memories because what they shared were the former lives that tormented them in Parchman. But the Guitar Man was not home or family, so they stood in front of him like he was a savior. And even though their memory of him was brief, it was a moment that their imagination could embrace to sow a fresh history, beyond the place where memory was suffocated by Parchman's creepers of sorrow.

The Guitar Man looked around himself as if he were not concerned that he did not know where to go. He looked at Fulton and Moondog and then led himself to the steps of the post office where he sat. No one knew at that moment that the Guitar Man would become the most popular and beloved of any gunman Parchman ever caged. So there he sat, alone, observing this new place. Its rhythms and moods. He listened to the walls and leaves and dirt and smells around him for what they would say. When the time arrived he would channel those voices into a song.

Fulton, Moondog, and Cuttino approached him. His eyes were closed as he inhaled Parchman. As if sensing that they were not going to depart, the Guitar Man opened his eyes and stared at them like an angry father awakened from his nap. Fulton stuttered as he spoke, "'Scuse us... we was just watchin' you, en you look familiar." The Guitar Man curled his brow, as if to say *don't we all*, and Fulton continued, "Have you ever played guitar in a place call Nagas in a town called Banks?"

The Guitar Man's stern eyes turned into a smile and he nodded, "You boys been to Nagas? Don't look like the type. Musta been a long time ago 'cause I ain't strummed there since nineteen hunred en five."

"It was a long time ago," Fulton agreed, "longer than that. We was just there one night, on our way to Hernando to work the railroad."

An air of familiarity filled the space between them. Fulton, Moondog, and even Cuttino felt like they had known the Guitar Man forever. There was something comforting in the sound of his voice, the way it wrapped itself around them and eased their aches. "We didn't get your name that night," Moondog continued, "nobody knew."

"Name's B.B. Washington. Nobody knows what the B.B. stands for. Not even me. But it's what comes before Washington. Bellie used to joke it stood for Black en Blue, 'cause Black is what I am en Blue is what I sing."

"Bellie your girl?" Fulton asked.

"She was. 'Til she ran off wit some milkmaid negro boy. I chased em for fourteen months before I finally tracked em down in Chickasaw County. I jes wanted to know why she stole away after we shared our lives for twenty years. I jes wanted to know why she woke up one day en took her heart from me en gave it to some boy half my age. But she wouldn't say a word, so I went crazy en told myself if I kent have her, nobody ken. I challenged that boy to a duel, knowin' he was too young to refuse, en I shot em dead before he could unholster hisself. I'll never forget that look in her eyes when she was watchin' his life bleed away from him. Those eyes told me what she couldn't put in words, they told me that she left me for him 'cause he was the boy I could never give her.

"Then they 'rested me for murder, en I ended up here three weeks later . . . damn, damn Parchman Farm."

B.B.'s last words shook Fulton. Not only was there this other world outside Parchman, but it was aware of it and spoke of it. Parchman possessed a certain abominable presence within Mississippi's colored consciousness; it was a place in a place, and he was a person in that place. And when Fulton discovered that B.B.

had been allocated to cage seven, he believed that B.B. had arrived for a specific purpose, and perhaps that purpose could save him.

B.B. slept six bunks in front of Fulton and three bunks to the left of Moondog. He was older than Fulton, but not as old as LaRue. Each morning Cuttino joined the three of them for breakfast and they lined up in the same work gang to thin the rising stalks, so they could grow tall and strong. They spent the other days with their cotton sacks over their backs, filling them with the kudzu, ivy, crab grass, monkey grass, and dandelions that pullulated even faster than the cotton. They ripped the weeds from the fields and then tilled them into the rows to enrich the buckshot.

For the most part B.B. worked in silence. He did not participate in the work songs; he chose to listen and absorb. However, sometimes he joined the others in imagining their lives after Parchman, or on bad days, imagining their deaths so that they could be released from the burden of surviving. Death was easy to imagine. Simple and glorious. Life took more work.

When dreaming of life, they all dreamed of freedom. Moondog dreamed of his Juke Joint. "Moonshine en dancin'. I'm standin' behind a forty-foot redwood bar wit an army a shine behind me. You ken taste my freedom in every drink I serve, and wit the money I make I ken buy a proper grave for Neshoba."

Cuttino spun his hopes around a general store, "In a town where nobody minds shoppin' from a colored, en where my boys ken go to school so they never gotta stock shelves like me. Then me en my wife grow old tellin' our grandchildren how life was when coloreds wasn't free."

Fulton dreamed of a sailboat. "White on the blue sea. Sailin' wit my Simbi en my Sweetest Queen to the kings who rule the four corners a the world. We're all drinkin' coconut milk en eatin' spiced delights. En each night we get to lay under the stars en think about the creatures lookin' down on us while we fall asleep."

B.B. dreamed of his next song. "In Chicago, not Memphis 'cause it's too close to Mississippi, in a four story Joint called B.B.'s where I rule the winds wit my guitar en my song. Black tuxedos en fat cigars. You ken see the sounds in the air, but you kent know how they gonna move you. You might lose your breath. Short skirts hoppin' and shiny shoes cloppin' to my Big Band. Big Band Washington. Chicago's King a the Blues."

After a few weeks, B.B. began to hum himself to sleep each night in the cage. No one minded because he hummed them to sleep as well. Cage seven slept better than any other cage in Parchman. The soothing cadence of his melodies calmed their harried minds and melted their aches like candles. Even the shackshooters stood silent, to listen. And once B.B. started humming, most of the gunmen started to dream again. Vivid dreams bleeding with the colors and sounds of other lives.

One dream repeated itself in Fulton's sleep. A dream of an ancient battlefield teeming with glistening warriors stretching to the ends of the horizon. They aligned to face each other, brothers and cousins and uncles on opposing sides with swords and spears and arrows drawn for blood. Fulton is the leader of one of the forces, and without knowing why, he feels compelled to enter a battle he cannot win. The tension oppresses the air, and then God like a little black boy dressed in a tattered loincloth appears inbetween them and begins to dance. He dances a supple, lyric dance without touching the ground. His limbs and eyes move like snakes, or like gypsy smoke. When the Black Boy God finishes his dance, his smiling eyes cast a final glance at the armies around him. And then with a fury he smashes one foot to the earth causing it to split open. He disappears into the widening rupture, and with the earth crumbling into empty space, the armies roar into warfare for the rights to whatever remains. With his sword trembling for blood, Fulton leads his army into its violent, delirious dance.

Then one day B.B. Washington sang. As if he had spent several weeks ingesting his new world, he opened his belly in the middle of the field in the middle of a work song, and everyone stopped to listen. It was not the words he sang which moved them, but the resonating volume with which his voice reverberated in their bones. He sang with the lungs of a hundred men, and everyone in his presence could only turn to listen. Sergeant Judson, III, James Willard, Jimmy Seyd, Gerrit Faulk, and Shaky Roach did not notice that no one was working because they were themselves entranced by the lyrical booming that human lungs could not contain ("It ain't from my lungs," B.B. would say with his hands on his healthy belly, "it's the furrows in my guts. 'Cause everything I've lived is there."). B.B. did not look up from his singing, but he knew that everyone had stopped to listen. Standing only a few feet from him, Fulton felt he might fall from the voice. He had never heard the ocean, but he knew it must reside in B.B.'s lungs -- furious and profound.

The guards returned the gunmen to work, but everyone continued to listen to the refrains of B.B.'s aural soliloquy. Soon, they could not even hear individual words, but only the sentences when they were finished, like trying to see a painting from its individual strokes. Some tried to hum with him, but most simply listened. B.B.'s face remained earthward. Duke Judson, III did not know how or what to think of B.B.'s song, but once he had torn himself from it, he understood that nothing would get done as long as B.B. was in his field singing. And yet, he wanted to hear more.

A week later, just before the fields were submerged in oceans of cotton and the harvest was to begin, Duke Judson, III approached Flood with a plan for B.B. Washington. Flood was already curious about B.B., so he was ready to listen. "No one can get any work done because they get so caught up listening to him, asking him for songs, and standing around like children wanting candy when he stops."

Duke Judson, III told Flood he had never heard anything like B.B.'s voice. Perhaps they could remove him from the field and task him with landscaping Flood's gardens. Judson did not have to argue long to convince Flood to accept his plan. Flood decided that B.B. would spend his day landscaping and brickmolding in Front Camp, and then he would spend his evenings singing to the Sergeants, Drivers, trusties, and Flood. Sergeant Judson was pleased, "I've heard if you put a guitar in his hand, he can play for days."

Flood turned pensive and responded, "But we can't just up and treat this negro better than the rest. That will sting, and that stinging means trouble. We'll have to legitimate his movement somehow."

Sergeant Judson looked afraid, but remained silent. Flood continued, "Nevertheless, I look forward to hearing this boy sing and play, and if he isn't what you say he is, then he's back in the fields."

Sergeant Judson left Flood's office satisfied, though Flood's sense of legitimization troubled him. Meanwhile, Flood was contemplating a plan that would facilitate B.B.'s transformation, a plan that positioned his own compassion as the only reason B.B. could remain in Parchman under more benign circumstances.

A week later Willard and Seyd told B.B. that he had missed his quota by fifty pounds three days in a row and would have to be punished. B.B. was incredulous, but helpless. Sergeant Judson threw him to the ground, and his Drivers lashed him a few times. Fulton and the other gunmen watched in terror. After six lashes, Sergeant Judson, III sent B.B. hobbling to the infirmary. Fulton watched as if his savior had been desecrated. A foul, acerbic bile rose into his mouth. It tasted like madness.

That night, B.B. lay in the infirmary on his stomach. The ruptures in his back burned like fire needles. Later, four shadows entered the room, and before he could turn to see them, they beat his legs with canes. The shadows left as silently as they arrived, leaving B.B. writhing with sorrow that he had ever loved at all.

Flood visited B.B. in the infirmary the next day and apologized on behalf of the attackers. B.B. moaned with the pain of his swollen shins. "My men are trained not to lose control," Flood said, "but sometimes, for whatever reason, they descend into fits of rage." B.B. responded with moans. Flood continued, "I feel bad, and I don't think it's right what's happened to you. So I'd like to make up for the incident. I'd like to take you out of the fields and let you come to Front Camp instead. After you heal of course. You can manage my garden for me instead of breaking your back picking cotton. What do you think of that?"

B.B. was not averse to Flood's idea, but he tensed his brow as he considered the negative implications of disassociation from the other gunmen. Like this song he once sang. A line somewhere about a snake that was killed by his younger brothers after he shed his first skin and they no longer recognized him.

"I also hear that you like to sing," Flood continued, "and that you can strum a guitar better than the best. How would you feel if I told you I would get you a guitar, and every night you could sing and strum for us right here in Front Camp."

"I guess I'd like to sing en play my guitar. I suppose it'd be nice to do that from time to time."

"Well then, I'll get you a guitar, and each night when your work is done, you can eat dinner in my kitchen with my servants, and then you can play and sing. If you'd like to, of course."

B.B. considered Flood's offer. As he saw it, he would be able to sing, and he would not have to die picking cotton. But one thing continued to trouble him, "let me play for the gunmen too. Not jes you en your guards. One night a week. Maybe Saturday nights. It'll give them somethin' to look forwad to, en they can relax en pick better cotton for it."

Flood clicked his teeth, wondering whether B.B. understood the desires that orchestrated the last few days, but ultimately chose to submit, "Very well. Saturday nights. Five nights for us, one night for them. I believe that's reasonable." Flood patted B.B. on the shoulder, and then departed, "Again, I'm sorry about your legs." B.B. turned to his other side to sleep.

Two weeks later B.B. was back in his cage, returning to a hero's welcome. "The world turned stale while you were gone," Fulton told B. B. as he helped him to his bunk. But B. B.'s return wasn't quite what the other gunmen were expecting. While B. B. slept and ate breakfast with his cagemates, as soon as the workday began, Gerrit or Shaky led him to Front Camp where he received a hoe, a shovel, and a spade to transform the front of Flood's mansion into a rolling landscape containing every flower that found habitat in the South. From canas to azaleas to dogwoods to tulips and lilies, Flood brought the plants to Parchman, and B.B. planted them into the rich, undulating earth that he had shaped like the heavy assonance of his guitar chords. Then, after a few weeks, Sergeant Judson allowed B.B. to walk to Front Camp unescorted, "See ya tonight," he would say at breakfast. B.B. felt like all the guards wanted him to like them, perhaps so to mollify the additional hatred the other gunmen felt for them since they had appropriated their hero. As for the gunmen, they would have fatally resented any other gunmen offered B.B.'s privileged segregation, but B.B. resided beyond the normal categories in which coloreds and whites resided. B.B.'s liminality, like a type of anonymity, preserved him; he was not this, and he was not that.

The only complaint from the guards was that B.B. would not repeat the songs they most enjoyed. He did not deny them from disdain, but songs arrived to him like a goddess on an auspicious night, and he could not be expected to reproduce that moment any more than a cotton stalk could be expected to produce identical bolls of cotton. There were notes and riffs that anchored his music, but most of what flowed from his fingers and lungs passed through him in the singular moment that he produced the sound and then vanished. B.B. played from the emotions yoked to the life he knew, immersed in the sounds of the earth around him that spoke in the whispers of rustling leaves. Those whispers were his music. His audience was of no consequence.

The trusties, Drivers, Sergeants, and Flood gathered each night after their dinner and sat on the other side of a redglowing fire. They watched the silhouettes of B.B. and his guitar, and they swam from their liquor into the pleasure of his musical shore. Soon enough, no one remained conscious to hear his music, though his melody swam into their dreams. When he was ready to sleep, B.B. walked himself to his cage where the shackshooters opened the door for him. He always left the guitar on his chair, where it sat until the next evening on the solitary side of the dying fire. A thick, chestnut guitar with young metal strings. Curved like the delicacy of a mother's hip, and rounded by the ancient impulse of its generative instinct. It was not his, because like the earth around him, it breathed a spirit that could never be possessed.

On Saturdays he played for the gunmen. More guards than were needed circled the gathering to prevent escape. Fulton, Moondog, and Cuttino sat in the front of the other side of the fire. Listening. He sounded like gypsy smoke to Fulton, moving with the simple sensations of a tobacco trance, born from the sarcophagus of a lover's memory. Spiritual, plangent, and emollient. B.B. would tell Fulton "The blues is philosophy, 'cause it enlightens the general through the explanation a the specific, en one thing the blues teaches you is that nuthin' ain't good or bad 'til you think 'bout it. Nuthin's blue 'til the blues sing it." All Fulton knew was that he felt compelled by B.B.'s guitar because he had lost his story; the attraction was mythological, and it spoke to him from a sourceless source. One day, B.B.'s music would compel him to chant the history of the world, like a poem.

LIFE'S ONLY PROMISE

Life's Only Promise

Now that Mississippi was where he wanted it to be, when his term as Governor ended J.K. Vardaman moved on to the United States Senate where he planned on continuing his crusade for the Southern way of life. He left Mississippi in the capable hands of his allies and entertained grandiose visions of crafting legislation that would ensure his grandchildren could grow up in a safe and proper Mississippi. Unfortunately for Vardaman, he didn't have much success in the Senate, and once he returned to Mississippi he was already forgotten, even though everything he had started remained just as he left it. Vardaman spent his last days fishing and smoking and when he finally died he was buried at the Lakewood Memorial Cemetery in Jackson.

But back when Vardaman first left, his opponents sensed a momentary instability in his racist superstructure, and new grassroots efforts emerged to enlighten Mississippians on notions of tolerance and equality. One such effort focused on educating Southern convicts on their basic human rights. So on a Sunday afternoon a crop duster flew over Parchman's Front Camp and dropped thousands of fliers which explained the "Rights of the Prisoner," and before Flood or any of the guards could shoot the plane from the sky or gather even a dozen of the fliers, the few gunmen who could read spread the word that they did not have to be in Parchman for twenty years just because they could not afford the court costs of a bogus indictment, and that with the help of an attorney and the Governor they could be pardoned from their sentence.

And fortunately for the gunmen, Vardaman's successor, Governor Edmund Noel, was a more moderate politician seeking to harmonize Mississippi's citizens and protect everyone's rights to private property, due process, and public education. Coloreds were still colored, and whites were still whites, but the differences could be maintained with civility. Nevertheless, though he was more moderate, Governor Noel had no intentions of disrupting Parchman and its tremendous profitability, but he did intend to placate some of the liberal concerns over its brutality so he could divert attention towards other issues, such as Mississippi's need for more roads.

Encouraged by these changes, liberal litigators journeyed to Parchman to help the gunmen gain their freedom, but they encountered an impediment, and that impediment was Flood's appropriation of the pardon process such that it became nearly impossible for a gunman to receive a pardon.

First, a gunman had to approach Flood and receive his support for commencing the pardon process. Second, Flood appointed the attorney who would plea the inmate's pardon before the Yazoo County appellant court. The appellant court then determined whether the case should be presented to the Governor, and then Governor Noel decided whether or nor to pardon the inmate. But the attorneys

Flood appointed and the appellant court to which they pled their cases were all allies of Flood and his South. A few gunmen were allowed to make it to the Governor, just enough to convince skeptics that the system was functioning, but most cases were dismissed only days after they had begun, and illiteracy did not help the gunmen understand the process and the contrivance of their failure. Separately, Flood re-motivated the diligence of his trusties by promising them full pardons for shooting dead any gunman who attempted to escape. Ten trusties were pardoned that year, to only three gunmen.

Like everyone else, Fulton, Moondog, Cuttino, and B.B. submitted their names for a pardon hearing with Flood. Three weeks later their names came to the top of the list. Flood conducted the hearings on Sundays in Front Camp after Kibel's service. He ascended the makeshift pulpit and called the names of the day's hearings. The named gunmen approached and awaited their turn. That day, Fulton, Moondog, Cuttino, and B.B. approached together and waited beneath Flood until he raised his face from his papers and spoke, "You four are applying for four pardons, correct?"

"Yessuh, Superintendent Flood, suh, we want to present our case together on account we been here... twelve years together, en B.B. three." Fulton spoke his sentence as if he were watching himself speak. Twelve years? Could that be correct? The word twelve did not sound like what it meant. It meant more than a third of his previous life. It meant his daughter had spent almost half her life without him. But it did not sound like any of those things. It sounded like some abstract sound unable to contain what it meant. So when he spoke, Fulton did not exactly comprehend what he was saying. He tried to think of some other word that meant twelve more than twelve did, but there was none.

"You, B.B., have not been here as long as the others and have more than half of your sentence remaining. What is the basis of your request?"

"I'm old, suh, en I been good while I been here. Now I want to find a home en die an honorable man. I only shot that boy for stealin my life from me. He coulda stole all my money, my clothes, en even my gitar. But not my life."

"No, B.B. There is no reason that justifies the killing of another man. No matter what he stole from you. You should have let it go. You should have found another life, if that's what she was to you. But you should not have killed that boy, so you will continue to serve your sentence."

B.B. stood dumbfounded for a few moments as the others lowered their faces. He held his guitar at his side and swallowed the air around him like a sedative. Then he turned and walked to the front of the chapel, where he sat on the ground and dug his nails into the dirt.

The other three remained, standing like statues in a garden awaiting Flood's adjudication. In short order, Flood determined that the three of them had no right to a pardon on account of their attempted escape, "I will personally ensure that the three of you suffer the remaining thirteen years of your sentences." Flood rustled through his papers, dismissed Fulton and the others, and called the next gunmen before him. But Fulton was not prepared to move. So Flood looked at them sternly, "That's it boys," he scowled, "your request is denied."

The words fell against their skin like jagged hail. They did not understand what had happened. Their hopes rose and fell like waves. Fulton offered a "But suh," but Flood had the Drivers remove them from his presence, leaving Fulton bereft of hope, bereft of future, sitting on his hands on the chapel steps next to B.B. contemplating twelve. The word circled around his head, like smoke, and he could not understand how it meant what it meant. It meant that he was forty-five. Forty-five. It meant Simbi was twenty-nine. She was almost the same age he was when he left her! The passage of time colluded in Fulton's mind. Was this his life? Could he be nothing more? Would he die here? Fulton no longer knew who he was. He no longer even knew what he looked like. He knew he must be gray, that he hunched and hobbled on his six toes, and that he ate with only a fraction of his original teeth, but he had not seen himself in over a decade (since he last saw his reflection in the marsh). He realized that twelve years had passed without his life moving any closer to where he wanted it to be. Time gone like burnt wood. And with over a decade of enduring Parchman's brutal assault on his body and mind, he was that much closer to his finality. Who was left that was Fulton? Who would be left after the remaining 13 years of his sentence? The absence swelled in his throat.

Empty of himself, that night Fulton returned to inhaling opium and paint thinner. He had quit after LaRue died, from reborn fears that the fumes would erase his memories, but now he no longer cared to remember. What use was memory if it inspired hope for what remained thirteen years away? What use was memory if he did not know whom it was remembering? He inhaled the thinner like a smoke screen over his consciousness. But residues always remained. Smells from the past triggered memories of the ghost that he was, which in turn haunted the ghost he had become. All around him, the shadows of his history returned with a clamoring. Fulton was left swirling in the void between his selves, empty of the awareness of who he was. Unpardoned.

Moondog and Cuttino saw LaRue's fate overwhelming Fulton. He began to fail his quota and sometimes smiled obliviously during his lashes. His friends tried to help him, but they could not penetrate his self-disjunction. He continued to sit with them on Sundays, but he no longer played dice. And he no longer played softball. He sat and stared at the directionlessness of his life. Occasionally he spoke, in a voice fit for delivering a speech, to whatever it was he was seeing at the time, "I couldn't name her. Her mama had to. But she died before she could. So them women named her after her grandmama. She died before she could name her.

Died before she was done comin' out," and he would continue with alternating crescendo and whisper, "but I couldn't name her. I couldn't even git her out. She was suffocatin'. Mama dead. Eyes just rolled up in her head. Blood everywhere. Mama dead. Baby stopped cryin' 'cause she was dyin'. Goddamit they yelled, git a knife they yelled. Cut her open en free that baby they yelled. Put her in my arms, en she could breathe. Heavy baby. But I couldn't name her. I couldn't decide what to call her the resta her life. She a heavy baby."

But though Fulton neared descent into the realm of broken tongues in the corner of his cage, the rain saved him. He needed time alone, and though he could not have it, the opium and the paint thinner helped fabricate a surrogate solitude once the rain came and the gunmen were locked in their cages for days. Storm clouds rumbled across the sky as if to wash all living creatures into the fabric of the earth, so that their decay might fertilize the next cycle of time. That was life's only promise. Lightning ruptured the gothic sky, water fell in rivers to the ground, and the agitated winds wailed to be released. Fulton could feel the rain melt away the calluses that had thickened over his mind. Everyone sat hour after hour listening to the heavens thumping against the cage. They gathered, switched bunks, and talked, but Fulton remained on his back, on his bunk, with his unblinking eyes, wide but blind. His thoughts recalled the rain on the railroad, the thumping against his tent. He recalled his dream. Then, for the first time since he received it, Fulton looked at the necklace around his neck. The ebb and tide of the universe resided within it, but all unfolding into itself, thus without consequence. He was correct then, to let himself slip away into the shadows of life. It was the only course. The dragon told him. This life is purposeless and nothing ever happens except its coming and going. But then why would the dragon have sought his dreams? Because dreams deny his universe, and that denial could redeem him. Because dreams utter a sound that cannot be silenced (since they are sung without breathing), and because it is too easy to remain obsessed with self-sorrow. That is what he told Simbi the night he left her. Realizing this, Fulton decided to return and listen to the others talking around him.

"Field's sure gonna be flooded," B.B. said.

"It's worse than the spring floods," Cuttino followed, "gonna ruin the resta that cotton."

"Rain like this gonna bust that levee at Mounds Landin'," Moondog continued, "or maybe even Pinnekoke, then we all be washed away."

"That won't be so bad," B.B. said, "we'll either be drowned or washed to freedom, maybe all the way to the Gulf."

Fulton rubbed his eyes and spoke, "That's the wrong way." He pointed to the north, "That's the way I wanna go. To my home." Home sounded like twelve when he said it. "That current ken swim me to my home. I know I'm there, waitin' for my return. En I will return." The others watched Fulton's return and smiled. They had missed him.

"Fulton's right," Cuttino chimed, "ken you imagine it? Finally returnin' after all these years, after holdin' that vision in your head day en night year after year en replayin' that reunion over en over in your mind."

"Then imagine no home to return to at all," B.B. said as he rolled his neck, "imagine your whole life is wanderin' 'til you die."

"You gotta home," Fulton responded, "we gonna leave here together, en you comin' home wit me en Moondog. My girl's gonna need a grandaddy."

They lay on their backs on their bunks in silence, listening to the rain. Its scent and sound suckled them, while the distant thunder reminded them of places beyond Parchman's consuming geography. The rain fell with abandon and released the scent of the earth's first moments. A scent that took them away from the present time of things. A time that reminded them who they truly were. Time alone.

LIFE'S ONLY PROMISE

Unfolding

Nothing else happened in 1908 except for the daily repetition of the previous day. A culture of routine. As quickly as gunmen died (from disease, heat stroke, fights, or shootings), new gunmen arrived each month. And as they baked and bled and broke and died, Parchman's gunmen all learned the secret of residing within a world emptied of human purpose.

Nothing happened again until the fall of 1909. It started one night as Superintendent Flood and B.B. Washington were dining on his back patio. Flood invited B.B. to dinner from time to time, out of curiosity to learn more about the life of a colored who was capable of such profound music. Flood was an ardent aesthetic, finding pleasure in the precision of Bach's concertos (which he played most nights on his rare gramophone while drinking his rare scotch) as well as in the reasoned brushstrokes of Raphael and Poisson. Flood descended from a family of plantation owners and often wished as a youth that a great painter would arrive to his mansion and capture the majesty of his family's flowing cotton fields. Flood tried himself to do so as a birthday gift to his mother, but he lacked the talents to transfer the inspiration in his eyes into the subtle movements of a brush. That was why he was so enamored with B.B., for B.B. seemed to paint his voice with the cotton empire around him.

But these mealtimes were not as pleasant for B.B. as they were for Flood. Not only was B.B. forced to secrecy, but also he had to undergo the awkwardness of watching other coloreds serve him. And on top of that, B.B. remained angry at Flood for not allowing him to pursue a pardon. As they dined, Flood tried to penetrate the mysteries he perceived in B.B.'s unique persona and its relationship to his music. But B.B. did not want to be probed and inspected. He did not want to explain his thoughts and inspirations to Flood, for he had never probed and inspected them himself. But he could not forgo the royal dinners Flood offered him (and Flood knew that) in place of the wretched sweet potatoes and greens he otherwise ate meal after meal, day after day. So he answered as best he could. Flood would ask, "Who taught you to play? Where do the chords and the words come from? Why would you shoot a man instead of taking him to a court of law to reconcile your disagreements?"

And B.B. would respond, "I taught myself . . . I don't know . . . I guess I thought a court a law couldn't reconcile that." The more Flood isolated and appropriated him, the more B.B. felt he had become stranded and alone. He lived in a penumbral solitude and resented the necessity of discourse with Flood. But never one to be obsessed with his own sorrow, one night B.B. decided to spend some of his political currency to secure some new privileges for the gunmen, right around the fall of 1909.

LIFE'S ONLY PROMISE

The Red House was his idea. Its shape and color and glory-be-to-god nights the gunmen spent in them, starting on a dewy spring evening in 1910, were all his idea. It was not as big as B.B. had imagined, because it had to remain smaller than the Superintendent's Mansion, but it was big enough for twenty rooms with twenty beds and a few couches in its dark foyer. The gunmen molded the bricks and built it that winter, not knowing what it was supposed to be. "Maybe it's a hotel," Cuttino joked, "so people ken come see how we live en die."

When B.B. had originally asked Flood for the Red House, he did not offer a lucid, cogent argument to justify it. Not a "it'll help curtail all the rapin'," or "it'll enhance the general happiness a the farm en therefore improve productivity." All he said was "Why not? It's our nature, ain't it? This would help us civilize it." Flood was not interested in providing comfort to negro convicts, and he certainly did not subscribe to B.B.'s logic, but he realized who was asking him and how much he had taken from him. He was compelled by his respect for him, and he assumed there would not be any real harm in the Red House. "O.K. You can have your house of visitation. They can build it this winter and receive guests once or twice a month. But the moment there's trouble I'm burning it down."

The gunmen built it and painted it red, and when it was ready to open, B.B. gathered the gunmen one Sunday evening in March, and he announced that, "According to Flood, this Red House makes Parchman Farm the first penitentiary in the history of prisons to allow conjugal visitation." The gunmen turned to each other in disbelief, and then they stared at B.B.'s sunrise smile. He began a song. *The Red House. The Tonk House. No longer stranger to the lovin' you knew. Behind the cattle barn. Before the fields. The Red House. The Tonk House. Come in en taste the lovin' you knew.*

The gunmen were allowed to wire their girls and wives, and in time they arrived each Sunday night on the Biloxi-Memphis local which stopped at Gordon Junction a few minutes before midnight. And each Sunday night, B.B. greeted them outside the Tonk House with his new song *The Midnight Rider*. It was the only song he ever sang more than once. Each gunman was allowed forty minutes. Those who were not wives found payment in smoke and drink. Cuttino and B.B. regularly enjoyed their forty minutes, but Fulton forbade both himself and Moondog from joining them until they used the new wire privileges to send a message to their families. So they wired to Anderson's post that they were alive in Parchman Farm and their families should head down 49 and visit them as soon as they harvest was done.

They sent several wires through the summer, but Anderson was still fighting the Government's postal requirements and continued to appropriate all postal communication that was intended for residents of his Land. Anderson would never allow the Government to insinuate itself into the governance of his ancestral territory. He owned the language that came to and left from his earth, as well as any discourse within it. So none of Fulton and Moondog's wires arrived to their families, and it was probably a blessing, for if Anderson had taken the time to receive and inspect the wires he would have evicted them.

By late summer, in the heat and anguish of the harvest (with corn this time as well), Moondog could not wait any longer, and he fled into the arms of an anonymous woman. Then Fulton was the only one, and the others teased him to submit. "Don't tell me you'd rather rub it," Cuttino would tease, "don't worry if you forgot, she'll show you how." And by October, when Fulton had not heard from his daughter, he finally crumbled and sought refuge in the embrace of a woman. Loneliness had overwhelmed him, and he needed to be held.

All that remained was to sniff some paint thinner to momentarily erase the memory of his Sweetest Queen. That done, he walked to the Tonk House. His friends smiled and shoved him, but Fulton remained focused like a man travelling to war. B.B. sat on the porch singing, and Cuttino led Fulton into the Tonk House to room eleven. They had arranged for a woman to wait within, and when they closed the door behind him he submitted to her bewitching odor, like the fragrance of blossoms unfolding their chalices to the sun.

Fulton descended onto the sweaty, crusty mattress with a woman whose name he did not know. He looked away from her eyes as he pressed his solitude against her hips, not making love, just feeling it. The woman struggled to breathe under his weight. She was aroused and frightened as he continued to press and press. She swooned, and he tightened as she called in siren whispers and raked his heaving back until the eruption conquered him and he crumbled atop her. Exhausted, he breathed deeply and curled into himself, eventually exhaling his contentment and then falling alseep into childhood dreams.

***

The profits from the harvest of 1909 surprised even Flood and Governor Noel. Meeting in Noel's office in Jackson, Flood reported the numbers, and Noel smiled and mused, "If people only understood how much can be made when you don't have to pay your labor. Classes will stratify themselves in all societies, so we may as well put people where they belong and profit from it. You know that Plato divided the people of his ideal society into classes, with a slave class that supported the rest. Gold, silver, and bronze I think. We are the Gold, Flood. They are the bronze." Flood recalled his classical studies and wondered why the connection had never occurred to him.

In only a few years, Parchman was exporting cotton to all over the country. Vardaman and Flood had erected an intricate network of contacts and shippers throughout the South, and through Parchman they were elevating Mississippi from the poorest to one of the richest states in the Reconstruction South (at least in terms of their coffers). Other states operated their own prison farms, from Florida to Georgia to Alabama, but none was as lean and precise as Parchman. Parchman was the model of convict leasing excellence.

But margins were being pressured by those convict farm copycats as well as by escalating Northern boycotts. So Noel and Flood had to commence a diversification of Parchman's products base to help secure their revenue stream. That winter, they would concentrate on a cannery, a slaughterhouse, and a cotton house. Foresight and adaptation. That is why they were great men.

But there was another pressure that would force them into an adaptation which they never envisioned possible. "Just one more thing Clinton," Governor Noel mumbled, "before you leave. Times are changing. Pressures from the North are growing again and may force us to populate Parchman with our own kind. To deflect the criticism. Take some of the wind out of their sails. No time soon. But the day may come. You know, sacrifice a little for the greater good. I'll talk to Long Chain and let you know." Flood was surprised and afraid. He knew that Vardaman would never bend the way Noel was, and Noel's malleability threatened to jeopardize his Mississippi.

But before any whites arrived in Parchman, something far more shocking happened. Shocking because no one, not even Flood, thought it could ever happen. Sunday, October, three minutes after three. B.B. had just stood to his feet after winning three rounds of dice in a row from Fulton, Moondog, and Cuttino, "Gotta stop now boys. Three's the world's lucky number, if I keep on I might roll snake eyes." Tiberius and two of his followers moved towards the chapel steps, and when no one was looking they led B.B. to the back wall of the cattle barn in front of the Tonk House and circled him like wolves. Not from spite, but from duty. B.B. had come to represent a dangerous imbalance in the order of things, crossing lines into a privileged world and disrupting the order of who he was and who he should be. He had denied his role, and ever since then, cows started eating each other, Tonk Women coupled like snakes, and the moon disappeared from a clear sky for hours. The sacrifice was for the order, to put everything back on its proper side of the world's straight line. So when they surrounded him, B.B. understood. He knew that Tiberius had traveled the underworld and been released from his flesh so that he could sense the disorder in things. At that moment, the sun was shining black light. B.B. opened his hands at his side.

Tiberius clawed his right hand and plunged into B.B.'s abdomen. He tore away a portion of sacrificial flesh, and the immolated blues man doubled over in agony. Then the two shamans fell on him with their teeth, tearing his shoulders and legs as Tiberius held his piece of B.B. over his head and drank the dripping blood, dousing him like rain. B.B. screamed and kicked, but his bones were too old, and those who happened by scurried away for fear of Tiberius' maleficence.

But Fulton and some of the guards heard the screams. Jumping from the chapel steps, Fulton sprinted to the cries and pounced on the attackers before anyone else had even turned the corner of the cattle barn. "Devils!" he yelled as he threw them from B.B.'s shredded body, his exposed, old bones glowing in the black sunlight. They were eating him like rotten wood. Their bloody mouths hissed as they recoiled, and Tiberius barked in accursed tongues at Fulton's interference. Fulton stood guard over B.B.'s body as Moondog, Cuttino, and several Drivers and trusties arrived with terror at what they saw. The guards held their rifles at Tiberius and his shamans but shuddered from his wide, white death stare.

"Animals!" one of the Drivers yelled as the other guards led the attackers to the clearing in front of Flood's Mansion. Fulton and Moondog carried B.B. to the infirmary while his attackers were stripped and thrown to the ground. Three Sergeants arrived with their whips and watched in disbelief as Fulton and Moondog supported B.B.'s dying moans. Everyone could see his old bones, exposed at the jaw, elbow, and ribs. White as those who imprisoned him.

Anger was thick in the air around the bloody faced captors. If Flood had been in Parchman, he would have whipped all three of them himself until they were dead, but he was with Noel in Tillatoba County recruiting cannery engineers. Fulton heard the first hissing crack from the infirmary and imagined their flesh opening to mourn. He wanted the Sergeants to whip them dead, and they would have, except that a moment later they saw something they never would have imagined seeing.

It was B.B. He heard the lashes begin, and as soon as his spinning mind settled, he broke himself from the infirmary table and ran with his remaining strength straight to the monsters who had almost killed him and threw himself in between them and the next lash. He received it in the neck, knocking him to the ground in exhaustion. Everyone stared, watching B.B.'s ruined carcass heave for breath. Only silence could behold the moment. B.B. raised his head, looked into the Sergeants' narrow eyes, and demanded, "Who are you to demand justice?" And then he collapsed. They carried him to the infirmary again, everyone wondering what the difference was between right and wrong.

Flood returned a week later, and when he was informed of the attack he boiled for blood, but his Sergeants told him how B.B. had forgiven his attackers. This time, Flood did not go to the infirmary to visit B.B., for he feared looking into eyes that would blame him for the unfolding of recent events. Flood knew that B.B. had never wanted to be the man he forced him to be, so he blamed himself for the attack. But he eventually cleansed his conscience by perceiving more fault in the dishonorable nature of negroes than in his own selfishness.

LIFE'S ONLY PROMISE

    A month after he entered the infirmary, B.B. emerged for the first time. Parchman had been without songs during his absence, and the silence was exhausting. But today, B.B. walked to his friends who were playing dice on the steps of the chapel. Across his arms, legs, and stomach, his injuries were covered by a purplish blueblack skin that stretched to cover the voids where his flesh once resided. His stomach remained grotesque, full on his right side but absent where the flesh was removed. B.B. held his ring-around shirt in his hand so everyone could see what he looked like and not waste time wondering. So they watched as he walked to his friends. When he arrived at their game he appeared like a child lost from his mother, but then he smiled and joked, "Bellie always told me to diet." Everyone laughed and Fulton helped him sit on the steps. He did not want to play dice, just to sit with them and listen. Those watching wondered when he would sing again.
    While B.B. spent the summer resting and recovering on the chapel steps, the other gunmen were deployed to the task of expanding the infrastructure of Parchman's new economy. Parchman would transcend cotton and become the center of the South's lumber, canned perishables, and meatpacking. Unfortunately for the gunmen, those whose hands would clothe, feed, and house the world were none of those who would participate in the rewards for doing so. The rewards were not conceived to distribute themselves beyond a few pairs of hands, hands that never tilled a field, picked a boll of cotton, or sweated a bead under the relentless furnace of the Mississppi sun. Not that the inequity occurred to the gunmen after the first few years of their lives, after they learned to expect little more from the world other than meager portions of food, clothing, and shelter unrelated in quality to their endless labor spent for the comfort and profit of others. They were well practiced in living through gestures that had no meaning. Wealth was not an entity they accumulated; wealth was having enough for each day. They were not the golden class.
    Parchman's cannery was completed in the spring of 1911, and the sawmill, slaughterhouse, smith house, and cotton house with cotton gins followed by 1915. Thus, by the harvest of 1916, not only did the gunmen have to pick the cotton, but also they had to gin and bale it for shipment. However, the gunmen did finally receive screens for their cage windows after a malaria outbreak killed one-hundred ninety-two gunmen in the summer of 1911. Trusties were appointed to oversee the operations of each new addition to Parchman's economy, and they in turn appointed those who would work under them. The new economy was refuge from the brutal fields, "You ken live ten years longer workin' in that cannery than in them fields," a gunman said. Some gunmen were appointed on the basis of prior skill, but most found themselves in the new economy by virtue of relationships and Tonk House favors to the trusties. Since Fulton, Moondog, and Cuttino had no prior skill and

were not interested in Tonk House favors, all three of them remained in the fields, planting and harvesting cotton, corn, okra, peas, and other greens as the market dictated.

But just as soon as the gunmen in Front Camp working for Parchman's less rigorous economy were enjoying the quality of their new lives, the day Flood feared arrived. None of the current gunmen ever imagined they would witness the day that they wore ring-arounds just like them. But they arrived one day with Long Chain Charlie, a new class of gunmen, in the summer of 1914. Only a handful. But they stood out like a negro at a Klan rally, like a rash on clear skin, or like a missing tooth in the front of your mouth. The gunmen stared at them when they walked through the front gate, and those new gunmen felt the weight of all those eyes on them.

White gunmen. Only a handful, but they were white and they were gunmen. Colored trusties pointed rifles in their faces and ordered them where to go and what to do. The other guards saw that the trusties had been waiting for this day all their lives, but as Flood instructed them, it was the new, if not temporary, nature of things. It was where History had led them, and now they were forced to live with it.

But whiteness was not without its benefits, even for a gunman. The handful of coloreds from Front Camp's industries were returned to the fields and replaced with the handful of white gunmen who had arrived. The colored gunmen cleared and cleaned cage eight for the white gunmen after the first harvest so that the white gunmen would not have to sleep and eat with them. Though they ordered and barked at them, most trusties dared not discipline a white gunman. The Drivers and Sergeants reserved that right, and in time, the whites replaced the colored trusties. Of course, the white gunmen did not play softball. But Kibel's God did not discriminate. White and colored gunmen knelt together each Sunday for his colorless service.

Even though they were separated from the coloreds and their lives were better, except during the harvest months when everyone was in the fields, the white gunmen wore a resentment on their faces that the other gunmen enjoyed. Two of them, in particular, were especially disenchanted with their fates. One was tall and fat with an angry beard and spurious eyes, while the other was tall and skinny with scars across his forehead and chin, like bookends. Since they were white and had less work to do, they had more time to brood over their time in Parchman, a brooding that fermented inside them and soured their composure. The larger had been a railroad worker and was sent to Parchman for killing two coloreds on the railroad. The thinner had not been doing much of anything, except occasionally raping a schoolgirl, until one day he had raped one too many and found himself in Parchman as well. Though neither had seen the other before they arrived, their angered and impatient temperaments drew them to each other as if they had been friends for years.

Each moment burrowed the pain of their indignity deeper and deeper into their minds. They were allocated to cage seven for the harvest, and their companioned displeasure curdled each day that they found themselves in the harvest fields, scowling at the sight of their bruised, bleeding, and pussed ankles and their boilingburned skin. *That's why whites ken never be slaves,* Fulton thought to himself, *'cause they'd burn to death.* And Gerrit feasted on them, kicking them to pick more and pick faster. They had been reduced to niggers, and they would not abide it.

So it was an issue of anger. Anger at the unraveling order of things. Anger that submitted to its self-serving transmutation into indignity. And indignity could not be denied, like an alligator that locates its prey and clamps its jaw across its neck. And so it was that on one particular day, the tall and fat and tall and thin white gunmen could no longer bear the barks and kicks of their trusty, Gerrit Faulk. The color of authority was on their side, and they knew that Gerrit's abuse reached only just beyond the limit of the vision of the nearest non-gunman white man. So when he had kicked them so hard on the back of the head that they were sure his nigger skin was rubbing off on them, when he had placed his rifle in their mouths one too many times and told them to work harder or he would blow off their faces, and when no other guard was in sight, the tall and skinny gunman threw himself into Gerrit's horse knocking him to the ground at the same moment that the other snatched his rifle and in a switchblade instant held it to his face. They stood over Gerrit with heaving disdain, "Open your mouth!" the tall and fat gunman said in slow, deliberate words. Gerrit turned his face away and closed his eyes as if to erase the universe. The tall and skinny gunman kicked him, "Open your fucking mouth!" The black gunmen gathered themselves around the scene and began to yell to Shaky and the Drivers for help.

"You fuckin' nigger! Open your goddamn mouth before I smash your skull!" Gerrit continued to turn his head back and forth away from the rifle's mouth, so the tall and fat gunman smashed his face anyway, opening a huge gash in his skull.

"No suh. No marstuh. Please suh. Please!"

The tall and fat gunman scowled at Gerrit and thrust the rifle into his mouth, gashing his lip and smashing his front teeth. Gerrit pleaded with him, begging in half-words for his life. But the tall fat gunman yelled down at him with a litany of hatred, "I'm gonna blow your head off you piece of shit nigger, I'm gonna blow you straight to nigger hell!" As the guards galloped towards them, only a few more words were left between the tall white gunman and his prey, "Now you remember, all you fuckin' niggers. Never forget what's what and who's who!" And then he ripped Parchman's precarious order with a gunblast that blew open Gerrit's head and splashed it against the faces of those who stood watching.

The Drivers and Sergeants arrived, but nothing much happened. The tall, fat white gunman had blasted Gerrit Faulk's face into a thousand pieces that settled to the ground and later melted through the stomachs of worms into the enriched buckshot which made cotton possible, and nothing much happened. Nothing much happened except that the tall white gunman and his tall skinny friend were made trusties. They were proud, strong, angry, and unstable, so they would make good trusties. The gunmen buried Gerrit behind the chapel, and Kibel later chided the remembrance of his spirit for his lack of discipline within the order of things. Like a stray dog. But the new white trusties did not escape his denouncement either. Kibel spoke against the decision to promote the murderers to trusties. He decried the miscarriage of justice and its impudent misapplication. Flood listened from his Mansion's third-story balcony and wondered why Parchman needed God's voice.

As Parchman's economy grew more complex, gunmen continued to arrive each month to support it, with another handful of white ones with each shipment. White gunmen filled the trusty population as well as the Front Camp economy, and a new order settled over Parchman, a stratification of kind and color, just like on the other side of the front gate. And just as Parchman seemed settled into its new rhythm and function, another surprise arrived just in time to support Parchman's growing population and infrastructure.

Cage thirteen was cleared for them and new uniforms with vertical black and white stripes were sewn. Up-an-downs. Most thought they were for the white gunmen, but they were not. The state legislature had expanded the penal code definitions of those who could be jailed and sent to state prison farms just in time to keep Parchman from wasting any additional cotton-picking or slaughterhouse labor on simple tasks like sewing a uniform or canning the vegetables. No need to waste fieldwork on less profitable infrastructure tasks. So they arrived with tasks awaiting them. The first female gunmen walked through the front gate with Long Chain Charlie in April, 1915. All colored. All terrified.

There were twenty-six of them, and they arrived in Long-Chain's one-hundred twenty-fifth shipment for a myriad of violent offenses. Everyone noticed them, standing in the middle of the line that stretched from the Administration Building like a flagellum. They walked in and then walked out in their up-and-downs, all allocated to cage thirteen. They drifted around Front Camp feeling the eyes press against them, nervous as if wandering through a dark forest from which death might spring for them at any moment. So they brandished deadly eyes and fangs to inspire caution in any hungry predator.

The guards enjoyed the unfolding drama, like introducing new chickens to an established pecking order. They and everyone else however, were wondering how it was that a woman had found her way to Parchman Farm. "What could they have done en why was they sent here?" Fulton asked B.B. Within minutes, Flood emerged from his Mansion to answer everyone's questions. He explained that the women were in Parchman for committing the most violent and unacceptable of crimes and that within Parchman their responsibilities would include sewing new uniforms and sheets, laundry, vegetable canning, cage cleaning, and cotton ginning. They would reside in cage thirteen, and any incident of assault against them would earn ten lashes and five years. "This is a bold experiment boys, a day on which you have the opportunity to demonstrate to all of us that you can be rehabilitated and trusted to return to society one day and behave like civilized people. Do not disappoint me." The female gunmen sat with their hands between their legs as he spoke, and they kept them there after he returned to his Mansion. "They're here 'cause the world requires symmetry, especially in its miseries," B.B. answered.

***

Thump. Thump. Thump against the cannery table. *God. God. Oooo. Stop, oh please.* "Mastuh, please!"

"Shut up nigger!" Slam. Slam. Slam his fist on her back with a shut up! *Please oh God. Please. Burns like my insides ripped. Like my heart ripped! God, my insides, my god.* Tears trembled like a childhood nightmare. Macabre sounds infected the air. Trembling like her body draped across a catafalque. *Sweet. Sweet Lord. Make it stop. Soon, please oh please soon . . .* He pressed his hands deep into her hips, pulling her as he struck again and again, the crimsoned scepter of his angry kingdom, into the unprepared furrows of his unwilling land. Fertile furrows. Furrowed. She squeezed her tears like water from a stone, hoping and praying that if they closed tight enough the world would disappear and leave her be. Safe. With time to rest her chin against her hand and wonder about everything except why it was that things were not otherwise. He not behind her like an ogre. Like an ogre and final oxen thrust he removed himself and returned to Front Camp. But he slammed her down with his fist when she tried to stand. This one a Driver. Two trusties behind. She swooned and tried to think of a song.

***

Parchman was peaking. From canned corn to salted beef and pork shipped in refrigerated cars, and of course, more and more ginned and baled cotton, more than the state of Mississippi had exported in five decades. The harvest elided color and kind. Everyone was in the fields, and the guards wielded their rifles and whips like celestial weaponry. They herded the gunmen like animals and galvanized their productivity with cattle prods.

    Meanwhile, Flood continued to push Parchman to realize its perfection as efficiently as rain falls to the earth, rises to the sky, and then falls again. Almost two-thousand eight hundred gunmen (guarded by over a hundred trusties, Drivers, and Sergeants) populated Parchman's fifteen cages and supported a self-sufficient system that deposited over one million dollars into Mississippi's state coffers in 1917. Flood entertained visions of a new, rich, proud Mississippi that would rival the quality of life of any state in the country. Not even the revered oil and steel industries of the North could generate profit margins like Parchman, all without using more than twenty-thousand acres and without polluting the country's water and air. Convict leasing would be recorded as the most successful concept in the history of industry since slavery. And Mississippi was realizing its perfection.

LIFE'S ONLY PROMISE

History Blues

Two more years passed and the summer of 1919 arrived. People at Parchman remembered that summer because Long Chain Charlie's shipments began to change. Long Chain himself had changed a few months earlier; the first Long Chain had retired and a new Long Chain, though just as large and disfigured as the former, assumed the mythic role. The new Long Chain Charlie's shipments did not differ in size or frequency, but in the schema of their coloration. Every ninth or tenth gunman brought through Parchman's gates was white. The first two shipments of the summer alone doubled the number of residents of cage eight, so the gunmen began to wonder and whisper in the fields, "Where all these whites comin' from... maybe it's the new govner... maybe the Nowth invaded again en this time they stayin'... no, no, no, I heard some a dem talkin' last week. It's some new law they breakin' which bringin' them here. They yellin' 'bout the govment en them purtans passin' laws violatin' they rights... I heard it too. Somethin' 'bout no more shine for nobody. So they up in arms bout the constitution en they rights. Right to do this en right to do that in the privacy of they home. But the govment sayin' it reckin' society, so they ain't no more for nobody. That's what I heard them sayin' anyway."

By the end of 1919 every bunk in cage eight was filled, and that meant there were more than enough white gunmen to fill the ranks of the trusties and oversee all the operations in Front Camp. In fact, the tall, fat gunman who had killed Gerrit Faulk, named K.W., had ascended all the way to chief hound trainer. And since he trained the hounds, he knew how to evade them, so one day he escaped to the east and was not recaptured until a year later. He returned to Parchman to a hero's ovation from the other white gunmen, and then escaped again and was not caught for eight months. He was a hero to the other whites and inspired several escape attempts among them. Parchman's Superintendent at that time was so exasperated with K.W. and his legend that he ordered some of his guards to convince K.W. to attempt a third escape, and when he did the guards were waiting and shot him dead. But K.W.'s legend at Parchman whispered in cage eight for years after his death and inspired more rebellion from that cage than any other cage in Parchman.

Nevertheless, the lives of the colored and the white gunmen were not entirely separate. Long before K.W. became a legend, one white gunman breached the barrier between the two populations. He approached B.B. one Saturday night when most of the gunmen were outside their cages with their opium or inside the Tonk House with their women. B.B. was sitting outside his cage playing his guitar for the first time since the attack. Over three-hundred gunmen from the nearby cages had gathered in front of him. Fulton, in particular, had been waiting for this moment so that he could chant Parchman's history to those too new to know it. In the midst of that moment, the white gunman walked towards B.B. Everyone present could smell that he did not carry himself with the same impervious air with which his peers walked amongst coloreds. They watched as he walked around the side of the group. Some of them even growled like wolves protecting their den. When he arrived before B.B., he lowered his head as if asking permission to speak. B.B. stopped playing and beckoned him with his hand. When the white gunman was standing before him, B.B. looked at him with a smile and asked, "So what unfortunate task brings you here?"

The white gunman looked around at the coloreds behind him and removed his hat with trembling hands. He spoke with words like water shuddering at the end of an icicle, "We, that is, some of the others, in our cage. Well. We were wondering, some of us, on the possibility of playin' in some of those softball games with ya'll. Maybe a couple of us on your team."

A surprising silence followed the question. B.B. considered the request and then responded, "What's your name?"

"Oliver Boone."

"En why did they send you Oliver to ask me if you could play softball wit us?"

"Well, no one really sent me, and I just figured you looked like the person to ask. What I mean to say is, there's just some of us."

"Come here all by yourself. Come here to ask me if you can mix with us in the softball games. Well, I don't think I'm the right person to be askin'."

B.B. looked past Oliver to the gunmen gathered beneath the floodlights, and he asked them, "What ya'll think? Should we play ball with Mr. Oliver Boone en his friends?"

A negative grumbling from the gunmen answered the question.

B.B. thought for a moment and then responded, "No, I don't believe that ya'lls the right person to ask either. All snakebit. I think the right person to be askin' is the capin a the best team in Parchman."

B.B. looked at Fulton, who was not pleased with the scrutiny B.B. had just thrust on him. Everyone focused on him with anticipation. Fulton thought to himself for a moment. He did not think of Vardaman, Long Chain, or the countless mobs when he responded, "Well. As capin a my team, I'm not sure that means I ken speak for all my teammates, but seems to me that if there ain't too many of you, we could find some place for you. If you're good enough."

Some of the gunmen gesticulated and challenged Fulton's decision, which Fulton was already beginning to regret. Then B.B. jumped to his feet and addressed the crowd in a voice louder than any of his songs, "Now hold on! Fulton's his team's capin, en he speaks for his team. If you don't want no whites on your team, then don't invite any. For those of you on Fulton's team who don't want no whites neither, why don't you stop en think for a minute. Now I know we're in Parchman en the world don't know en don't care what happens here, but Oliver en Fulton is tryin' to show you the way to make things better, so quit your growlin' en maybe next Sunday will be the start a better times."

The crowd's anger dissolved, and B.B. returned to his guitar. Fulton began to orate the history of tobacco leaves, and Oliver Boone returned to his cage with good news for his friends.

A month later, thirty white gunmen were playing in the softball league while the other one-hundred forty white gunmen watched. And like many of the black gunmen, most of them watched with displeasure. There were occasional fights and arguments and attacks in the night against Oliver Boone and his friends. But cage eight continued to participate in the softball games, and in time those who disapproved lost the energy to perpetuate their disdain. Nevertheless, B.B.'s words did not prove prophetic. White gunmen were still white and coloreds were still colored as far as the guards, Flood, and Mississippi's system of jurisprudence were concerned. Still, it was a bold experiment, and B.B. was proud to have fathered the prison world's first system of conjugal visitation as well as the South's first racially integrated softball team.

All the while, the ranks of the guards of Parchman Farm had remained relatively intact, at least until now. While thousands of gunmen had come and died in fifteen years, the Sergeants, Drivers, and trusties were fixtures in Parchman. Some retired and were replaced by their sons, others fell ill and died, but much like Long Chain Charlie, though the faces changed, the people were the same, decade after decade. Of course, Flood had been at Parchman since it was a watery soup, and he assumed he would remain its Superintendent for another ten years. But when Mississippi's new, moderate Governor, Theodore Bilbo, heard the stories of the internal violence, manner of punishment, and mortality rate of Parchman's gunmen, he invited Superintendent Flood to his Mansion in Jackson for a talk.

"I'll be brief Flood," Bilbo said as he scratched the neck of his calico cat, "I'm relieving you of your duties as Superintendent of Parchman."

Flood was irate, but helpless. He cursed Bilbo and his myopia, "You don't know what Parchman is. You want all the money and the glory without the reality of how to get them. You can't run Parchman like a nursery and hope to put a million dollars in our accounts. You're gonna find out the hard way, and I'm gonna watch you fall." Flood stormed out barely able to catch his fuming breath.

But Governor Bilbo had his plans. He replaced Flood with the son of the owner of Mississippi's largest cotton distributor, Caesar Johnstone. The Johnstones shipped more cotton to more places than any distributor outside of the Dunavants in Georgia. They shipped primarily to the Northeast and Far West along with monthly shipments from Biloxi to South America and Europe. For the past decade they had shipped more and more of Parchman's cotton and had expressed interest in privatizing the operation under their control, but Vardaman, Noel, and Bilbo had been unwilling to consider the notion. Parchman was the key to their respective claims that they were enhancing the quality of life of their voters. But with increasing competition from other penal farms, Governor Bilbo decided it was time to strengthen the bond between the Johnstones and Parchman. Caesar Johnstone would be allowed to operate Parchman however he wished, provided he maintained certain standards of civility. And for his services he had the right to allocate up to eighty percent of Parchman's cotton production for distribution by his family. In that way, Governor Bilbo ensured he would be associated with Mississippi's aristocratic renaissance for years to come.

Johnstone arrived the same morning Flood departed. Flood left that morning in a new Ford with his belongings in a pickup behind him. Since it was a Wednesday, no one was in Front Camp to see him leave. It was late October and it was cold. Flood left with his face to the ground, angry and humiliated. He was unsure what he was going to do with himself when he woke up the next morning.

Caesar Johnstone arrived a few hours later and ordered all the gunmen from the fields to Front Camp. He awaited them on his third-story balcony, rocking in a rocking chair and smoking the pipe his great-great grandfather was given by James Hamilton for losing a bet on who would be elected the second President of the United States. Hamilton, in turn, had received the pipe from Alexis de Tocqueville as a momento of the Old World's rebirth into the New. The Johnstone's had passed the pipe from first born to first born and smoked only North Carolina grown tobacco from its ancient bowl. So on his balcony, while he was awaiting his gunmen, Caesar Johnstone was smoking the history of his arrival at Parchman, stretching through centuries and across seas. He gazed at his new empire and the potential riches in its soil. It all awaited the creation of a context by those perspicacious and disciplined enough to exploit it. That was the earth's ancient secret. Not how seeds sprout and reach a hundred feet to the sky, not how continents drift and collide along the depths of their volcanic crusts, nor how the rains fall to nourish living things that then die, evaporate, and become rain again. None of this. The earth's most true and ancient secret was that it could be appropriated by the life it supports for profit. That's what Johnstone's family had seen since the day it arrived on America's untapped shores. There is no poetry in the falling of a sleepy leaf to the earth; there is only the transference of wealth. Johnstone considered it his duty, like his father's before him, to seize the earth's treasured potential. And the negro's duty was to churn and upturn the earth's treasures for him.

So Johnstone watched as the gunmen and their guards emerged from the fields. From his balcony they seemed as diminutive in potentiality as in stature. They emerged like ants to receive further instruction. Johnstone smiled and exhaled his contentment, *I am more than a man, I am more than this moment of mine, my name is more than the word that refers to me.* The Sergeants and Drivers knew who Johnstone was, but the trusties and the gunmen had no idea who this man smoking his pipe on Flood's balcony presumed to be, like he owned the state and the air people breathed. Johnstone enjoyed watching the gunmen fill the space in front of his mansion; their substance and volume made him feel heavy against the world, so that it could never disregard him. He weighed as much as all of them because he held all their destinies in his hands.

Johnstone allowed them to wait and wonder and watch him inhale his pipe with leisurely disregard. At length he arose, as the sun was beginning to set, and he appeared in a shadowed silhouette, just like Flood did in the sunrise before their first punishment, only this time more scarlet than yellow, "My name is Caesar Johnstone. Superintendent Johnstone." He waited for them to wonder. "The former superintendent has retired and returned to his home. I have assumed the duties of his position. Things will be as they have been. For now. I will be inspecting the fields and the activities in Front Camp and will institute changes as I see fit." He paused again and inhaled his pipe like the first breath after too much time underwater. He searched the eyes of his gunmen and saw the uncertainties he wanted to see. "You are all here in Parchman because at some point you were caught and prosecuted for affronting the civility of our society. The work you do is designed to teach you the discipline and self-control required to return you as productive and civilized members of Mississippi society. For those reasons I will be reviewing the status of your *Red House* with your Sergeants to determine whether it is counter-productive to our efforts here." He inhaled again and looked past them to the forest and the sky beyond it. The gunmen below looked up into the descending sun and tried to discern the shape of the voice they heard, but because they were squinting into the sunset, all they could see was the new shadow of authority that resided in the Superintendent's Mansion.

Fulton turned his face from the sound and looked at B.B. because he realized his friend would suffer the most significant consequences of the new voice atop the Superintendent's balcony -- the severed bond between B.B. and that voice. He saw the fear unfolding on B.B's face, curling its wrinkles with each new iteration of consequence. He saw that this new form would not be interested in meaningless landscaping. The last of B.B.'s few black hairs were frightened to gray and his face sank. Fulton placed his hand on B.B.'s shoulder and assured him, "We'll watch your quota. Don't worry. We'll watch your quota."

Three days later Johnstone burned down the Red House and gathered all the gunmen to witness the blaze. The fire itself burned red, and Kibel said that the sin made it so. Though its exterior was dry and weather beaten, the interior of the Red House was moist with indulgence, so it burned without a cracking and popping, but with a hissing instead. Johnstone watched from behind the gunmen atop his black, intemperate steed, and he thought to himself that his workers would have more energy to make him more wealthy.

With the Red House gone, the boys and the men who looked like boys slept in peril once again. The female gunmen did not sleep in peril, but they had always been and remained in danger once out of their cage, not from the other gunmen, but from everyone else at Parchman, except Kibel. As in the years before the Red house, every week or so a twelve year old boy turned up dead behind the sawmill or cannery. The perpetrators were only a few, and most had an idea of who they were. But no one could do anything about it, for if they were not Sergeants, Drivers, or trusties, they were gunmen who were attached to gangs -- the Clips, the Grays, the Shines, or the Blackbones -- which were all far too dangerous for anyone to challenge.

The gangs had been with Parchman since its first days. The guards had a vague notion of their presence but never interfered because they seemed to help maintain order with a minimum of violence. Flood drew the analogy to wild wolves that organize themselves in packs to demarcate boundaries and maintain order among competing interests. And the truth was that there had been only four gang related conflagrations in the seventeen years during which gangs had organized themselves at Parchman.

One evening with B.B. humbly strumming his blues, Fulton found himself chanting the history of Parchman's gangs to his audience. He, Moondog, and Cuttino were three of maybe thirty gunmen who had been in Parchman since its birth, and gangs were the first entity to unfold from it. Fulton felt it was his responsibility to relate Parchman's history to the next generations, to those who lived after its beginning and before its end. Fulton felt History preserved within him, as if he were the verbal conduit of the stories around him, like B.B. once was. Chanting helped him understand his placement within the passage of Parchman's life, and he hoped his stories helped the others like they helped him. He hoped his sound was heard.

"There was two of them. The first two gangs. They was created by Parchmans foundin' gunmen, en they was responsible for the first en most bloody gang war ever. All the gunmen lived in two cages in them days, en almost everybody belonged to them two gangs, The Fathers a the East en The Fathers a the West. They was created by two enemies from they lives before Parchman. One had burned the land en cabin a the other 'cause the other had raped his daughter. The judge sent them both to prison en Long Chain railed em here. Govner Vardman said they was perfect examples a the kind a disregard for essential human morals that Parchman could rebilitate.

"The Fathers a the East en The Fathers a the West didnt do much a consequence for the first year after they was bown. I remember Cuttino en me was in the cage a the Fathers a the East. We didn't join at first. I don't know that we ever did, 'cept that after a time everyone in them two cages was considered the Father a one place or thother. That was just how things divided themselves up back at the beginnin', before some a you was even born.

"Times was difficult then, en the gangs helped us through... course we didn't call ourselves gangs then, that name came years later when people started lookin' back. But we would sing songs outside our cages on Saturday nights, en they would sing songs outside theirs. Sundays at the service we sat in our groups on either side of the congregation while Kibel preached brotherhood en morality en turnin' the other cheek. En before we knew it, we all hated each other as much as the founders did. We hated them for rapin' our daughter, en they hated us for burnin' they crops en they cabins. Some hated more than others, but we all hated, 'cause when a man looks at you day after day like he wants to open your chest wit his hands en eat your beatin' heart, you start to feel the same way, en you kent help but hate him.

"For the first year, no one dared provoke thother. The founders told us 'bout the glorious day when we would revenge the injustices en cleanse our ancestors. We would line up in the field en face each other, man to man, each wit his devil on the other side. En our ancesters would be behind us, throwin' themselves in our fists when we swung. That's the day I feared 'cause my brother Moondog was on the other side. It may sound crazy, but that's how we felt, en in our anger we didn't know what else to think. We had all been stolen from our former lives en brought here where we slept in shit en drained icy water day after day wit others droppin' en dyin' day after day, en we didn't know what this place was en what it had planned for us en whether we would ever see our former lives again. That's why we saw the devil in our brother en why we was ready to open his chest wit our hands."

Fulton paused. The memories of his words knotted in his chest. Cuttino passed him some shine that slipped like a soothing sunbeam down his chest and melted the knots. Moondog threw another log on the fire. The three of them sat together, at the head of Parchman's history, venerated by those who listened.

"But," Fulton continued, "we drained en drained that Great Swamp even though every day it seemed endless, like it drownin' the whole world. It was only years later that this place was all divided up into this function en that function en each to its kind. But as the Great Swamp was getting thinner and thinner 'til only a thin layer a muddy waters remained across the top of the land, somethin' 'bout that made things get worse. The words a the founders grew more en more angry. We was caught in a frenzy en blamed all our unhappiness on the other side. They was the devils, en our freedom was waiting on the other side a they death.

"So the night arrived; a clear Saturday night in the fall when the Great Swamp was finally drained en we saw the earth beneath it. Though it was a Saturday night en though they was all drunk by midnight, to this day nobody knows what happened to the Drivers en the shackshooters that night to keep us from the Great War. But they was not wit us, not until they could hear us in the fields wit our roarin' en bangin' meant to raise the dead. We stared at each other across the fields. Then everythin' went silent, en we realized that they ancestors was our ancestors too en we was fightin' ourselves. But it was too late to turn away from the future we was fightin for. En wit our blood boilin' for blood, for the chance to take hold our lives in our hands en fight for our destiny, our founder told us he saw the ghost a his raped daughter standin' in the middle a the battlefield, en she was the sign a the goodness en justice of the blood we was goin' to spill.

"So we ran wit our fists held like claws en our screamin' like thunder. It musta been our initial clashin' that boomed loud enough to wake them guards from wherever they was, 'cause it wasn't ten minutes later that they rode wit guns blazin' into the fields. But we kept clawin' en tearin' each other apart. In jes them few minutes the fields was already filled wit bodies. En when they shot at us to stop, we jes kept fightin' harder en harder. One of them fell on me, en I was trapped under him for a few seconds when another came wit a stone raised over his head lookin at me like fire was in his veins ready to crush my head. But Cuttino smashed him across the face wit a log en freed me from the ground.

"After a while we didn't even know who we was fightin'. The air was swirlin' wit our anger en our blood en smellin' like Shiloh the mornin' after. Even the muddy marsh turned muddy red. It was only after our anger began to burn away that they separated us from each other. We was delirious wit blood en death en didn't know who or where we was. Everythin' was dyin', en the new earth beneath the Great Swamp drank our blood. Two-hundred en twenty a us lined up that night, en only sixty survived. Our ancestor's vengeance took half a hour.

"We was under strict lock en key for the next six months while Long Chain replenished our cages en started to fill the others. Both the founders was killed in the Great War, en locked up en confused as we was, no one stepped into their shoes, so The Fathers a the East en The Fathers a the West just faded away. Soon enough, people stopped talkin' 'bout them en 'bout that night en 'bout all the reasons we used to hate each other. I used to fall asleep thinkin' a all the lives we kilt en wonderin' what my family would say if they knew what I'd done.

"Then there was the Great Flood a the winter a nineteen-hundred eight. The Pinnekoke Levee gave way en we was covered by a foot a water in our cages. So we had to drain all that water en rebuild the levee again. En by the time the harvest a 1909 was upon us, a few survivers a the Great War began conceivin' new gangs. The Blackbones en the Shines was the first two, Sons a the Fathers. Moondog,

Cuttino, en me didn't join the gangs the second time, en we tried to warn the newcomers a what had happened the last time there was gangs in Parchman. But they didn't wanna learn from the past, like it never happened, en soon enough another gang here en another gang there popped up, en those is the gangs we have today. But for the most part they kept to filchin' thinner or just recreatin' together. It's the Blackbones en the Shines who get into all that hurtin'. But since they're the oldest en the biggest gangs, kent nobody do nuthin' 'bout it.

"Anyway, that's how gangs was born here at Parchman Farm en that's how things been ever since, each separatin' to the kind that suits him."

LIFE'S ONLY PROMISE

The Silence of Residue

Parchman continued to churn its gunmen, and B.B. barely managed to drag himself through the next harvest. Along with their own quotas, Fulton, Moondog, and Cuttino combined to pick half of B.B.'s quota each day. The Sergeants did convince Johnstone to allow B.B. to play one or two nights a week, but his music had grown laborious to him. Some nights he feared it. The winds and voices of the sourceless source around him no longer inspired his lungs and danced his fingers. His guitar was heavy and unfocused. Sometimes he just strummed a C or an A as if he did not know what else a guitar could do. Fortunately, he did not need to sing because Fulton remained compelled to chant the history of the world. And the gunmen listened with rapture. B.B. enjoyed the chanting too, because it distracted him from his gradual dilapidation.

Nevertheless, like LaRue before him, B.B. began to mutter bizarre, distant words in the fields and in his bunk at night. He no longer led the booming chorus of cage seven's work songs, and it was not clear to Fulton that he could even hear the others while they were singing. He simply tucked his face against his shoulder and muttered. Soon enough, Fulton almost had to knock him off his feet to get his attention, and even then he would stare seemingly unaware of who he was and where he was, or with the face of a desperate child lost in a strange place with no understanding of how to return home. "B.B.... B.B., I say! Do you hear me? It's me. It's Fulton." If and when he responded, his words were spoken to someone else, "I got your money Lee. I played all night. So take your money." He popped in and out of the awareness of who he was. And then on Saturdays he played his guitar like asthma. Fulton chanted his histories anyway, as if B.B.'s spirit had swum into him.

"It wasn't always that men was gettin' sick en dyin'. Oh no. Not at all. There was a day when men walked to en fro en lived forever. They was born from the Great Earth Mother who lived at the end a the sea, en through time they traveled en filled the earth. They filled they time buildin' monuments to they Great Earth Mother en writin' the history a they thinkings for her next children to read. But one day the Endless Water Snake who was wrapped 'round the world approached the Great Earth Mother en slept wit her. He was coiled round her for years. All her children was furious, so when the Endless Water Snake finally released the Great Earth Mother, they kilt him, en it rained en rained for days. Not the gentle rain that feeds the crops, but the violent rain that destroys everything. But they revenge was too late.

The Great Earth Mother gave birth to a vicious snake baby who went forth en stung his human brothers dead. When they came after him he hid in his mother's womb en she begged her sons to spare him. She knew he was no good, but he was her child too. By en by, the snake child went forth time en time again en soon enough he had poisoned the entire earth dead so that no men was left alive. Darkness fell across the world, en the Great Earth Mother sobbed en sobbed her loss. En as she sobbed, her snake child who had grown into a snake man slept with her. She took him into her even though she knew what he had done, en when their love was over he died. When she gave birth she had twins. One was a snake like you see today en the other was a baby just like ours. But somethin' was wrong wit the baby.

It fell ill en grew old while the snake child remained strong en youthful. The Great Earth Mother knew the truth en she sobbed. She knew the snake had stolen her immortality for its half a her womb. In that way, when snakes get sick or old, they jes leave they bodies behind en are born again. But when a man gets sick or old, he kent shed hisself like his snake brothers do, so he dies. That's the story a how men lost they immortality. And that's why even today, if you look into a white sky, you can see them snakes swimmin' 'bout in your eyes, so you always know who introduced you to death."

Fulton, Moondog, and Cuttino did what they could to ease B.B.'s remaining days. They carried him through the harvest in the summer and convinced his audience to allow him to sleep Saturday nights in the winter. They sat with him at the eating table or inside the cage and hoped that their presence comforted him. Sometimes he would speak, "I ken see your breath. See mine too. Means we warm inside. That's how we different from the rest. We know we warm inside. It's the heat, so they say, that can melt your sins away. When it's time. Even when its bonechillin' cold outside. Then you can pass through a needle a hay. Ain't nuthin' left a man when his sins is all burned away. Ain't nuthin' left, cept a tuft a ash." Then B. B. would sleep, and he seemed to be the only gunman in any cage at Parchman Farm whose teeth did not chatter all night.

The new gunmen who arrived each month did not know who B.B. Washington was, and they would never learn, especially after Fulton found him one morning eating the neck of his guitar, metal strings and all. One of these gunmen who arrived in cage seven was a particularly large and irascible colored named Rosco. He slept in a bunk in between Fulton and Moondog and told everyone that he was in Parchman for train robbery and attempted rape, "I did try to rob that train, but there wasn't no rape unless they thought I was tryin' to tonk the train." Rosco was one of the only men Fulton had ever seen who was as large as Moondog, but he was neither as gentle nor as kind as his friend. He spent each day in the field brooding over his failed robbery and planning how he would succeed next time, "Problem was Kee. Kent trust nobody. Not even if you known em twenty years. Kee was late. Weak en scared. Got away too. Probably tonkin' my woman en laughin' at me now. I'm killin' them both the day I'm free." Fulton tried to mute

Rosco's rantings, but his anger always ensnared him, like a rope around his neck, and forced him to inhale his rage.

So it should not have surprised anyone that it was Rosco, that suffocating day in July, who finally did what no gunman or guard had ever considered doing since Tiberius. They were at the Waterboy's Wagon, inhaling buckets of water to cool themselves and their swollen hands. During the harvest, the gunmen were unshackled during water breaks so that they did not trample the cotton as they gathered for water. Fulton, as usual, was fighting for water to take to B.B., while B.B. was standing aside from the group, bent over in exhaustion and thirst, with his open hands nervously twitching at his sides. But on this day as B.B. waited for his water, the world suddenly began to spin desperately around him, so in uncontrollable fear he charged at the Waterboy's Wagon, climbing over the others and barking slurred vowels. In the process he raked Rosco across the back of the neck, and Rosco spun with a punch that dropped B.B. to the ground, knocking out his two front teeth. Rosco cursed in pain, but nobody noticed him or B.B., who was twitching like a frightened child. B.B. heaved and watched his blood drip down his chest. The trusties were fifty yards away sipping their water in the shade when Rosco charged at B.B. with all the anger in his life, "Git up old man! Git up en get your beatin'!" Rosco raised B.B., who shouted, "No no, I ken, I kent, I kent..." and then bashed him with an uppercut to the chin that snapped his head back like a twig. B.B.'s knees buckled and he collapsed.

At that moment Fulton turned with water and called for B.B., but he saw Rosco atop him, tearing into his head and face with his teeth. Fulton ran at Rosco and pounced on him, flailing his fists and teeth into the giant gunman, but Rosco threw him off with his tree-trunk legs. Then Moondog noticed the melee, and he rushed at Rosco, knocking him off B.B. The two immense men grappled like jungle beasts, while Fulton kicked at Rosco from behind. Their anger was boiling beneath the blazing day, and the sight of B.B.'s bloodied body burned Moondog and Fulton's rage beyond delirium. Then two trusties arrived with their rifles and warned, "Stand down Fulton, and let them settle this."

Moondog and Rosco locked against each other with the force of rhinos. When they spun apart they each jumped to their feet and filled their heaving chests with air before charging again. As their fight raged, they both became bloody, bruised, and exhausted. Fulton watched his friend fighting his fight as he tended to B.B., who was still on the ground whispering disconnected sounds. The warriors crashed blows upon each other like juggernauts. Blows to the face, the legs, the chest that would have broken any other man. They crashed and rolled across several rows of cotton, but the trusties did not mind since they were more interested in the fight.

The combatants spun apart again and then stood face to face panting for breath. As they sized each other, searching for submission in the other's eyes, Moondog instinctively sensed a moment in which he could gain an advantage. In the blink of Rosco's eyes, Monndog struck at his legs like a snake, lifted him off the ground in the same motion, and flipped him backwards over his head while twisting his own torso so that he could crash on top of him as he slammed him to the ground. Rosco was dizzy from the blow, and Moondog seized the dizzy moment to wrap his thick arms around Rosco's neck and squeeze with the strength of all the hatred that had boiled within him since the day his brother was lynched. He was erupting into the world. He screamed as he pressed and squeezed Rosco's neck in between his bulging arms. He screamed for his brother, he screamed for B.B., and he screamed for the other life he wanted to live.

Moondog's screams resonated through the fields as he twisted and jerked and crushed Rosco's neck, attempting to sever it from its trembling connection to the remainder of his spine. His chord of consciousness. Moondog wanted to feel that moment, when by his bare and brute hands he cracked Rosco's neck, sending a flashing shock of paralysis throughout his body. He wanted to watch consciousness leak from Rosco like blood. So he turned and squeezed and continued to roar, immersed in the intensity of his strength. Focused like a wild cat on its prey. Focused on his strength and his screaming until the moment it ended with one last burst of hatred. It was a moment like the blink of a shooting star, when both he and Rosco realized that a life was going to expire, a fragile moment when with the strength of all his anger and with a final scream, Moondog snapped Rosco's neck sideways and his ominous body fell limp in Moondog's arms. For a moment, it appeared that Moondog was cradling the lifeless body. Then he rose to his feet and joined Fulton in tending to B.B. He was on his back spitting blood on his face. His eyes rolled into their sockets as he tried to speak, but his words were amorphous and misspoken, as if trying to form themselves for the first time. Fulton and Moondog attempted to raise him, but he did not want to move. Fulton removed his shirt and applied pressure to B.B.'s gushing forehead and cheek. He was bleeding like a farm animal as he moaned, "Ken... kent! Iooooooo... Kent haare."

Fulton grew desperate, "B.B. stop! Lissen! Stop en Lissen! Ken you git up?... B.B.... Ken you git up?" Fulton slowed his words as he began to realize what was wrong. B.B. had grown silent, and a single tear fell from his eye, sliding down the curves of his face and mixing with his blood. The tear told Fulton what B.B. was suffering, and Fulton dropped his head in submission to the baleful purpose of the world. A heavy, solitary silence hung over the fields, and Fulton realized that silence had consumed B.B. without remorse or mercy. His head dropped under the dysteleological weight of his realization, "He kent hear us," Fulton softly spoke to Moondog, "he kent hear anythin'."

Moondog dropped his head in sorrow.

B.B.'s face tightened as the pain of Rosco's attack needled within him. It was as if his body were slowly discovering each new place that Rosco had bled. First the gash across his forehead like a cropper's sickle. Then the hole in his cheek. Then his broken ribs. Meanwhile, the earth beneath him received his scarlet oblations. Fulton and Moondog attempted to bandage his wounds with their ring-arounds and tried to lift him to relocate him to the infirmary. But B.B. pleaded, "Leaf mae, leaf mae."

Fulton looked into B.B.'s eyes and realized that he understood everything. He understood that his blood was spilling like an hourglass, inching him closer and closer to emptiness. He understood that there was a moment, now fixed in its placement, which designated his finitude. So they each took hold of his hands, and Fulton rested B.B.'s head in his lap to wait with him. He reached for the pail of water he had fought for and slowly poured it over B.B.'s head. Moondog placed his body to shade B.B. from the merciless sun. His wounds were already rotting.

B.B.'s face was struggling with something to say, so they sat with him patiently, not caring whether they received lashes for failing their quota that day. Perhaps he wanted to tell them he was afraid to die. Perhaps he wanted to tell them he feared losing himself to the emptiness that was consuming him before he tasted freedom again. Or perhaps he wanted to tell them that he was not afraid at all. That the second, solitary tear trembling from his eye was a tear of release from the burdens of his dreams and the immeasurable pain with which they had haunted him each day of his (caged) life. Their fond memory of him would be fulfillment enough. Perhaps that was why, as he listened to the footsteps of his final moment tapping behind him, he placed his hands on their chests, and with a final, gentle suspiration, exhaled his consciousness into their hearts, so that if they ever stood before the tyranny of unfulfilled dreams, they could open their chests to reveal him as witness to their purpose and value on earth. His eyes closed and said, "Thank you," just before his hands fell open to the ground.

LIFE'S ONLY PROMISE

Serpents and Words

Less than a month after Rosco killed B.B. and Moondog killed Rosco, another gunman arrived in cage seven who had the look of a wolf in his eyes. His name was Otis Ottley, and he suffered from a feverish brooding like a fish racing back and forth in madness against its reflection in a bowl. Otis paced and grumbled and tried to force more than he could see into his vulpine eyes. That was why he could not sit still, and why he rocked back and forth in his bunk at night. And though Fulton initially thought that Rosco's spirit had returned in the form of Otis, something about his manner reminded him more of Mongoose. His was a spirit that would rather die than be caged.

Within weeks, Otis had gathered a group of gunmen who whispered with him each night. They all muttered angry, delirious words.

"What they sayin' all night," Cuttino wondered.

"Don't know," another responded.

"Sound like they plannin' somethin'," Fulton added.

"Probably gonna try to escape en get us all kilt," Moondog continued.

"I don't want no parta that," Cuttino said, "I don't wanna be locked up in here like last time, or have another ten years added to my sentence jes cause somebody else in my cage tried to escape."

"What you gonna do?" Fulton asked, "you kent deny a man his chance to escape."

"No," Moondog responded, "but he ken protect his right not to suffer 'cause of it."

"That's right." Cuttino echoed.

"I don't know..." Fulton brooded, "I jes don't think we got the right to interfere. What you gonna do, turn them in to the trusties?"

"No. I don't know. Maybe. Maybe I'll get ten years taken off if I do."

"Yeah, 'cept it'll be 'cause Otis finds out en rips your head off."

"Well then," Cuttino surmised, "what you sayin' is it's either ten or twenty or thirty more years here, or gettin' my head ripped off next week, en gettin' ten years off my sentence. Tellin' don't sound so bad to me."

They all sat in silence after Cuttino's reductive analysis of what could be. It seemed too simple. His words were unencumbered by the contingencies and considerations which otherwise complicate decisions of significance. If only the actual complexities and countermomentums of existence could be sloughed off from time to time and the simple "this" or "that" of a decision could manifest itself for the simple choosing, like when you're snakebit. But that is why words are so deadly. Fulton saw Cuttino's words twisting (like smoke, like mist, like a snake) like so many words he had heard before, and that is why he had no faith in words, especially when spoken by someone to whom he was subordinate. At times, he even found it difficult to trust his own words. Did he understand and believe what he was saying? Or was he saying it precisely to delude himself? And then there were numbers. Numbers were especially onerous. Numbers like twelve years, or three dollars a barrell, because they invariably revealed themselves to have been veils disguising less desirable numbers. Words fatigued Fulton. They required incessant vigilance, and even then they could spell disaster. And yet, Fulton wondered what else there was.

For this reason Fulton feared Cuttino's last sentence. It was sufficiently simple and lucid to appear to have securely signified itself without any unexpected redirection or evasion of meaning. On the contrary, Cuttino's last sentence seemed locked and directed straight at its obvious target. Twenty years, no head, two years. After eighteen years, headlessness seemed a meaningless price to pay for the possibility of two years, especially when inaction could leave them swimming in purgatorial shit for a week with a few more years added to their sentences, courtesy of Parchman's uniquely pernicious justice. Cuttino's sentence painted the possibilities all too clearly, leaving Fulton both disconcerted and beguiled.

A few weeks after Cuttino frightened Fulton with his simple and pointed words, after the shackshooters had fallen asleep and owls began to hoot at the stars, Otis and his followers awakened the inhabitants of cage seven and gathered their sleepblinky eyes and their sleeplazy bones into the far corner of the cage. Otis stood in the corner with four men flanking either side of him along with two dozen others flanking them. Fulton, Moondog, and Cuttino stood at the center of the gathering of gunmen and asked, "Why you done woke all us up?" They spoke for the group because they were the elders; that is, because no one had been in Parchman longer than they had, and that meant they were wise and strong.

But as he had since the day he arrived, Otis was looking at Fulton with eyes that betrayed his disregard for Fulton's history in Parchman. Otis did not see wisdom and strength in Fulton's longevity, instead he saw a weak, abiding boy who was unable or unwilling to seize his fate and effect a better life for himself, or die trying. He knew that Fulton, Moondog, and Cuttino had tried to escape and had endured countless brutalities, but that their continued existence in cage seven instead of either being free or being dead manifested the true weakness of their spirits. Therein, Otis saw Fulton, Moondog, and Cuttino as dangerous influences on the gunmen, convincing them that it is acceptable to submit to the ways of things and that life, in its own mysterious ways, will one day respond with justice for the lives of tormented men. Fulton was a plague to Otis and the freedom of his people, cannibalizing their destinies.

When he addressed cage seven Otis spoke strong words, "I am Otis Ottley. These are my First Men. In each cage except thirteen and eight I have Second Men who organize our people. We are over five hundred gunmen, and we call ourselves The Liberators, and the time has arrived for you to join us in our liberation."

No one said anything. Some were too tired, some did not know what Otis was saying, and some like Fulton knew exactly what he was saying, but no one said anything. No one said anything after Otis Ottley's proclamation, so he said it again, "Liberation. Liberation. Don't you want to be free?"

"How come we ain't heard nuthin' 'til now?"

"Because you have not been listening. These words should have been ringing in your ears louder than the clanking of your shackles each day that you were worked to death so they can be rich. These words should have been ringing in your sleep louder than your nightmares. If you haven't heard them til now, it's because you haven't been listening."

"You got some plan?... words is one thing, but escapin' without dyin' or gettin' ten more years is another."

"I only need your courage to join us in our war for freedom. I only need your hearts to die fighting for your freedom."

A general murmur and grumbling spread across the gathering -- "I only got one more year... I remember what happened last time we tried... why you so different from the rest?"

Otis allowed the questions to surface, watching Fulton. Fulton remained silent in observation, as if seeking to locate his own mind in the resolution of the debate. He did not know whether he was ready for another war, or whether war was purposeful at all. At length, Otis addressed his audience in a whisper loud enough to silence theirs, "Brothers. Listen. Think of how much you've lost since you've been here. Don't allow your fear to shackle you to this evil earth year after year after year of your precious life. Think of how much you've lost since you've been here. All the time you could have been free. Some of you have been here longer than others have been alive. Do the rest of you want to wake up and say that to yourselves one day? Won't you free yourself if you have the chance? This place is worse than the slavery your ancestors endured. And when you finally die, there's thousands of other niggers out there waiting to be arrested to take your place. Maybe your son or your daughter. That's what nigger means. But we are not niggers! They created niggers. And slaves and King Cotton. They made all these things different from themselves, from what they should be if they had just left the world alone. But we are different because we will change it all back. We are different because we are unified in our fight. In other parts of this country, coloreds have jobs and live free and send their children to school. Why should we be so different here? Why should we be denied our freedom and our right to a better life? We are strong, and our sweat and blood should be spilled for our gain, not for their fat, lazy pockets. Join me. Join us. Take your freedom in your fists and hold it tight. Liberate yourself so your ancestors can finally look at this world and smile. It seems obvious to me -- Freedom or Death -- but not this animal life with them kicking us like stray dogs."

Still there was silence. Otis spoke with fiery words, but there was still silence. The only sound in the cage was the suspiring chorus of wintry breathing. There was enough chill in the autumn air and enough moonlight beaming from the window to illuminate the mystic panting of their breaths.

Though there was silence, their minds were churning. Fulton felt himself in the center of a vortex of doubt, again. Cuttino's words a few days before, and now this. Though he knew words grew more serene with age (or was it that they decayed?), Otis' young, whirlwind words raced along his spine and awakened forbidden voices within him. The others looked to Fulton for guidance, but he was tumbling within an internal labyrinth of resurrected emotions that he had buried after their failed escape. Life. Freedom. Daughter. All interred long ago beneath the thick callous of his former consciousness. But now in the mist he saw their ghosts circling around him crying, "Vengeance!" like poison in his ears, pricking his fear like mosquitoes.

He slipped deeper and deeper into a dizzying whirlwind of distant voices from his forgotten former self, *Fulton! Fulton! Redeem me. Fulton! Fulton! Avenge me.* Fulton looked at Moondog and Cuttino and searched their troubled introspection for the strength to hear the voices haunting him. But ultimately it was something that he smelled at that moment, a sanguine scent from a time of freedom, of nights on his porch with the memory of love, that awakened the passions of his slumbering courage. He did not know from where or how the scent arrived, but when it filled his lungs, it released the constriction that had choked his breath for too many years, precluding him from once again announcing to the world, "I am Fulton... Freedom or Death."

Fulton's proclamation settled it. Otis and Fulton met eyes in the darkness and shared recognition of the task awaiting them. Otis had already erected a network of information dissemination throughout the cages. They used Sundays to communicate. The Second Men placed themselves throughout Front Camp, playing dice, napping, or spinning tales, while the First Men walked with other members in groups of three or four and mumbled sentences or phrases to the Second Men as they walked by, just loudly enough to communicate their utterances, "Elders have joined... gather flames... in six Saturdays jes before midnight... swarm to Front Camp... our numbers gonna free us... freedom for The Liberators... glory to our ancestors... spread the word."

***

Autumn adorned itself with winter's crystal jewelry as the day of liberation approached. But not everyone was a Liberator. Most of the other gangs had joined the Liberators, but others remained separated through fear or disbelief or the opportunities that resided in opposition to their success. So they were betrayed. They had been too cautious for a white gunmen to have ever overheard their plans, and it was not one of their own who betrayed them (which later surprised Otis, for as a martyr he assumed his own brothers would betray him, and he planned for it). But it was another, a man whose muted presence since Mongoose's death had all but erased his face in the minds of those who once feared his spectral eyes and curses. Nor was he called what he was called before, and that also helped others to forget. His new name was Isaiah, and the minds of those who feared him had since been too fatigued to relocate their memories of Tiberius into him, even though his shadowy form and ravenous face remained the same. Fulton still had occasional nightmares of Tiberius, as a demon with black claws and fangs shredding the flesh of trees as he fled from him through a forest. But Fulton held no fear of Isaiah, for he was just another man, and that was exactly how Isaiah wanted it.

From the margins of his six remaining followers, Isaiah learned of The Liberators and their plans, and so he conceived his own plan by which their failure entailed his freedom. He discovered three weeks before the planned escape, and two weeks later he and his followers were prepared to sacrifice The Liberators to save themselves. It was that simple. All he had to do was walk up to Johnstone's Mansion and exchange The Liberators and their plans for his freedom. Johnstone would have to accept, for their plan required him to know the details and not just stand ready to improvise a counter-offensive. Besides, "What's seven gunmen gone to the lesson those hundreds en hundreds, maybe a thousand, will learn when you slaughter they plans? They'll never think to escape again. They'll fear you en they'll fear the world even more for conspirin' 'gainst their escape."

Johnstone sat in his chair looking for the holes in Isaiah's argument, but more than that, Johnstone remained unconvinced that it was appropriate to consider any dealings with a colored. "I could just stand a hundred guards with rifles outside your cages or in the fields and shoot the head off anyone who tried to escape.

"I told you. That won't work. They've planned for that. They expect you to find out somethin's goin' down. But you're gonna need to know what it is if you gonna stop them. You gonna have to trust me. Seven or a thousand. That's all you should be thinkin' 'bout."

"And what makes you think you can trust me to let you go?"

"Nuthin'. I got another plan for myself if you renege on your word to me."

Johnstone smirked at Isaiah's brazen confidence, almost too confident to trust.

"Look. I got nuthin' to gain by comin' here riskin' my head en lyin' to you. If you decide I'm spittin' shit at you, you'll find a way to have my head. That's a lot a risk unless I knew I had information that was well worth your trustin' me."

Johnstone remained silent. Isaiah's logic seemed too logical to be the truth. And his confidence was either a clever mask or the face of power in the knowledge he possessed.

"Seven or a thousand. On my terms or at my embarrassment. Everything about you tells me not to trust you, but everything you say indicates I have nothing to lose by trusting you. If you weren't a negro maybe you could have been a politician, maybe Governor, or maybe even one of those two-faced Northern politicians. They had the gall to message Governor Bilbo and me last week that they want to investigate our pardon process since none of you animals is receiving a pardon. Maybe it's time I convinced our Governor to grant a few. Maybe seven. For meritorious service to the sanctity of the State of Mississippi. Maybe that will satisfy them for a while. I suppose you're right Isaiah, I suppose it is worth trusting you, whether or not you are spittin' shit."

"Yes suh. Of course suh."

"Now all that remains is for you to tell me exactly what these negroes have concocted that is so smart that a thousand of them would escape. And when, of course, they are planning to do so."

"Yes suh. Of course suh. Won't take but a few minutes suh."

The Redemption Tree

They had been gathering flammable liquids for months, mostly gasoline and paint thinner, in the small, single-serving size liquor bottles (conveniently made from thinner glass after Prohibition in order to save money) that the guards left strewn across Front Camp every Saturday night. They had some larger fifths and Jeroboams that they used for storage, hidden beneath the bubbling of each cage's shit swamp. The guards eventually discovered the smuggling, but since they were accustomed to the gunmen's abuse of thinner and gasoline they thought nothing of it. In this way, little by little The Liberators gathered and stored gallons and gallons of gasoline and paint thinner in the small Jack Daniel's one-sippers which they hid from the nightly frisks in the one place no trusty or shackshooter was willing to look. And after all the months and all the gathering, when the Thursday before the Saturday night of The Liberators' planned escape arrived, the winter air thickened into a moist, silver mist that turned Parchman's floodlights into ghostly beams glowing through a midnight underworld. There was no moon or sky, just the glowing eyebeams of the floodlights and the circular swirling of the mist.

Looking into the mist, Fulton thought he was looking into the world of the dead. He remembered the last time these ghostly mists descended to the world of men, and even though he knew there was nothing he could do, he rose from his bunk and pushed through the night to Otis' bunk. He awakened Otis and whispered through the mist, as if it were listening, "I gotta bad feelin' 'bout our plan. Somethin' bad's in the air en it knows what we doin'."

"What do you mean Fulton? Only two days left, and now you want to tell me, at this point, that you have a bad feeling?"

"We gotta make a change. Wait another week, change the plan somehow. This one's been figured."

"Another week?" No! No. As sure as I'm a caged nigger we will not delay. What's wrong with you Fulton? I thought you were ready for this. And now you want to wait? Our lives are too short Fulton."

"No. That's not how it is. I want this; I want it for all a us jes like I did before. But I've seen these nights, en I've smelt this smell. They turn the world against us. That's why we gotta change the plan. They're here now 'cause they know, en they waitin' for Saturday to ruin us."

Otis paused to examine the weight of the man behind Fulton's words. He wanted to believe that fear was responsible for Fulton's indecision, but there was something in his eyes, behind the mist, and something in his voice, unfaltering and determined, that manifested his courage. Otis knew that at this point he could proceed without Fulton, but many, out of veneration for his wisdom, would wonder, and that pause could cost them lives. Otis placed his hand against Fulton's chest.

He did not feel the desperate thumping of a frightened man, nor the listless rhythms of an old one, instead he felt a chorus of voices bearing witness to the wisdom of his intentions. Otis recoiled his hand and spoke, "I understand. But we will not wait. We go tomorrow. A day early. Send the word. Those who don't hear will understand when the time arrives. Two hours after midnight. Tomorrow. Same as on Saturday, with the whistle of the overnight to Kansas City."

Then Otis shared a secret with Fulton. There was a tree, in the forest, that could help save them. "My mother, Jazzmine, told me the night before Long Chain brought me here that she would pick a tree due north of the front gate and mark it with a white X at its base and mark the trees that led up to it with white dots. She told me she would hollow the base of the tree and fill it with rifles and pistols and bullets for me, so if I fled and made it to that tree I could defend myself. She called it the Redemption Tree." Otis knew that his mother knew what Parchman looked like because some of the daughters of her friends used to visit the Tonk House, but he did not know that like them, she would have to prostitute herself for months to save the money to get the guns and bullets for him. "If we are separated during the escape, I'll leave a rifle for you so you can defend yourself and make it to freedom. And if you can make it to Kosciusko by Wednesday, my brother will be waiting with a pickup to drive us to any other state except godawful christforsaken noplace for negroes Mississippi."

"Thanks, Otis. I'll see you at the Redemption Tree." Fulton returned to his bunk, and as he fell asleep, he tried to convince himself that this time he had outplanned the evil that always seemed to outplan him.

Johnstone could not let them burn to death. That was the difficult part. The loss would be too great, and they knew that. That was why their plan would work. So instead he called one hundred State Militia Men to join the other guards in forming a midnight perimeter around Front Camp as well as around each cage. That way, when they tried to burst through their blaze, they would be met by unforseen and overwhelming counter fire that would be enough to drive them back to their cages, just in time to hose water onto the fires. Johnstone informed his guards of the plan Friday morning, who in turn were to inform the shackshooters when they relieved them Saturday morning. He ordered the State Militia Men to arrive in Scott that afternoon where they would remain until late Saturday night. At that point they would ride to Parchman to erect their barriers at midnight with orders "to shoot anything that moves that isn't the color of day."

But the mists of suspicion had draped Fulton's dreams in funeral shrouds one too many times, so by Friday afternoon he and Otis had already informed three-fourths of The Liberators of the change in plans. For the remainder of that winter afternoon, The Liberators passed mischevious smiles to their guards, who knew more than The Liberators were aware, but did not know that The Liberators, in turn, knew something different from what the guards thought they knew. Everyone waited for the hours and minutes to pass to the glorious moment in which each expected to crush the other. For one, the moment would validate History; for the other it signified the inversion of the philosophy that had germinated from that History, however local and transient that inversion may be. And when the Liberators returned to their cages that night, each whispered as he entered, "For the last time."

During those nervewracking hours before escape, some imagined the return to their former lives with nostalgic smiles, while others rolled the plan over and over in their minds inspecting the details for unforseen dangers.

Fulton, Moondog, and Cuttino spent the hours of anticipation whispering to each other. They had endured these moments before.

"How you feelin' Moondog?"

"Strong."

"I kent believe we doin' this again. Feel like I'm watchin' myself in a dream."

"Me too. Like I'm somewhere in between. Like I'm watchin' myself go through this witout any fear or worry for the outcome a what I do. I don't like it, but it's helpin' me stay calm."

"Me too. Guess that's how life is when you're old."

For some it was sooner than expected, for others it was long after, but when the whistle blew, everyone was ready. They descended like secrets from their beds and reached into the shit swamp for as many single-sip, pints, and fifths as they could carry while others passed around the matches and lighters they had stowed in their bunks. They punched each bottle through the cap with stray springs from their mattresses, and then tore their ring-arounds and stuffed the shreds into the caps. They worked with precise movements, and within minutes they were ready and waiting.

Otis stood at the head of the cage peering out at the two shackshooters resting against water barrels a few yards from the cage. A small fire burned between them and danced an orange glow across their faces. Firecolor eyes. Otis uttered one last prayer, that he had not overestimated the economic sensibilities of his captors, and then he looked back to his First Men who stood at the back of the cage with the largest bottles of gasoline and thinner. He raised his hand and seized the air within it in an urgent fist and whispered, "Freedom or death," and he dropped his fist to his side. A moment later a furious conflagration erupted in the back of the cage. A few seconds after that, everyone was at the front of the cage desperately clamoring for release. Half a mile away, and half a mile beyond that, shackshooters gawked at the decision before them. Open the cage and watch them run amuck, or stand firm and watch them all burn to death. No one wanted to explain to Johnstone that he had sat and watched two hundred gunmen burn to death, so with grave trepidation each pair of shackshooters moved forward to the front door of their cages. The shackshooters at cage seven approached the front door, while the gunmen within continued to scream for mercy, "Don't let us burn to death!... Open the door! Please! Please have mercy!... Oh sweet God have mercy!"

The fire raced through the cage expelling dense clouds of black, sooty smoke within which the screaming gunmen coughed and choked. There was a moment, seemingly infinite, during which Otis, Fulton, and all the other Liberators feared that the shooters would not open the doors. They were at the front, and they looked into the faces on the privileged side of the inferno, screaming from their choking lungs for mercy to swoop down and free them, just this once, from the necessity of their accursed fate. And so it did, this once, as the shackshooters unlocked the black, smokespewing door, releasing the gunmen from their caged inferno.

Otis and Fulton pushed through the door. The shackshooters stood back with their rifles pointed to ensure an orderly exodus from the cage, but from behind the billowing smoke funnel that was released when the door opened, two fiery missiles landed in their chests and burst on impact, engulfing their unsuspecting targets in an explosion of flames. The gunmen streamed out of the cage and encircled the shackshooters as they screamed until the relentless flames dropped them to their knees in prostrating submission to their fates. They appeared as if praying to the Fire God for mercy, having sacrificed themselves to his flame.

Twelve of the fourteen other cages erupted into flames and emptied their contents around the same time that Otis, Fulton, Moondog, Cuttino, and the rest of cage seven found themselves outside of their cage and on the verge of freedom. But at that same moment the Sergeants, Drivers, and trusties were fanning out from Front Camp, and Johnstone was in the Post Office wiring the Militia Men in Scott to charge at Parchman and shoot every gunman they saw. As the gunmen fled into the night, some for the fields and others for the forest that led to Gordon Junction, they were expecting the galloping arrival of the guards. They ignited their Freedom Flames and rained fire on those who chased after them. Gunmen were shot, guards were burned alive, and chaos consumed the heart of the Yazoo Delta.

Fulton, Moondog, Cuttino, Otis, and three of his First Men managed to burn their way into Front Camp, only to stop slackjaw-stunned dead in their tracks at the vision of a hundred thundering Militia Men swarming towards them across the very earth over which they had planned to escape. Ruined, only ten minutes into their plan, ten minutes into freedom (so much can happen in ten minutes, and so little in ten years). They bowed their heads in exhaustion and disbelief, "How did they... where... how many bottles... eight, nine, ten..." They remained hidden in the shadows of the wooded perimeter just fifty feet from the front gate, from the other world where freedom and former lives awaited. They looked around and saw other gunmen who had broken free also stop in disbelief, with Parchman's guards closing from behind and the Militia Men from the front. A cursed nigger sandwich. Fulton was bent over and his lungs were heaving, but he raised himself and spoke as if to children, "We ain't got no choice now. We kent go back. Freedom or death. If them en alla us charge, maybe some will get through en carry our freedom wit em."

"Freedom or death," Otis softly proclaimed, as if finally understanding the words. The seven of them charged through the front gate and fanned into the night with the Militia Men galloping towards them only a hundred feet away. Others saw them and charged as well. It was a plan of numbers. If they traded one for one, or even one for two or three, then many of them would still run free. They screamed as they ran, and the Militia Men lowered their rifles to fire.

They lit and threw their remaining Freedom Flames as they fled. Some hit, some missed, but all of them blazed fear into the horses causing them to break their formation and gallop out of control in all directions. The Militia Men struggled to corral their steeds back towards the front gate (from where dozens of gunmen were pouring out and Johnstone was blasting at them like ants from his third-story balcony) to intercept the fleeing gunmen. Parchman was ablaze with chaos and confusion. Fulton, Moondog, Cuttino, Otis, and three of his First Men ran for the forest while maintaining a distance of about fifty feet between them. They and several others penetrated the Militia's crumbling wall of defense, so several Militia Men had to turn around and pursue them from behind. But by the time they had broken free, Fulton's group had almost exhausted its Freedom Flames, and since Fulton did not have any more himself he concentrated on the darkness in front of him and listened to the heaving of his breathing.

At that moment he imagined his body as a singular, lithe muscle evolved for this sprint to freedom. Though fifty-one years old and with only six toes, he was running as fast as Otis and the others. Moondog and Cuttino labored several yards behind, but they remained focused on speeding the passage of the ground beneath them, scanning through the darkness for roots, stones, or holes that could trip them.

The Militia Men were navigating the flames and closing from behind, but Fulton and the others were only a hundred yards from the dark forest that stretched to Gordon Junction. At this time of night and without the hounds, who were back at Parchman unleashed into the fields to retrieve the fleeing gunmen, it would be impossible for horseback Militia to track them through the forest, which after the railroad at Gordon Junction, stretched for miles past Scott, past the Big Black River, almost to Alabama. The hunters would be spread too thin and too wide to focus on all of them, and that dispersion could signify their success.

As they continued to flee, bullets were nipping at their heels and zipping past their ears. *Jes twenty more steps* Fulton counted. *Twenty to freedom. Oh God, jes give me twenty more.* But there was more mathematics than "twenty" to consider.

There was also the probability that given a fixed volume of space in which the bullets were flying, and given a fixed volume of space within that space that the fleeing gunmen occupied, one of the bullets would strike one of them before they entered the forest. Fulton did not need a mathematician to know that the chances were not slim, but he was hoping that the bullet would strike one of the people for whom he would not feel compelled to stop. He knew that his freedom resided outside the margins of that possibility.

When Fulton and Otis were not more than ten yards from the thick, dark forest, Fulton shuddered when he heard, not one, not two, but three simultaneous howls just behind him. He turned and saw three men on the ground, each struggling to drag himself forward even though he had been shot in the arm or the leg or the back. And two of them were Moondog and Cuttino. His friends were forty feet from each other with the Militia Men closing from less than two hundred yards behind. Fulton and Otis caught each other's eyes; Fulton was equidistant from his friends, but Otis was closer to Cuttino. "You get Cuttino!" Fulton yelled at Otis while he ran for Moondog. He knew that they could never retrieve their friends and escape into the forest in time, and even if they did, the slow trail of blood would be easy to track.

But the greater knowledge that overcame him was that he could not continue without them, for their fates would forever haunt him. Fulton ran at Moondog, but then turned and saw Otis standing frozen. "Otis! Get him now!" But Otis remained still, afraid to look at Fulton, like he was betraying his ancestors. Fulton yelled at Otis, "C'mon Otis! Get him!" But Otis had already chosen another path. He did not ask for forgiveness as he turned his face from Fulton's and fled into the forest, leaving Fulton just enough time to be faced with the suffocating decision of choosing which of his two friends he would try to save, and which other he would condemn to certain capture, torture, and death.

He felt both their faces beseech him in the darkness, and though both of them had saved his life before, he had only a few seconds to decide whom he would save and whom he would condemn. Since it was his former life to which he was fleeing, he pulled his face away from Cuttino and ran towards Moondog, raised him from the ground, and dashed towards the forest, where he hoped Otis had found his Redemption Tree and remembered to leave them a rifle or two. The Militia Men were closing from no more than forty yards, gathering fallen gunmen as they advanced. The moment before they entered the forest, Fulton turned and saw Cuttino reaching from the ground as if to grasp beyond the critical distance between himself and his liberation, just as the Militia arrived at him and his spirit expired from his defeated face.

Fulton and Moondog reached the forest edge with a few Militia Men closing on them. Moondog's right leg was shattered, so Fulton labored to carry him through the forest. He yelled for Otis, "Get your guns! They comin' from behind! Get your guns en shoot em!" But as he trudged forward, Fulton could not see or hear from the darkness imposed by the ominous trees. He heard the Militia Men dismounting and saw their distant torches ignite. He saw the orbs dancing behind them in frantic pursuit, "You gotta leave me," Moondog pleaded, "go on home. You kent make it carryin' me."

"No chance! Shuttup en run!"

"Listen! If you drag me, we both get caught, en I'm dyin' anyway. You gotta make it home to mind both our families."

"No Moondog! I kent sleep in my bed in my home knowin' I left you here to die. We goin' together or not at all."

Moondog was silent for a few steps, and then spoke again, "Then I jes hope Otis remembered to leave us some guns."

"Me too."

They stumbled through the forest like an unbalanced, three-legged beast dragging along a limp tail. They heard the yelling and the gunshots behind them as the dancing orbs captured the other gunmen. The lights were closing and occasional bullets whizzed past their ears. They no longer screamed for Otis to defend them; they prayed that he was not far ahead as they followed the white-dotted trees towards the Redemption Tree.

They never found Otis, and when they arrived at the Redemption Tree with gasps of anticipation, they uncovered the hollow and discovered nothing. Their hearts sank from their throats into the roots of the Redemption Tree, and Fulton screamed to the sky and the trees and the animals and the serpentine mists that tormented his miserable life. Moondog collapsed and placed his face in his hands, "Oh god, my god." The orbs were dancing nearer and louder.

"What now?" Moondog whispered.

Fulton raised his friend from the ground, and the three-legged creature with two heads and a limp tail struggled a few yards forward and then fell again. At that moment they both realized that Fulton's opportunity for freedom had slipped from his hands the moment he returned for Moondog. On the ground, Moondog began to feel the intense pain of his shattered leg, but the greater agony swelling within him was the fear that Fulton would resent his decision to return, and in turn, would resent him. But Fulton's mind was elsewhere, somewhere on the shores of a distant isle with his Sweetest Queen. He raised Moondog from the ground and returned them to the Redemption Tree, where they sat and waited. The will-o-wisp orbs danced towards them through the cool, misty forest and began to grumble as if they could smell their struggling prey. As before, freedom was moments away. As before, it was a fluke that foiled them. As before, Fulton wondered what hope would deceive him next and convince him to survive.

LIFE'S ONLY PROMISE

The three-legged two-headed creature sat and waited, and looked into the night sky as if before the time ghosts had been banished from the earth. Waves of clouds passed one after the other under the moon. It watched the dancing wisps emerge and become lanterns held by angry arms. It watched them shout and gesticulate at them as they approached, and it sat, a shadowy solitude at the base of the Redemption Tree. It watched the six rifles lower to its face, and it prayed to be shot. It had drunk too many horrors and now felt as hollow as the forsaken emptiness in the hollow of the Redemption Tree.

"Where the others?"

"Ain't no others. We the farthest gone."

A rifle crashed across its right skull, spraygushing its blood into the moonbeam air.

"I said, where the others and where they headed?"

"Don't know. Jes ran like the rest. That's all I know."

"Let's just shoot em and move on."

"No. We have our orders. Drag em back to the farm with the rest, and keep hunting." Gunshots and screams sounded in the distance, and the air began to smell of ash, the kind of ash liberated to the sky from the violent burning of an unfulfilled dream.

The creature was tied to the back of a horse, dragged to Parchman, and thrown on a pile of similarly gathered creatures, all shattered and returned to writhe. A circle of armed guards held them for what awaited them. As he lay in the pile, with bodies beneath and atop him, Fulton hoped that the minute he had delayed the Militia Men was enough for Otis to run free. Maybe the shots they heard were his own, and now he was flying into the night with their freedoms in his legs.

They writhed and moaned for days at the center of Front Camp. They were piled atop each other, and several died from blood loss, infection, dehydration, suffocation, or the hopelessness of their lives. Those who had not been in Parchman long enough to lose their noses died from the very smell of the pile. As the days passed, more and more gunmen were dragged into Front Camp by guards or Militia Men and dumped atop the pile of broken bodies and dying dreams. Johnstone spent hours each day sitting on his perch watching the gunmen suffer, while the remaining gunmen, mostly from cages eight and thirteen, began rebuilding the cages, which were only skeletons of ash. Johnstone was furious, but thankful they had not attempted their escape during the harvest. On occasion, he rose from his perch, waved aside his guards, and fired his rifle into the mass of bodies six or seven times, watching them scream and squirm in horror. Bodies that died were left where they lay.

Even if a gunman tried to run free in the hopes that he would be shot, the guards were ordered to beat him senseless and return him to the pile. It was never cold enough at night to freeze, but it was cold enough to drive madness into the stem of a gunman's consciousness, leaving him swirling in a ghostly nausea. Like Johnstone, Fulton was thankful it was not summer; the heat would have baked them all.

When their urinating, defecating, decaying stench had grown too noisome for him to endure, Johnstone descended from his perch and ordered the gunmen raised to their feet (or foot) so he could administer their punishment, "For their ferocious, destructive, and murderous acts." The gunmen who were still alive were hosed clean. The others were piled beside the chapel to be burned, and Cuttino's remains were among them. Over two hundred of them stood in a line in the center of Front Camp, and since it was Sunday, the other gunmen arrived for their morning service, but despite Kibel's protestations, Johnstone ordered them to sit on the ground across from the line of dying gunmen. Johnstone replaced Kibel atop his podium pulpit and addressed the line of gunmen with a fulminating voice, "As of today, one-hundred ninety-one gunmen have escaped and are not yet accounted for. Two-hundred thirty-seven are dead, and two-hundred and four stand in line before me. Well done. Quite a show."

Behind Johnstone several of the Sergeants began draping ropes across the nearest branches. "The reason you are standing before me, about to receive your punishment, is that I half-trusted one of you, and one of you made the mistake of half-trusting me. Two-half trusts make one distrust, and that's what I should have done." He turned to one of his Sergeants and whispered to him. The Sergeant walked towards the crowd of gunmen. When Isaiah saw the Sergeant moving towards him he jumped up as if to run, but then he simply stood and waited. The Sergeant arrived at him and crashed his rifle across his face, knocking him to the ground and knocking four of his teeth from his doomed mouth. Isaiah and his followers were brought before Johnstone, and Johnstone pierced their eyes with an acerbic stare, "Maybe you were misinformed, maybe you misinformed me. Either way, since I never fully trust a nigger I was able to avoid a complete disaster, but you will have no such luck."

In the moment of his destruction, Isaiah looked at his followers and ordered them, "Stand tall en vanquish your fear."

Johnstone laughed and told Isaiah, "You don't have long to fear; you'll be the first I lynch."

They were led to the ropes, dangling from the skeletal trees. The trees seemed to be humming a requiem from the sound of the wind that passed between them. The Sergeants positioned their necks inside the nooses, and from his Pulpit of Justice, Johnstone ordered, "Take em up nice and slow." They rose from the earth like the souls of fallen soldiers to the heavens. Slowly. Their necks bulged, and they twitched and kicked their limbs like marionettes. Fulton pulled Moondog around the gunman in between them and held him next to his shoulder. Moondog's shattered leg was contorted and limp beneath him and had begun to fester and puss. His pain was incessant. Fulton hated seeing his friend suffer so deeply. After a few minutes Isaiah began spitting half-words no one could understand. He was the last to expire, and then all of them were dangling from the trees, their heads meekly fallen to one side.

"Lower them."

They were lowered and piled next to the chapel. Fulton turned to Moondog in desperate fear, "It's my dream! It's my dream! Whichever is alive must care for them 'til the end. Promise me. Whichever is alive must survive."

Fulton's desperation frightened Moondog, but he answered with a firmness intended to ease his frantic friend, "I promise."

"I promise."

Johnstone had only begun. Many more would feel their last breaths burned from their lungs as they left the world suspended between heaven and earth, the most forsaken of realms in which to die. Bereft of both earth and ancestors. "Take em. Half of em, and string em up like the dogs they are. The rest of you, watch and remember. Think of their dead bodies and fatherless families the next time you feel like leaving here before your proper time."

The entire line of gunmen felt their hearts knot. Fulton and Moondog stood at the far side of the line from which the Sergeants began selecting which gunmen would be hanged. They both closed their eyes as the voices neared, "You, you, you, you." Sometimes they picked two in a row, sometimes they skipped a few, so no one knew who was dead and who was alive until he was yanked from the line. As the voice neared and neared, Fulton saw his life like a cloudy, gray sky behind his closed eyes, and he whispered a prayer for the happiness of his family. And then the voice neared, louder and louder, "You, you." His heart raced; it thumped against its agonized walls, as if being punched by a demon from inside.

Oh dear lord, I ain't got much time... the voice was louder, *if it's time for me to leave here...* louder and louder and only a few men away, *please spare him en give him the strength to survive...* the voice was atop him like thunder, *en protect my girl from the evil things that happen to us in this world...* and then the voice grew softer. He opened his eyes and saw Moondog's back, being dragged away to the hungry ropes in the trees. He also saw Moondog's right hand in a fist at his side, held tight with the fear of death, but also with the transfer of pride intended to buoy Fulton's flagging will to live.

It lasted for hours. They had twenty ropes but over a hundred gunmen. Twenty would rise up, twitch, bulge, and then dangle for half an hour. Then they were lowered, piled with the others aside the chapel, and another twenty were raised. Kibel did his best to plead with Johnstone for mercy. He had never witnessed such horror. He stood beneath the dangling, dying bodies with his head half turned, and he endeavored to bandage their souls before the sight of God. In between the lynchings he pleaded with Johnstone, "In what context of justice can their crimes justify such punishment? You have no right to steal their lives, for the Law is a code of mercy and benevolence, not gratuitous murder. By these actions you are reducing justice to vengeance, and such a reduction is a harbinger of doom for all mankind."

But Johnstone was unmoved. So in these desperate moments, Kibel understood for the first time what it meant to be a darker child of God. He understood for the first time the hopeless dread of the kenotic world in which they fret and die. Every word of his preaching was emptied by a context of such unjust possibility, and the power of God was helpless to save them. Kibel's apostatic heart collapsed like a dead weight in his chest, and before the lynchings ended, he lowered his face from the sky and wandered from Parchman into a world bereft of any image or relation to the sacrosanct, "The world of men is drunk with power and the delusion of significance. This conceit is our doom." He was last seen wandering the empty forests and plains of Mississippi like a ghost without a place to rest.

All the while, the guards kicked the other gunmen and forced them to watch, especially after each group expired and there was nothing but dangling, wintry silence. Fulton could not bear to look, so he unfocused his eyes. He looked past the lynchings at something beyond them so that he could not see their agonized faces and final twitches before their heads fell to one side. And when Moondog was positioned and raised from the earth, neither could look at the other. Tears unfocused Fulton's eyes, and Moondog closed his, afraid to see the world as he was stolen from it, and from his dear friend. Once he was raised, the burning and choking kept him from thinking of all that he was losing. He huffed like a bull for each ounce of air, but his immense weight constricted the chaffing rope into his strained neck. Moondog fought himself to remain alive, for just another instant, for just another moment on earth, but gravity sealed his fate. Fragmented visions of his life blinked though his mind -- his sons and his wife, Neshoba dangling like this before him, the land that sustained and destroyed him, and his pure and profound friendship with Fulton. He had failed them all.

Soon Moondog was the last gunman twitching with life, and he sensed the moment like a gift, so he tried to leave his final breath in the world on his own terms. He reached into the ancestral strength of the winds within him, opened his lids to meet Fulton's eyes, and struggled to exhale his final words to his friend, "The rope of ignorance is thick like a tree, but it can never suffocate our cry for Freedom." But nothing more than a choking cough emerged from his lips, and his final thought in life expired unsaid. When Fulton saw Moondog's head fall lifeless to one side, he wished instead that he had died.

***

Winter twilight had descended on Parchman by the time the last gunmen were lowered and deposited on the pile of former lives. The trees were raw from the scarring of a thousand dying kicks, and absolute solitude inscribed itself in the beating hearts of those made to bear witness. That day would forever haunt the dreamless dreams of everyone who resided on the living side of Parchman's punishment. They all wished their mind's eye blinded so they could sleep in darkness. And though they considered it, not one of them dared to banish those convulsive images by taking his own life. It would be an offense against their memory, which it was their duty to preserve in conscious life.

Ten years were added to the sentences of the recaptured gunmen who were not lynched. The remainder of the winter was long and quiet, save for the echoes of Long Chain Charlie's monthly refilling of Parchman's depleted population and the banging of hammers as the cages were rebuilt. It took the gunmen three weeks to reconstruct their cages, and during that time they slept outside, huddled around small fires.

Then Fulton was re-assigned to the slaughterhouse. He took living pigs and drove the slaughter poles through their mouths and out the other end. He skinned, gutted, cleaned, and salted them for their shipment (in refrigerated cars) to various pork distributors.

Since the day Moondog died, Fulton had not said a word. He was stoic and silent. He no longer knew anyone, and he no longer wanted to. The wailing of the pigs and the deathspray of their innards seemed no different from a whipoorwill's night serenade. He felt purposeless in the world, and the only reasons he remained alive were his promise to Moondog and the image of his dying fist. Nothing else inhabited the forlorn chambers of his heart.

But his mind did not pass the time without reflection. The slaughterhouse forced him to consider his carnivory and wonder what the difference was between it and what History had done to him. Perhaps if he stopped eating meat, History would stop eating his. And during the spring of the next harvest Fulton realized that he was fifty-two years old. "Fifty-two" like "twelve." He was a young man when he arrived, and now he was nearing LaRue and B.B.'s ages. Old man. He had traveled from father to grandfather during his nineteen years in Parchman, and he still had almost two decades to serve. He often laid in his bunk at night and thought about all that he had lost, about his grayed hair and missing teeth, about his absent friends and endless pains, and all of this did not add to more than half of what he was expected to endure at Parchman. For the first time since his Sweetest Queen died, he cried. Tears flowed from the floodgates of his tormented life, and they melted the bitter tension between who he was and who he wanted to be and the ever-thickening reality that he could do little to abrogate the differences between them. He shed a tear for each remaining year of his sentence and he did not speak words again until 1935.

Sharpening the Dagger

Despite Parchman's insularity, word of the escape and of Johnstone's punishment arrived to empathetic and shocked ears, primarily through the story of one gunman named Alton Fifer. Alton had been a gunman at Parchman for eleven years when Governor Bilbo pardoned him because the woman he was supposed to have raped later confessed that she had not been raped at all, but that her father forced her to lie because he suspected Alton of stealing eggs from his hen house. Alton had not been one of the gunmen who followed Otis to freedom or death, but the moment he was pardoned, the editor of the *Yazoo Daily*, Oren Loklen, defied death threats and printed Alton's story and the story of Johnstone's brutal punishment. In that way, Alton became the first word ever to leave Parchman and be heard.

The Southern response was muffled. Even for Governor Bilbo, outrage eventually turned to resignation. Bilbo was at the mercy of cotton economics, so removing Johnstone would mean removing Parchman's cash flow which would mean removing himself from office. But Alton's story arrived in the North to more determined ears. Students wrote to congressmen decrying the medieval ethics of Mississippi's leaders and the hypocrisy of a nation not only founded on the inalienable freedoms of men, but also re-emerged from a bloody self-confrontation that re-established the universality of those rights for *all* men. Meanwhile, Mississippi had created a world worse than slavery. Would the nation's leaders remain idly disinterested until the country arrived at another breaking point of self-massacre?

These voices of opposition finally crept into the President's Office, with Alton Fifer standing meekly beside them. President Coolidge listened to the attorneys and advisors describing what a man like Alton had endured at Parchman Farm. The President listened as he stroked the neck of his golden retriever, and at the end, he looked at Alton and asked, "So what is it exactly that you want?"

"Mr. President, Suh," Alton responded, "all we wants is to be free like the rest, free from fear that our lives can be ruined at anytime . . . even dogs is treated better than us."

The President looked at his retriever and then at Alton. The former glowed with contentment, and the latter was chapped and worn like desert flesh. President Coolidge dismissed everyone from his office except his Secretary of State.

"How long have we known about this?"

"A long time Mr. President, I suppose."

"It's how things are down there. Right?"

"So we've said. But lynching a hundred men? Arresting and convicting without due process? That man Alton lost eleven years of his life for a crime he didn't commit."

"I see. I see how it works. It starts at the top, but the top starts at the bottom. Governor Bilbo was elected by the people of his state, and that is who he represents. He may have been the one to pardon Alton, but he won't change anything as long as his voters dont want him to."

"Even if his state operates an unconstitutional penal farm?"

"It's not unconstitutional until there's a lawsuit that thinks so, and no judge in Mississippi would ever let such a lawsuit breathe a word to a jury."

"That's why things have been the way they've been. That's how democracy works."

"But there are things we could do. It might not be too difficult to scare some of those judges out of their seats, even one would be enough, and get some of our own men down there, and we could also put some pressure on Bilbo, or lobby against his re-election. And we can certainly prosecute Johnstone for cruel and unconstitutional punishment. I want to see that man behind bars."

"Or maybe in those fields picking cotton."

***

Twelve months later not much had changed in Mississippi. Alton Fifer was given a job in the nation's capital with the Postal Office, and a few racist adjudicators were pressured into retirement. Johnstone was prosecuted in Federal Court by the newly appointed Jackson District Attorney Loral Brewer in the courtroom of Loral's colleague and newly appointed Mississippi Supreme Court Chief Justice Tom Talper for the murder of over one hundred men. He was convicted after a seven month trial, but he received a pardon from Governor Bilbo and returned to his father's house to help manage the family's cotton distribution business. Governor Bilbo appointed Tom "Big Boss" Zaras, a prominent landowner from Jackson, as the third Superintendent of Parchman Farm in the twentieth year of its existence.

Big Boss spoke with a voice as commanding as any Superintendent before him even though he was smaller than all of them. He wore a black suit, even on the hottest summer days, and with his almost emaciated frame he appeared more like a reaper than a man. But he was not frail. He walked the fields once or twice a week inspecting the harvest and barking instructions. And even though Big Boss seemed delicate, the gunmen feared his word.

The gunmen discovered that Big Boss' Parchman was a strict but fair place. He curtailed the liberties of both guards and gunmen in the interests of better production. Governor Bilbo offered Bog Boss a profit-sharing plan whereby the growth of Parchman's profits directly swelled his own pockets, and since he had his eye on a fifteen thousand acre tobacco plantation in Virginia he was well motivated to ensure Parchman's continued success. So Big Boss moved the Saturday midnight curfew to ten, and he ordered the previously uncurfewed guards into their cabins by midnight. Participation in Softball Sunday was denied for failure to meet a quota on any single day, and any gunmen caught sniffing thinner would receive ten lashes. Big Boss no longer maintained the pretense that Parchman's existence was predicated on the rehabilitation of wayward citizens, "This is not a nursery and this is not a jail. This is a Mississippi business, and you're here as the labor force of this business because you were unwilling to abide by the rules of living as free citizens in Mississippi. Nevertheless, you'll be treated fairly until you break my rules. After that, I'll eat you alive."

In the stoic self-detachment that had consumed him since Moondog's death, Fulton quietly submitted to Big Boss's new order, though his aging body was not as complicit. In Big Boss's second year, Fulton turned fifty-four, and he began to suffer the physical ailments of a body that was crumbling under the decades of abuse it had endured, like his cabin back home. Fulton suffered from shoulder stiffness and excruciating lower back pains that kept him tossing in discomfort night after night. Headaches sliced his mind in the middle of the day, he continued to wheeze and choke with asthma, and his eyes burned every minute of the day. Once the harvest returned and everyone was back in the fields, more often than not he failed his quota, and he received several lashes for his failure. But he continued, day after day, harvest after harvest, without any particular purpose except for the necessity that permeated him, born and sustained from his memory of Moondog's dying fist.

Fulton no longer counted the days to the moment of his liberation from Parchman, and he no longer felt the weight of himself moving in the world. This zombied Fulton lost his relationship to the earth. *Liloba* was empty, a weightless void over which he floated with indifference. *Liloba* had betrayed him and seemed accomplice to the unending miseries of his life. Torn from *liloba*, Fulton was torn from himself. Devoured by *Liloba*, Fulton was devoured by himself. He was the undead specter of his former dreams, and only the ghost of the earth remained.
Despite the fact that little changed in Mississippi after Alton's story, there was one set of ears that heard the story and awoke from years of self-imposed deafness, and those ears belonged to Dr. Kenneth Adelson. Adelson had sat on his screened porch suffering from chronic bronchitis and had not listened to human words ever since that foul day in Scott, Mississippi when History could not discern the difference between heroes and monsters. But when Dr. Adelson heard Alton Fifer's name, he remembered a little colored boy whom he treated in Tillatoba County for chicken

pox, before Vardaman's public health cuts forced him to remove his practice from poor, colored communities. Adelson remembered Alton's bright eyes and angelic smile, and he remembered Alton was not afraid of his injection and that when he grew up he wanted to be a doctor too, so he could make people's pains go away.

On the day he heard Alton's story, Dr. Adelson cried. He cried because he remembered a day when he believed he could change the world so that a colored boy like Alton could become a doctor, and he cried because he realized that his father was one of a multitude of fathers whose ghosts would be absolved only when that day arrived. So with what life remained in him, Dr. Adelson dreamt one final plan. He had read about Loral Brewer's and Judge Talper's prosecution and conviction of Caesar Johnstone, so he contacted them and asked if they would want to hear his plan. They did, and they listened as if the world knew why they had arrived in Mississippi and sent Dr. Adelson to guide them. "Can you believe our good fortune," Loral said to Judge Talper later as they sipped apple cider, "this Dr. Adelson is going to help us save years."

"Yes he will," Talper responded as he licked his beer-foamed lips, "his plan is perfect."

For his part, Adelson sought Talper and Brewer because if Vardaman had taught him one thing, it was that plans were only as secure as the power of the man who makes them. So now, with the proper minds in the proper places, and with power and a plan on his side, Adelson felt alive and purposeful for the first time in years. And this time he tasted victory, for he reasoned that if last time consciousness could not change the Law, then it must be the case that this time the Law could change consciousness.

Part of Adelson's plan was to slowly slice and claw at Parchman in preparation for his final, violent strike. So unfortunately for Governor Bilbo and Big Boss and all their friends, Adelson again traversed Mississippi with stories of Parchman's brutalities, and once again he galvanized a significant consciousness against Parchman and the other state convict farms. He argued that the "Coloreds are being arrested on phantom charges, sentenced to outrageous terms in prison, and then brutally exploited for the profit of the state until the sentences of their phantom crimes outlived their phantom lives." Again, he exposed convict leasing as virtual enslavement.

Meanwhile, his enemies responded with a different picture. There were no phantom charges nor segregation of the law designed to incarcerate coloreds. The sentences, while occasionally aggressive, were on the whole standard and fair, and when lengthy sentences arose it was pursuant to the specific turpitude of the defendant as well as a deterrent to others. As for the convict labor, the defendants argued that the convicts worked comparable hours to regular members of society and that working to improve the condition of the state by generating funds for schools, roads, and lower taxes was the least a violator of the sanctity of the state could do. Most of the inmates at these convict leasing farms were murderers and rapists. Working for the welfare of the state they had violated was their duty.

While Adelson's viewpoint remained the minority, the increased public scrutiny of the inequitable nature of Southern law and the depravity of the inmates' lives began to wear on Penitentiary Superintendents. In Mississippi, Adelson and his followers lambasted Big Boss and picketed outside his businesses until the just-and-fair Big Boss was ready to wage war on anyone and everyone bold enough to stand between him and his Virginia tobacco plantation.

Adelson's protestors, called the *Constitutionalists*, marched again on Parchman's gates and demanded the just treatment of all citizens of the United States and for the recognition that even "convicted" murderers and rapists retain some basic human rights. Many of the *Constitutionalists* and their families turned up shot or otherwise brutalized, but some hope was nevertheless germinating behind Parchman's front gate. And sensing that hope was swelling in his prison population, Big Boss suspended the softball games and banned all gunmen from Front Camp until the protestors left, two weeks later.

Then, as if by design, the Depression of 1929 hit the country like a brick across the head, shifting regional attention away from prisoner's rights to the stunning impoverishment the country was suffering. As a result, Parchman's defenders found new support for the money it generated to help buffer the state against escalating unemployment and inflation, and therein Parchman found respite from public scrutiny for a few more years. But that was still just in time for Adelson's final plan.

So for the time being, Long Chain Charlie continued rounding up new gunmen, and Parchman continued producing cotton, canned vegetables, and salted meats. The new faces all looked the same to Fulton, the same as LaRue, B.B., Cuttino, Mongoose, and Moondog. He had seen their faces a thousand times, and he knew their destinies before they were born. Fulton often thought of his friends before falling to sleep and told them that he also walked amongst the dead. *I see you there, in his glowy eyes, en you too, in his tired wrinkles. En you, when you was a child. I see all a you 'cause we live in the same place. Ain't no diffrence 'tween us. We all walkin' the rounds together.*

LIFE'S ONLY PROMISE

The Phantoms of Justice

Immersed as he was in his somnambulistic detachment from the world, Fulton did not notice Tennie Crump when he arrived at Parchman in the autumn of 1931, even though he slept only a few bunks away. But Fulton was not alone, for even those who were not yet erased from the world also failed to notice him because he was a surprisingly unremarkable young colored -- plain, even mundane in appearance, and short with obvious eyes. Tennie seemed the type of simple person whom you could look at and feel that you knew everything there was to know about him. And that is precisely why he arrived at Parchman Farm. He cultivated his anonymity. He worked just hard enough, and he carried a likeable trustable demeanor from his cage into the field and back again. No one even remembered that Tennie kept a journal under his pillow in which he inscribed the day's events each night.

Despite his mission of anonymity, within a few months Tennie abandoned his transparence in order to write for his fellow gunmen since he was one of a handful of colored gunmen who could read and write. On Sundays several gunmen gathered around him and dictated their letters. Fulton occasionally walked along the perimeter of the gatherings with his arms folded and his head down. He recalled the letters LaRue wrote for him and thought to himself that Tennie's efforts were doomed because words could not escape Parchman. One day when Tennie called for him, Fulton turned and scurried away. "Don't mind him," one of the gunmen said, "he been a crazy old man since anyone can remember."

"How long's he been here?" Tennie asked.

"Don't know, nobody know . . . longer than anybody," a gunman answered.

Tennie watched Fulton scamper away into the shadows, and he realized Fulton was the exact gunman he needed to ensure success.

Meanwhile, unfortunately for Tennie, now that Adelson had soured Big Boss into waging war against anyone who seemed an enemy of Parchman's success, Big Boss became concerned with Tennire's epistolary sessions. Tennie was no longer invisible, and Big Boss warned Tennie "Nothing good's gonna come of your letters, so you better stop writing." Big Boss also ordered his Sergeants to fix a suspicious eye on Tennie, "He could be planning an escape. I don't trust him. I don't like the look in his eye. It's too hungry."

But Tennie refused to submit. The gunmen needed him, and he was after all, in Parchman to save them. So Big Boss ordered his favorite Sergeant, a man named Dexter, to administer his favorite punishment on Tennie to "Fatten him up so he doesn't look so hungry." Sergeant Dexter was a garish, six-and-a-half foot, grizzled white man who defined his superiority to the colored race by raping each and every colored man, woman, and child he could wrap his meaty hands around. Sergeant

Dexter raped and beat Tennie four nights in a row, and each night when Tennie returned bloodcrusted and broken, Fulton thought of Topeka. On the fourth night Tennie wrote in his journal, "Raped again. Beaten bad. More ribs broken. Nose is broken. Some teeth knocked out. Head is going to explode. Wish I were dead. Wish I had never done this. August 29, 1932."

So Tennie stopped writing letters, and the likeable trustable smile across his face was replaced with a sour scowl and tombstone eyes. He was also informed that twelve months had been added to his two year sentence for disobeying penitentiary rules. He began missing his quota and received lashes for it, and in his swelling misery he often crawled into his bunk to sleep without writing anything in his journal. He could no longer bear to relive each day.

Sensing the urgency of his agenda, Tennie focused on Fulton. He watched him lying on his bunk on his back sleeping with his eyes open. The others told Tennie that nobody knew anything about him except that he had been at Parchman longer than they had been alive. All his friends had died through the years, and no one understood how he continued to live and how he managed to pick his cotton and slaughter his pigs day after day, year after year, with his back bent and his ankles shredded by his shackles. He did not even eat any more except for an occasional biscuit and tea. He appeared as if time had nibbled away his flesh to the bone, leaving only his wrinkled skin, gray hair, and baggydark eyes. But that was why Fulton was critical to Tennie's purpose, for he had suffered it all.

That Sunday Tennie found Fulton sitting alone behind the chapel staring into the indifferent ground. "Name's Tennie, sir. Tennie Crump." Fulton remained silent with his eyes wrapped around a rigid blade of crabgrass. "I've been wanting to talk to you since I got here, but they all say you ain't talked to nobody in years." Tennie waited for him to respond, and he saw other gunmen shaking their heads at his attempt to speak to Fulton. "They call you Old Daddy. I don't know if you mind, but that's what I'll call you cause my own daddy died when I was a boy. He didn't have the chance to be old. My mama raised me. She worked as a seamstress then came home and fed me. Made sure I did my studies. She used to put my head in her lap and tell me all her dreams were in me. She worked and worked and sent me to college. Up in Nashville."

"Only four coloreds in the whole school. Broke her heart after two years when I told her I had to do this. Told me all her dreams would die if I died and there would be nothing left of her." Tennie felt like his words were passing through Fulton unheard. "I, uh, I need your help Old Daddy. I'm not here because of what they think. I was sent here by a lawyer named Brewer. To keep a record and find witnesses. For a trial. We mean to end this place. We mean to drag it before the Law and be rid of it. You've been here longer than anyone, you've seen and endured everything, so I need you to bear witness in a court of law to what you have suffered. You can finally speak how you've been beaten and worked like a dog." Fulton raised his face to Tennie's and gazed towards him, but not at him. Tennie continued, "don't you want to be heard? Don't you want to be the voice that brings justice to these people? If not for yourself then for all the others before and the thousands powerless to follow." Fulton rubbed his dry, burning eyes and returned his face to the crabgrass, drybrown as it clung to the arid earth beneath it. Both desiccated. It the parched grass, he the parched man.

Discouraged but not resigned, Tennie returned to the group of gunmen he had already recruited. He had almost a dozen; almost enough. The case would wind its way through the federal docket for another year, so he had time.

As Fulton watched Tennie return to his other witnesses, he felt from all his experiences that History was not ready for Tennie's vision. But Tennie had shaken him with one observation. He did want to speak. But for all his life, whenever he presumed to do so, his voice had suffocated into an inaudible whisper. He had embraced similar words, the words that Tennie embraced now, like Otis and Mongoose before him, but they were always fated to silence by their powerless design. Words without the weight of consequence. Words unheard.

Meanwhile, Big Boss shed the remainder of his system of fairness and began implementing a Draconian efficiency in Parchman in an attempt to palliate Mississippi's Depression frenzied impoverishment. He felt the pressure to be a hero to Mississippi and also to maintain his own wealth. Big Boss worked his gunmen from before sunrise to after sunset six days a week in order to squeeze every ounce of cotton out of Parchman. More gunmen than ever collapsed from sunstroke, shackle poisoning, dysentery, malaria, violence, and heart failure. Talk of creating another large-scale convict leasing farm began to simmer in Jackson, and construction would have begun within a year had not Tennie Crump and his colleagues redirected national attention to the inhumanities of Parchman Farm, with the unforseen help of the new Governor of Mississippi, Mike Conner.

Governor Conner was inducted to office in October 1932, and he was not in office four weeks when he began instituting violently contested policies of equality for coloreds and women. Equalities of education, opportunity, and treatment under the Law. Conner was not an absolute revolutionary; he understood that change would need to filter slowly into the consciousness of his state. And though he enjoyed the firm support of thousands of Mississippi citizens, his enemies could not understand how he had won the election. No one Big Boss knew wanted Conner alive, and none of the coloreds dared to vote, so everyone concluded that Roosevelt's government was responsible for his victory. Once in office, Conner appointed his constituents to the positions in which he wanted them, and in turn his constituents informed him of a case crawling up the state's docket called Case 102b. The People v. Parchman Farm. Governor Conner never went to Parchman, but in public appearances he exhorted the case as the first step towards the healing and liberation of Mississippi. And most important, the case would save him from having to unilaterally depose Big Boss and challenge Parchman's existence. Conner thanked the fates for his good fortune. The victory of Case 102b would condense years of rhetoric into one moment of distilled revolution. This would be his crown and the victory of his life's crusade.

In response, death threats and scandal became a regular part of Governor Conner's daily routine. Every day the papers were inked with stories of scandal and improprieties littering Conner's character and calling for his resignation. But Conner laughed at most of them, "Hell, I was a poor school boy in Oxford when they say I was having an affair with that Grenada woman," or "Now how could I have been embezzeling money up North thirty years ago if I was working on the railroad right here in Mississippi?" Conner shrugged off the death threats and the scandals as if destiny were his ally. To his loyal (and harassed) followers he assured, "History is ready for us. We have arrived at the time in our Country's life of the awakening of a new consciousness. A consciousness of acceptance, not prejudice, a consciousness of equality, not inferiority, and a consciousness of inclusion, not separation." Conner envisioned supplanting Mississippi's endless rows of cotton with the symmetries of social equality, beginning with Case 102b.

But Big Boss learned about Case 102b too, and he also decided the case would be the crown of his victory. Big Boss learned that the case alleged that Parchman grotesquely violated the eighth and fourteenth amendments of the Constitution, so he hired several attorneys to learn more about the case to help ensure its failure. Big Boss also contacted colleagues throughout the Mississippi judicial system to slow Case 102b's progress through the federal docket. As a result, after eight months, a court date for opening statements in Case 102b was set for ten months later, February 10, 1934. And just as Adelson, Talper, and Brewer were pleasantly surprised by the arrival of Governor Conner and his ardent support of Case 102b, so too was Big Boss surprised by the arrival of a critical piece of information that would threaten to dramatically alter the lives of Case 102b and everyone associated with it.

It was the coldest night in ten years in Nashville with a record nineteen inches of snow blanketing the unprepared streets. Federal attorney Kutcher Todd, Big Boss's niece's husband, wrapped himself in three layers of wool and marched to the Law Building at Vanderbilt University. He had traveled from Jackson to deliver a lecture on the fourteenth amendment. Because of the snowstorm, which stretched from south of Jackson to St. Louis, only a handful of students and professors arrived for Kutcher Todd's lecture. In his lecture, Todd made the case for the exclusion of coloreds from the entitlement of due process under the fourteenth amendment by explaining that the colored, by his nature, lived outside the parameters of the social contract and resided instead in a chaotic state of nature, and as such, did not reside within the same ontological and legal parameters as normal citizens.

After his speech, Todd was in a restroom stall emptying himself when he overheard two students. He was intrigued by their conversation, but he could not follow its context, until the last sentence, the only sentence he needed to remember. He tried to rush out of the stall and find the students, but by the time he readied himself, the students had left the restroom and returned to the crowd that remained outside debating the salient points of his speech. Nevertheless, Todd remembered the important, final sentence, and before returning to Jackson, he dispatched a messenger with a message (since the storm had interrupted phone and wire services) to his wife's uncle, Big Boss, that said little more than the sentence he overheard while in the stall at Vanderbilt, "Well, if what I've heard about that informant at Parchman is true, Mr. Todd might be eating his words about due process one day."

Tennie Crump was playing dice with the five gunmen who were still alive to testify in Case 102b when Kutcher Todd's messenger rode into Front Camp towards the Superintendent's Mansion. Moses Maloo was the oldest of Tennie's witnesses; that is, he had the most gray hair, and he had been in Parchman for seven years of a life sentence for murder. He looked up from the game of dice as the messenger galloped across the earthy slush, "That messenger done read his message. I ken tell. En wit that look on his face it ain't good news for somebody." The others watched the messenger dismount at Big Boss's Mansion and approach the guards at its front door. Tennie dismissed the possibility that the messenger possessed words that could undo him. He knew his name was nowhere to be found. But what could he do if they did know something? A chilled wind passed through him as if no flesh resided in between him and his spine. He shuddered and threw his dice.

When he read the letter, Big Boss felt violated and wanted to lash a hundred gunmen to death. When he came to Parchman he tried to be fair, but again the world was not allowing him to be. He dismissed the messenger and sent for his Sergeants. As he awaited them, he looked out his office window at the gunmen scattered below and wondered who his enemy was. With all the voodoo and the gangs, how could he separate one from the rest? How could he look at any one of them and know he was the infiltrator? His Sergeants would have to find this gunman, and if they could not, more desperate measures would need to be taken. "I don't care how you do it, so long as you find him. Spy on them. Eavesdrop in the fields. Look to see who's hiding something behind his face. He will be young, and idealistic, and foolish. He will make a mistake. You just have to be there when he does. And when you discover him, you come to me and let me know. I want to deal with him myself. It's February now, and we have until November or December before this case reaches a courtroom. Nobody but Conner and this judge wants to hurry the case, and we will ruin them both at the last minute, when it's too late.

And that's the day this nigger and his nigger friends will find themselves wishing they were born smarter than niggers." Big Boss paused to call in a female gunman to warm his breakfast tea. "You go find the gunman who has my severed neck in his eyes."

Spiritual Leprosy

March arrived with bags of cotton seeds for sowing. Mountains of seeds, the unborn fabric of Southern wealth. The Sergeants informed the Drivers, but not the trusties, of the presence of the viral gunman described in Kutcher's letter, and they were ordered to remain vigilant for surreptitious gatherings or suspicious words. They resurrected Sergeant Tipton's relationship with Jarvis Small, and in the next six months they uncovered fourteen suspects who were tortured to death before they confessed any relationship with Case 102b. Bodies appeared at the side of the Chapel for burial with fingernails removed, eyes gouged, or limbs burned. All in plain view (now that Kibel and his God had abandoned Parchman), so that the other gunmen could see, and fear. And even if one of the gunmen had admitted a relationship to the case, Big Boss would have kept searching anyway.

Meanwhile, Tennie was frantic. He was certain that all those gunmen were dying because someone thought they were him. He was petrified that Big Boss would discover him, so he all but ended any additional discourse with his witnesses, except for the occasional reassurance that their mission remained intact and that he would be informed when the case arrived in court. But the deaths of the others haunted him, and he cursed the day his silence cost them their lives. There could be no justice in a world that unfolded such consequence, and that being the case, there may be no justice for them when their day in court finally arrived. In that event, their sacrifice would be purposeless.

In the peak of the September harvest during a water break, Tennie approached Fulton again. He asked him for his help, "I'm afraid, Fulton. Lots of men are dying, and I'm afraid it's because of me. I hear them screaming when I sleep. I hear their families screaming too. If they get me, we need you to lead these men into that courtroom. We need you to bear witness to the entire history of this place." The Water Boy wheeled his wagon to their cage, and as usual Tennie brought water for himself and Fulton, just as Fulton had once brought water for B.B. Fulton sipped the water and felt it cool his brittle bones. "Please Fulton, just say something. Just let me know if they get me you'll make sure this fight is finished. It's not for me or them or the rest of us, but for our children and the world they inherit." Fulton raised his face from the ground and squinted into the sun. He took one more sip of water and then poured the remainder onto the ground.

Winter arrived late, with the scent of ghosts in the breeze, and Big Boss continued to interrogate a new gunman every week, anyone who looked like he might be the conspirator who meant to unravel the South, crumble its time-thickened foundation with the myopic disgruntlement of a minority's agenda. Week after week, another would-be assassin assassinated. Like Vardaman before him, Big Boss reasoned that History was, after all, the province of the empowered.

Science, philosophy, and art all flourished in stratified societies, in a world separated by God, by biology, by History, into its distinct kinds. Thus, equality is the enemy of difference and the conspirator against progress. And since Big Boss's search for that conspirator had brought him close to the new year without success, he would have to take more desperate measures very soon. The next day.

That night as he lay in his bunk, Tennie thought about the gunmen who had slept in his bunk before him. Were they at home with their families, or were they melting into the earth behind the chapel to be reborn in the first blooms of the next harvest? Which one would he be? Then he imagined his last day of life. Would he see it approaching miles away like a dark storm rumbling across the flat horizon, or would it take him in a flash, before he had a moment to recognize what it was? He was unsure which he dreaded more.

That was one of the differences between Fulton and the other gunmen; Fulton no longer thought about the ends of things, nor the beginnings or middles. Time no longer arranged itself in a linear movement. Instead, Fulton lived in an eternal present during which everything that had happened and all the unborn possibilities of the future recoiled into themselves. The only thing he saw behind his eyelids was the emptiness that resided after everything in the world became dark and unremarkable. Inside, there were no more daughters and friends and things that were lost. Inside, Fulton resided in the calm emptiness at the center of the world's self-destructive hurricane. For that reason, when the hurricane swirled into Parchman the next day unleashing the horrors of History's potential like an apocalypse, Fulton remained inside and silent, within the placid center of the maelstrom. He was nothing more than a disjoined witness to the day which none of the others would ever forget, December 25, 1934.

They were all sitting outside their cages eating Parchman's traditional Christmas supper. The women had cooked for two days, turkey and ham with collards, gravy, biscuits, and pecan pie. The open sun helped warm the winter afternoon, but Fulton could not taste the sun in his lemon tea. Since Kibel had left Parchman, the Christmas suppers no longer included an evening gathering and prayer for salvation. Kibel's podium pulpit remained standing but was cold and abandoned. Parchman was the garden in which God no longer resided.

Tennie sat next to Fulton and asked him, "More collards?" *Collards. No more collars. Collars round your neck. Kent swallow. Round Moondog this day. He sing slow songs under the tree. Round his brother this day. Collar got me here this day. Bein' too close. Shot 'em when it won't choke. I kent do it. Hear him all night. Won't choke neither. Breath too strong. That's why he breathe shine. Like the clouds like my smoke. Dreams I send to the world to come find me this day. Take me home like the railroad. Railroad got me here this day. Dreams bury wit his daddy. Sometimes I see em at night, sometimes in the sky where they don't wanna leave. We try to leave this day. We try to leave again. See the fires from the trees. No freedom at the Redemption Tree. Freedom's only in a collar.*

"Everybody up. Drop your food. Big Boss wants you in Front Camp, now!"

Every gunman, black, white, female, old, and young gathered into the yard in front of Big Boss' Mansion. Drivers and trusties were perched atop the surrounding buildings, and all sixty of Parchman's Sergeants were standing on Big Boss's patio porch. Tennie felt his knees buckle. He feared the purpose of this gathering, and he did not know how much longer he could endure living in such fear. At length, Big Boss emerged from his Mansion with a silver plated pistol in his hand and a scowl across his face. He waited until he could feel their hearts thumping in the air around them. Then he addressed them, "I would like to wish you all a happy Christmas Day, but in order for it to be happy, one of you must step forward." *She's happy when we sail. All round the world. We eat Christmas dinner wit the Queen a Spain.* "I would like to wait for another day, but they told me the trial is set to start in two weeks. Those of you who can make this a happy Christmas Day know what I am referring to."

Tennie, Moses, and the other witnesses felt their pulses arrest, their throats constrict, and sweat begin to bead across their foreheads. *I see they heads on high. Silver spirits who keep my dreams locked underground.* "So now the day has arrived when all this will end. There will be no trial. At least not the one that you and the Governor think. I don't have time to waste," *Supper time! Bed time! School time! Cotton Time! Time to wake up. Time for water. Time is runnin' out...* "So I'm going to do this the quickest way I know how." Half the Sergeants walked into the crowd and each took one gunman by the arm and dragged him to the ground in front of Big Boss.

One of the Sergeants had initially seized Tennie's arm, but then released him to take hold of the frightened gunman hiding behind him. Tennie thought he would collapse. Thirty gunmen were dropped to the ground in front of Big Boss; one of them was white and three were women. "Stand up!" Big Boss ordered. "Face the other way, to your fellow gunmen." *There ain't no other ways. They all go the same place.* "I'm going to shoot one of these gunmen every thirty seconds until you show yourself to me, and prove to me you are who you are. So speak up now or I'll be shooting all day."

His words hit the gunmen like a collective concussion. One of the thirty felt his immanent mortality overcome him, so he fled towards the front gate. Not ten steps later a hissing shriek burst through his head and dropped him to the ground. "That's one." *Jes one baby. We gotta have jes one. One day, a son, to inherit our lives. I know you afraid from your mama. But you ain't got her weak heart. You gotta heart like a lion. Jes like our boy gonna have. He gonna be a strong boy.* The others remained standing, backs to him, fearful and taut. They awaited the terrible sound of the clicking shaft. They watched the blood spill from the other's head and steam upon the icy earth.

Bang! Another fell. *Rainin' hard tonight. Thunder won't stop. If the levee go the whole crop go. Then we owe him three harvests. You too small to help. More en more a us owned by him more en more. I hope that thunder don't blow the levee down.* Bang! Another fell, and then another. They fell to the ground and spilled their opened heads. No secrets inside. "You must have one fantastic case to stand there and let me shoot all these gunmen without saying a word." *Words don't mean no nuthin' nohow anyway.*

Tennie's mind was failing and he began mumbling nervously. Bang! This time a woman. Then one of the remaining yelled, "Please brother, show yourself," and the white one added, "Don't stand there like a coward while we die!" *We all dyin', from the birth. Livin's just findin' diffrent ways to be dyin'.* Big Boss raised his pistol level to the remaining heads and waved it back and forth, wondering who he would shoot next. "Twenty-two, twenty-three, twenty-four... there are only a few more seconds in between this moment and another tragedy."

Ain't no tragedy possible in a world where some is born niggers en others ain't. Ain't no tragedy possible in a world where evrythin' I do is already undone. Then the voice spoke, "Stop! It's me. I'm the one you want, Case 102b." Big Boss lowered his pistol and everyone turned with a gasp towards the voice. Tennie turned too, because it was Moses Maloo who walked forward to stand face to face with his Big Boss. Big Boss eyed Moses in silence, Moses did not look back, and Tennie gaped in disbelief. For the first time since he arrived at Parchman he understood what their freedom really meant. It did not mean an end to the abuses and the pain. It did not mean the opportunity to return home. Freedom meant the end of situations like this. Freedom meant the return of the destinies that Mississippi had appropriated centuries before. Freedom meant the end of spiritual leprosy.

As he looked at Moses, wondering why his enemy was so old, Big Boss nevertheless saw the glorious funeral of this momentary turbulence in Mississippi's history. "And the others? Where are they?"

"There ain't but one other, en you already shot em dead."

"I know there are more, now call them forward."

"There ain't no others. Wasn't nobody willin' to take the risk, or believe we could win."

Big Boss pressed his silver pistol against Moses' forehead, "I'm gonna ask you once more, and them I'm gonna empty your miserable brains to the ground. Where are the others?"

"You ken shoot me en all the rest all day. Only thing that'll happen is you'll have no gunmen left en eventually someone's gonna come askin' why there's a thousand gunmen wit holes in they heads."

They both knew who that someone was, and the reference infuriated Big Boss. His hand flexed and slowly pulled the trigger half way back, when just as quickly his face calmed and he placed his pistol in its holster. "You know what, I don't care anymore. I don't even care enough to torture you to death just to make sure you're not lyin'. I've killed a few gunmen today. Even if there are conspirators left among you and they still have the guts to try their luck against me and the State of Mississippi and think that all of a sudden things are gonna change. You take me on when the time comes and we'll see together who gets justice and who doesn't." Big Boss punched Moses in the face and then kicked him in the groin. "Maybe it would be appropriate to crucify you, but you don't even deserve the sanctity of the reference. Hang him! And make sure the rest of them see it." Big Boss turned and walked into his Mansion, where he climbed up the stairs and told himself he had just saved Mississippi.

The guards kicked and beat Moses Maloo over to the Lynching Trees, which were still bruised from a few years before. They noosed his neck and lynched him. Fortunately for Moses, he was old and had a weak neck, so he only suffocated for a few moments before dying. Crows were picking at his remains before he was lowered and buried beside the chapel along with the others who died that day. The lynching of Moses Maloo was the first lynching that Tennie had ever seen, and nothing he had read prepared him for it. Not even the pictures. For several weeks after, he awoke to suffocating nightmares that he was being lynched, and he screamed for air to breathe while pulling at his neck to release it from the collar's ghostly constriction.

Two of Tennie's witnesses decided not to proceed with their roles in Case 102b. They did not care who Judge Talper and Loral Brewer were; as far as they were concerned, justice resided in Big Boss' hands. The defection left Tennie with two witnesses, and he was certain that he would have little success in trying to recruit more. So he tried to convince Fulton one more time, and even though the sacrifice of Moses Maloo illuminated images of the precious lives that his sacrifice meant to save, Fulton nevertheless remained silent and resistant to Tennie's requests. *It's still a world a black en white. So it's best to be invisible.*

LIFE'S ONLY PROMISE

Fragments

The next week, a wobbling and wheezing Dr. Adelson, Judge Talper, and Loral Brewer requested an audience with Governor Conner and revealed the plan behind Case 102b. Conner counted his lucky stars and smiled as if the heavens finally possessed colored gods. Then, on January 7, 1935, Governor Mike Conner, District Attorney Loral Brewer, and thirty State Troopers rode into Parchman Farm in a Ford Model T and six military jeeps. Governor Conner marched into the Superintendent's Mansion and requested the presence of Tennie Crump. Big Boss clenched his teeth and asked, "Why do you need this gunman?"

"I have a pardon for his release and the release of several others."

"Which others?"

"Kindly bring Tennie Crump to me before my men have to go find him themselves."

Big Boss led Governor Conner outside his Mansion and one of his Sergeants told him that Tennie worked in the slaughterhouse. So they walked to the slaughterhouse, and Big Boss instructed the Sergeant on duty to bring Tennie Crump forward. Tennie was working with Fulton in the skinning pit when he heard the words he had feared ever since Sergeant Dexter punished him for writing letters, "Tennie Crump, Big Boss wants to see you right now." For a few moments, Tennie feared his life was about to end in the slaughterhouse, yet he almost felt relieved to be rid of the anxiety and paranoia with which he had lived for the past months. As he approached the front of the building he saw several white men gathered around each other, and he saw Big Boss's face, whose expression was commensurate with the squealing and shrill yelping of the pigs.

Just as he was preparing for his end, Tennie arrived at the front of the slaughterhouse and saw Loral Brewer. He figured the other was the Governor, and he felt the weight of a thousand deaths lifted from his chest. He had survived. But he did not smile.

"This here's Tennie Crump."

"Thank you Sergeant. You may return to your duties. Tennie, I am Governor Conner and this man to my right is Jackson District Attorney Loral Brewer."

"Pleased to meet you both, suh."

"Now Tennie, you were a student before coming here, right?"

"Yessuh, Mr. Governor, suh."

"And there are others?"

"Yessuh, two suh."

"Two?"

"Yessuh, only two, suh."

"And their names?"

"CC Turl and Tommy Snipes."

Governor Conner opened his briefcase and removed three Certificates of Gubernatorial Pardon and wrote the three names on them, "these men are receiving pardons. The appellant courts have overturned their convictions as mistrials. Please unshackle the other men and bring them to the front gate." Before Big Boss's reddening face could erupt, Governor Conner turned and walked to the front gate with his hand around Tennie Crump's arm.

Big Boss brought the other gunmen to the front gate and watched them climb into the military jeeps. He called Conner's name and walked towards him, face to face. Conner was steady, and his eyes were like knives. Big Boss addressed him with muffled rage, "I know what this is, Conner. I know about the case."

"I know you know, and that only adds to my pleasure."

"You're the only Governor to challenge what this place means. Don't you know that I pay your salary?"

"The time for this place has ended. These men and their case mark the beginning of a new era for Mississippi. Your era will be archived as an ignorant age whose conceit awakened Justice from her careless slumber."

"Over my dead body."

"You'll have to offer more than that to redeem their suffering."

Conner turned from Big Boss and climbed into his car. As his enemies exited Parchman, Big Boss brooded under the gravity of the moment. He saw a rift rupturing in History's horizon, and for the first time in his life he was unsure on which side of the rift he was standing. Meanwhile, Fulton had walked out of the skinning pit and was also standing in Front Camp. He wondered whether Tennie would be the second word to leave Parchman, and be heard.

***

Though all the potential jurors were white, Judge Talper and Loral Brewer almost entirely controlled the jury's selection for their benefit, so when the case finally began, Brewer painted Talper's courtroom with the morbid colors he knew would assault the jury's sensibilities. He portrayed a Mississippi that was born from prejudicial monsters who wore the guise of civility and philosophy to justify their hunger. The jury felt as if it was listening to the impossible testimonies of an impossible place, especially when Tennie read excerpts from his journal. The prosecutor was relentless, "Describe a summer day in the fields of Parchman Farm... describe the sexual abuses you endured... describe what happened when you failed your quota... describe your living conditions... describe mealtimes in the fields." Governor Conner and Dr. Adelson sat through every minute of the testimony, watching Loral Brewer open the innards of Parchman Farm for everyone to see, and they saw the devoured remnants of a thousand colored lives.

But the defense attorney, Douglas Kerr, did not surrender. Though his rebuttal witnesses, including Flood, Johnstone, and a dozen Sergeants and Drivers, testified that their disciplinary policies were predicated on the brutal, boorish, animalistic, amoral behavior of the negro race, though Douglas Kerr argued that the stories related in the courtroom were the grossly exaggerated fables of three misguided inmates, and though he announced that in fact some coloreds themselves had been promoted to enforce Parchman's rules, the jury continued to frown at the defense's self-serving testimony and the air of entitlement with which it spoke. And since Kerr could not risk revealing the plot behind Case 102b to the courtroom for fear of the gunmens' testimony of Big Boss's Christmas Day executions, the defense's position became increasingly tenuous.

However, one argument remained which Kerr had saved until his case became desperate, and this argument would be difficult for the jury to ignore. With Big Boss' permission, Kerr argued that everything heard in the courtroom described conditions in Parchman only during Big Boss' tenure as Superintendent. Tennie, CC and Tommy had been in Parchman only a few years, and as such, whatever injustices they described were not constituent to Parchman, but were only the recent mistakes of its recent keepers. Thus, the jury could find fault with those keepers, but not with the entirety of Parchman Farm. At that point, Kerr moved to split the defendant into two entities, Tom Zaras and Parchman Farm, and to judge each of them separately. Despite Brewer's objection, the law compelled Judge Talper to grant the motion. Everyone understood what the motion meant, and at that moment Tennie dropped his head and told himself that Fulton's silence would cost them the case after all. And so the time arrived, after forty-one days of testimony, for both attorneys to present their closing arguments to Judge Talper's Court of Justice.

Prosecutor Loral Brewer began, "There are not many words that can convey the atrocities and injustices suffered by the gunmen of Parchman Farm. You have heard of a thousand deaths. Death by lashing, death by overwork, death by disease, and death by cruel punishment. You have heard of the mockery of our law. Children sentenced to five years for stealing candy, men who have grown old and died in Parchman without ever being convicted of a crime, and the swelling of sentences without due process of any kind. And though we may not have all these men alive and before us to speak their suffering, can there be any doubt that what these three witnesses describe has always been true of Parchman Farm. The laws of men cannot respond to all their cries for justice, but we can at least gesture to address their grievous chorus of affliction.

"The eighth and fourteenth amendments of our country, a nation born from the bloodied womb of our liberation from tyranny, protect our citizens from cruel and unusual punishment and from any abridgment of said citizen's right to life, liberty, property, and due process under the Law. Is there any doubt that the gunmen of Parchman Farm, like their enslaved ancestors before them, have suffered a thousand years of a thousand crimes? Our Constitution was conceived as a malleable doctrine, able to guide our pursuit of life and liberty throughout the progress of our nation. That is why our governance is the envy and culmination of History. And with this gift at our disposal, shall we spit in the face of our forefathers' sacrifices with this lack of vigilance over that nation of liberty that they conceived?

"There is no doubt that we have failed our nation, our History, and our forefathers with the existence of Parchman Farm. There is no doubt that we have failed the colored citizen who was assured equality of rights and opportunity under the law of our land. And there is no doubt that we have failed the progress of History by digressing to a medieval rule of law that oppresses the many for the wealth of the few. It will not be easy for you to initiate the enlightenment of Mississippi's consciousness to the nightmares of its monstrous sleep. It will not be easy for you to stand in the face of ignorance and maintain the justice of your wisdom. But you must make your stand today. In Arkansas, Governor George Donaghey abolished convict leasing twenty-two years ago, and yet our state languishes unenlightened and behind the law. The future of our State rests on the superior wisdom we are asking you to manifest today. Do not accept the way of things, and do not submit to the beguiling ease of deferring justice to another time. Imagine yourselves on the other side of History and ask yourselves for what you would pray each night. You would pray for a nation of justice and liberty for your children, just as these men and their forefathers have knelt and prayed each night for decades. Not until today has Mississippi been poised to answer their unheard prayers. And our answer can only be the abolition of this monstrous institution. We only hope that you will open your hearts to their cries and answer them with God's eternal justice."

Brewer took his seat, and the courtroom awaited Kerr's response. Brewer had spoken with composed, reasoned words that were not overwhelmed by emotive energy. The judge and jury had listened, watching the words form in his mouth. And now, Douglas Kerr walked to the center of the courtroom and offered his response, "My colleague is correct about one thing, justice resides in the eyes of the wise. So let us consider this: when you switch your child for violating the norms of good behavior, is it reasonable for the child to cry injustice? We punish our children to ensure that they grow into moral, law-abiding citizens of our community. The same is true of adults who break the law. They are punished to rehabilitate their civility. And throughout History, society has conceived punishments to fit the crime. Parchman Farm is nothing more than the manifestation of this historical truth. And if the offender continues to offend, harsher punishments must be administered. Parchman Farm is nothing more than the manifestation of this logical truth.

"But Parchman has deviated from History in one, important way. Parchman's creators accepted the assumption that the violator of civil sanctity owes a debt, not only to justice, but also to the society he violated. The violation of civil sanctity requires punishment; the debt incurred to society requires recompense. Therein, Parchman was conceived as the place where these violators would serve their punishment and also work to repay their debt to the society they offended. It is not enough that the rapist and murderer simply sit in a jail sucking our tax money; no, he should be forced to repay his debt to society. This is Parchman's philosophy and charter. Its convicts spend their sentences canning vegetables, packing meat, and baling cotton so that the profits of their labor may be used to repay their civil debts. Does not the rapist owe us better roads and lower taxes? Does not the murderer owe us new churches and new schools? Instead of vilifying the charter of Parchman Farm, we should be applauding the wealth it has added to our society, especially during these difficult economic times, when all of you must know someone without a job or a means to provide.

"Like any institution, abuses may arise. But these are the aberrations of single individuals and should not discredit the greater institution. If you disagree with something the President does, does that discredit the Presidency? We may choose to erect a means of vigilance, but let us not destroy Parchman simply because of the recent mistakes of a few men. We are entering an age of tempestuous change, but before we lose ourselves to the whirlwinds of modernity, let us take a moment to reconstitute and reaffirm the ancient institutions that have sustained our happiness thus far. The purpose of History is in our appreciation of the tests of time, a test our way of life has passed through war, poverty, and now, through this shortsighted challenge to the spirit of our society. I know that you will agree. Thank you."

Before adjourning his courtroom for the jury's deliberations, Judge Talper instructed his jury to consider the violations of the inmates' eighth and fourteenth amendment rights separately for Parchman Farm and Tom Zaras. Two days later the jury emerged from its deliberations, but not before Dr. Adelson's bronchitis finally squeezed the last breath of air from his ragged lungs and he died. He had been lying on his back on his bed unable to sleep when he realized he had only a few breaths remaining. He counted them down slowly, like ocean waves tumbling into the shore. When he arrived at his final breath, he filled his lungs with as much wind as he could, placed his father's visage in his mind, and exhaled all the battles of his life into the realization that victory and defeat were never anything more than differently spelled words.

The night before the jury announced its verdict, Dr. Adelson was buried. After the funeral, Governor Conner and Loral Brewer sat on a bench in the cemetery and gazed at the land of the dead. Conner thought about how many of them, like Adelson, died before their dreams, and for the first time since he began his crusade for justice, he wondered what justice really meant.

"Tell me, Loral, what do liberty and justice mean?"

"What do you mean Governor?"

"I mean, in the last few months you and I and others have been repeating these words like we had discovered the name of God. I've heard their sounds so often that I don't know what they mean anymore."

"Are you saying that the meaning of liberty is in its sound?"

"No. That's not what I mean. I know that liberty means something like freedom from oppression and that justice means something like the impartial administration of morality and law. I know this in my mind, but in that courtroom you pronounced the need for justice and liberty and liberty and justice, and soon all I heard was sounds, not the condition or place or time in which these qualities exist."

"I suppose they are abstract notions without a time or a place. They only define themselves in the moments of their recognized actualization, when you witness a court uphold the law or when you see a colored man living without fear and with the rights to vote, to own property, and to provide for his living. That's what they are and that's what we're fighting for."

"So then liberty and justice are confined to moments. That's what troubles me. I always understood them to be a state of being or a state of affairs. But oppression and injustice outnumber their opposites a hundred to one. We can't change Mississippi's philosophy of being. All we can do is fight a moment here or a moment there, and that will leave us forever lacking achievement of what we have spent our lives fighting for. And it's exactly this fact that might undo us, the fact that justice and injustice are only moments. If you were on that jury could you say that all of Parchman is unjust based on the testimonies of those inmates who have only been there the last two years?"

"Following the strict letter of the law . . . I don't know. It's certainly the case that everything they talked about before they arrived in Parchman was hearsay, and the only reason the court heard any of it was because Talper was the judge."

"It only takes one member of that jury who is not already prejudiced towards our sense of justice to undo us."

"That's why it's very hard to change the law."

"That's why I dont know what my crusade means any more."

Governor Conner left the cemetery that night afraid that the law had no purpose and that no one could ever understand its meandering course through the ravines of time. He no longer understood his crusade, and he knew that he would probably leave the earth before he succeeded, but he remained thankful for privilege of freedom to die trying.

The next day the past, present, and future filed into the Supreme Court of Jackson, Mississippi to witness the jury's decision. The courtroom was called to order, Chief Justice Talper ascended to his chair, and then everyone sat and remained silent. Talper's mouth was cotton dry as he looked to the Jury and asked, "Has the Jury reached a verdict on the matter of Parchman Farm's violation of the eighth and fourteenth amendment rights of its inmates?"

"Yes, your honor, we have," the jury's foreman replied.

"And has the jury reached a verdict on the matter of Tom Zaras' violation of the eighth and fourteenth amendment rights of the inmates of Parchman Farm?"

"Yes, your honor, we have."

"Will the bailiff please relay the verdicts."

The bailiff retrieved the envelope from the jury's foreman and delivered it to Judge Talper. Governor Conner watched the envelope like destiny. He watched Tennie and the other gunmen whose hearts were in their throats, and he watched Big Boss and his Sergeants, who seemed indifferent to the envelope's contents. After receiving the envelope, Talper read its contents with an expressionless face. Then he addressed his courtroom, "Will the defendants please rise. Mr. Foreman, in the case of the People versus Parchman Farm, on the matter of said Farm's violation of the eighth amendment rights of the plaintiffs, how do you find?"

"Not guilty, your honor." The words crashed like hammers into Conner, Brewer, and Tennie's chests, and a grumbling murmur filled the courtroom.

"And on the matter of Parchman Farm's violation of the fourteenth amendment rights of the plaintiffs, how do you find?"

"Not guilty, your honor." A second murmur followed the foreman's words. Some were elated, others felt destroyed.

"Very Well. Now, on the matter of Tom Zaras' violation of the eighth amendment rights of the plaintiffs, how do you find?"

"Guilty, your honor." The entire courtroom acted as if it had not heard the decision.

"And on the matter of Tom Zaras' violation of the fourteenth amendment rights of the plaintiffs, how do you find?"

"Guilty, your honor."

The defendants looked at each other and then at their attorney. Tennie, the other gunmen, Conner, and the rest of the courtroom did not know how to respond. They had not lost, but neither had they won. They looked to Talper's face to try to understand what the decision meant, but even he appeared sorrowfully perplexed. After a few moments, Judge Talper addressed the defendants with heavy, solemn words, "We will reconvene in one week for the sentencing of Tom Zaras. But this is not an ordinary case with precedents and statutes to guide me. This courtroom has simultaneously declared today that Tom Zaras has violated the rights of his inmates, but also that there is not sufficient evidence to declare that the philosophy of our state has fallen behind the laws of our nation and that there is no disjunction between the evolution of these laws and the stasis of our entrenched prejudice. To you, the Sergeants of Parchman Farm, I return you to your jobs, but not without my plea that the time has arrived for you to free your minds of the prejudice of your ancestors and try to unlearn the hatred you inherited from our past. As for you, Tom Zaras, your sentencing will be in my courtroom one week from today at eleven am. This court is adjourned."

The bailiff called the court to order, and Judge Talper exited with the fragments of justice in his hands. Three hours later, when the courtroom was dark and empty, Governor Conner remained sitting alone, with the half-victory of his crusade still thumping in his chest. Though he had not won, he offered this day to all the faces known and unknown who had spent their lives fighting the fangs of oppression even as they clamped shut through the center of their dreams. And yet, his half-victory was more precious than anyone could know. For Conner held a secret from the world, and if the world would know it, then he, his allies, and all their progress would crumble into the resurrected jaws of their enemies. So Governor Conner sat with his secret in the darkness of the Court of Law, in the shadows of justice.

One week later, Big Boss arrived in Judge Talper's Courtroom for his sentencing. He sat with his attorney and wore an unconcerned smile as he filed his nails. In turns, he looked over his shoulder at Tennie and the other gunmen and foresaw their dismemberment and slow burning in a fire. Then he looked at Conner. Their eyes met, and Big Boss winked as if he expected to leave the Courtroom unscathed, like a magic trick.

Judge Talper arrived, and without wasting time, motion, or words, he delivered the context of his sentencing, "This has not been an easy week. I have prayed each night for the wisdom to fashion a sentence that will manifest the will and purpose of the law. But the law is never absent of context, and you, Superintendent Zaras, and the thousands like you whose philosophy saturates our moment, you are the inextricable component to our context. Even when at odds with you, the law cannot locate itself outside of you. This is where my own wisdom manifests its impoverishment. I cannot presume to possess the perspicacity to adjudicate this localized rupture between you and the law. I only fear that when the rupture closes, the law will not have changed the consciousness of Mississippi with which it has disagreed on this instance, and therein my sentence would become meaningless."

As Judge Talper spoke, Tennie and Conner closed their eyes. They expected Talper's words to be stronger, but he seemed to be speaking as if he already expected his words to be undone. Nevertheless, once his thoughts had been heard, Talper asked Zaras to rise and he delivered his sentence, "Superintendent Zaras, due to your violent disregard of the constitutional rights of your inmates, this Court decrees that you are hereby relieved of your station as Superintendent of Parchman Farm and shall be replaced by a Superintendent of the Governor's appointment. You are sentenced to twenty years in prison without parole, to be served in Parchman Farm."

Before Talper could bang his gavel, and before the irony of his sentence could sink into the courtroom, Douglas Kerr jumped to his feet, "Your Honor, my client is filing a motion to appeal your decision." The courtroom erupted with angry cries and Talper banged his gavel as if beating an animal into submission.

When the courtroom calmed, Talper announced, "Very well mister Kerr. Bail is set at one thousand dollars. This court is adjourned." Talper banged his gavel and stormed from his courtroom with such exasperation that the winners felt that they had not won anything at all.

Big Boss paid his bail, and within a few weeks, his appeal was heard by all five Justices of the Mississippi Supreme Court. In a three-to-two decision, Talper's lower court decision was overturned. Big Boss returned home and still had enough money to buy a six thousand acre tobacco plantation in Virginia.

Nevertheless, for the moment, Governor Conner had been given the latitude to make as much as he could of his half-victory in Case 102b. The next day, he appointed a member of his advisory staff, Eli Cade, as the next Superintendent of Parchman Farm. Cade called all the gunmen to Front Camp and told them about Case 102b, about Tennie's testinmony, the jury's verdicts, and Talper's sentencing. He also told them that Governor Conner had decided to voyage to Parchman in two weeks to personally review each inmate's case and pardon anyone he judged to have served more than his just sentence, starting with cage one and working up. He called it Liberation Week.

Most of Big Boss' Sergeants retired with his departure, and Cade replaced them with a dozen new Sergeants who neither hated coloreds, nor were bothered by the thinning difference between them and their colored inmates. They abrogated the unwritten policies incensing violence and distrust between inmate and guard, and they abolished the position of trusty. They established a maximum workday of eight hours and excused the old or sick from their labor. The inmates of Parchman Farm felt that a dark, nightmarish layer of reality was sloughed away and a new world was born. They felt that if they did their work and behaved well, they could trust in humane treatment and the proper termination of their sentences. But then, at the same time, all the colored inmates knew that they were still reborn the color of night, and some part of their world would always fear the dark.

And true to their and Talper's fears, as Parchman's profitability eroded under Cade's more lenient rules, Conner's enemies ensured that he lost the next election. He was replaced by Hugh White, who ran on a platform promising to return Mississippi to its glorious past, like Vardaman once promised. Governor White replaced Cade with one of his own allies, and soon enough Parchman was once again working its gunmen to death and trusties were once again shooting gunmen to get pardoned, as if nothing had ever changed.

But for the time being, Fulton observed Parchman's modest transformation under Cade and awaited the moment of the Governor's arrival for Liberation Week. He waited like one awaits sleep on a stormy night. A few days after Cade arrived, Fulton was moved from the slaughterhouse to the cannery along with several of the other older inmates to work with the female inmates canning Parchman's vegetables.

And with Conner's Liberation Week on the horizon, hope was timidly reborn in Fulton's eyes, but he did not dare imagine what awaited him if freedom came his way. He did not dare forsee his hopes, for that vision had inevitably projected itself into whatever realm of the universe was responsible for the unraveling of nearly every dream he ever had. So he resolved to wait, to defer, with an indifferent, emotionless, empty, evenmind. But sometimes a glimmer of hope would escape his eyes, and he would turn to watch it shade from vermilion to gray as it descended with the sunset into the earth to sleep.

The Silence that Circles Breathing

Each Sunday afternoon Superintendent Cade sat on his porch in a rocking chair and narrated the great historical events of the century to his gunmen. On the day before Governor Conner arrived at Parchman, Fulton listened to Superintendent Cade orate the story of the Great War, which had raged from 1914 to 1919 and painted Europe's soil with the bloodied innards of young boys who died far away from the understanding of their purpose. Fulton was thankful he was not one of them, and he lowered his head with the sadness that the entire world seemed plagued with purposelessness. As he listened to the story of the Great War, Fulton thought to himself that those soldiers in those trenches lived and died a lot like coloreds in Mississippi. *We live in the earth too, en everyday the sky showers down ruin on us, en we don't know where it's fallin 'til it's too late. Then after a while we don't understand no more why we livin' en what we fightin' for.* In that way, the end is mercy.

That night Fulton dreamt about the trenches and all the faces buried in them. As he walked through the trenches they transformed into a rounded belly filled with water, within which floated the various faces of his past. Uma, his grandmother, Moondog, Neshoba, Stoka, LaRue, B.B., Mongoose, Cuttino, and countless others. They floated silently in the waters, though they seemed to be trying to speak. Fulton walked through the length of the belly retracing the history of his life. The endless legion of desperate faces, like masks, began to frighten him, so he reached his hand forward and tried to speak to them, but nothing emerged. He tried to ask them why were they here? Could they leave? Was his daughter here? He tried to scream, but nothing emerged. And so the faces remained silent, and in their silence they menaced him like the cacophony of a thousand shackles.

Fulton continued to walk forward through the faces, wondering how long the belly would stretch. Walking on and on in a circle. Then after what seemed like ten lifetimes, the belly coiled upwards. There was light, and the faces disappeared. Moving forward he saw that he was in a canyon. Spiked mountains lined the horizon. Then he heard a rumbling roar that sent him spinning through the dark, thick space outside the canyon. He fell without a ripple into an endless ocean colored like an empty night, like his daughter's newborn eyes. He floated atop this plumbless, dark expanse of water whose secrets he could never know. Then he looked up and saw the face of a dragon, whose eyes opened like blossoms and burned the light of the universe. The dragon roared again and filled Fulton's lungs with winds from the four ends of space, and then he was able to speak.

"Who are you?"

The dragon glowed in silence as its tongue (or was that its tail?) dripped from its mouth into the waters, as if simultaneously drinking and expelling the unformed space around it. At length, it responded, "I am History, and there are no other Gods before me. I am the lyrical sound that exhales and inhales the world, and the expanse of conscious time is the pause between my breathing. That pause is the moment within me, coiled like a moat of silence around the living and the dead."

"Why are they trapped inside? Where is my daughter? All I ever asked was that she have a better life than mine."

"Seek to bear fruit, and it will consume you. Disregard these phantoms, and I can never torment you."

"But your saying so doesn't change me."

"Because you color the indifferent world with your individual dreams and then fall prey to the drama and calamity you project. It is your nature, and you are its slaves."

"Then you have breathed the winds of words into me, and I fail to find the purpose in speaking."

"Silence is the substance of all things. Neither your loudest roar nor the passing of epochs are ever heard. You may choose to slay me, but a thousand more will spring from my slain body."

"I don't understand."

"Look to your necklace, and you will understand. Look inside and you will understand. I can only give birth to ghosts."

The dragon curled its head within its cosmic coils, and the light of the universe disappeared, leaving Fulton floating alone in unending darkness, left only to embrace the weight of his solitude. He could not move in any direction, and he was no longer certain whether his eyes were opened or closed. He wandered as if for years, ruminating. He looked at his necklace and then he looked inside, and all he saw was darkness, and all he heard was the fading echo of his unheard question as it recoiled into the cavernous chambers of the abyss within him. At that moment Fulton realized that every torment in his life was seeded in his fury to make a sound (to ask, to slay, to create a difference); but instead, living was never anything more than the decay of that sound. Thus, only the silence of questionlessness could offer him rest.

***

Governor Conner arrived the next day and prepared his Mercy Court in Superintendent Cade's office. Superintendent Cade informed Conner that Parchman housed over two-thousand four-hundred inmates, and he would need six weeks to review all their cases. But Conner only had a few more months remaining in his first term, and he knew that the time he spent at Parchman freeing its gunmen was time he was not spending campaigning for what precious votes remained for him after Case 102b and the higher taxes and fewer churches that would be the consequences of his crusade for prison gentility and colored equality. So he decided to focus Liberation Week on the oldest and youngest inmates as well as any inmate who had been at Parchman over ten years.

Cade's Sergeants combed Parchman's records for every inmate who met the criteria of the Mercy Court, and beginning with cage one, each file was delivered to Conner, and the inmates were brought to the Mercy Court in the Superintendent's Mansion. Though it was March, every inmate was ordered out of the fields to wait at his cage for the possibility that his name would be called. So as they waited, the inmates reached into their collective memories of courts and laws in order to formulate the arguments for their release. They whispered outside their cages, "I heard the govner freein' us that ain't suppose to be here or been here too long... I hear he only lettin' the white folks go... I heard he already let Charlie Bennet from cage two free en gave him a hundred forty dollars... yeah, walked right outta the front gate wit his ring-arounds on... he been here longer than anybody 'cept Fulton... walked right out the front gate."

The Mercy Court was open each day from sunrise to sunset, evaluating cage after cage of inmates too old, too young, or too innocent to have been in Parchman at all. As he presided over his Mercy Court, Governor Conner choked with shame with almost every case, and with every case he grew more and more agitated because he knew there were probably ten other cases just like the last one, but he could never remedy them because he could not pardon the dead. But he did what he could. He freed three homeless boys, Jabo Dean, Pratt Read, and Homer Read - nine, nine, and ten - after they had spent eighteen months in Parchman for urinating in a public area. He took one look at their morose faces and understood how fiercely they had been abused. Little Pratt Read did not even speak during the hearing, he simply sat twitching his head and waving his lonely hand across his face as if to clear away insects.

Conner presided over countless cases of mishandled justice and abuse of the law, such as the case of Rudy Randolph. It began on the Wednesday of Liberation Week, when a retired Mississippi Judge named R.B. Smith arrived at Parchman, after having heard about Conner's Mercy Court. He requested the Governor's presence and asked about an inmate named Rudy Randolph. When Randolph arrived in the Mercy Court, he almost collapsed at the sight of the judge who had sentenced him to prison fifteen years ago. Retired Judge R.B. Smith asked Randolph to present his case for Pardon to Governor Conner. Randolph did not understand, but he stuttered his argument nevertheless.

It was 1920. He was seeing a woman who already had a little girl from another man. One day he caught her giving his money to that man, so he left her. The next thing he knew, she accused him of raping her little girl.

"Were you guilty?" Conner asked.

"Govner, suh, they found me guilty, but I wasn't."

"Did you plead guilty?"

"The lawyer told me if I didn't my sentence would be worse."

"Did you hire a lawyer, or did they appoint one?"

"The 'pointed one, suh."

Then R.B. Smith interceded, "I was the Judge in Randolph's case. The woman was named Nora, and she and the girl testified that Randolph had raped the girl. Even though it was a case of colored on colored crime, the moral outrage of the rape of a ten year old girl pressured me into sentencing Randolph to life in prison. The case was closed and justice was served. But then the next year I tried a case in Rome. It was a rape case, and the victim turned out to be that same little girl. I was suspicious, so I had her examined. The doctor said she had never been entered."

Conner's face boiled red, "And you let this man languish here for fourteen more years of his life?!"

"Yes sir. I know sir."

"You know? What do you know? Life is our most precious gift, and the role of law is to protect it, not squander it." Conner was too furious to continue. He pardoned Rudy Randolph, who like the others, walked out of Parchman's front gate into a world which he did not recognize and which did not offer him an obvious place to rest.

It was later that day, March 28, 1935 when one of Superintendent Cade's Sergeants at cage seven announced, "Fulton Chapman. Governor Conner is calling you to the Mercy Court." Fulton had tried not to think of this moment since the beginning of Liberation Week, but his hopes had nevertheless been palpitating within him, re-awakening the constriction around his lungs and leaving him bent and wheezing all day. He tried to keep his mind empty, but he could not help pondering how he would return home, what he would find, and how he would pass whatever years remained for him. What would Simbi be wearing when he returned? How would her face shine? Would his heart collapse the moment he embraced her? As he walked from his cage to the Superintendent's Mansion, Fulton looked across at the front gate and recalled himself when he arrived at Parchman over thirty years ago. Young, strong, hopeful, and full of dreams which spilled from his eyes. That was what he remembered, not the muddy mind and soggy heart which were bemoaning how an instant could so violently redirect his entire life.

Fulton climbed the stairs to the Mercy Court as Governor Conner rubbed his eyes and awaited his thirty-eighth hearing of the day. The Sergeant stopped Fulton outside the court's closed door and removed his shackles. Then he opened the door and instructed Fulton to enter. Fulton walked into the Mercy Court with his face to his feet and his open hands twitching by his side. He remained bent and wheezing. Governor Conner's face was buried in papers looking for the next file, 7-32, when the wheezing and a sense of an ancient familiarity raised his face to Fulton's just as the same feeling raised Fulton's to his. Their revenant eyes met as if seeing each other after a thousand thousand years, and the ghosts of their former selves awakened in fearful reunion.

"Oh God, my God, Fulton."

The weight of disbelief overwhelmed Fulton and further knotted his breathing into a staggered gurgling. Conner jumped to his feet and dismissed the guards from the room. He approached Fulton with a child's trepidation, "It, it's you, isn't it? Can it be? After all this . . . time?"

Fulton's world went dark, but he knew it was him when he saw the caduceus hilt of the dragon dagger still at his side. He could not move or speak. Conner reached his hand to Fulton's arm, touching him as if to ensure he was real. As if for hours, they stood staring into each other's faces.

"Fulton, it's me, it's Jay."

After a pause, Fulton spoke his first words since Moondog was murdered, "I see. I know. En I don't know whether to smile or die."

Governor Conner led Fulton to the desk and seated him in the chair across from him. They looked at what each other had become. Fulton's hands twitched in his lap. Conner's heart sank as he recalled their friendship on the railroad and how disparate the trajectory of their lives had been. He wore pressed, elegant clothes and was Governor of a land that had forced Fulton through the cannibalizing sieve of its prejudice, leaving him thin-fleshed, gray, and sunken beneath his tattered ring-arounds. Conner pressed his face into his hands to hide from the undead specter before him. He remembered a proud, strong man who once saw magic in the night sky.

"Oh God, Fulton, please don't tell me you've been here since..."

"Since a few weeks after that night in Jackson."

"But that was thirty years ago! Oh God, Fulton, how could this be, how could the world?"

"The hows and whys lost they meanin' a long time ago, en I woulda taken my life then if it wasn't an offense 'gainst the earth."

"Your family. Your daughter."

"I banished them from my heart long ago."

"But I couldn't find you. I searched, but I couldn't find what they had done to you. Vardaman kept me locked a few weeks, then he let me go. Later I heard you had all been lynched. So I searched for your cabin and told her. Simbi. I told her you got sick but that you left her money. I gave her everything I had, and I visited every few months for years giving her whatever I had. I was lost, Fulton. I didn't understand. I know she cried and cried, but Orlando cared for her. I haven't seen them for years though, right before I decided to run for Governor." Conner paused so Fulton could understand. He wanted Fulton to ask a question, but Fulton remained silent, and old.

"You have a granddaughter, named Maya, after her great-grandmother. She was six the last time I saw her. She was beautiful..."

"No more."

"I'm sorry."

"But... I wrote letters."

"She never said anything. We would have come instantly!"

"No more."

They sat in silence, one in disbelief at what the other had become, the other in the presence of the failure of everything his life had labored to fight. At length, Fulton asked, "Why are you doin' this?"

Conner sat back in his chair and inhaled a deep breath of thought. "I have a secret Fulton. One that only my dead parents know, and I have used this secret against this world for years. I'm just like you Fulton, I'm colored." Though the expression on his face did not change, Fulton felt the world unravel around him. It was the last thing he wanted to hear.

"I know I look as white as any white man, but I am colored. My grandparents were slaves, and their owner killed my grandfather and raped my grandmother. She had my father, and when he died of smallpox, the slaveowner's son raped my mother. I was born so white he ordered the physician to kill me that night. But my father's closest friend overheard their plan, so at my mother's request he took me from her and fled into the night across the Wolf River all the way to Oklahoma. He raised me there and told me about my history and my special skin. I spent my childhood locked inside our cabin, lest someone find a colored was raising a white boy. When I was ten he sent me to an orphanage, and that's when I started wandering. I searched for my mother but never found her."

Conner paused again to gather his thoughts. He was telling a story that had remained buried within him all his life. And though Fulton could not believe what Conner was saying, that only a few shades of color demarcated the difference between his life and Conner's, he sat and listened with an empty expression like a mask on his face. So Conner continued, "After I heard you were dead, I wandered for a few weeks, until I remembered what you said about your daughter, about how when she felt sad she imagined herself as President and made the world just. And I remembered that you said I was the only white man you ever met who you'd want to be Governor. And that's when I realized what was missing from my life. Dreams. So I made up my mind to become Governor, just like you said, and I fought and fought and succeeded. I was changing the world Fulton. And with Case 102b I fought and fought and thought I succeeded again. But looking at you, now,

I see I have always failed. My life, my gift, and everything I dreamed has failed."

Tears swelled in Conner's eyes as he spoke. He closed them, and the tears gently overran the contours of his secret face. He was choked as he continued, "I know it's no consolation that I pardon you today Fulton. I know nothing can redeem your loss."

Fulton stood from his chair and looked down at Conner, stolid and bereft, "You will understand if I ken never see you again."

Conner nodded. Fulton turned and left the Mercy Court. When he arrived at the front gate, one of the Sergeants ran up from behind and offered him two-hundred dollars from the State of Mississippi, but Fulton refused, "I'm sure one of its citizens would kill me for it before I even walked ten minutes from here, 'sides, I don't acknowledge the debt."

Fulton passed through the front gate and did not turn to look back. He coughed and wheezed as he walked away, for he was overwhelmed by the sensation of his unfettered movement and the knowledge that finally, after thirty years, he was walking down a dusty road, towards the sunset, towards his former life, towards home.

LIFE'S ONLY PROMISE

Footsteps of the Revenant

He had no money, and he was not in a hurry, so he walked all the way home. Barefoot and gaunt from the cachexia of colored existence, he hid his face from the world underneath his gray, full-brimmed hat, and he retraced the thousand anterior footsteps that had traversed this same barren horizon of being shortly before him. He trudged home like a palimpsest of purposeless dreams. A few hours into his journey, the heavens opened like a swollen belly, and rain fell in waves across the body of the earth. The tempest cooled Fulton's lungs and eased his breathing while its heavy, gray presence melted the horizon and awakened a furious commingling of heaven and earth. Fulton pondered the deluge, wondering whether the Pinnekoke Levee would collapse and return Parchman to the watery chaos from which it was born.

Three days later the rain continued to fall, and Fulton continued to walk home, though he did not walk alone. A procession of black ants had paraded alongside him since the rain began. It stretched ten-thousand ants long and carried lotus flowers on its back with a morning glory at the front and a pine needle at the end. Fulton watched the ants and was happy for their company, but he concentrated on his movement forward and on the cool, silky rain that melted the knots and aches of his life.

After the third day the rain cleared and the heavens and earth redistinguished themselves. A rainbow ascended from the horizon and coiled in chromatic luminescence around the world. When he could see again, Fulton saw that he was only two days down 304 from his home. The dew-moistened landscape awakened his senses from their extended dormancy. He inhaled the fresh, reborn scent of the washed earth and recalled the evenings on his porch with Moondog and the glowing fragrance of his tobacco dreams. The sweet songs of the whippoorwills, the sonorous whispers of wind past his ears, and the sensation of freedom held like an infant in his hands all enervated memories of the sweetness of life that had been interred within him for thirty years. The Mississippi landscape was endless and breezy around him, budding with the newborn colors of spring.

He passed through Banks and saw the snakes and zombies and a man unloading tobacco at the rail junction. The man was not Coltrane, so instead he imagined Coltrane sitting with B.B. singing poetry to the dead.

As he continued, everywhere he looked kudzu ravaged the landscape, suffocating for miles and miles a horizon that seemed to be whimpering for release. And then he saw familiar trees. He saw the fig tree under which he conceived Simbi, and the tree next to the schoolhouse where she used to add and subtract each winter. And later, just to the west he saw the Lynching Tree where Old Willie still sat. His eyes were open and his mouth harp remained at his side, but Fulton could not discern whether he was dead or alive, so he walked up to Old Willie and sat next to him under the tree. He was old, emaciated, and gray, and he still awaited an answer.

"Where you been?"

"Parchman."

"I ain't hearda that. What's it like?"

"It's what life is like without the sweet things."

Fulton sat with Old Willie for a night. He fell asleep and dreamt of the subtle shapes of his previous lives. When he awoke he looked at Old Willie and said, "That was me."

Upon awakening, Fulton understood that as long as Old Willie wanted an answer, he could never rest. But he did not want to tell Old Willie that the trees did not hear his song. He did not want to tell Old Willie that dragonslayers and saints abide the same fate, and that the only difference between them is their temperament. And he did not want to tell Old Willie that the destiny of the world requires someone to abide its curse, that someone's neck must remain exposed when History tightens its noose. Moondog had learned all this as a child, the day he buried his mouth harp beneath the Lynching Tree. That was the day he realized there was no difference between the living and the dead, for they are both the silent residue that binds the cycle of time. That was the day he awakened and the Lynching Tree became his Redemption Tree. And today, Fulton understood as well. He understood the emptiness of all being and the consequent myopia that causes all suffering. Fulton hoped one day the Lynching Tree would awaken Old Willie too, so he could await with serenity the second verse of the couplet that announces the end of time.

On the morning of the seventh day of his walk, Fulton saw the hill atop which Anderson's Mansion stood. He saw the sharecropping plains below and the cabins dotting their perimeter. Everything appeared the same. As he turned off 304 at the fated crossroads and onto the dirt road that led to his cabin, he watched the procession of ants crawl into the earth while their lotus flowers blew into the clear sky. A spring breeze floated from the south across his face, and no other sound disturbed the silence of the morning, as if all living things had stopped to witness Fulton's reunion with his former life.

There was a pool of clear water a few yards before his cabin. Fulton looked in it and saw himself for the first time in thirty years. What should he feel? To look at his weathered, wrinkled, gray face and his life-sunken eyes, to see a man he did not recognize, emptied of the life he once understood. What should he feel? This was he. And there was his porch and his rocking chair. And there still, that was his daughter's flower garden, and beyond it still the fields that had sustained his family on earth. Memories more heavy than the birth of his child. Memories more heavy than the History that made pain their only origin. Memories of the family he left. They must be here; he must be here, and he has returned for them.

As he walked towards the cabin he saw something new in front of the flower garden, kneeling at a patch of disturbed dirt with a burnt stump remaining where the apple tree used to be – a little girl with drooping pigtails, tracing lonely circles around her belly button as she stared at the churned earth with a bereft sadness that gloomed the otherwise familiar twinkle in her eyes. She noticed his presence, a wrinkled, shoeless figure hiding beneath a hat like the scary man in a dream. She rose to her feet and ran to the cabin yelling, "Daddy! Daddy!" A man emerged from the cabin; he saw the tattered figure standing motionless with his open hands palsied by his side and his face hidden from the world. He sent his daughter into the house and approached the tattered man. "What you need stranger?"

The other remained silent, hidden, and choked by uncertainty. The voice did not sound familiar to him. It was angry and shaken. "I said, what you need stranger? Kent you see we got things to attend to?" The other did not raise his face, afraid. The angry, shaken father descended from his porch and seized the shovel laying in the yard near the churned earth. "I ain't gonna ask you but one more time, then you gonna be on your way, one way or thother. What do you need here, stranger?"

After an interminable moment, the tattered figure answered from beneath his hat, "I don't need nuthin'. Jes hopin' to come here en find my family."

The father was confused and impatient. The weight of another sadness tormented him and left him unprepared for what he saw when the tattered figure raised its face from beneath its hat and allowed the sun to illuminate the aged, gray, sunken face of his daughter's grandfather. Fulton saw Orlando's eyes widen like the morning sun, just before his knees buckled and he collapsed into Fulton's open arms. The embrace of his son slew the nightmares of his former life and raised the ghost of the gentle father who had raised his daughter in his heart and then left one fated, unforgiven day with dreams of soon returning with a better life.

Orlando cleared the tears in his eyes and tried to speak through his emotion-choked throat, "How ken this be? We thought you were dead. Where you been... all these years?"

"I will tell you everything in time. For now, call my daughter here so I ken see her again."

Orlando's face collapsed. He closed his eyes and lowered his head in disbelief that the world would force him to announce to her father that his return after thirty years was one week too late. But Fulton understood, *That burnt tree over there, en the disturbed earth.*

"Oh God Fulton, how ken I . . ."

"It's Ok. It was expected."

Orlando told Fulton that she and their daughter, Maya, had grown very ill and that Simbi had passed away last week from the disease. None of the doctors knew what it was, so none of them knew how to treat it. But Fulton looked at the burnt spike remains of the apple tree next to the flower garden, and he saw the innocence violated from Maya's eyes, and he understood what had truly happened. He knew what they had done to the girl, and he knew that his daughter had responded with the fury of her ancestral motherhood. Only a spike of the apple tree remained, charred black like the skin of she who was tied there and like the nightmares of those forced to watch. She was, after all, Uma's daughter, and like her, returned to ash.

Fulton asked Orlando to call Maya. She arrived nervously at her father's side, with eyes much older than the twelve years they had been on the earth. Orlando told her who the stranger was and that he had come to help take care of her. Fulton kneeled to her and smiled. He took her thin hand in his, and he felt his fatherhood reborn within her, "Have you ever been to the far coast a Africa or visited the Queen a the East Wind?"

"No suh."

"Well then, I'm gonna take you there on a ship across the ocean, after we sit down with your mama en help her rest." Fulton kissed her on the forehead. He looked at the cabin in front of him as if it were a painting; he was afraid to walk towards it like it was home.

That night Fulton lay down in the bed of his fatherhood. He reclined like a deity afloat celestial waters in a blissful state of waking consciousness. Then he slipped beneath the veil of sleep, where the vivid shapes of dreams caressed his rest, until all the dreams vanished and he was immersed in a dreamless slumber. He floated within a placid condition of quiescent, undifferentiated consciousness wherein the experiences of the last thirty years melted into an emptiness and the cessation of particulars. And then he arrived at the tranquility of the transcendent silence that followed. Serene and breathless. The topos and meaning of his necklace. He flowed into a pristine consciousness, and in that tranquility his emptied mind became the speculum of the universe.

The next morning, Fulton awoke and shaved his face and head. He felt emptied, light enough to flow in the wind until the wind died. Like a tuft of ash. He felt emptied of his condition of original debt -- debt to ancestors, debt to progeny, debt to *liloba*, debt to History, and debt to circumstance, because he knew that there was never anything to which those original debts could bind.

Emptied, he walked outside and sat at the foot of his daughter's grave. He lit a small fire and watched in silence with his open hands calm atop his knees. He sat for twelve days, motionless, without eating or drinking, and the crescent moon decorated the sky like a jewel each night. Maya occasionally sat beside him and watched his penance.

Then on the twelfth day, Simbi's flower garden blossomed roses, lubem lilies, irises, and tulips like a child's eyes opening to the world. Fulton turned to Maya and told her, "Life is the journey that prepares us to join our ancestors."

At Fulton's request, Maya gathered flowers from the garden and spread them across her mother's grave. They fell from her fingers like mist, not like tears. Then Fulton asked her for butter, which he poured on the fire, releasing an ambrosial smoke that formed gentle, cream-colored clouds into the otherwise clear blue sky. A sweet rain fell like feathers from the clouds, but Fulton's fire remained calmly lit. During that afternoon, several animals gathered around them. A calf, an eagle, and a serpent formed an inner circle around the fire. The eagle and the serpent interwove themselves with the tension of lovers, and the calf rested with its head on the ground. Fulton bowed his head and brought both his hands together above the ash as if in prayer. The fire ripened to a towering blaze, and the spirits of all ghosts emerged from the smoke, ancestors and their demons alike.

Watching them, Fulton understood that they continued to wander because gesture and sound had been extinguished from the world. He saw all of them, but he fixed his eyes on his grandmother, his daughter, and his Sweetest Queen. They were beautiful.

Then Fulton asked Maya to bring him tears from the Weeping Well, and after they drank, Fulton whispered into the calf's ear. The pillar of fire subsided, the rain cleared, and a rainbow emerged from the grave of ash and stretched its arms beyond the cycle of preceding lives. Twilight descended. The earth swooned and exhaled the history of its empty dreams, like winds from the dragon's belly. Fulton inhaled these winds and blew them into the unfulfilled wanderings of his sleepless host. Accepting his breath, the ghosts embraced the serenity of their silent role in the world's desperate, purposeless drama, and it was only then that a portion of the forgiven earth opened beneath the ash and invited them all to recline and sleep, until the undulating meter of History recoiled into the next inhalation of time.

LIFE'S ONLY PROMISE

Epilogue

Despite the efforts of those like Governor Conner, Parchman Farm remained relatively the same until 1972. When an inmate named Danny Bennet, a white, former high school football star, was beaten to death by his Parchman guards, a civil rights attorney named Roy Harber journeyed to Parchman to investigate. He was shocked by what he discovered. Despite the fact that Parchman's guards beat and murdered many of Harber's potential witnesses, on Febraury 8, 1971 Harber filed suit on behalf of four Parchman inmates -- Nazareth Gates, Willie Holmes, Matthew Winter, and Hal Zachery -- for violation of their first, eighth, thirteenth, and fourteenth amendment rights. Judge William Keady ruled for the plaintiff in the case of *Gates v. Collier*. However, Parchman and its keepers fought the *Gates* decision for four more years, but Keady persevered and in 1976 Mississippi created a Department of Corrections to oversee Parchman Farm and ensure its adherence to the rule of law. Today, you can still visit Parchman by driving down a thin, dirt road just off highway 49 in Mississippi.